PRAISE FOR
DAUGHTER OF THE SWORD

"A noir modern Tokyo overwhelmed by the shadows of Japanese history . . . a compelling multifaceted vision of a remarkable culture, and a great page-turner."
— Stephen Baxter, author of *Bronze Summer*

"*Daughter of the Sword* really captured my imagination. The interweaving of historical Japanese adventure and modern police procedural, Tokyo-style, caught me from two unexpected directions."
— Jay Lake, author of *Endurance*

"Effortlessly combines history and legend with a modern procedural . . . will have you staying up late to finish it."
— Diana Rowland, author of *Touch of the Demon*

"An authentic and riveting thrill ride through both ancient and modern Japan. Definitely a winner."
— Kylie Chan, author of *Hell to Heaven*

"Bein's gripping debut is a meticulously researched, highly detailed blend of urban and historical fantasy set in modern Tokyo. . . . Bein's scrupulous attention to verisimilitude helps bring all the settings to life, respectfully showcasing Japan's distinctive cultures and attitudes."
— *Publishers Weekly* (starred review)

continued . . .

"One of the best debuts I have ever read . . . an epic tale that heralds the emergence of a major talent." —Fantasy Book Critic

"A great police procedural urban fantasy that deftly rotates between Mariko in present-day Japan and other warriors in past eras." —Genre Go Round Reviews

"*Daughter of the Sword* reads like James Clavell's *Shogun* would have if it had been crossed with high fantasy by way of a police procedural." —Otherwhere Gazette

"Magic swords and samurai set alongside drugs and modern Tokyo and all blending in together to produce an engrossing and original story." —Under the Covers

"I loved the plot of this book. . . . I would recommend it to those who like fantasy and those who take an interest in Japanese culture." —Book Chick City

"*Daughter of the Sword* is a gritty and compelling police procedural . . . written in beautiful and exotic detail." —All Things Urban Fantasy

"If you love reading about faraway places, historical fiction, and fantasy, this book should definitely be on your list." —Literal Addiction

YEAR
OF THE
DEMON

A NOVEL OF THE FATED BLADES

STEVE BEIN

A ROC BOOK

ROC
Published by the Penguin Group
Penguin Group (USA) LLC, 375 Hudson Street,
New York, New York 10014

USA | Canada | UK | Ireland | Australia | New Zealand | India | South Africa | China
penguin.com
A Penguin Random House Company

First published by Roc, an imprint of New American Library,
a division of Penguin Group (USA) LLC

First Printing, October 2013

LIBRARY OF CONGRESS CATALOGING-IN-PUBLICATION DATA:
Bein, Steve.
Year of the demon: a novel of the fated blades/Steve Bein.
p. cm.
ISBN 978-0-451-46519-1 (pbk.)
1. Women detectives—Japan—Tokyo—Fiction. 2. Detective and mystery stories.
I. Title.
PS3602.E385Y43 2013
813'.6—dc23   2013018673

Printed in the United States of America
1   3   5   7   9   10   8   6   4   2

Set in Adobe Garamond Pro   •   Designed by Elke Sigal

R eaders have been telling me they'd like a little guidance how to pronounce all the Japanese names they find in my work. Ask, dear reader, and ye shall receive. Three general rules tell you most of what you need to know:

1. The first syllable usually gets the emphasis (so it's MA-ri-ko, not Ma-RI-ko).
2. Consonants are almost always pronounced just like English consonants.
3. Vowels are almost always pronounced just like Hawaiian vowels.

Yes, I know, you probably know about as much Hawaiian as you do Japanese, but the words you do know cover most of the bases: if you can pronounce *aloha*, *hula*, *Waikiki*, and *King Kamehameha*, you've got your vowels. Barring that, if you took a Romance language in high school, you're good to go. Or, if you prefer lists and tables:

a as in *father*
ae as in *taekwondo*
ai as in *aisle*
ao as in *cacao*
e as in *ballet*

ei as in *neighbor*
i as in *machine*
o as in *open*
u as in *super*

There are two vowel sounds we don't have in English: *ō* and *ū*. Just ignore them. My Japanese teachers would slap me on the wrist for saying that, but unless you're studying Japanese yourself, the difference between the short vowels (*o* and *u*) and the long vowels (*ō* and *ū*) is so subtle that you might not even hear it. The reason I include the long vowels in my books is that spelling errors make me squirm. What can I say? I've spent my entire adult life in higher education.

As for consonants, *g* is always a hard *g* (like *gum*, not *gym*) and almost everything else is just like you'd hear it in English. There's one well-known exception: Japanese people learning English often have a hard time distinguishing *L*'s from *R*'s. The reason for this is that there is neither an L sound nor an R sound in Japanese. The *ri* of Mariko is somewhere between *ree*, *lee*, and *dee*. The choice to Romanize with an *r* was more or less arbitrary, and it actually had more to do with Portuguese than with English. (Fun fact: if linguistic history had gone just a little further in that direction, this could have been a book about Marico Oxiro, not Mariko Oshiro.)

Finally, for those who want to know not just how to pronounce the Japanese words but also what they mean, you'll find a glossary at the end of this book.

BOOK ONE

HEISEI ERA, THE YEAR 22

(2010 CE)

I

Detective Sergeant Oshiro Mariko adjusted the straps on her vest, twisting her body side to side to snug the fit tighter. The thing was uncomfortable, and not just physically. Mariko hadn't had to wear a bulletproof vest since academy. Even then it had been for training purposes only; she'd never strapped one on in anticipation of being shot at.

"Boys and girls, listen up," Lieutenant Sakakibara said, his voice deep and sharp. He was a good twenty centimeters taller than Mariko, with a high forehead and a Sonny Chiba haircut that sat on his head like a helmet. He looked perfectly at ease in his body armor, and despite the heavy SWAT team presence, there was no doubt that the staging area was his to command. "Our stash house belongs to the Kamaguchi-gumi, and that means armed and dangerous. Our CI confirms at least two automatic weapons on-site."

That sent a wave of murmurs through the sea of cops surrounding him. CIs were renowned for their lousy intelligence. Narcs with holstered pistols, SWAT guys with their M4 rifles pointed casually at the ground, all of them were shaking their heads. They all spoke fluent covert-informantese, and in that surreal language "at least two" meant "somewhere between zero and ten."

Mariko was the shortest one in the crowd, and if she looked a little taller with her helmet on, everyone else looked taller still. Police work attracted the cowboys, and the boys really got their six-guns on when they got to armor up and kick down doors. Being the only woman on the team was alienating at the best of times, and now, surrounded by unruly giants, Mariko felt like a teenager again, awkward, soft-spoken, trapped in the midst of raucous, rowdy adults and just old enough to understand how out of place she was.

It was no good dwelling on how she felt like a *gaijin*, so she returned her attention to Lieutenant Sakakibara. "There's going to be a lot of strange equipment in there," he said, though he hardly needed to. SWAT had downloaded images of all the machines they were likely to encounter. The target was a packing and shipping company, an excellent front for running dope, guns—damn near anything, really—and the machinery they'd have on-site would offer cover and concealment galore. Everyone knew that, but Sakakibara was good police: he looked out for his team. "Weird shadows," he said, "lots of little nooks and crannies, lots of corners to clear. You make sure you clear every last one of them. Execute the fundamentals, people."

Again, everyone knew it, and again, everyone needed the reminder. Mariko marveled at how some of the most specialized training in the world boiled down to just getting the basics right. In that respect SWAT operations were no different than basketball or playing piano.

"B-team, D-team," Sakakibara said, "you need to hit the ground running. I want to own the whole damn structure in the first five seconds. Understand?"

"Yes, sir," said twelve cops in unison.

"C-team, same goes for you, but don't you forget"—Sakakibara pointed straight at Mariko as he spoke—"Detective Sergeant New Guy is a part of your element. The Kamaguchi-gumi has put out a contract on her. I won't have her getting shot on my watch, got it?"

"Yes, sir," Mariko said with the rest of C-team.

The first of the vans started up with a roar, and the sound made Mariko's heart jump. She chided herself; she was thinking too much about those automatic weapons, and now even the rumble of a diesel engine sounded like machine gun fire. She reached down for the SIG

Sauer P230 at her hip, taking yet another look down the pipe of the pistol she already knew she'd charged.

"The seven-oh-three gets here in"—Sakakibara checked his huge black diver's watch—"six minutes. That gives you five and a half to get where you need to be. Now mount up."

"Yes, sir," the whole team said, and Mariko started jogging toward the B and C van. The rest of her element fell in behind her.

When she reached the dark back corner of the van her heart was racing, and she knew it wasn't because of a ten-meter jog. Her hand drifted to the holster on her hip, satisfying an irrational need to confirm that her SIG was even there. Running her left thumb over the ridges of her pistol's hammer, she absently wondered why the movement should still feel strange to her. It wasn't as if she hadn't logged the hours retraining herself to shoot as a lefty; at last count she'd expended about two thousand rounds on the pistol range. She hadn't yet hit the same scores she'd been shooting right-handed, and that idea weighed on her, heavier than the ceramic plating of the body armor that now made her shoulders ache. Despite all the training, somehow her brain couldn't even get used to the fact that when she held something in her right hand, she held it with four fingers, not five.

Thinking about her missing finger made her think about the last time she had to point a pistol at a human being. Fuchida Shūzō had cost her more than her trigger finger. She'd actually flatlined after he rammed his *katana* through her gut, and she had matching scars on her belly and back to prove it. But more than this, he'd scarred her self-confidence. Everyone on the force knew they could die in this line of work, but Mariko *had* died, if only for a few minutes, and ever since then she wondered how things might have gone if she'd pulled that trigger even a tenth of a second earlier—if she'd put a nine-millimeter hole right in his breastbone, if she'd spared herself the weeks of rehab, if she'd earned herself a bit of detached soul-searching about the ethics of killing in the line of duty rather than ruminations on everything she'd done wrong to let things get that far.

Those ruminations plagued her day and night, and images of Fuchida and his sword flashed in her mind every time she visited the pistol range. Sometimes it got so bad that she couldn't even pull the trigger. The more she *needed* to hit the target dead center, the more she got mired in the fear of failure, and once she fell that deep into her own head, she couldn't even put the next shot on the paper.

Her former sensei, Yamada Yasuo, had a term for that: paralysis through analysis. Swordsmanship and marksmanship were exactly the same: the more you thought about what you were doing, the less likely you were to do it right. So long as Mariko trapped herself in doubting her marksmanship, she was a danger to herself and others.

Now, listening to her pulse hammer against her eardrums, she worried she might freeze up when those van doors opened and her team had to move. Two thousand rounds she'd slung downrange, trying to train her left hand to do its job, and two thousand times she'd failed. Now other cops were counting on her, and if she failed tonight the way she did with Fuchida, it might be one of *their* lives on the line. She drew back the slide on her again, knowing it wasn't necessary, needing to do it anyway.

She felt a tap on her shoulder pad and looked up. "Hey," Han said, "you think you checked that weapon enough yet?"

It was a little embarrassing being caught in the act, but the fact that he'd noticed was reassuring. Han and Mariko were partners now, and his attention to detail might save her ass someday. She'd already made a habit of noting the details about him. He always put his helmet on at the last minute. He tended to bounce a little on the balls of his feet when he was nervous. He had an app on his phone that gave him inning-by-inning updates on his Yomiuri Giants. The TMPD patch Velcroed to the front of his bulletproof vest was old, curling at the corners. Hers was curling a bit too—the vests usually sat in storage, sometimes for years, and who would ever bother to peel the patches off?—but Han's patch had a weaker hold on his chest, probably because he caught the curled-up corner of it with his thumb every time he reached up to brush his floppy hair away from his ear. He wore his hair longer than regulations allowed, and his sideburns—longer and bushier than Mariko had ever seen on a Japanese man—were against regs too. But violating the personal grooming protocol was one of the perks when you worked undercover, and Han made the most of it. He'd have worn a beard and mustache too, if only he could grow them, but his boyish face didn't allow him that luxury.

"I'm pretty sure that chambered round hasn't gone anywhere," he said. "Then again, I haven't checked it myself. You mind checking it for me?"

"Smart-ass."

Han grinned. "Guilty as charged."

She noticed he was bouncing a little on the balls of his feet, and since he didn't make any noise Mariko knew he'd strapped everything down tight. The SWAT guys that filled the rest of the van were equally silent—no mean feat given the close quarters and the sheer numbers of magazines, flash-bangs, gas masks, and radios they'd affixed to their armor.

The floor rumbled, someone pulled the door shut, and they were off. The lone red lightbulb cast weird shadows. There was an electric tension in the air, a palpable enthusiasm silenced of necessity but champing at the bit. "Han," Mariko whispered, "you ever had to wear a vest before?"

"Sure. At my brother's wedding."

"You know what I mean."

"Not since academy."

"Me neither," said Mariko. She lowered her voice even more and said, "Does it make you scared, knowing they have submachine guns in there?"

"Well, *yeah*."

Mariko took a deep breath through her nose and held it awhile before blowing it out. It felt good to have someone on the team she didn't have to be defensive with. With everyone else she was always on her guard, because everyone else was all too willing to see her as a girly-girl if she ever showed a moment's weakness. But she and Han could tell each other the truth—even if only in private—and while she wouldn't be caught dead whining to him, just being able to admit she was scared lessened her fear somehow.

"Jump-off point in one minute," the driver said.

That palpable, silenced excitement mounted. It was strange, feeling that much nervous energy restrained by cops who were otherwise as rowdy as hormone-addled frat boys. She couldn't see them well in the red light, but somehow Mariko knew even the SWAT guys were tensing up. "Han," Mariko said, "you put your lid on yet?"

"Nope."

"Well, put it on, damn it. I don't want to tell the LT C-team didn't hit their door on time because my partner bobbled his helmet while he was getting out of the van."

"Jump-off in twenty," said the driver. The doors opened up and suddenly the cabin filled with light and industrial stink. Acrid paint smells told Mariko there had to be an auto body shop nearby, and a wind out of the west carried all the smog that should have been marinating Tokyo and Yokohama. Or maybe that was the exhaust from teams A and D, which pulled away faster and faster as Mariko's van slowed to a halt.

Then she was following Han, her heart pounding just as hard as her heels pounded the pavement. She wished her gear wasn't so heavy, wished her goggles weren't fogging up so soon, wished she'd spent a little less time on the pistol range and a little more time training for her next triathlon.

But just like running a tri, this too proved to be a case of pre-race jitters. She overtook Han as they turned the corner into a narrow alley. She could have passed the SWAT operators too, but she reminded herself that it was their job to breach the target, her job to seize the dope once the target was secure.

As they passed a shabby, weather-beaten, wood plank fence, Mariko got her first look at their target. It was a two-story slab of beige bricks nearly identical to the buildings beside it. There were six of them, lined up like the pips of a die on a dirty, seldom-used lot. Apart from being a tenth as high as most of the buildings in the neighborhood, the target and its little siblings were utterly without character. Light shone through most of the windows, which was good; it was easy to see perps behind them.

Mariko kept the darkened windows in her peripheral vision as she ran. Her focus was on the back door, and on the empty expanse of concrete between her and it. It was the only exposed stretch of their approach, but there was no getting to the C-side of the target, the back side, except to cross it. If the buildings on this dirty lot were the six pips on a die, the target building was the lower right pip and C-team was just rounding the lower left. Running right past the two were the twin tracks of the Chuō-Sobu Line, where the *clackety-clack, clackety-clack* of the 7:03 was getting louder and louder by the second. There was no crossing the train tracks—they were fenced, and the chief of police had nixed SWAT's plan to just cut through the fences and approach the C-side directly—and so the only way to the back door was to cross that shooting gallery of a parking lot.

Mariko's team tucked themselves into a corner to catch their breath. They waited for the train for the same reason they'd been so careful in strapping their gear down tight: speed and surprise were their only sure defense against automatic fire. The helmet and vest were half armor, half security blanket; every cop knew there was no protection against a lucky shot. Submachine guns could spit out a *lot* of potentially lucky shots.

Mariko heard a little *snik* behind her and turned around to see Han adjusting the straps of the helmet he'd just put on. He shot her a wink and a grin. "Go time."

The train was upon them before she knew it, and then they were running again. Off to Mariko's left, A-team's big black van roared through the parking lot and B-team was almost to the B-side windows. As Mariko's element reached the C-side door, the SWAT guy with the ram—a heavy goddamn thing by the look of it; Mariko could hardly believe he'd kept pace with the rest of the team—charged the door and laid into it.

The ram bounced back.

He hammered the door again, but the ram bounced off like it was made of rubber. "Shit," Mariko said. So much for owning the building in the first five seconds.

Now that the train had gone, she could hear shouting, shattering windows, the explosion of flash-bangs. Now two SWAT guys were on the ram, beating the holy hell out of the door. They were supposed to have made their breach by now. A-team would already have punched right through the front door, and if Mariko's team couldn't punch their door, their suspects would only have A-team to shoot at.

Mariko didn't like the thought of volunteering to draw some of that fire, but the whole point of converging on the target at once was to overwhelm and confuse the opposition. Besides, the longer her suspects had to think, the more time they had to find weapons or flush product down the toilet.

She pulled a flash-bang grenade from her belt and set it on the windowsill behind her. "Get down," she said, and she tried to hide her whole body under her helmet.

White light consumed the world. The concussion was enough to buckle her knees. It sounded like Armageddon, but it sure blew the hell out of the window. Mariko hopped through the gap, Han following like her own shadow.

For Mariko the world narrowed to whatever her pistol could see. She put her front sight on the empty doorway, then this corner, then that one, not checking the other two because that was Han's area and she knew he'd do it right. The furniture didn't even register to her except as cover.

With the room cleared she and Han made for the hall, looking for the bathroom. When they raided residences, that was where perps disposed of product, and there was no reason a commercial storefront's toilets couldn't be used for the same purpose. Mariko reached the hallway just in time to see the C-side door exploding inward, finally succumbing to the ram. Two of her SWAT guys breached and held. The other two followed Mariko and Han.

Footsteps thundered on a flight of stairs somewhere nearby. So many voices were shouting through Mariko's earpiece that she couldn't keep them straight. She rounded a corner and saw a balding man in a maroon track suit closing a door behind him. She only got a glimpse of the room on the other side of the door, but she thought she saw some kind of heavy machinery back there.

In an instant Han had a pistol on the suspect too, shouting at him to get down, and both SWAT guys had him in the wavering glow of the flashlights undermounted on the barrels of their M4s. The man in the track suit gave all four cops a cocky smile, held his hands up near his head, and let something small and shiny fall from his right hand.

Keys.

That arrogant smile told Mariko all she needed to know. Her suspect didn't care about being arrested. All he had to do was stand there getting handcuffed long enough for some machine on the other side of that door to destroy all of her precious evidence.

She rushed the perp. Still wearing that cocksure smile, he stood with his hands in front of him, as if to offer his wrists. It was the sort of pose she'd only seen in people who had been handcuffed before. Mariko took the tiniest bit of delight in seeing his eyes widen a bit as she drew near. Apparently he assumed she'd slow down before she reached him. But body armor wasn't just for stopping bullets.

She hit him like a wrecking ball. They crashed through the locked door, which, unlike the reinforced door that had repelled the battering ram, was just an interior door like the ones she'd expect to find in the average apartment. She let her shoulder pad sink into her suspect's solar plexus, rolling right over it and up to her feet. Han would be on the guy; Mariko didn't need to look back and check. She didn't recognize any of the weird machines standing in front of her—and there were a lot of them—but she didn't need to. She just hit the STOP button on the one that was mixing a bunch of white powder.

She learned afterward that the machine was for making those biodegradable packing peanuts, and that doing so involved turning cornstarch into tiny little pellets, which were then subjected to extremely high heat to expand them to their peanutty volume. She also learned that mixing highly combustible amphetamines into the cornstarch wasn't exactly a foolproof method to make a whole lot of speed disappear, but if you let the laced cornstarch hit the pellet processor, it was a great way to flood the building with noxious gases and make the whole neighborhood smell like ammonia for a week. In the moment, though, Mariko stood with her hands on her hips, panting a bit and smiling down at the guy she'd just blasted through the door.

Frowning at the splintered doorframe, Han said, "You know, Mariko, I thought we worked pretty well as a team, but I have to tell you I didn't see that one coming."

Mariko grinned at him, enjoying her adrenaline high. "Opened the door, didn't it?"

"Yeah. But you know, these do that too." He jingled the perp's keys at her. "And these don't give the SWAT guys heart attacks and make them hope they can clear the big roomful of weird-ass machines before someone puts a bullet in the chick they're supposed to protect."

SWAT had indeed cleared the rest of the factory floor, and judging by the chatter coming over the wire, the operation was over. It seemed impossible. "Han, how long did this thing take?"

"What, the op?"

"Yeah."

He shrugged. "Starting from when we first hit the back door? I don't know. A minute, maybe? No, less than that, I think."

"Me too. Call it forty-five seconds."

"Okay. So what?"

"So," Mariko said, "was that the best forty-five seconds or what? Damn, I love this job."

2

Mariko sat on the edge of the desk in the shipping company's sales office and waited for her verbal beating.

It was inevitable. She'd violated standard operating procedure, and cops who violated SOP suffered a thorough pummeling by a commanding officer. Han knew it too, and he sat beside her on the broad desktop, arms folded across the peeling TMPD patch on his chest, equally resigned to the same fate. "Hey, check that out," he said, as if making small talk could distract them from their impending fate. "You think we can get these guys on weapons possession?"

Mariko had been looking at the same thing: a weather-beaten *katana*, obviously ancient, sitting on an elegant wooden holder on the shelf that ran the perimeter of the room, forty centimeters or so below the tiles of the drop ceiling. It was a shelf designed for collections, but this was a collection that defied categorization. Another *katana*, this one of spring steel, coupled with a little placard verifying its authenticity as an actual prop used in filming Kurosawa's *Yojimbo*. An iron demon mask pitted with rust and age. A series of ceramic samurai figurines that looked more like action figures than art. A bronze helmet, its studded laths worn green with age, clearly a fragile piece that ought to have been behind glass in a museum. A wooden Fudō statue of the same vintage, lacquered in red, his trademark sword and lariat wrought in solid gold. An autographed head shot of Toshiro Mifune. *Hanzō the Razor* on LaserDisc, also autographed. One after

the next, a parade of miscellany circumnavigating an otherwise coherent and cohesive room.

Mariko gazed absently at the old iron mask while rehearsing what
she'd say in her own defense. The facts were plain: if she hadn't
breached the target when she did, she and her element might never
have seen their perp closing that door behind him. They would simply
have put a rifle on the locked door, cleared the rest of the building, and
only then punched the factory floor, after they'd collected a full complement. Impeccable tactics, but it might have made the difference
between having a bunch of hard evidence mixed into a hopper full of
cornstarch and having hazmat teams evacuating the neighborhood
while every hospital in town was choked with a glut of narcs and
SWAT cops getting treated for chemical burns of the eyes, sinuses,
and lungs.

All perfectly sound observations. All of them irrelevant if either she
or Han had sustained an injury. SOP was SOP, and breaking it
brought down the Hammer of God, regardless of whether anyone
actually got hurt.

Han must have been entertaining similar thoughts. His right foot
was doing a sewing machine impression, and he rapped his thumbs
nervously on the top of his helmet, which he held in his lap. "Hey,"
she said, "does that demon mask look familiar to you?"

"Huh?" She'd snapped him out of some distant reverie. "Uh, no,
not really. You?"

"Yeah, but I can't place it." Mariko frowned. The more she looked
at it, the more she was certain she ought to recognize the mask. It was
like seeing the face of an old high school classmate, someone she ought
to know but whose name maddeningly escaped her. Suddenly she
found Han's little drumbeat against his helmet distracting. She was
about to ask him to stop when Sakakibara stormed into the office.

Instantly both of them stood to attention. "There they are," Sakakibara said, "Butch and Sundance."

Sakakibara never called anyone by name. He rarely took the
trouble even to tell people which nicknames applied to them; he just

made them up on the fly and expected everyone else to sort it out. Sometimes he'd give someone three or four names a day; other times the first nickname would stick like a steel-tipped dart and hang on for years.

He marched around them to drop heavily into the salesman's chair behind the big desk. "The SWAT commander says I'm to suspend you for a month without pay and bust both of you back to general patrol. Says it's no good for you to run around trying to get yourselves killed while his boys are trying to do their job. He's not wrong about that."

"Sir," Mariko said, "if we had breached even ten seconds later than we did—"

Sakakibara fixed her with a glare. "Who the hell gave you permission to speak?"

"Sorry, sir."

"Which one of you pulled the stunt with the flash-bang?"

"I did, sir." Mariko said it quickly, knowing that Han might well take the hit for her if she left him the opportunity. He'd been with Narcotics for eight years already, serving under Sakakibara for five of those. The LT was likely to go easier on a seasoned veteran than the newest addition to his team.

"The SWAT guys are having a fit over that, believe you me," Sakakibara said. "Any guesses as to why?"

Mariko had a few. Broken glass was a hazard, period; there was a reason the SWAT operators all wore Kevlar gloves and Nomex hoods. And Mariko got lucky that she'd ported a carpeted room with her flash-bang. Crossing a glass-strewn linoleum floor was like tap-dancing on marbles.

But Sakakibara didn't give her a chance to reply. "If you ask me, I figure it's because none of them thought of it first. Wish I was there to see it; it must have been pretty damn cool."

"It was," Han said. Mariko just looked at the floor, struggling to restrain a grin.

"All right, chalk one up for Batgirl. So blah, blah, blah, don't do that again, consider yourselves chastised. Now sit your munchkin asses down."

Mariko and Han did as they were told, taking the two swivel chairs facing the desk. The chairs and the desk were a matching set, and they would have been at the height of fashion if this were 1981. Mariko allowed these details to pass by more or less unnoticed, as she was still trying to figure out the nickname. "Munchkin" was simple—Han was a head shorter than their LT and Mariko was shorter still—but "Batgirl" took a little longer. The stunt with the window. With the flash-bang. That she got from her belt. Utility belt. Batgirl.

Mariko hoped that wouldn't be the nickname that stuck.

"Either of you know the name Urano Sōseki?" Mariko and Han both shook their heads. "Well, you're about to," Sakakibara said. "He's your buyer. Runs this place for the Kamaguchi-gumi. You'll find him out back in the ambo. Did I hear it right? Did you Justice League him through a door?"

"Yes, sir." Mariko didn't know whether to feel proud or ashamed.

Sakakibara gave her an approving nod. "Not bad for a munchkin. Anyway, like I was saying, Neck Brace-san is your principal buyer. We've got five of his crew too, but they're little fish. You'll want to talk to them eventually, but get to Neck Brace before they wheel him out of here."

"Sir," Mariko said, "I could swear I heard an ambulance leaving five or ten minutes ago. Are you sure he's still here?"

Sakakibara looked at her with unfeigned surprise, and more than a little disdain. "Are you questioning my judgment?"

"Sorry, sir."

"You've got pretty big balls for a chick."

At first Mariko read his tone as angry, but she changed her mind when he gave her a wry, snorting chuckle. "Not that I have to explain myself to you, but yes, we had two ambos on scene. The one you heard was running your seller to the OR. Neck Brace and his boys roughed the guy up pretty good."

Mariko frowned. "Do we know why?"

"That's your job to figure out."

"Sir," Han said, "does this mean you're giving us this case?"

"Put that together all by yourself, did you? I figure Frodo here would be hungry for it, seeing as it's Kamaguchis buying serious weight and it's Kamaguchis that put the hit out on her. What do you say, Frodo? You want these guys or not?"

Mariko could only assume *she* was Frodo, though for the moment she was less concerned about the nickname and more concerned about Sakakibara's loaded question. She had a history with the Kamaguchi-gumi, all right. Not of her own design; they just took it personally when a cop got famous by taking down one of their own. Fuchida Shūzō—the man who chopped off Mariko's trigger finger, the one whose crazed face flashed before her eyes every time she went down to the pistol range to retrain her left hand—was once a street enforcer under Kamaguchi Ryusuke.

Mariko had killed Fuchida out of sheer self-preservation, an offense that a high-ranking underboss like Kamaguchi Ryusuke wouldn't usually take personally. Everyone had a right to self-defense, a right that Kamaguchi had exercised himself on more than one occasion, always with lethal effect. Word on the street was that Kamaguchi would have preferred to write off Fuchida's death as an unfortunate cost of doing business. Fuchida had been getting uppity anyway, and it wasn't as if Mariko was some contract killer from a rival clan. But thanks to Fuchida's predilection for swords and a couple of bizarre twists of fate, Mariko had killed him in an honest-to-God duel, and that was the sort of thing that splashed Mariko's picture and the phrase "samurai showdown" all over the nightly news for a week. Kamaguchi Ryusuke *had* to put out a contract on her after that. In his line of work it was just saving face.

He'd passed the job off to his youngest son, Hanzō, known on the streets as the Bulldog. Like his father, the Bulldog had an underbite and a big, muscular frame. Mariko remembered his photos from her debrief with Organized Crime. His father had a reputation for being cool, levelheaded, and tenaciously territorial, but the Bulldog was only known for a brutish, sloppy brand of bloodshed that had become his signature. OC had long suspected him of being the Kamaguchi-gumi's go-to guy when it came to vendetta killings. Now it seemed he'd signed on to even the score on Fuchida Shūzō.

It made Mariko's heart do somersaults just to think of the fight with Fuchida. Somehow the thought of a bounty on her head was less scary. Troubling as it was, the idea of a hit man out there somewhere was still an abstract concept, while the vision of a madman trying to hack her to pieces was all too vivid. She wished it were otherwise. It was embarrassing to be afraid of things in the past, things that could no longer hurt her. She wished she could be as worried about the hit man as Han and Sakakibara seemed to be, but that wasn't what kept her up at night.

Either way, the lieutenant's question was clear. It wasn't *Would you like this case?* but rather *Are you man enough to take this case?* And there could be only one answer to that. "Damn right, sir. Let me at them."

Sakakibara gave a single, curt, approving nod. "Good. Like I said, your buyer's out back. If you pass the SWAT commander on the way there, do me a favor—hell, do yourselves a favor—and look like I just gave you a royal ass-whupping."

The ambulance was parked in the loading dock, and to get to the loading dock Mariko and Han had to pass through the splintered wreckage of the door Mariko had bashed down. She felt a cold little thrill of adrenaline at the sight of it.

They crossed the factory floor, which was cavernous, and Mariko imagined it must have been deafening when all the machines were running. As it was, the only sounds came from the sparse population of cops that had migrated into the room. One of the cops sat idly with a rifle across his lap and eight or nine perps sitting against the wall in front of him, most with their heads bowed, all with their hands zip-tied behind their backs. A gaggle of narcs had gathered around the machine that, until Mariko had shut it down, had been processing an admixture of cornstarch and amphetamines into a thick white goo. Mariko had a quick word with them before she and Han proceeded to their suspect.

"Hey, by the way," Han said, "what gives with 'Frodo'?"

Mariko shrugged. "Because I'm short?"

"Nah. That was 'munchkin.'"

The fact that he didn't ask about "Batgirl" probably meant that he'd figured it out already, and not for the first time, Mariko was glad to know she and her partner thought so much alike. For one thing, it helped them work as a team, and for another, Han was a veteran narc and good police; if Mariko thought like him, it meant she was thinking in the right ways.

She opened the door to the loading dock and was greeted by a blue cloud of diesel smoke. Inevitably, in the tradition of cops and firefighters everywhere, the paramedics had left their vehicle's engine running. Through the haze Mariko looked down on Urano Sōseki. They'd strapped him to a backboard and, as Sakakibara's nickname foretold, he was bound in a neck brace. A cop sat next to him in the ambulance, still armored just as Han and Mariko were; SWAT's tactical medic, no doubt. Unintelligible voices squawked over the paramedics' comms, different from the chatter coming in over the SWAT and narc channels. Straining in his neck brace to see who had just come in, Urano said, "You again."

"Me again," said Mariko, jogging jauntily down the short flight of stairs to where the ambulance was parked. In the tone a doctor would use with a six-year-old patient, she said, "And how are you feeling today?"

"I been bowled over by a piece of snatch before, but never quite like that. You want to go for another roll with me?"

Lovely, Mariko thought, but she didn't let it show on her face. Han ignored him too, for which Mariko was eternally grateful. She didn't need anyone leaping to her defense as if she were some kind of damsel in distress. There weren't many cops that understood that—not very many *men* who understood it—and once again Mariko was glad to have Han as her partner.

The tactical medic wasn't as enlightened. He thapped Urano in the forehead with a knuckle and said, "Shut up."

Han hopped up in the back of the ambulance and sat down next to Urano. "So," he said, "I guess you know you're going to prison for a while."

"You got nothing on me," said Urano.

"I don't know about that," Mariko said. "There's all that speed in your cornstarch hopper. That's got to count for something."

Urano snorted. "It's not mine."

"Sorry," Han said, "that's not the way this works. See, if it's illegal and it's in your building, we've got you on possession."

Mariko nodded. "Felony possession, since our guys are saying you've got quite a bit of it in there. How much did they say, Han?"

"At least fifty kilos," said Han. "Maybe more."

"That's right. Urano-san, did you know that machine in there has a scale built into it?" He didn't need her to connect the rest of the dots. There was an inventory log too, and nothing could be easier than checking the weight of what was actually in the machine against the weight of the bags some factory worker had recorded pouring into the machine.

"You got nothing," said Urano. "We didn't pay for it. It's not ours."

"Really?" Han said. "So, what, some guy just came by and decided to *donate* a whole bunch of speed?"

"It's not ours," said Urano, his patience fading fast. He tried to sit up to look Han in the eye; a jolt of pain slammed him flat on his back. "Not ours," he grunted. "We told that little shit not to bring it by here. He said you were coming. I told him we'd set up another meet. The dumb bastard came by anyway."

"And that's why you and your boys beat the hell out of him," said Mariko.

"So we get to add aggravated battery to the possession charge," said Han.

"Not possession. It's not ours." Another shot of pain made Urano wince. "Book me on the assault thing. Fine. He deserved it. But we didn't pay for the shit. We don't even got any money around here. Go look. You see any big stacks of bills, you tell me; I could use them. But we got nothing. We bought nothing. So *you* got nothing."

"You keep saying that," said Han. "We'll have to sit down and chat sometime about how the drug trade works."

"But maybe downtown," said Mariko.

"Yeah," said Han, "and maybe after you go see a doctor. You look like someone kicked your ass."

Mariko and Han sat on the concrete lip of the dock as they watched the ambulance pull away. Han fished through his pockets for a pack of cigarettes. Lighting up, he said, "You think he's telling the truth about the cash?"

"I didn't see anything."

"Me neither." He said it with a knowing tone. When it came to narcotics, no one wanted to tell the truth. Users, dealers, suppliers, all of them lied—and not just to cops, but to their own loved ones and even to themselves. Mariko knew that all too well, as did anyone with a history of addiction in the family. Mariko prided herself on her ability to detect when someone was lying to her, and if anything, Han was better at it than she was. Eight years on Narcotics meant eight years of seeing through the smokescreens.

"So what are these guys selling the dope for, if not for cash? A hostage, maybe?"

"I don't like it," Mariko said. "Why piss off the hostage takers? You've got to deliver payment on *their* terms, *neh*?"

"Good point."

"But what, then? You can't have a drug buy with no money."

"Yeah," Han said around his cigarette, "but you're not supposed to have dealers show up to a blown sting either. Urano said his guy knew we were coming."

"Which means his guy doesn't mind pissing off the Kamaguchi-gumi. He's got to be out of his mind."

"Or desperate."

"Lucky to be alive either way. Assuming he survives, that is."

"Right," said Han. "Sakakibara said the dude's in surgery, *neh*?"

Mariko nodded. "So we've got a seller who's willing to take enormous risks—"

"Enormous by dope slingers' standards. Not exactly my grandma's sewing circle."

"Exactly," she said. "And a buyer who's willing to beat his supplier half to death. Is this case making any sense to you?"

"Nope."

"Me neither." Mariko chuckled and shook her head. "But you're interested, *neh*?"

"Oh yeah."

"Me too."

3

Mariko could smell herself in the elevator. She was sweaty, her matted hair felt as if it still had a helmet strapped onto it, and she smelled faintly of Fourth of July fireworks.

She was the only person in the whole apartment building who would have drawn that comparison. She was the only one who had ever celebrated the Fourth of July, because she was the only one who spent her childhood in the States. It was strange, thinking of fireworks she hadn't smelled since junior high, and she wondered why on earth her hair would suddenly share that smell. Then she remembered the flash-bang going off right above her head.

The elevator announced her floor with a canned voice that sounded just like the woman who narrated those airline safety videos. Mariko hauled herself out of the elevator and tromped down the narrow corridor to her apartment. Her boots felt like they were made of lead and she wanted nothing more than to take a hot shower and collapse into bed. But that was a pipe dream. She'd won enough races and tussled with enough bad guys to know her body's reaction to an adrenaline high. She wasn't going to sleep anytime soon.

That was all right, because she had some research to do.

But the shower came first. Then she flicked on the electric teapot, and when it clicked itself off she poured boiling water into two extruded polystyrene containers of Cup Noodles. It was something of a post-workout ritual for her, planting herself on the bed, savoring the soy sauce smell of instant ramen, and cracking open one of her old sensei's notebooks. Usually her evening workouts involved swords, not bulldozing bad guys through locked doors, but the cool-down ritual was equally effective in either case.

Professor Yamada Yasuo, her first kenjutsu teacher, had earned himself a seat in the pantheon of Japan's greatest medieval historians. He harbored a fascination with the material culture of the samurai that began with his first week in army boot camp and stayed with him until his dying day, leading him to earn black belts in every sword art Japan had to offer. Fate had a cruel sense of irony: Yamada-sensei died of a vicious sword wound, and at the hand of his own student, no less. Fuchida Shūzō was a butcher and a sociopath, and after killing Yamada, he'd forced Mariko into the sword fight that cost Mariko her finger and Fuchida his life. Mariko wasn't religious, but she knew fate's cruel irony when she saw it: living by the sword and dying by the sword and all that.

She had the honor of being Yamada's last kenjutsu student, and also of being the inheritor of all of his notebooks. He'd written everything by hand—had never even owned a computer—and most of his work was over Mariko's head. In fact, much of it was over the heads of the many tenured and gray-haired history professors whose dissertation committees he'd chaired back when they were in school, but even so, Mariko enjoyed working her way through his notes. She thought of them as her way to have a little conversation with him.

Tonight, however, she was looking for something specific. That demon mask, the one on the office shelf in the packing plant, was familiar somehow. At first she thought it might have been a pop culture thing—growing up overseas, she'd missed out on a lot of her generation's icons—but Han hadn't recognized it either. That made her think the mask must have been somewhere in Yamada-sensei's many scribblings.

She had hundreds of his notebooks, stacked in tightly packed banker's boxes along the far wall of her tiny bedroom. She had no space for them, but neither could she bear to part with them. She liked coming home to him, even if all she had left of him was his old notes and his sword. Glorious Victory Unsought, the final masterpiece of Master Inazuma, rested in the sword rack she'd installed over her bed. It was enormous, a horseman's weapon, and it threatened to pull out the mounting screws with its weight. That in and of itself might have been tempting fate's sense of irony—in a land of earthquakes, a swordswoman was unwise to sleep directly under her weapon—but the sword was so long that this was the only wall it would fit on.

She was skimming tonight, not reading, and she worked her way through five volumes in the time it took her to finish her dinner. It was on the last page of the last notebook that she found what she was looking for.

The demon mask stared back at her. Its long, curving fangs were sharper than its stubby horns, its face wrought in a permanent grimace. It had a sharp row of incisors but no lower jaw, as it covered only the top half of the face, like something one might wear to a masquerade ball.

Yamada-sensei must have sketched it when he was younger, before he lost his vision. He'd surrounded it with notes, including guesses at its weight and size, and also the names of some historical figures attached to it. Mariko only recognized one of the names: Hideyoshi, one of the *San Eiketsu*, the Three Unifiers. Toyotomi Hideyoshi, Oda Nobunaga, and Tokugawa Ieyasu were the founding fathers of her country, three great warlords who united dozens of warring fiefdoms and turned them into one pacified empire. If not for them, there would be no Japan.

A thrill of adrenaline clenched Mariko's stomach and froze her breath in her lungs. It was the same feeling she would expect after narrowly missing what should have been a fatal car crash. Not two hours ago, she'd raided that packing plant with a small army of cops. What if the Kamaguchis had initiated a firefight? Both sides had automatic weapons. This was the kind of artifact that Indiana Jones would risk his life to recover, and one stray bullet could have destroyed it forever.

It was uncanny that she should own the only notebook with a sketch of this mask and that she *just so happened* to be in the same room with the mask. Not so long ago, she would have called it a spooky coincidence, but this was Yamada's notebook, and her time with him had been weird enough that she'd stopped using the word *coincidence* when it came to him.

Of course it was possible that Yamada's mask had nothing to do with the mask she'd seen tonight. More than possible, in fact. Probable. Almost certain. There were thousands of masks in Japanese history, tens of thousands, and as a historian and a lover of medieval artifacts, Yamada would have had an interest in any number of them. But his particular speciality—his raison d'être, in fact—was studying the artifacts that no one else dared to study lest they be accused of believing in magic. Mariko wasn't ready to believe in magic, but she did believe in fate. Her experience with Yamada left her no other choice. And that meant she had to admit the possibility that she and the mask were fated to cross paths.

A strange catharsis settled over her. She'd satisfied her curiosity about the mask. She'd reinforced her faith in her own powers of recollection, association, and deduction—never a bad thing for the only female detective in a department run by chauvinism and prejudice. And she'd forged a new connection with her departed sensei. She didn't like believing in fate. It was too close to astrology for her, too trippy-hippy, so if she had to suffer her new belief, it was good to find more evidence in support of it.

And it was good to find *something* that made sense tonight. It was weird enough to cross paths with an artifact like the mask, and her new narcotics case was weirder still. A buy with no cash. A supplier with no fear of cops or yakuzas. Nothing about the case made sense. It was the kind of thing to keep her up all night, staring at the ceiling and working over one failed theory after the next. Catharsis was the best sleeping aid she knew of. As tired as she was, it couldn't have come at a better time.

4

The instant she awoke, she knew something was wrong.

It was impossible to say what tipped her off. It might have been some scent in the air, noticeable only on a subliminal level. Mariko couldn't say for sure. It wasn't her alarm clock—it hadn't gone off yet—and there was no other noise in her apartment. Mariko only knew that something wasn't right. And that was before she saw Glorious Victory was missing.

Her sword was always the first thing she saw in the morning, right above her head as soon as she awoke. And now it was gone. An intruder had been in her apartment. He'd been standing right over her, in her bed, asleep. He could have done anything to her. And he'd stolen the most valuable thing she'd ever own.

The sight of the empty sword rack hit her like a hammer in the chest, but she didn't have time to think about it. Someone had been in her apartment. Her only safe place wasn't safe anymore. Someone had been in her apartment.

Her pistol was at work, locked in a desk drawer. Her Cheetah stun baton was on the little wall-mounted bookshelf above her kitchen table. Her gaze flew wildly around the room, looking for a weapon. There was nothing. The intruder might still be *in her home* and she was unarmed—and caught in panties and a T-shirt, no less. She'd never felt more vulnerable.

The best weapon she could find was her alarm clock—battery

powered, not heavy enough to really hurt anyone, but it was the best she could do. She gripped it like a cavewoman's brain-clubbing rock and got a sight line on her kitchen. It was clear. She traded the clock for the Cheetah, then opened a drawer with her free hand and dug around for her biggest kitchen knife. It seemed cheap, flimsy, almost toylike now that she needed to use it for self-defense. But she was as heavily armed as she could make herself, so she checked the last hiding place in her apartment: her bathroom. It was empty.

She went to relock her door, only to find it was already locked. She'd actually hoped she'd forgotten to lock it the night before, because now the truth was clear: she wasn't safe at all. Not here. Her doors and windows were no protection. Someone had been standing over her in her bed. He could have beaten her with her own stun baton. He could have put that flimsy knife to her throat. Raped her. Killed her. *Anything.*

Noise erupted behind her. She whirled, her breath frozen, her heart pierced by a million icy needles. She brought her feeble weapons to bear, but only in vain. It was just her alarm clock.

It buzzed irritably on her countertop, louder than it had ever been. In truth it only seemed that way, and Mariko knew it. She was jumpy. The damn thing had taken her by surprise.

She killed it and slumped to the floor. Her back pressed against her front door, and the cold of the floor tiles seeped into her feet and her ass. She felt naked. What now? she thought. Call the cops? You *are* the cops. Call Mom? Saori? They wouldn't be any help. But Mariko had to call *someone*. She didn't want to deal with this on her own.

That in itself was an alien instinct. Self-reliance was one of her strong suits, maybe her strongest. But this invasion of privacy had shaken her to the core.

Dialing 110 was the right thing to do after a burglary. It was what she would have advised anyone else to do. But Mariko didn't do it. She grabbed her phone and dialed Han. "Get to my place as quick as you can," she said. "Bring a fingerprinting kit with you, and don't touch my door until you dust it."

"Screw the prints," Han said, "how are *you*?"

"I told you, I'm fine," Mariko said. They both knew she was lying and they both knew why, and Mariko wished Han could just leave it at that. "What did you find on my doorknob?"

"Prints all over it—most of them yours, probably, but we know your guy definitely didn't wipe it clean. No scarring around the keyhole, so I don't think he used a bump key. No scuffs on the frame near the jamb either, so I don't think he worked the bolt. But I've got this funny suspicion that you knew all of that already. What's going on here?"

"Weird stuff. Ninja stuff." Mariko took the fingerprinting kit from him and started dusting her apartment, starting with the sword rack in the bedroom. "I checked with the night watchman; only four people came in or out all night, and they all live here. The security cameras tell the same story. My windows are all intact, all locked from the inside—"

"Which hardly matters, since you live on the seventeenth floor—"

"But I checked anyway, just to be thorough. And you're going to love this: the door chain was latched too."

"What? That's impossible."

"Clearly not."

"Come on. How could he—?"

"I don't know, Han. All I know is that when I come home I always slide the chain on the little thingy, and when I woke up this morning, the chain was on the little thingy."

Han poked his head in her bedroom. "So your perp couldn't have come through the door."

"Nope."

"And he couldn't have come through a window."

"Not unless he knows how to relock them from outside."

Han scanned the room, maybe looking for additional entries and exits. "So what'd he do, pass through the wall?"

"Kind of looks that way, doesn't it? And he walked out of here with a sword this big." She spread her arms as wide as they would go. "Not exactly inconspicuous. I've had the radio on ever since I called you. No reports of a ninja creeping through the neighborhood with a giant sword."

"To hell with the radio. You need to call Mulder and Scully. This isn't a home invasion, it's a damn *X-Files* episode." He studied her for a second. "Shit, Mariko, I'm sorry. This has to be scary as hell for you."

"I'm not exactly thrilled about it, no." She looked away from him, and pressed her eyes shut and her lips together as if sheer force of will could keep her face from going red. She didn't want to have this conversation with another cop—not even with Han, the one person she trusted more than anyone else on the force.

"Did he . . . I mean, are you okay? Like, *okay* okay?"

Mariko swallowed. "If you're asking what I think you're asking, no, he didn't rape me."

Han sighed as if she'd just lifted a parked car off his chest. His relief was so palpable that she even felt some of it herself. *This* was why he'd earned her trust. Any other man in the department would have pressured her to go in for a rape kit. Han took her at her word, and he did it because he treated her like an adult. Lots of the other guys respected her, but they did it the same way they'd respect a high school athlete doing something amazing, something only the pros should be able to do.

So when he felt relieved, it wasn't fatherly or brotherly or anything else. It was plain old *thank God you're okay*, and that meant the world to her. Given the morning she was having, it almost made her cry.

But that wasn't something she was going to do, even in front of him. She busied herself with studying the crime scene so she'd have something other than her emotions to think about. Her eyes passed over Yamada-sensei's sketch of the demon mask, in the notebook she'd left faceup and sprawled open the night before.

She winced at the thought of what damage she'd done to the spine of the notebook, leaving it sit open like that for hours. It was the most trivial concern imaginable, and yet it niggled at her, so she reached down to close the book. As she did so, the next page flopped over, and on the overleaf she saw Yamada's handwriting running like a banner at the top of the page: *What is the connection between the mask and Glorious Victory Unsought?*

She sat heavily on the bed. Kamaguchi Hanzō—the man who had a contract on her life, the man whose drug den she'd raided the night before, the man whose brutality on the streets had earned him the name Bulldog—owned an ancient mask that was somehow related to her sword. A sword that was now missing. A sword that had been taken by someone standing over her bed as she slept.

"Oh, hell," she said.

"What?" Han said.

"It was the Bulldog. I think he's sending me a message." Mariko handed Han the notebook, opened to the page with the mask. "Remember the shelf of antiques in his office? All medieval stuff, most of it related to the samurai. My sword would fit right in."

"So what, last night he decided to expand his collection?" Han thought about it for a second. "I don't like it. I mean, there's a hit out on you, right? If he's going to take all the trouble to break into your place, why not just shoot you?"

"Gee, thanks. You really know how to help a girl feel safe."

Han winced as if he just felt the squish of dog crap under his shoe. "Sorry. But you know what I'm getting at. Why not collect a double payday? The sword plus the bounty?"

"I don't know. Like I said, I think he's trying to send me a message. But I'm damned if I know how to read it."

Han looked back at the door, then at the windows, his boyish face scrunched up in thought. "There's something else: that message of his is in the wrong language. I mean, the dude's got a list of priors going back twenty, twenty-five years, almost all of them violent crimes. Now picture a guy like that breaking into your apartment. How is he going to do it?"

Mariko thought of the Bulldog's photo on the top sheet in his file.

Broad shoulders, ferocious eyes, an underbite like a wild boar's. Not the type to run a stealth mission. "Good point," she said. "Kicking down the door and shoving a shotgun in your mouth is more his speed."

"Exactly. This ninja stuff is just weird."

"So is his dope deal." Mariko ticked off each point on her fingers: "No cash on hand for the buy. A dealer who knows there's a sting and shows up anyway. Kamaguchi-gumi enforcers who don't mind beating the hell out of their supplier but somehow grow a conscience when it comes to killing him—"

"I don't know about that," Han said. "Last time I checked, the dude was still in surgery."

"Yeah, but you know what I mean. They could have killed him, but instead they just roughed him up. We've got a drug deal with no money and no logical motives for the buyers or the sellers. And now the buyer just *happens* to break into my apartment on the very same night? Why wait this long? If Kamaguchi knows where I live, he could have aced me weeks ago."

"And if he wanted to hock your sword for drug money, he could have kicked in your door whenever he wanted."

"Exactly. But instead he waits until the very night I'm involved in a raid on his speed operation, and then he does all of this elaborate ninja shit."

Han shook his head. "I don't get it. You?"

"Not a clue."

"But you're interested, aren't you?"

"Ten percent interested, ninety percent pissed off." Mariko clenched her fists in frustration. "This guy broke into my *home*, Han. And from the look of it, he can do it whenever he wants. Can you understand what that means to a woman who lives alone? Where the hell am I supposed to sleep tonight?"

Han took a deep breath, as if he were getting ready to jump off a cliff. Then, just before offering the invitation Mariko knew was coming, he deflated. He couldn't put her up at his place. That was a line male and female partners couldn't cross, and both of them knew it. The department's prohibition against "fraternization between officers" was admittedly old-fashioned, and Han had no qualms about bucking bullshit regulations when he had a mind to, but Mariko didn't stray outside the lines. She counted herself lucky to have a commanding officer who was willing to let her kick down doors instead of pushing paperwork, and she wasn't about to jeopardize that.

Besides, the real problem wasn't Mariko's accommodations; it was the break-in, the upside-down drug bust, the price on Mariko's head. Somehow they'd all become interconnected. Whatever the connection was, it had Mariko feeling so vulnerable that she hadn't even mustered the courage to take a shower. The thought of trapping herself in a tiny room, naked and cornered, was too unsettling.

She pulled her cell phone from the pocket of her jeans and checked the time. She and Han had half an hour before Lieutenant Sakakibara would bust their asses for being late to work. No time for a shower now. She stepped past Han, poked her head into the bathroom, and studied her reflection in the mirror. Her short, choppy, bed-head hair stuck out in a hundred different directions.

"That's just great," she said, cranking on the hot water. She'd have to run her head under the faucet and call it good. "Han, do me a huge favor and stand guard outside my door for two minutes, would you? If you see any ninjas in the hallway, shoot to kill."

Han grinned. "You got it." He made a show of racking the slide on his pistol for dramatic effect.

She forced a laugh, pushed him into the hallway, and locked the door. It wasn't even six thirty yet and it was already shaping up to be one hell of a day.

BOOK TWO

AZUCHI-MOMOYAMA PERIOD, THE YEAR 21

(1588 CE)

5

Shichio sat in his writing room with three scrolls sprawled before him, wholly covering the lacquered red top of his knee-high desk. One showed a map of Suruga, Kai, and Shinano—northern provinces, nuts as yet uncracked. One was a map of Kyushu, dotted with personnel deployments. The third listed all the fortifications and garrisons in the Kansai, along with their troop strengths. Tonight's puzzle was sorting out which regiments to disband in order to replace the casualties across all the other wounded divisions. It was taxing work, but Shichio was only too happy to leave his battlefield days behind him. He was far better suited to solving logistics problems than to all those sweaty, dirty, bloody days in the field.

It was late and the hallway on the opposite side of his shoji door had been dark for hours. Now something in the hall glowed like a foxfire, hovering at chest height, indistinct through the rice-paper windows. The shining orange ball bobbed right and left, up and down, making its way slowly to his study. It swelled in both size and brightness, then settled near the floor, close enough to the shoji now that Shichio could make out the blurry outlines of a dancing candle flame. He sighed and laid down his writing brush. "Must you disturb me yet again?" he said.

"Begging your pardon, General," said a voice so meek it could only belong to Jun, his adjutant. "There's someone here you should see."

"Do you plan to tell me this someone's name?"

"I don't know it, sir."

Shichio saw through the shoji as a kneeling shadow bowed low. "Jun, am I usually in the habit of answering summons from unidentified callers? No. Go away."

"Begging your pardon, sir, but you ordered me to send for you for this one."

"Ah. Him."

Shichio rose, Jun sliding the shoji open even as he did so. The hallway was dark but for Jun's candle and empty but for Jun, who was so slight of build that he could hardly be said to be there at all. Shichio took an object wrapped in silk from his shelf and tested its weight in his hand. It was no bigger than a sushi plate, but it was as heavy as if it were made of stone. He stepped out into the corridor. "So? Where is he?"

"Just this way, General."

Jun popped to his feet and scurried off down the corridor. His candle caused yellow flares to shine here and there on the walls, bouncing its light off the gold leaf that seemed to cover every last panel and rafter in the entire Jurakudai. Shichio smelled incense and wondered if the wind was carrying the scent from the nearby Hongwanji temple or if Hashiba had sent his incense bearers running through the halls yet again. Shichio would have done almost anything for Hashiba, but first and foremost he'd like to give Hashiba some advice in decorating this garish monstrosity.

As Jun led him across a gravel courtyard under the three-quarter moon, Shichio saw the lunar reflection in the gold leaf on the roof tiles. By the gods and buddhas, Shichio thought, who gilds roof tiles? It was so overwrought.

But such decisions were not Shichio's to make. Perhaps he would get to design a palace of his own one day. Now and then Hashiba spoke idly of invading China. If he did invade, perhaps Shichio would go and make a name for himself there. Perhaps he would besiege some city, and ride in triumphantly after it fell. He could seize the most elegant mansion in the most peaceable quarter, and make a proper palace of it.

Tasteful colors, unembellished roof tiles, and an art collection to rival the Emperor's. But until then he would enjoy the comforts of the Jurakudai, such as they were.

The man kneeling in the courtyard enjoyed precious little comfort. His elbows were tied behind his back with jute rope, each wrist bound to the opposite forearm. He wore no armor, and the gravel must have been punishing his knees. But he had the body of a soldier: broad arms, broad neck, a sturdy torso, and a shaved head. Shichio did not recognize him.

Until the man looked up at him. Then Shichio could see the scar running straight across his forehead, halfway between his eyebrows and the top of his forehead. It was thin, the scar, but even by moonlight it was unmistakable.

"Bring him inside," said Shichio. "Now."

Jun seized the prisoner by one of his elbows and tried to herd him toward the nearest building. The prisoner did not move. He had the muscles of a career soldier and the belly of a retired veteran; the reedy Jun could not hope to move him. But the prisoner conducted himself with honor: no doubt he saw that Jun or Shichio could summon other, larger men, and so rather than risking the indignity of being dragged off, he stood of his own accord and followed Shichio solemnly.

Shichio marched ahead, sliding open the first shoji he came across and slipping out of his sandals to enter the audience chamber within. Jun halted at the door, and with a tug he bade the prisoner to stop too.

"Well?" said Shichio.

His adjutant looked at the tatami floor. "Sir, he's shod. And his feet are dusty."

"Then you'll have to clean the tatami later, won't you? Or if that's too much trouble, I could just have you skinned and hang your filthy pelt on the wall. That ought to be enough to distract visitors from the floor, don't you think?"

Jun swallowed and shoved the prisoner into the audience chamber.

Shichio was about to tell him to shut the door when he saw it was already too late. Hashiba was crossing the courtyard, heading straight for him. Mio Yasumasa, that old fat oaf, trailed two or three paces behind. General Mio towered over Hashiba like a snowcapped mountain. Of course it was hard to find a grown man shorter than Hashiba, but Mio seemed to lord his size over him, stomping like an elephant and wearing his armor for almost every occasion. What possible need could he have to be armored tonight? Here, in the most secure building in the Kansai? Yet the huge *sode* at his shoulders made him seem all the broader, and the *haidate* bouncing on his huge and ponderous thighs made it sound as if an army were approaching.

Hashiba smiled when he saw Shichio. The moonlight deepened the shadows in his face, sharpening his features and reminding Shichio why Hashiba's enemies seldom called him by his rightful name, Imperial Regent and Chief Minister Toyotomi no Hideyoshi. More often they called him the Monkey King. His face was too long below the nose, his cheekbones too sharp, his teeth too pointed. To Shichio he looked not so much like a monkey as like one of those little wrinkle-faced dogs from Peiping that women ought to find ugly but find adorable instead. Too ugly to be ugly.

"General Shichio," Hashiba said as he drew near, his voice jolly and booming—as much to be heard over Mio's clattering as to indicate his mood, Shichio thought. "Who's our guest?"

Shichio had no way of answering that question. He certainly couldn't tell the truth; if this man was who he thought he was—if he'd gotten that scar across his forehead the way Shichio thought he had—then Shichio might as well cut his own throat as tell the truth about who the man was and how he'd come here. And lying was no good either. Every now and again Hashiba forgave someone who betrayed him, but the fact that he did so made his punishments all the more terrifying. One never knew which Toyotomi Hideyoshi was going to hand down judgment.

It was Jun who rescued him. "My lord regent, this man was overheard maligning your name."

Hashiba laughed. "And for this you invite him into my house?"

"My lord regent," said Jun, bowing low, "some of your loyal soldiers were extolling your virtues at a roadside tavern. This one had been drinking like a whale—"

"As had my loyal soldiers, no doubt."

"I'm sure you're right, my lord." Jun bowed even lower. "This one, he drank too much and he contradicted your soldiers. They said you were a master tactician on the battlefield. This one said his master outmaneuvered you."

"So he's a braggart. My dear Juntaro-san, if you brought all such men to my attention I'd never have a spare minute to sleep." Hashiba chuckled. "And that's to say nothing of doing what I prefer to be doing in my bed rather than sleeping."

Jun prostrated himself lower still. If he could have sunk through the floorboards, he would have. "My lord regent, to be more specific, he said his master outmaneuvered you as if your armies had passed out drunk on the field of battle."

"And if I were to make an example out of all such braggarts, I'd never have time to march my armies anywhere. Or to do any drinking." Hashiba laughed again. "You dragged this man all the way here for nothing, my boy. Where did you say you found him?"

"At a tavern on the road to Mikawa, my lord."

"Mikawa." Hashiba's smile vanished instantly. "He's one of Tokugawa's men?"

Shichio butted in before Jun could speak. "I think not. He wears neither the crest nor the colors. Don't worry. I will get to the bottom of who he is and where he hails from."

Just like that, the smile returned—but it was a wicked smile now. "See that you do," Hashiba said. His eyes were warm, but his voice was cold; it was so hard to tell what he would do next.

He clasped his hands together with a loud clap. "So. Gentlemen. The audience with the emperor was a success. He's given me his blessing to conquer the north. The weather is clear and the moon is bright. A perfect night all around for singing, drinking, and finding eager young fillies to mount."

Mio bowed and assented. "A capital idea," said Shichio. "Would you mind terribly if we spoke for a minute first? Alone?"

Hashiba reached up to slap Mio's massive spaulder, then punched Jun on his bony arm. "Summon the girls and the sake," he said, all friendliness and light now. "We'll sit on the moon-viewing deck. Oh, and, Jun, see to it that these tatami are replaced. Your prisoner's gone and trodden all over them with his dirty boots."

Jun bowed, gave Shichio the tiniest of glances, and made himself scarce. General Mio gave a curt bow and headed toward the moon tower. Shichio stepped into the audience chamber and Hashiba followed, sliding the shoji shut behind him.

"Hashiba-dono," Shichio said.

"Not here."

"We're alone."

Hashiba looked at the prisoner, who stood proudly despite his bound arms and the dust of the road on his clothing.

"This man is no one," said Shichio, hooking a finger under Hashiba's chin to pull his gaze back to his own face. "But if you're worried about him talking, we can arrange to have his tongue cut out, can't we?"

Hashiba took half a step backward. Usually he liked these little hints at violence. They made him feel powerful. But not tonight. "Who is he, Shichio? You're up to something."

"He's no one. I swear to you. But I think he has information about an abbey of the Ikkō sect."

"Nonsense. We doused that fire years ago."

"Perhaps. But even a single ember can give birth to a forest fire, *neh*?"

"Ask Mio. He was around before your time. He'll tell you: we put them to the sword by the thousands. Believe me, the Ikkō Ikki are no threat to anyone."

Shichio made a pouting face. "Let me ask this one anyway."

Hashiba smirked. "Why? You've got no taste for asking questions anyhow—at least not in the way that guarantees the right answers."

Shichio suppressed a shudder. He'd seen the fruits of Hashiba's favored method. He'd seen the horrors of the battlefield too. Hashiba's technique was indescribably, nightmarishly worse.

And despite Shichio's efforts to conceal his revulsion, Hashiba saw through his mask. "You see?" he said. "All I have to do is mention *real* questioning and your blood runs cold."

Hashiba had him cornered. But if there was one thing Shichio was good at, it was turning a position of weakness into a position of strength. "If I do it your way, you'll let me ask my questions?"

Hashiba sighed. "If this is Tokugawa's man, it'll be nothing but trouble for me."

"Come, now. He'll never miss one man, will he?"

"Lord Penny-Pincher? He'd notice if a horsefly went missing. And taking the north will be troublesome enough without goading its best strategist."

"Please, Hashiba-dono, *please.* . . ."

Another sigh. Hashiba looked at the prisoner for a moment, pensive, probably calculating benefits and risks. At last he said, "He cannot leave here alive."

"Oh, thank you, Hashiba-dono."

"You can thank me later. When you're done with him, come on up to watch the moon with me." He looked down at Shichio's hand and the heavy, cloth-bound, platelike thing it was holding. "Bring that with you."

"Count on it."

Then Hashiba was gone and Shichio was alone with his prisoner. "I'm not going to tell you a damn thing," the prisoner said.

"Oh, we already know that's not true, don't we? Yes, we do. It only takes a few drinks to get you talking. Well, I won't be giving you much to drink, but you'll find Lord Toyotomi's other methods are equally tongue-loosening. Now, you're not going to be so stupid as to run, are you?"

The man stuck out his chin and squared his shoulders.

"No? Good. Our destination isn't far. I'd just as soon ask you my questions here—they're going to replace the floors in this room anyway, aren't they? You might as well do all your bleeding here. But you heard the regent."

The prisoner followed obediently to the little outbuilding near the slaughterhouse—not that he had much choice, being prodded along by two of Shichio's bodyguards. He blanched when he saw the table, and ground his teeth as they stripped him of his clothes, but otherwise no sign of fear showed in him. He knelt before Shichio not as one showing obeisance but as one prepared to commit seppuku. His eyes were already on Shichio's *wakizashi*.

Shichio looked down at the sword, then back at his captive. "You samurai! Your thoughts always run straight to bloodletting, don't they?" He slapped the man's face. "You disgust me. You should praise your swords for their elegance, their craftsmanship, but no. You smear them in gore. Why can't you butchers understand? These swords of yours, they're works of art."

He began to unwrap the thin, heavy thing he'd been holding all this time, the one he'd taken from the shelf in his study. "Unlike you, I appreciate artistry. Let me show you my favorite piece."

He took his time peeling back the silk. As the folds of cloth fell away, the face of a demon gradually emerged. It was a mask—or rather a half mask, only big enough to cover him from his forehead to his upper lip. It was a very old thing. Rusty orange accented the recesses: the furrows in its brow, the wrinkles around its scowling eyes. It was the perishability of the mask that made it so beautiful, like icicles sparkling in the very sunlight that would melt them.

The moment his fingertips brushed its rough brown skin, Shichio found himself thinking of blades, of piercing and stabbing. The mask always had that effect on him. Indeed, prior to owning the mask, he'd never seen swords as beautiful. Now he couldn't understand why he hadn't appreciated them before. So graceful. So powerful. He found them quite fascinating.

He stood before his prisoner and donned the mask, binding it tightly in place with leather thongs. He slid his fingertips over the short iron horns jabbing up from his forehead, ran his tongue over the sharp row of fangs that extended down just as far as his own teeth. The prisoner's eyes widened. He shrank away from the mask. It was a subtle thing, the smallest retreat in military history, but the fear was visible in him now. Shichio found it delicious.

"It gives me no pleasure," he said. "The bloodshed, that is. To tell you the truth, even the smell of it sickens me. And the thought of tying a man to a table, making him utterly defenseless, and *then* bleeding him—it's simply monstrous, isn't it? And yet I must do as my regent commands. But you understand that, don't you? Yes. Yes, I think you do."

Shichio gave him a compassionate smile, stroked the man's cheek, passed his fingers through the man's hair. His prisoner pulled away from his touch. It was so easy to terrify these men, these fearless worthies of the samurai caste. They thought nothing of pain, they held death in contempt, and yet the mere sight of a lunatic gave them pause. This one had no idea what to make of Shichio and his mask, and in the structured world of the soldier, to be unpredictable was to be utterly mad. The largest cobra and fiercest tiger were nothing in comparison. Animals had instincts. Their intentions were easily known. Not so with a madman.

The fact that he wore a demonic mask did not necessarily make him a madman. It was the loving caress that made his prisoner shudder. Even Shichio's bodyguards recoiled at the sight.

"Now, then," Shichio said, "you were listening earlier, *neh*? When Jun explained who you are to the regent? Of course you were. Now you're going to tell me about the things Jun left out. About that scar on your forehead. About the man who gave it to you. About his friend, the monk."

The prisoner was quaking uncontrollably now. Was he trying to assess what the masked lunatic would do next? Was he evaluating escape strategies? Wondering how many swords and spears stood between this room and the streets of Kyoto, or how far he'd make it with his arms tied behind his back? Shichio was dying to know.

He took the prisoner's chin between his thumb and forefinger and bent down close enough to kiss him. "Tell me about the monk," he whispered. "Tell me about the house of Okuma."

6

The challenger's *bokken* smashed across the knuckles of Daigoro's right hand. Daigoro backed away, but the pain did not. As his challenger circled him, Daigoro flexed the top two fingers experimentally. Pain shot through them as if they were made of broken glass. Two broken bones, maybe more. He'd have to wait until the end of the duel to be sure.

Daigoro limped to his right, mirroring his opponent's movement. Sora Samanosuke was a cagey fighter. He retreated more often than he advanced and he feinted more often than striking true. The tip of his sword fluttered like a hummingbird. Daigoro knocked it aside, chopped down at the wrists, but Sora backed away. Daigoro lunged, pressing his opponent back, trying to catch him on his heels. Sora circled. Daigoro's sword chopped high, aiming for the temple. Sora parried and cut low.

His *bokken* struck just above the knee. Daigoro felt his leg buckle and could only roll into the fall.

"Point, Sora," said Katsushima Goemon. In that very instant he was in the center of the courtyard, separating the two opponents. The sheer speed of his movement drew a gasp from Daigoro. Half a heartbeat earlier, Katsushima had been kneeling in the judge's position, yet despite the gray in his topknot and bushy sideburns, he moved as swiftly as any bird of prey. Even on the best of days, it took Daigoro the space of several breaths to rise from kneeling.

Today was not the best of days. Pain burned like a torch in his right hand, and of course his right leg was no help. Even at birth it was skinnier than either of his arms, and now with only one good hand and one good leg, it was just another weight he had to move to get himself back to standing.

The sand of the courtyard was warm under his palm. The wind made the trees whisper on all sides of the Okuma compound, and a dust devil whirled in one corner of the compound's weathered wooden walls. Daigoro could smell the salt of the ocean on the breeze, and the promise of spring rain, though the only clouds were far toward the horizon. On the opposite side of the courtyard sat Lord Sora, resplendent in his yellow kimono and bright orange *haori*. His long white beard swayed in the breeze as he regarded the combatants, and suddenly Daigoro felt ashamed of his sand-dusted *hakama*.

At length Daigoro managed to get to his feet, and with his wooden sword trembling in the two usable fingers of his right hand, he bowed to Sora Samanosuke. The champion of the Sora clan returned the bow and both fighters retired to their sides of the courtyard, Daigoro limping and Sora all but floating. He'd been the underdog, and now his chest swelled with pride.

"What have I told you about patience?" Katsushima said as Daigoro lowered himself to a kneeling position. "You mustn't press a fighter who wants to be pressed. You're letting him draw you off your guard."

Daigoro opened his mouth to respond, then bit down hard as ice-cold spikes of pain lanced through his right hand. He looked down to see Tomo, his baby-faced retainer, peeling his fingers away from his *bokken*'s grip. Tomo looked up, his ever-present smile bending into a wince. "I'm so sorry, Okuma-dono. Setting the bones is best done quickly."

Daigoro wondered how a simple potter's boy could know that. But he could also imagine the pain Tomo would have inflicted by taking his time in straightening the fingers. Better to do it as Tomo had done: swiftly, in one go. Daigoro fought down a wave of nausea and tried to center his concentration somewhere else—*anywhere* else, anywhere other than his hand.

"I cannot understand you," Katsushima said, his tone sharper than it should have been. He might have been thirty years' Daigoro's senior, but Daigoro was the lord of the house. Then again, Katsushima had sworn no oaths to House Okuma. He'd taken no payment for services rendered. It was true that he'd been acting as Daigoro's swordmaster, and he'd taken on the role of mentor in a more general sense, but strictly speaking he was more of a houseguest. The man was *rōnin*, plain and simple.

"This is your seventh straight loss with the *bokken*," Katsushima said, "and the seventeenth in your last twenty duels. Yet with steel you're untouchable. Why?"

Because I don't want to kill anyone, Daigoro thought. Because so long as I don't wish to kill anyone, Glorious Victory Unsought will never let me lose. And because once you're in the habit of dueling with steel, playing with *bokken* is about as serious as monkeys chasing each other through the treetops. This is a game, and one I only play because I have to.

Then that ice-cold pain hammered deep down into the bones of his hand. He looked down and saw Tomo had tied the top two fingers together. They were purple and swollen, but Tomo's sure hands and a long cotton ribbon would see them bound as painlessly as possible. Some game, Daigoro thought.

"Your focus is as leaky as an old grass roof," said Katsushima. "Listen to me. Why can you not show the same patience with wood as you do with steel? You never overextend yourself with Glorious Victory. You could have had this Sora boy and you gave the match away."

"No," Daigoro said, and he was about to explain why Katsushima was wrong, but then he remembered: Katsushima didn't believe in enchanted blades. Tales of magic were for farmers' wives, he said, and now was not the time to rekindle that debate. Daigoro had to prepare himself for a very different conversation.

So instead he said, "It hardly matters now." He had taken the first point but lost the last two. In a few moments Katsushima would call out both fighters and announce Sora the winner. But on the positive side, Daigoro thought—still trying to keep his mind off his ruined right hand—at least the Soras won't ask me to duel with steel. Glorious Victory is too heavy for me even at my best. Today I'm not sure I could even keep her tip off the ground.

Katsushima shook his head, gave the tiniest of snorts, and returned to the center of the courtyard. "Fighters, bow!"

Daigoro stood, *bokken* in his left hand and cold, piercing pain in his right, and bowed. "Fighters, approach!" said Katsushima, and the two duelists marched in lockstep with each other to meet Katsushima in the middle.

"Winner, Sora Samanosuke."

And that's that, thought Daigoro, bowing deeply to his opponent. Now we can get down to what's important. He'd never had much taste for dueling. For years he'd wondered whether he might have felt differently if he'd been born tall and strong like his father or brother, but at the moment he wondered only about how quickly he might have been able to get down to business if everyone else weren't so taken with duels.

Glorious Victory Unsought was half the trouble. It was his father's sword, a genuine Inazuma blade, but even without it his father would still have been famous as a warrior, a diplomat, and a tactician. It was probably his fame that had gotten him killed. It was his sword that got Daigoro's elder brother Ichirō killed—well, that and Ichirō's ego, Daigoro supposed, but certainly these damnable duels were no help. Challengers came from far and wide to face House Okuma's famed Inazuma blade. Now only Daigoro remained to face them. Ichirō's death condemned Daigoro to a lifelong sentence of working day and night to uphold their father's reputation.

Daigoro still didn't understand why the clan leaders had agreed to name him Izu-no-kami, Lord Protector of Izu. At sixteen Daigoro was not only the youngest of the five lords protector; he could have been a grandson to any one of them. Okuma Tetsurō had left such a lofty reputation for his son to live up to, and Daigoro was not yet accustomed to shaving his pate.

"My lords," Daigoro said, "it has been my honor to be defeated by such an agile warrior. Now, if you would like to join me for dinner—"

"Not so fast," said Lord Sora. He stood and approached the fighters, his yellow kimono flowing behind him and the broad orange shoulders of his *haori* all but glowing in the sun. Sora Izu-no-kami Nobushige was another lord protector of Izu, and had held that station since even Daigoro's father was a little boy. Despite his many years his white topknot had not thinned at all, and his red face still seemed as though he'd just left the forge that made him famous. Upon arrival at the Okuma compound, Lord Sora and his grandson had presented Daigoro with two of their clan's famed *yoroi*, breastplates so well crafted that they were said to be able to deflect even the musket balls of the southern barbarians. Daigoro could not help thinking that the gift was made too late; had the Soras provided their unique armor a year earlier, they could have been meeting with Daigoro's father today.

Years of hefting and hammering had made Lord Sora's body strong, but the decades afterward had slowed him considerably. "My grandson is unsatisfied," he said, almost shouting because he'd made so little progress across the courtyard. Daigoro noted the old man's shuffling steps with sympathy; he wasn't much faster himself. But he also noted that between Lord Sora's shouting and his perpetually red face, it was impossible to read the man's emotions.

"He believes the famed Bear Cub of Izu has not fought at his most bearlike," said Lord Sora, still booming. "He believes our young lord has gone easy on him so that our parley will go smoothly. I am sure the young lord will explain to him why this is a misperception."

At least *that* wasn't hard to read. Daigoro was certain the doubts hadn't come from Samanosuke at all. They came from the old man.

And the solution to all of this could have been so easy. Daigoro had but to hike up the hem of his *hakama* and show the Soras the wrist-thin leg concealed within. But to reveal his own weakness would have brought shame on both his clan and his father's memory. Only a handful knew the son of Okuma Tetsurō was a cripple.

So instead he said, "My lords, my prowess has indeed been spoken of highly—more highly than it should have been. I assure you, I fought my best."

"Then how is it that my grandson bested you so easily? Your reputation precedes you, Okuma-dono. Everyone knows you are undefeated in duels with live steel. If my grandson were so inclined, he might come to the conclusion that you have insulted our house. That you were toying with him. Even that you let him win in order to secure a better price on Sora *yoroi*."

And one might also conclude, Daigoro thought, that you deliberately read the worst into every situation, the better to drive up the price of your precious armor. Or that you believe two broken fingers is too small a price to pay for nothing more than the honor of dining with you. Or that your grandson's life is no price at all, that it will be good enough for your house if one of your lineage dies on Inazuma steel.

But Daigoro could say none of it. He could only try to keep from shaking his head, to hold his breath rather than let out a scoff. Lord Sora was close now, standing shoulder to broad shoulder with Katsushima. Daigoro hoped he'd contained himself well enough, because the old man was close enough to see the slightest hint of disrespect.

"I don't suppose," Daigoro said, his tone less gracious than it should have been, "that your grandson would like to come here and voice his concerns himself."

Sora's red cheeks wrinkled in the wake of a thin, spreading smile. "I fear he may have lost his composure."

"He certainly wouldn't want to do that," said Katsushima, giving Daigoro a piercing stare.

"No, indeed," said Daigoro. "No, he would not." Stubborn old bastard, he thought. Damn you for making me do this. "But perhaps he might be willing to face me in a second duel?"

Sora's white eyebrows pushed up toward his topknot. "Why,

Okuma-dono, what sort of a barbarian do you take him for? He has his honor to think of. It wouldn't do to challenge a man he's just beaten."

"Of course not," said Daigoro, grinding his teeth. "I mean to say that, if he would be so gracious, I would be honored if he would accept my invitation to fight me steel to steel."

A triumphant light gleamed in Lord Sora's beady black eyes. "Samanosuke," he called, not even bothering to look back, "ready your *katana*."

Daigoro limped back to the veranda where Tomo and Glorious Victory stood waiting. Tomo regarded him with a smile that conveyed more worry than gladness. His hair was disheveled and he was wringing something in his hands, something too small and slender for Daigoro to see.

"Tomo, I'll need you to do something more for these fingers. There's no way I can hold—"

"It's all well in hand, sir." Now Tomo's smile was boyish again, widening as he presented Daigoro with a closed fist. He opened his hand with a flourish, revealing a short, curved length of copper.

"Tomo, is that your hairpin?"

"No longer, sir. It's your splint. May I see your hand?"

The metal matched the length of Daigoro's middle finger precisely. How Tomo had managed that was beyond Daigoro's ken. It hurt like hellfire when Tomo unwrapped the bandage he'd laid before, and when he bent misshapen fingers to match the curve of the copper, it was everything Daigoro could do not to wail like a little child. But the metal was a lot stronger than broken bone—maybe even strong enough to hold the weight of an *ōdachi*, Daigoro thought. If I don't pass out first.

A few quick wraps with the cotton bandage and Daigoro's broken fingers vanished, replaced by a fat, swollen, pain-ridden tongue, curled in just the shape needed to grip a sword. "By the Buddha, that stings," said Daigoro. He wiped the last unbidden tears from his eyes and willed his clenching jaws to relax. "You're a miracle worker, Tomo."

"If you're lucky, he'll kill you, sir. And if not, I'm going to have to reset those fingers after the duel."

Daigoro pushed himself to his feet, babying his right hand. He needed Tomo's help to draw Glorious Victory, whose blade was nearly twice the length of his arm. He saw Samanosuke's eyes widen as the two of them came to the center of the courtyard.

"Take your stance," Katsushima said, and Daigoro's right thigh quivered as he centered his sword. He found himself overgripping with his left hand, the better to take weight out of the right. The pain coming from those two fingers was blinding. Daigoro raised Glorious Victory to a high guard, the blade pointing straight at the sun, leaving his vitals wide open in an effort to take more weight off his maimed right hand.

Samanosuke hovered like a bee, well out of range. His *katana* was scarcely half the length of Daigoro's *ōdachi*, and he was too crafty a fighter to simply wade in looking to score a quick kill. Had he ever faced a horseman's sword before? Did he know Daigoro's high guard sacrificed most of his reach? Daigoro couldn't be sure.

Samanosuke ventured in closer. Daigoro held his stance. Another step and Samanosuke was close enough to strike. Their eyes met. Samanosuke lunged.

Daigoro had been so focused on Samanosuke's blade that he never saw his mother rush onto the battlefield.

She looked like a madwoman, her hair billowing smokelike in every direction, and she grabbed Samanosuke from behind. "No no no no no," she shrieked, her hands digging into Samanosuke's elbows like iron hooks. Samanosuke had to struggle just to keep his footing.

Daigoro was paralyzed. He couldn't lower his blade lest Samanosuke think he was attacking him. Nor could he simply toss his father's sword aside like an old chicken bone. His scabbard was a good ten paces away. "Mother!" he shouted, his sword standing uselessly in his high guard.

"Not my baby," she wailed. "Not my baby mybabymybaby—"

At last Katsushima took a hold of her, prying her hands off Samanosuke one by one. Moments later Tomo was on her too, and together they wrestled her back into the house.

"What is the meaning of this?" Lord Sora bellowed. Daigoro and Samanosuke still had their swords in hand. Formally speaking, their duel was still in progress, but any other semblance of formality had scattered to the winds. Now Lord Sora was shuffling into the fray, blustering as only he could. "Is this how you come to be undefeated? Do you Okumas allow your women to do your fighting?"

Daigoro lowered his weapon, taking care to point it away from everyone else so that no one could mistake it for an attack. "My lords," he said, "you must accept our most abject apologies. Within the past year my mother lost her husband and her firstborn. No doubt you've heard how my brother Ichirō died, *neh*?"

Still visibly shaken, Samanosuke gave a nervous nod. "In a duel."

"A duel just like this one."

The truth was worse, though Daigoro had no mind to share family secrets. Ichirō's name meant "firstborn son." Daigoro's meant "fifth son." Their mother had miscarried two boys in between, but of course no woman could have named her next child "fourth son." Four was the number of death. Daigoro's mother had wanted to give her fourth son a girl's name instead, for clearly some curse hung like a pall over the boys of House Okuma. Perhaps a girl's name might deceive the evil gods and spirits. But her husband would not allow it, and so she'd named her next child Daigoro, despite the fact that he was not the fifth. The curse had already disfigured his leg; she would not hang the number of death on her newborn as well.

The thought of losing him shook her like an earthquake. Three of her four boys had already been taken before their time, and now the sight of her last living son facing live steel had shattered her completely.

"My lords," Daigoro said, "I beg your understanding. She is beside herself with grief. Sometimes she does not know what she does."

Samanosuke nodded, more sure of himself this time, but his grandfather was incensed. "I should think not," he boomed. "I've never seen anything so disgraceful."

"I give you my word, she will not interfere again. My men will see to it."

"They should have seen to it the first time!"

"Quite right, Lord Sora. They should have. Rest assured that the responsible parties will be punished most harshly. In the meantime, please, if the Buddha's compassion means anything to you, have pity on a poor woman who has lost more than she can bear."

The breath coming from Lord Sora's nose was as loud as a bellows. His huge red fists reminded Daigoro of the demonic Fudō statues standing guard over so many temples, the ones that had scared Daigoro so deeply as a little boy. He was a storm front in human form, and he even brought the rain with him: those dark clouds on the horizon had already reached the compound, blotting out the sun. "This is an outrage, Okuma. Most of the daimyo in Izu are younger than me, and you're younger than the lot, but I've never, *ever* heard a daimyo called 'my baby' before. If you think we're going to stand for an embarrassment like this—think what the other clans will say, a Sora beaten in a duel by a, by a—this, this won't stand at all—"

It was all blustering from there. Daigoro offered apologies on behalf of his entire family. He offered to make good on his invitation to duel, the next time at the Sora compound. He offered a roof over the Soras' heads. But though Samanosuke seemed amenable, his grandfather opted for a long ride home in the rain.

7

That night Daigoro sat in the teahouse, which had been prepared for many more guests than Tomo, Katsushima, and himself. Low tables ran the perimeter of the room, each one bedecked with chopsticks, a bowl for pickles, another for soup, another for rice, a space left for where the fish platters would be served, and a little bizen teacup. Daigoro supposed it was actually a mercy that his guests had left in a huff. Were they present, he would have been obliged to bottle up his suffering during their meal. As it was, Tomo could get straight to resetting his broken finger bones.

He winced and bit down hard, eyes watering, as Tomo pried the last of the fragments into place. "Terribly sorry, sir," Tomo said, looking up with a compassionate smile. In truth Daigoro could not recall a time when he had not seen Tomo smiling. Fever, dog bites, even typhoons, nothing could sour his expression. He'd probably even smile if someone rammed a dagger in his chest. It was his way of dealing with the world's tribulations, and in that sense he and Tomo weren't so different. As a born samurai, Daigoro was expected to hide any pain or dismay behind a mask of equanimity. Tomo was lowborn, yet took refuge in his smile just as Daigoro took refuge in feigned serenity.

Daigoro blushed, ashamed that he'd allowed his mask to fall. Tomo finished with the fingers, binding them between thin strips of bamboo. It hurt like Fudō himself was crushing them with his great red teeth, but Daigoro managed to keep his mask on. "Thank you, Tomo. I believe you've saved my hand."

"It's nothing, sir."

"Good night."

"Good night, Okuma-dono."

Daigoro watched as the potter's boy took his leave, keeping close to the walls to avoid the heavy raindrops that still drummed against the outermost edge of the veranda. They hammered the clay tiles of the teahouse roof so steadily that it was difficult to hear anything else.

"So," Katsushima said over the rain. "Today could have gone better."

Daigoro chuckled, his spirits as dark and damp as the night. "Do you think so? I was hoping the rumor that my mother bested Samanosuke would spread like wildfire. Just think how everyone will fear the Okumas if their unarmed women can defeat swordsmen."

Katsushima groaned. "What happened there? Why was she even out of her bedroom?"

"What does it matter? The damage is done."

"What are you going to do about it?"

"I've dismissed all of her attendants, of course. At least her chamberlain had the good graces to spare me from making a proper example of him. He was a good man, and I shouldn't have liked to execute him at all. He was sensible enough to retire to the orchard and throw himself off the cliff."

"I wasn't asking about the attendants."

"Yes," Daigoro said with a sigh. "My mother. Obviously she'll be kept under watch until we can find more competent replacements."

"No," Katsushima said. Daigoro heard a distinctly chiding tone in his voice. "Your pressing problem is the Soras. And soon enough the Inoues. When do they come?"

Daigoro's shoulders sank. "In less than a week. Not nearly enough time to patch things over with the Soras. And as bullies go, I'm told Lord Sora pales in comparison to Lord Inoue. I've spoiled everything, Katsushima. How did my father ever manage to keep these people in line?"

"You haven't spoiled everything. The Soras did leave two of their famed *yoroi* as a gesture of goodwill."

"That was none of my doing. They gave us those before we even sat down to tea. And I'm going to need a lot more than two breastplates if I'm to buy peace with the Inoues."

Daigoro looked out at the raindrops spattering the faces of every puddle in the courtyard. "It looks like Izu is going to drown tonight, Katsushima, but the truth is this place is more like a field of dry grass. It only takes a spark to start a wildfire, and this damned rivalry between the Soras and Inoues is sending sparks flying everywhere." Daigoro pounded his fist on the table—his good fist; the right still burned like hell. "I've botched everything I can botch. And because of today, tomorrow will be worse."

"Patience," said Katsushima.

8

Lord Inoue entered the Okuma compound on the back of an enormous white mare. He was a small man, scarcely taller than Daigoro, and compensated for it with a tall hat, voluminous robes, and *daishō* much shorter than average, as if someone might mistake him for being larger by mistaking his swords to be of normal length. To Daigoro's mind he wore not clothing so much as a costume. He made quite an impressive entrance, but Daigoro wondered if he'd given forethought to what would come immediately after entering. His horse was far too long-legged for him, so the samurai of the Okuma honor guard had no choice but to find somewhere else to look as the lord lowered himself off his horse, at one point dangling with both feet off the ground.

"*This* is the fearsome Inoue Shigekazu?" Daigoro whispered under his breath.

Katsushima, standing beside him, sniffed. "This is the man he wants you to see. A feint, exactly the same as in fighting. Tread carefully."

Daigoro nodded. "My mother is secure?"

"Tomo is watching her himself. Well, Tomo and a host of personal guards."

Daigoro felt his gut go cold. It was one year to the day since they'd received word of his father's death. He should have been comforting his mother, not locking her away like a common criminal. "Today will be especially hard for her," he whispered. "She cannot be allowed to disturb the audience with Inoue, but see to it that she is not treated harshly."

"I'll round up that old healer of yours. Poppy's tears should keep her quiet."

Lord Inoue, having finally reached the ground, approached Daigoro with a bodyguard of eight samurai, all of them his sons. All were dressed in black and silver, and Inoue's sideburns and thin mustache were also black traced through with silver. His darting eyes followed Katsushima, then flicked to Daigoro, then to the roof, the well, the shadows below the veranda. Daigoro had heard the man was paranoid, but the rumors hadn't prepared him for this. He moved as if assassins lurked in every corner.

At last Lord Inoue reached the short staircase leading up to the broad, shady veranda that surrounded the main house. He gave Daigoro a deep and graceful bow. "Okuma-sama. I do hope your mother is feeling better."

Daigoro willed his face to remain passive. How had Inoue heard of last week's debacle with the Soras? His spy network was said to have eyes and ears everywhere, but Daigoro had taken steps to quarantine that information. He'd shut down the entire Okuma compound, allowing no one who had seen the duel with Sora Samanosuke to go beyond the gate. Surely the Soras had said nothing; not only did they stand to be hurt by the story, but they despised the Inoues. Who had talked?

"Mother is quite well," Daigoro said, bowing back. His right hand accidentally brushed against the leg of his *hakama*, shooting spears of pain through his broken fingers. "I thank you for your concern. Come, shall we sit? You've been on the road a long time."

They took their tea in a long tatami room overlooking the sea. The shoji were open, admitting a gentle breeze and the sedating smell of the camphor grove behind the compound. "Ahhh," said Inoue, sipping his tea. "The sky is blue. The gulls are calling. What a beautiful day to talk about spies."

Daigoro gave a polite laugh, glossing over his guest's faux pas. "It seems we've finished with the preliminaries. Of course you're right, Inoue-sama. My family would benefit from allying with your intelligence network."

"As would everyone else. Even Toyotomi no Hideyoshi, the emperor's new chief minister and regent, has been making inquiries. Tell me, Okuma-sama, what can you offer that even the likes of Toyotomi cannot?"

Daigoro knew what Inoue was after. The cagey old daimyo was one of the first on the islands to see the tactical merit of the southern barbarians' muskets and matchlocks. Inoue's musketry battalions might have been what first prompted Lord Sora to develop a breastplate capable of deflecting musket balls. And since Inoue was paranoid, he could not set aside the fear of assassination by musket. He simply had to have Sora *yoroi*, and not just for himself. He had countless sons, and high-ranking officers too. All of them needed protection. But Sora would not trade with him. So long as only Sora commanders were safe from gunfire, the Soras had an advantage to counterbalance Inoue's firepower.

Lord Sora's initial refusal to sell had swollen into open enmity, the kind that showered sparks all over the dry, grassy field that was Izu. Daigoro wanted to prevent a wildfire, and had he not failed with the Soras, he could have sold Sora armor to the Inoues. He could have forged a link between the two houses, protecting the Inoues while making the Soras rich. Everyone would win. But his mother had smashed it all to pieces. More importantly, Daigoro had failed to repair what she'd broken. He was sure his father would have found a solution, some answer Daigoro hadn't been able to see himself.

So Daigoro knew exactly what Lord Inoue was angling for, and Inoue was aware of that before coming here, and both of them knew full well that Daigoro could not afford to give up what Inoue would ask of him. *I do hope your mother is feeling better.* That was no social formality, no idle comment in passing. It was an announcement: you had negotiations with the Soras and your mother made a shambles of them. You tried to outflank me and you failed. And you still need what I know, so now I can ask anything I want from you.

And Daigoro knew what Lord Inoue wanted. First and foremost he wanted the armor, but since he'd known he wouldn't find that here, there was only one other thing the house of Okuma could offer, only one gift as valuable as the intelligence the Inoue spies could deliver. Daigoro knew what it was, and he knew his family couldn't afford to part with it.

He met Inoue's gaze. Those darting eyes were as still as stones now. As dangerous as musket balls. They saw too much.

"Lord Inoue, as long as we're dispensing with the formalities, may I dare to venture a guess on what General Toyotomi has promised you?"

Those eyes glistened. The slightest of smiles touched the corners of Inoue's lips. He cocked his head, shifted on his cushion, and gave Daigoro an appraising look. "Does my young lord wish to compete with me in the field of information gathering?"

"I do."

"Please. Regale me."

Daigoro swallowed. His pulse quickened, but he could no longer back down. "I think Toyotomi offered his own hand in marriage. He is already married, of course, but even a regent's concubine is still an honorable station. I wouldn't want to hazard a guess on which one of your daughters you offered, since you have so many—all beautiful and charming, no doubt, but I daresay you would offer someone young enough to promise many children. Am I far wrong?"

Inoue's eyes narrowed. His smile became a thin, flat line.

"Aha," said Daigoro. "Now, it's been some years since I've had the honor of spending time with your daughters, but perhaps you'll recall your Kameko was my grammar teacher. I remember how happy she was each time you gave her another brother or sister. As prolific as you've been, Lord Inoue, I can't imagine you're wanting for daughters of marriageable age. You'll have a fifteen- or sixteen-year-old who's perfect for the regent. She could provide him almost as many sons as you have."

That last was a gross exaggeration. Toyotomi would need an entire village of women to produce the sons Inoue Shigekazu had fathered. Behind the lord's back, people joked that Inoue's intelligence network was so vast because he had a son or daughter married into every house from here to China. Another facet of his paranoia, Daigoro supposed; who better as a bodyguard than your own flesh and blood? Who better to command your battalions, manage your grain stores, prepare your food? No little girl of Inoue's could ever hope to outproduce her own father, the man who counted children the way most men counted rice.

But certainly Inoue had offered one of them to Toyotomi. Daigoro could see it in his face. His black and silver eyebrows lowered ever so slightly; his gaze darted out to the horizon and back. Daigoro had struck the bull's-eye dead center.

And now he feared what came next. Because he'd botched the Sora negotiations, the most valuable thing the Okumas could offer House Inoue was a marriage. And in that discussion Inoue held all the cards. He had no shortage of daughters to marry off, and Daigoro could only offer his own hand.

Only a few months ago, he would have been more than happy to submit to a marriage for his family's political benefit. Back then, Ichirō was the clan's prize. But now Ichirō was dead, leaving Daigoro as the eldest son of the Okumas. The costs and benefits of marriage were totally different now.

Daigoro cleared his throat. "I believe we were discussing a prospective wedding between one of your daughters and the lord regent."

Inoue shrugged. "We were speculating idly about such possibilities, yes. But more pressing, my young lord, is whom you might marry. You're the head of your house now. Shameful for such a powerful daimyo to be unwed, *neh*?"

Not as shameful as squandering my family's most valuable bargaining chip, Daigoro thought. "I'm sixteen, Lord Inoue. I still have a year or two before bachelorhood becomes unseemly." And a year or two to draw other allies close with the possibility of marriage. As soon as I'm spoken for, my family loses its best asset.

"Is that the fashion these days? Forgive me. I'm an old man; I do not see such affairs with the same eyes as you younger folk. Perhaps remaining unwed is not as shameful for you as it is for those of the older generations—mine, for example, or even your mother's."

Inoue's narrow eyes twinkled. The lines around his mouth deepened, as if he were trying to restrain a smile. "Speak plainly," Daigoro said.

"As you wish. How long has your mother been without a husband? A year? Longer?"

"What does it matter? She's no dowager. The responsibility for House Okuma falls to me."

"So it does. So it does. But if my young lord wanted to leave his prospects for marriage open, he might well marry off his mother instead, *neh*? Think of what a weight it would lift from you, not having to worry about her any longer. She's started feeling the effects of her years, I imagine. It was a long time ago that I was her age, but I remember well enough."

Daigoro thought of those wrinkles at her eyes, of how they'd multiplied in the last year. And he thought of how easily Lord Inoue could manipulate the Okumas if he managed to marry a son to their matriarch. Inoue was wrong: she wasn't so old that her years were a heavy burden. The wrinkles came with worry, not age. Her grief was so heavy that it threatened to crush the life out of her. She was in no state to be married off, least of all to a bully from the Inoues.

And that meant Daigoro's hand became all the more valuable. Not only could he forge a much-needed alliance; he could also protect his mother against predatory suitors—above all the predators from the wolf pack called House Inoue.

Lord Inoue's eyes twinkled all the more brightly. "My young lord, I sense your hesitation. But as you said before, my sons are not the only ones seeking marriage; I have daughters too. You mentioned my Kameko, for instance. I daresay you know her well enough to remember how intelligent and graceful she is. An ideal wife for a bright young man such as yourself."

Daigoro remembered. Kameko was as gentle a soul as any man could hope to meet. And as busy as Daigoro was in learning how to govern his clan and maintain stability in Izu, he had no time for courtship. That made Inoue Kameko a sound choice. He knew her. She'd taught him to read and write, and later taught him poetry and calligraphy. She was patient, sweet, kind, and conscientious.

And she was thirty years Daigoro's senior. She would bear no sons, and the Okumas desperately needed sons.

That shifted Daigoro's thoughts in a different direction. The last time he'd seen Inoue Kameko was at his brother Ichirō's funeral. With her was a younger sister, one whom Daigoro guessed to be close to his own age. Kameko had attended out of respect for Ichirō, also a former student of hers, and the little sister was there as her attendant. But what was her name?

He could see her clearly in his mind's eye. She'd worn white, with tiny red leaves woven into the silk. The leaves were red, *aka*, for *aki*, autumn. . . .

"Akiko," Daigoro said. "What of her? She came to my brother's funeral. That was very generous of her. As I recall, she's unmarried, *neh*?"

Inoue's eyes narrowed. Vertical lines furrowed between his eyebrows. He sipped his tea rather than speaking. There were only so many reasons for a reaction like that. Daigoro had backed him into a corner. But how?

However he'd done it, it wouldn't do to let up now. The girl was obviously precious, the brightest star in her father's sky. And she was important for some reason. But Daigoro couldn't see what it was. He struggled to keep the uncertainty out of his voice, to speak as congenially as if Inoue were his oldest friend. "How old is your Akiko? I'd have guessed she's close to my age, but if I may speak frankly, her face is as pure and bright as it must have been on her first birthday. It's hard to guess the age of a beautiful girl like her."

Lord Inoue finished his tea. Daigoro filled his cup for him, never taking his eyes off Inoue's face. The wizened little daimyo studiously avoided his gaze. "Marriageable age for certain," Daigoro said. "Unless you've got a husband in mind for her already. General Toyotomi, perhaps?"

Inoue's gaze darted to the floor, then the wall, the teacup, the tabletop. Aha, Daigoro thought. I've got you. "Well, no matter," he said, his tone rosy and light. "If she's spoken for, she's spoken for. Still, I wonder how one so young could have angered her father so much that he'd be willing to toss her out like a mud-stained kimono."

That got Inoue to look up. "What do you mean?"

"Come now, Inoue-sama. Even the regent must bow to the coin. Toyotomi presses the war far and wide, but he seldom fights. More often he treats, *neh*?"

"You dare ask *me*? If it were not for me, no one in Izu would know the name Toyotomi, much less his exploits."

It was a gross exaggeration, but Daigoro was happy to see he'd struck a nerve. He bowed, and in his most apologetic tone he said, "Of course. I meant only to point out that this is a man who buys his victories by giving lands to those who concede defeat. He expands his empire without expanding his purse. It's risky, *neh*?"

"Risky?" Inoue scoffed. "It's damned clever—and I thought you were bright enough to understand just how clever. Don't you see? A defeated daimyo who retains his own territory thinks he's won. He thinks mustering troops at Toyotomi's command is no hardship, when in fact all the fool has done is to ensure that he'll always be the one who pays to keep Toyotomi's army fed. If the regent asks for ten thousand troops, then that is how many the local lord must assemble, and in the meantime the man has ten thousand bellies to fill."

"Begging your pardon, Lord Inoue, but the risk I spoke of isn't Toyotomi's. It belongs to his womenfolk. How many wives and concubines must he have by now? Imagine what it must cost to keep them clothed and housed in a style that befits the regent's own household." Daigoro paused for a moment, to let Inoue envision just how lavish that lifestyle must be. "It might not go so badly for your daughter if General Toyotomi were constantly expanding his personal wealth, but he isn't. Akiko will be the smallest cub in a litter already starving for its mother's milk. By this point those women must be clawing at each other for the smallest bauble. But no doubt you've foreseen all of this, which only leaves me to wonder how awful a daughter's crime must be for her own father to throw her to the wolves."

"Hm." Inoue smoothed his slender mustache with a thumb and fingertip. He was otherwise speechless for a long, pregnant moment.

At last he said, "You see much for a boy of your years. You impress me. And I would not see my daughter become a discarded concubine living in a hovel."

"Like any loving father," Daigoro said.

"If I were to offer you Akiko's hand in marriage, would you accept?"

Daigoro blinked and looked out at the sky. Had he just outmaneuvered the great Inoue Shigekazu, or had Inoue outmaneuvered him? Daigoro's first goal had been to gain the benefit of Inoue's spy network. A marriage to the apple of his eye would accomplish that. But his next most important goal was to retain his family's most powerful asset: his own bachelorhood, and with it the possibility of alliance through marriage. Now, rather than trying to avoid wedding a barren daughter, he'd pressured Inoue into offering him his most desirable daughter. Or had he? Perhaps Inoue played the fool all along, hoping to get Daigoro to push him to just this conclusion.

Either way, Inoue had asked the question, and he'd asked it from a position of weakness. Had this been a duel, Inoue would have been on his back, disarmed and helpless. No man of honor could kill him in such a position. In effect, Inoue was begging him for mercy. And a true follower of *bushidō* had no choice but to grant his wish.

Father, I wish you were here, Daigoro thought. I wish you could tell me the right thing to do. He had no doubt that his family would be stronger with the countless eyes and ears of the Inoues. Nor did he have any doubt that the old man seated across from him would bully his new son-in-law whenever and however he could.

Equally doubtless was the fact that if Daigoro said no to Akiko's hand, Inoue would take it personally. He'd borne his silly grudge against the Soras for decades. No doubt he would use the full might of his spy network to hurt the Okumas. He might even look for new ways to marry his children to Daigoro *and* Daigoro's mother. Daigoro wasn't even sure he'd outfoxed the old man this time around; he certainly didn't know how many more times he could pull it off.

And there was the last consideration: what Izu needed now, more than ever and more than anything, was stability. As lord protector of Izu, Daigoro knew his duty. A marriage between his clan and the Inoues would bring stability.

What should I do, Father? Compromise our family's position in order to stabilize Izu? Or compromise Izu in order to leave our family better positioned for the future?

Daigoro had no idea what his father would say. He knew only that his father had an aphorism, one he'd repeated countless times through Daigoro's childhood: *A samurai makes every decision in the space of seven breaths.* The path of *bushidō* was not for the hesitant.

The feast that evening was a thing of beauty. The Okuma cooks truly outdid themselves: roasted sparrows so delicate that they almost melted in the mouth; soft tofu artfully sculpted and dyed; shrimp flecked with gold; sushi of every description: squid and octopus, lobster and roe, eel and egg. Sake flowed. Toasts were made. The scullery maids would be washing dishes until sunrise.

Then came the musicians, and clapping and dancing, and after much prodding Lord Inoue stood up to sing. Even Daigoro's mother seemed to be having a good time—owing in part to the poppy's tears, no doubt, but only in part. Daigoro himself could have used some of her medicine; his broken fingers still felt like they were made of broken pottery. He watched his mother singing along and smiled. If anyone ever needed cause for celebration, it was her.

An hour into the festivities, Daigoro finally allowed Katsushima to corner him. "I'm pleased to hear you'll finally be dipping your wick," Katsushima said, "but are you certain you've made the right choice?"

Daigoro bent closer, the better to be heard over the *shamisen* and *shakuhachi* players. "No. But with Akiko as the dowry, Inoue could have bought a greater house than ours. He sacrificed and we sacrificed."

"Who sacrificed more?"

"I don't know yet. But Mother is having fun, and that's something I wasn't sure I could buy for any price."

Katsushima's face darkened. "She is a liability."

"She is my mother. What would you have me do? Marry her off instead?"

"No." Katsushima said it a bit too quickly. "As dangerous as it is to keep her around, it is more dangerous to let her go."

"Well, what, then?"

Katsushima said nothing to that, but Daigoro was afraid he could guess the answer. Katsushima had no family. He was as free as a wave on the sea. But he was right. Daigoro's mother might be at peace for the rest of the evening, but he knew how vulnerable she was. She made the whole clan vulnerable. She'd already spoiled things with the Soras, and because of her condition she'd forced Daigoro to bind himself to the daughter of a petty, overbearing, power-seeking spymaster. The Okumas were weaker so long as Daigoro's mother was among them.

Just like that, the music sounded flat to his ears and the sake soured in his mouth. Someone like Katsushima might have married her off just to make her another clan's problem, then cut all ties so she couldn't be used against him. That certainly would have been an easier solution. But even Katsushima could see it wasn't so easy to cut emotional ties. And if she couldn't be kept around and she couldn't be let go, there was only one other solution.

It would have been so easy. Daigoro had a hundred different sword hands he could assign to the task. In truth it was the only sensible alternative he had. And Daigoro would never forgive himself for thinking of it.

9

fter the most dizzying month of his life, Daigoro found himself on a balmy evening sitting next to his new wife. Cicadas chirped merrily outside the compound walls and the sunset painted the western sky with a thousand shades of orange. Akiko sat beside him on the lip of the veranda, her perfume as sweet as apple blossoms. He still felt as if he barely knew her—their wedding was the first time they'd spent more than an hour in each other's company, and that had been only a week ago—but so far he had the impression that they'd get along well. She made him laugh, and that simple fact made him realize he hadn't had much occasion for laughter in over a year. It was good to have laughter back in his life.

Better still, seeing his leg hadn't upset her in the slightest. It looked more like a skinned snake than anything else, and prior to last week the very thought of marriage had inspired dreadful thoughts of trying to hide his leg from his wife for the rest of their lives together. He couldn't bear seeing a woman's revulsion at the sight of it, but how could he conceal his leg from someone who would see him daily in his smallclothes? Perhaps Akiko had been forewarned about it. Or perhaps it had taken her by surprise when she first undressed him and she sincerely wasn't put off. Daigoro didn't care which one it was. He felt only an overflowing swell of gratitude that she hadn't reacted sourly.

And the discovery of sex made his life immeasurably better. He'd understood the mechanics of it well enough, and for his fourteenth birthday Ichirō had even taken him to visit a brothel. But at that age he'd been even more embarrassed of his leg than he was now, and so the prostitute had only stripped herself naked and slipped her hand down the front of his *hakama*. Daigoro's wedding night came as a nigh-religious revelation. Akiko was equally eager, and despite a touch of neophyte clumsiness in some of their experimentations, so far they hadn't experimented fewer than six times a day.

Yet there remained the incessant affairs of state—this clan bickering with that one, Lord This and Lord That feuding over some perceived slight—and the affairs of House Okuma too. First and foremost was the wedding, the planning of which had consumed every spare moment beforehand and the paying for which promised to occupy him for some weeks to come. Between all of that and the constant temptation to chase Akiko back to the bedroom, Daigoro hardly had time to eat. He hadn't so much as unsheathed Glorious Victory, to say nothing of training, though for that his battered right hand was supremely grateful.

Akiko ran a fingertip across his shoulder blades and handed him the next envelope. She had what seemed like an unending supply of them, some delivered personally at their wedding, others trickling in as the riders came and went with each passing day. Daigoro opened the newest envelope—it was cleverly folded to blossom like a flower—and discovered it was from Lord Yasuda, Daigoro's favorite among all the Okuma allies. Daigoro thought of him more as an uncle than a military asset. Sadly, he was an aging uncle, and his many years were finally catching up with him. He'd taken sick, and so he hadn't been able to attend the wedding even though the Yasuda compound was less than half a day's ride away. Nevertheless, Lord Yasuda's gift was most generous: nine beautiful horses, three stallions and six mares, along with wishes for many foals and many children. The aging lord himself had a new great-grandson, and expressed his wishes that Daigoro and Akiko quickly make for him a playmate close to his own age.

"Oh!" Akiko chirped. "Look, a delivery from the regent himself."

"How about that?" Daigoro said. "I wouldn't have thought news of our little wedding would have made it so high in the sky."

"And to think the sun and the moon didn't think to give us anything. How scandalous!"

She broke the wax *kiri* blossom seal, and watched eagerly as Daigoro took it from her and read. "Oh, hell," he said.

"Is that what the regent thinks of marriage? It hasn't been bad so far."

Daigoro chuckled, but only halfheartedly. "Tomo," he said, not needing to raise his voice; unless the boy was off on some errand, he was always within earshot. "Find Katsushima-san for me, would you?"

"Is it trouble?" asked Akiko.

"The worst kind. An execution order."

Akiko gasped. "The imperial regent wants you to commit seppuku?"

Daigoro shook his head, giving the letter a puzzled look. "No. He orders me to kill the abbot of Kattō-ji."

"What? Why?"

"It doesn't say. It says only to send his head back to Kyoto."

It was his wife's turn to frown. She read the regent's missive for herself, and by the end Daigoro saw her forehead furrow with the same consternation he'd felt as he was reading. "Who is this monk?" she asked.

"You met him briefly."

"What, the old man who blessed our wedding?"

That and more, Daigoro thought. He admired the abbot. He knew the old monk had once been samurai, and that meant he might well have made some enemies on the battlefield. It was even possible that he had faced General Toyotomi. Could he have been involved in one of Toyotomi's defeats?

Daigoro dismissed the thought. Even if it were true, all past offenses were absolved as soon as one took the cloth. Why should anyone call for his head now? And why would someone of such a lofty position even deign to remember that the abbot existed?

"Daigoro, this is dated two weeks ago."

"I know."

"He could have you killed just for failing to respond." She shook the letter at him like a stick. "This is Toyotomi Hideyoshi we're talking about. Patience and fair-mindedness aren't what he's known for."

"I know, Aki. Just listen—"

"How did this happen? Does he send you so many letters from him that you can just *forget* one?"

Daigoro wasn't accustomed to being reprimanded by a woman his own age. He wondered if this was what married life had in store for him, though he had to admit there was love in her agitation. After only seven days together, she cared enough for him to get upset when she saw him threatened.

Even so, he was glad to see Katsushima walk up behind her and snatch the letter from her fingers. He'd taken her entirely by surprise—his footfalls were as muted as his personality—and that made her catch her breath long enough for Daigoro to get a word in.

"Aki, listen to me. Suppose it took a week's time for this to come from Kyoto. That would have it arrive on our wedding day—to be lost in the confusion, *neh*?"

"And then to be tossed in with all the other letters and gifts. . . . Merciful Buddha, Daigoro. What are we going to do?"

"Only the obvious," Katsushima said. He reexamined the *kiri* blossom imprinted in the broken seal, studied the letter once more, then handed it back with a fatalistic shrug. "Best to get it over with." Out of old and indelible habit, his thumb flicked out to loosen his sword in its sheath.

"I won't," Daigoro said.

Katsushima gave a curt bow. "I understand. It's harder when you have a personal connection. Lend me a horse and I'll see it done."

"You misunderstand me. I have no interest in beheading an innocent man."

"Buddhas have mercy," Akiko said, "you don't mean to defy the regent, do you? When she noticed the look she'd drawn from Katsushima, she glared right back. "Don't you look at me like that. Do you think just because I'm a woman I can't understand affairs of state?"

Katsushima snorted. "You're a girl, not a woman. And the answer to your question is yes."

Akiko was on her feet in an instant, fists on her hips. "If I am a girl, then my *daddy* is the most powerful spymaster between here and Kyoto."

If Daigoro thought she had her hackles up before, that was nothing compared to now. She stood over him with all the tenacity of a she-wolf defending her cubs. Daigoro found he rather liked it.

And she wasn't finished. "Do you think that sword of yours is the only kind of weapon? A precocious little *girl* can lower a man's defenses in ways no sword ever could. I've served my father as a courier since I was old enough to count to ten."

Katsushima wore an expression Daigoro had never seen in him before. He looked startled and chastised and bemused all at once, as if he'd knocked over a buzzing hornet's nest only to release a swarm of angry butterflies. His look did not lessen Akiko's temper.

"Aki," Daigoro said, tugging her sleeve, "sit next to me, would you, please? I need you to tell me what you make of all this nonsense about the river and the flood."

She gave Katsushima a defiant little squint and sat down, snatching the letter from Daigoro's hand. He smiled and was glad she didn't see it; her feistiness was adorable, but it wouldn't do for her to know he felt that way. Not yet. "Here," he told her, pointing to the passage in question. *"Whatever is too heavy for the river to carry off is easily washed away by the floodwaters."*

"It sounds like His Lordship fancies himself a poet," Katsushima said.

Akiko harrumphed. "It sounds to me like His Lordship offers you an ultimatum: either you take the abbot's head or he'll send a battalion to come and get it."

"And perhaps conduct other business while they're here," Daigoro said, filling in the rest. "Like flooding the house of any upstart lordling who defied his will."

"It makes no sense," Akiko said. She studied the letter again, as if she hoped to find some explanation that hadn't been written there before. "Why should a daimyo halfway across the empire want this man killed?"

"I don't know," Daigoro said, but in truth he had no attention to spare for that particular riddle. He had questions of his own to answer. How had so much gone so wrong in so little time? His father had managed the squabbling lords of Izu for decades without mishap. Now, just a year after his death, Izu was fraying at the edges and the Okumas had drawn the ire of the most powerful warlord the islands had ever seen. Daigoro cursed himself. This was not the path his father had laid out for him. If Glorious Victory Unsought was too heavy for him to wield, leadership of the clan was heavy enough to crush him like an insect.

He could almost feel his father's mantle hanging on him, a stone yoke pressing down on his shoulders and straining his heart. His bones ached under the weight of it. His only goal was to protect his clan and preserve their honor, and his every decision had achieved just the opposite.

"I cannot understand your hesitation," Katsushima said. "The right path is clear."

"It's anything but," said Daigoro. "Do you really expect me to ride up the hill and murder an innocent man?"

"Of course."

Akiko let out a little gasp. A tiny, distant part of Daigoro's mind wondered at the difference between true samurai and those whose families maintained the station but not the code. Akiko had a fierce heart, to be sure, and Daigoro grew fonder and fonder of her by the day, but her father was a craven who hid behind his walls, just like his father before him. Inoue Shigekazu was a potent ally, but never on the battlefield. Clearly he'd never spoken of killing and dying as Katsushima spoke of it, or else Akiko would not have reacted as she did.

It was enough for Daigoro that her father had his spies and informants—and, of course, his topknot. Had the Inoues not been samurai, marrying Akiko would never have crossed Daigoro's mind. As well marry a pine tree as marry a peasant. The very concept didn't exist, at least not in the true samurai's mind. Katsushima was one of those. Daigoro's father had been too, and it was Daigoro's sole aspiration to become one himself. But in this case he could not emulate his new mentor.

"Katsushima-san, this is not the honorable path. I cannot agree with you."

"And I cannot fathom how your morality can prevent you from doing the right thing." It was clear in his tone that his patience was fading fast. "Why are you afraid to do what is necessary?"

"And why are *you* so bold as to speak to my husband that way?" Akiko was back on her feet. "You are a servant of this house!"

For his part, Katsushima showed admirable reserve—or else Akiko's outburst made his dwindling patience seem admirable by comparison. He only looked up at Akiko, who, since she stood on the veranda and he stood in the garden, loomed over him like a giant— but one made of flower petals, as far as Katsushima was concerned.

Daigoro touched Akiko gently on the hand. "He is no servant. He stays because he is welcome to stay, and because he chooses to. I count him as a friend and a counselor, but Katsushima-san has never sworn an oath to my banner."

"Nor will I," said Katsushima. "But if you ask me to, I will ride to Kattō-ji and return before sundown with the old man's head in a sack. If you would not have your own men spill his blood, send me."

"And if I don't send you? Will you do it of your own accord?"

Katsushima did not need to think about it for long. "No. The decision is yours. I will not make it for you."

Daigoro nodded, relieved that he would not have to find a way to restrain a man he respected. "It's wrong, Katsushima-san. He's committed no crime."

"Are you sure of that? Sure enough to kneel beside him before the *kaishaku?* Because that's what you'll be doing if you defy the regent: you'll sentence yourself to execution."

Once again that tiny, distant voice in Daigoro's mind voiced its observations about the differences in social stations. Only a *rōnin* would speak of being *sentenced* to death. Daigoro, lord of his house, would not wait for a higher lord's sentencing; if he'd done wrong, he would already have plunged his sword into his belly.

But for all of that, Katsushima made a good point. Daigoro had no idea what history the regent and the abbot shared. For that matter, he didn't even know the abbot's name. How many conversations had he ever shared with the old man? Three? Four? The abbot had impressed Daigoro from their first meeting, and had offered him valuable spiritual guidance, but for all of that Daigoro didn't really *know* anything about him. He had been samurai, yes, but for whom? He had seen battle, yes, and he'd even faced Daigoro's own father, but how had he conducted himself on the battlefield? With honor? Without? Had he dishonored the great Toyotomi himself? How?

Daigoro could answer none of those questions. All he could do was order a horse to be saddled so he could pay a visit to Kattō-ji.

10

"**O**kuma-dono," the abbot said when he opened the gate in the temple's garden wall. "What a surprise! It's late."

He held a thin taper; its flickering flame caused his many wrinkles to deepen with shadow. The evening had become quite chilly, but the bald abbot wore neither a hat nor an overrobe. "May I come in?" Daigoro said.

"Of course, of course."

Upon stepping through Kattō-ji's gate, Daigoro saw the moonlight playing on the broken skin of the huge, twisted, ancient pine that dominated the courtyard. The rocks surrounding the pine had been raked to form concentric waves around the fat, gnarled roots, like ripples retreating from stomping feet in a shallow pool. Here and there a candle flame quivered behind paper windows, but for the most part the abbey was dark and still.

"Please, sit, Okuma-dono. What can I do for you on this beautiful night?"

The abbot sat down on a short staircase that ascended to the meditation hall. Daigoro lowered himself to sit beside him, his right knee wobbling as he did so, his right hand protesting loudly as he used it to balance himself as he sat. He looked at the abbot, whose unbroken hands rested on two good knees, and found himself envious of the old man's health. And just how old was he? Sixty? Eighty? Daigoro couldn't be sure. He only knew that he himself was just sixteen and this wizened abbot got around more easily than he did.

"I've received a missive," said Daigoro. "From General Toyotomi, the new regent."

Daigoro studied the abbot's face as he delivered this news. The abbot's eyebrows rose at the mention of Toyotomi. Then his face became even more serene than it was already—and that was saying something, for this was a man who could teach the moonlit stones in the rock garden about serenity.

"Do you know him?" said Daigoro.

"The answer to that depends on what you mean by 'know.' I've never met him face-to-face."

"But you met him on the battlefield."

Again the eyebrows rose. "Ah," said the abbot. "Now, that's an interesting insight. What led you to it?"

"He wants me to deliver your head in a sack."

"Does he, now?"

Daigoro marveled at the abbot's tranquility. Yes, the old man had been samurai, and yes, he had been practicing Zen for years, but even so, he might still have let slip a hint of distress upon learning that the most powerful man in the empire wanted him dead. Once again Daigoro found himself envious.

And yet he was frustrated too. The abbot had an annoying habit of not answering questions, and the answers to tonight's questions might keep both of their heads firmly on their necks.

"So you met him in battle," Daigoro said, prodding.

"Yes, you could say that. In a sense the battlefield is the only place where one can truly meet another man. There his true face is unmasked. But asking your question that way will cause my answer to mislead you."

Daigoro didn't feel misled, but neither could he ignore the abbot's warning. He felt his frustration mounting and took a deep breath in an attempt to quell it. "Sir," he said at last, "would you please enlighten me as to how you know Toyotomi Hideyoshi?"

"You asked whether I met him in battle. That can mean two things, *neh*? Did I fight him in battle? No. Did I see his true face in battle? Yes."

"So you served under him."

"Not under him. Under one of his commanders, a man named Shichio. You may not know of him, but I assure you, that letter you received was his, not Hideyoshi's."

"You say you've never met the regent face-to-face," said Daigoro, "and yet you refer to him and his commander by their first names. Why?"

"Shichio is Shichio. Hideyoshi is not Hideyoshi, but he is not not-Hideyoshi."

Again the frustration swelled in Daigoro's belly. He felt it pulsing in his neck, hot enough to choke him. It pulsed in his broken fingers too, biting at their sore and swollen flesh. It was all he could do to retain the thinnest shell of politeness. "You'll have to tell me what you mean by that."

"Shichio is Shichio because he has no other name. He comes from peasant stock. Have you ever heard of a peasant with a surname?"

"Of course not."

"And Hideyoshi has as many names as the sky has stars. 'Hideyoshi' is as good as any of them."

Daigoro was ready to growl. More than anything he wanted to shout, *Damn you, unclog your doddering ears and listen to me.* Instead he said, "Perhaps I should be clearer. A man with hundreds of thousands of troops at his beck and call wants me to kill you. If I refuse, he'll call for my head as well. I need for you not to speak in riddles anymore."

"Oh, but I'm not," said the abbot, his face as innocent as a newborn kitten. "The man you call 'the regent' changes names as often as most men change clothing. When I fought under him his name was Hideyoshi. Before that it was Hashiba, and before that the Bald Rat, and before that it was Kinoshita, and before that it was who-knows-what. Now it is the Monkey King, or Imperial Regent, or Chief Minister. Most recently it is Toyotomi Hideyoshi. Who knows what name his mother gave him? I call him by the name he had when I met him."

"Very well," said Daigoro. "I am grateful for your explanation, but you'll forgive me if I feel I'm no closer to understanding why this man should want me to deliver your head."

"I've explained that already, *neh*? He doesn't. Shichio does."

Daigoro closed his eyes. It was all he could do not to strangle the abbot. "All right," he said through gritted teeth, "so why does Shichio want your head?"

"I expect he's recently met a man with a scar across his forehead. Years ago I watched that man receive his scar. As a result, an army of ghosts handed Shichio a defeat, and because Shichio was routed, Hideyoshi lost the day as well. And if Hideyoshi were ever to learn of this story, I expect he would seek Shichio's head, not mine."

Daigoro pounded his knee with his fist. "Damn you and your bewildering words! Is this as plainly as you can speak?"

"My lord, if you'll just wait one moment more—"

"I'm through with waiting. Don't you understand? I could end this conversation with one stroke of my sword. And I'd be better off if I did it, too. I have only to deliver your head and life will suddenly become very easy—for me, for my family, for the whole damned peninsula. Yet you want to play more word games. Enough with these stories and fairy tales! I don't want to hear another word of any ghost armies."

"Not even if it was your father's ghost army?"

Daigoro groaned, massaging his forehead with his left hand. He was ready to shout at the old monk again—how dare he play on Daigoro's heartstrings by dredging up memories of his father?—but then he remembered: his father and the abbot once faced each other in war.

Daigoro knew virtually nothing of that encounter, nor of any of his father's battlefield exploits. His father had never spoken much of war; he'd always been careful not to glorify it overmuch for his sons. He'd never been one to test his mettle by entering into needless combat—or so was Daigoro's impression anyway. Daigoro's guesses vastly outweighed what he knew for certain.

And with the pressures of running the clan pushing in on him from every side, now more than ever Daigoro needed to *know* what his father was like. His father had always known what to do. The right path had always been clear to him, and so what Daigoro needed was to know his father's mind.

"Very well," Daigoro said. He pushed himself to his feet because he'd burned up what little tolerance he had left for sitting still. "Tell me about my father. But on the Buddha's mercy, I beg you, be brief and be clear."

The abbot bowed his head. "What do you know of Hideyoshi?"

"He is a master tactician. A master manipulator too, they say, more likely to win a battle with words than with swords. He is said to be uncommonly ugly, uncommonly canny, and uncommonly fond of both drinking and pillowing. And now that Oda Nobunaga is dead, he is the greatest general this side of China."

"The greatest? I think not. Better to call him the mightiest. But let us begin where you began. Do you know where he garnered his reputation of being a master tactician?"

"Of course. He conquered the whole of Shikoku in a matter of months. Kyushu in a matter of weeks."

The abbot shrugged. "Unimpressive. Swift victories come easily against unprepared enemies, and more easily still when enemies decide to become allies instead. One does not become a great general by bribing greedy men."

"What of his battle at Takamatsu Castle? As I heard it, he was trapped between the fortress and an incoming force of superior numbers. Survival would have been an admirable goal in and of itself, yet Toyotomi outmaneuvered both sides and claimed victory on the day. There are other examples. The list goes on and on."

"So it does. But those who compose the list tend to leave out his defeats. I was witness to one of them."

"I asked you to be brief," said Daigoro.

"Yes, yes. We were camped at Gakuden, in Owari. Not far south lay a hill called Komaki, where Tokugawa Ieyasu had just established a garrison and headquarters. Do you know Tokugawa?"

"Of course. My father fought with him in the Battle of Mikatagahara. The Tokugawas have looked favorably on us ever since."

The abbot nodded and smiled. "If ever you get the chance, ask Lord Tokugawa what your father did to earn House Okuma such special favor. But that story is for another time. For now, Tokugawa is at Komaki and Hideyoshi is in Gakuden—as am I, serving as a scout under his commander, Shichio. *Neh?*"

"Go on."

"You mentioned that Hideyoshi is a master manipulator. His man Shichio makes him look like a deaf mute. Shichio knew that Tokugawa harbored a great love for his homeland of Mikawa, and that with so many Tokugawa divisions in Komaki, Mikawa was relatively undefended."

Daigoro nodded. "He attacked Mikawa?"

"No, but he enticed another general into doing so. Shichio is not the type to stretch out his neck where others might take a swipe at it. He finds it safer to voice his ideas through others, taking credit when they succeed and laying the fault with them when they fail."

"This story does not seem to be getting any shorter."

"Forgive me. Shichio manipulated a general named Ikeda Nobuteru into attacking Mikawa. Hideyoshi approved, and sent Ikeda, his sons, and Shichio to spearhead the assault. We rode out expecting little resistance. Little did we know that one of Tokugawa's minor allies, an unknown daimyo named Okuma Tetsurō, had anticipated a move against Mikawa. He placed informants weeks in advance, in every village surrounding Mikawa, and he received word of our sortie almost as soon as we set out. So there we were, the hammer's head, expecting to strike an overripe melon and finding an anvil instead." The abbot dropped a fist into his palm.

Daigoro nodded. "So instead of striking directly at the enemy's heart . . ."

"We marched straight into a Tokugawa slaughterhouse. Ikeda, his son, and his son-in-law were killed before we knew it. But Shichio is not one to lead the charge. He remained in the rearguard, and deployed me and four other riders to scout out a flanking option. To our right we found only a swollen river. To the left a forest of banner poles, all bearing the bear claw of Okuma."

"So you retreated?"

"Oh no. I don't wish to cause offense, my young Bear Cub, but yours was a minor house in this war. Tokugawa's advance was the one we had to fear. If the little house of Okuma were the only one guarding his flank, we thought we might press through."

"But Father anticipated that too, didn't he?"

The abbot gave a wry chuckle. "He was just getting started. All of a sudden we were surrounded on all sides, a hundred arrows trained on our throats. He stripped us, dressed two of his men in our armor, and mounted them on our horses. They rode back to tell Shichio their comrades had been slain and the Tokugawas could not be flanked. Shichio fled with what little remained of his column. He reported to Hideyoshi, who made a hasty retreat. Hideyoshi is embarrassed by it to this day."

Daigoro smiled. Never before had he heard a tale in which the name Okuma loomed as large as names like Tokugawa and Toyotomi. Those were the houses that defined the shape of the empire. To think a little-known horseman from Izu had lent his banners to the cause! Daigoro had never felt such pride.

But now that he thought about it, he saw the story had holes. "You know too much for a common cavalryman. You must have had Hideyoshi's ear, or Shichio's at the very least."

"I was Shichio's top-ranking scout. Of course I had his ear."

"Then how could he mistake my father's rider for you?"

"Aha," said the abbot, as proud as Daigoro's own father had been when one of his sons tamed his first horse. "Very good, my lord. How many head wounds have you seen?"

"What?"

"The forehead bleeds terribly when cut. A slice above the eyebrows masks a man's face so completely that even his own brother might not recognize him."

"Hm," Daigoro said. At first it sounded like the utmost betrayal: his father had bloodied his own men. Worse, he did it for the sake of deceit. Daigoro wondered what it would feel like to draw a sharp knife across his own forehead, and worse yet, what it would feel like to order another man to do the same. But then he saw the truth: any one of his samurai would do it without hesitation. It was the samurai's duty to obey, and the lord's duty never to give an order unworthy of obeisance.

Still, Daigoro wondered how desperate a situation would have to be to order his men to mutilate their own faces. Was such an order ever just? Yes. He had to admit it was conceivable. But could he live with giving the order? Daigoro hoped he would never have to find out.

"I'm disappointed," Daigoro said.

"In your father?"

"Never. My disappointment is with you. You've left out the army of ghosts you promised me."

The abbot's cheeks crinkled in a smile. "Begging your pardon, Okuma-dono, but I haven't. The ghosts were critical to the story."

Daigoro thought for a moment. Then he said, "To your right was the river, and to the left . . ."

"Precisely. Imagine my shame when I learned the forest of Okuma banner poles was just that: banner poles, with no battalions beneath them. Your father dedicated nearly all of his men to the ambush, with just a handful deployed over the next rise to give the illusion of an army."

"His ghost army."

The abbot chuckled and shook his head. "As I say, imagine my shame. My own master routed, not by Tokugawa's legions but by the imaginary army of an insignificant house. Bested without a single sword being drawn. Your father showed me what it truly meant to be samurai. Well, I couldn't very well keep my topknot after that."

"So what happened?"

"I asked him permission to shave my head. He did me the greatest honor of my life: he cut off my topknot with Glorious Victory Un-sought, the very sword you carry today. I joined the monastery. My four comrades were taken as prisoners. The two samurai who cut their own foreheads at your father's command were rewarded handsomely for their bravery and selflessness. And one of them, it seems, has been dwelling too much on the old days."

"What do you mean?"

"Some years ago your father released his four prisoners. Hideyoshi had become too powerful for your father to risk his ire, and the pris-oners could no longer do any harm—at least not to the house of Okuma. But Shichio had them crucified anyway. All of them. Why?"

"Because they knew the truth," Daigoro guessed. Thinking aloud, he said, "But that would only matter if . . . no. It can't be. Are you suggesting that Shichio still hasn't told his master what happened that day?"

"Never forget, Okuma-dono, Hideyoshi and Shichio are both the sons of farmers. They were not raised as you were, born to a code. Shichio tells the truth only when it suits him."

"So even to this day Hideyoshi thinks he was routed by Tokugawa Ieyasu?"

"A name great enough to rival his own," said the abbot. "Even that must vex him terribly. Imagine Shichio's fate if Hideyoshi were ever to learn exactly how he was defeated. Imagine his wrath if he ever learned his most embarrassing defeat should have been a victory."

Daigoro thought about it and felt his heart swell with pride. One of the regent's top generals, living in fear of execution simply because he was outfoxed by Okuma Tetsurō. Execution was no way for a samurai to die, but this Shichio deserved no better. If he were truly samurai, he would have opened his own belly years ago, in the very hour that he failed.

"Be careful what you take joy in, young Bear Cub." Daigoro looked up and saw the abbot studying his face. "The Red Bear of Izu earned an enemy in Hideyoshi's court. Now you have inherited that enemy. One of your father's men has been telling tales of the old days."

"No. Our men are loyal."

"What else explains my death warrant? Shichio has learned that I am still alive. I attended to your father's funeral and your brother's; any one of your men could have seen me there."

"I won't believe it."

"Then you are in need of another explanation. Your father's scouts were young men when they deceived Shichio. Unless some accident has befallen them, there is no reason to doubt they still live."

"No." Daigoro searched his memory, trying to envision an Okuma samurai with a scar across his forehead. No faces came to mind—but then, Daigoro did not know his every vassal. He knew every man at his own compound, but the Okumas had lesser houses too, scattered across southern Izu.

"Perhaps one of them was drunk," the abbot said. "Perhaps he felt you slighted him somehow. Perhaps he felt House Okuma has somehow become unworthy of his loyalty."

Oh no, Daigoro thought. Mother.

The debacle with the Soras had cost Daigoro the most, but it was hardly the first of its kind. Her outbursts were becoming more frequent, more acute, and all too often they happened in public. Could that have been enough to turn a loyal samurai astray? Daigoro hated to think so. But after losing his father and his brother, House Okuma was undoubtedly weaker. Now its matriarch was a madwoman, its lord her crippled teenage son.

No. Loyalty was loyalty. It if failed even once, it did not exist at all. Father had trained his men better than that. Hadn't he?

"Somehow Shichio knows I am alive," the abbot said, as if he read Daigoro's thoughts. "How else might he have discovered this?"

"Augury," said Daigoro. "Divination. A *kami* speaking to him in his dreams."

"Perhaps. But the more likely explanation is one of this world. A loyal man uttering one word too many after drink loosened his tongue. One of Shichio's own men, crossing paths with yours by happenstance, recognizing a scar."

"What does it have to do with you? You took on the cloth. A man's old crimes are cut away when he shaves his head."

"Among the honorable, yes."

"Well, then, this is easy," said Daigoro. "Hideyoshi was named regent. Perhaps he wasn't born samurai, but he is certainly samurai now. He has no choice but to live up to it. I'll tell Hideyoshi the truth, he'll take Shichio's head, and this ridiculous drama will come to an end."

"You are more than welcome to try. But do remember, Shichio manipulates men as deftly as a potter shapes clay. If you tell Hideyoshi the truth, you will also have to tell him it was your father who bested him in his most public defeat. And more than bested: *duped.* What will Shichio be able to shape out of your story?"

"Nothing. The emperor bestowed Hideyoshi with name and title. Let Shichio weave his webs; Hideyoshi will cut through them with a sword. He is samurai now."

"And yet you've taken to calling him Hideyoshi rather than General Toyotomi."

Daigoro grunted and stared at the pebbles in the rock garden. The abbot had a point. Even the emperor could not change what a man was in his heart. The world might regard Hideyoshi as a trueborn samurai, but Daigoro doubted whether one who was born a peasant could ever walk the *bushidō* path.

"So what am I to do?"

"Behead me. Save your family and yourself. Buy peace."

"No. You've committed no sin."

"Oh, but I have."

"I won't accept that. Yes, all of us have done wrong in our lives, but you've done no wrong by Shichio—and even if you had, all your crimes were absolved when you took on the tonsure."

The abbot shrugged. "That's as may be. But if the price of peace is the head of one innocent man, I think any daimyo in the land would consider it a bargain."

"No. It's wrong." But even as he heard himself say it, Daigoro knew it was the easiest path. The abbot had no family, nor even any fear of death. He had embraced his own impermanence. Outside the walls of Kattō-ji, the world would scarcely notice his passing. And in taking his head, Daigoro could appease this Shichio, a man with the might of a warlord but the conscience of a petty thief. Who knew what he might do if he felt slighted? Daigoro couldn't even guess. All his life Daigoro had striven to live up to his name, his birth, his father's image. He had no idea what went on in the minds of dishonorable men.

Daigoro took his leave, and allowed his mare to set her own slow pace on the ride back down to the Okuma compound. He was thankful to be alone in making this decision. Tomo was a good servant and a better friend, but he was lowborn. And Katsushima had strayed from the path as soon as he dedicated himself to his sword over his master. Neither of them could fully understand what *bushidō* demanded.

If it were as simple as delivering his own head to Hideyoshi, Daigoro would have known what to do. Self-sacrifice in the name of family came as naturally to him as breathing. But killing an innocent man in the name of family smacked of cowardice, not selflessness. And yet the abbot was right. Usually peace was bought with the blood of thousands. Heroes died for it. Why could a monk not be as heroic as any samurai? The abbot had offered his own neck and offered it freely. He'd neither insisted nor shied away. Daigoro could ask no more of any soldier in his command.

But the abbot was no soldier. He'd renounced the sword, and in so doing he'd put himself on the opposite side of a line Daigoro was loath to cross. Peace, at the cost of moral compromise. Principle, at the cost of endangering his family.

Daigoro knew what he had to do. He just didn't know what to do with the fear. Too often doing the right thing had made him suffer. This time it made him tremble.

11

Shichio's favorite room in the Jurakudai was the highest deck of the moon tower. Hashiba liked it too, but for very different reasons. Hashiba enjoyed the view of the city; the lofty perspective made him feel more powerful, and the quiet made him feel more at peace. Shichio liked the moon tower for its austerity. It was one of the only places in the entire palace that hadn't yet been gilded and painted and overdone. Hashiba was oddly embarrassed by that fact; he seemed to equate ostentation with wealth, and, by extension, tastefulness with poverty. That meant the upper deck of the moon tower was an intimate place for him, a good place for dalliances and for private meetings with his closest advisers.

Shichio was content to serve in both capacities. At the moment that meant wiping Hashiba clean after they'd finished. The demon mask seemed suddenly heavier—or rather, Shichio suddenly felt its weight on his neck muscles, now that he wasn't otherwise distracted—and so he shifted it to sit atop his head. Moonlight streamed in through the open walls, and a cool breeze raised goose bumps all up and down Shichio's naked, sweat-slicked body. Hashiba never seemed to feel the cold. He was tougher than Shichio, in that way and many others.

"Look at you," Hashiba said, chuckling. He bunched Shichio's silken kimono in his fist and threw it at him. "Why do you carry on this way? I've concubines enough. Why not invite a few of them up here to warm you?"

Shichio understood the subtext well enough. Hashiba didn't understand that sex might be like the moon tower for them: enjoyable for two very different reasons. For him, real men did the penetrating, not the receiving, and so he found their liaisons shameful—not for himself, but for Shichio. That was why he wanted a consort to join them: so that Shichio could be the conqueror for once. But there were two ways of conquering too. That was something else Hashiba didn't understand.

"Tell me," Shichio said, "has there been any word from that Okuma boy?"

Hashiba laughed. "Him again? We can bring some of our own boys up here some night if you like."

Shichio's hand slipped down to the inside of Hashiba's upper thigh. "Come on. Tell me."

Hashiba sighed. "He married. I can only assume it was to forge an alliance with that Inoue clan. That's good. I can use one to apply leverage against the other."

"I don't care who some bumpkin boy shares his bed with. I want to know about my present."

"Ah. That." Hashiba folded a pillow under his head and settled back in. "I'm sorry, I don't have any monk's heads for you. Don't we have enough monks around here? Go march on Mount Hiei. Collecting a few heads up there will help keep the rest of the monasteries in line."

Shichio made a pouting face. "I don't want *a* head, I want *his* head."

"Well, you can't have it."

Shichio slipped the mask off his head. "You're certain of that?"

"What is it with that mask of yours?" Hashiba pushed Shichio's hand away, got to his feet, and strode forward to look down at his capital city. His shadow bisected a broad rectangle of moonlight on the floor. "You're too fond of that thing," he said. "You pet it like a house cat."

Shichio was surprised to discover it was true. His thumb was running over the tips of the mask's teeth, over and over, wholly independently of his will. It was an unconscious habit, but now that Hashiba had drawn his attention to it, Shichio recognized that caressing the mask and speaking of violence were two faces of one coin. Visions of swords, of stabbing and being stabbed, of penetrating and being penetrated. The mask inspired these things in him. That was why he wore it during their liaisons, and why all this talk of beheading had aroused similar feelings. Shichio felt himself begin to stiffen.

"It's the craftsmanship," he said, still stroking the mask. "Come back here. Look at how expressive it is. In gold, this kind of detail is pedestrian, but in iron? Never. It's as rare as anything. It's the most rugged sort of beauty, don't you think?"

Just like you, Shichio thought to himself, but Hashiba's musings went in a different direction. "I think I should have buried it right beside the assassin you took it from."

Shichio remembered that night all too well. It was the first time he'd killed a man. It was the night he made himself valuable to Hashiba, the night his fortunes started changing for the better. Rightly or wrongly, Shichio attributed his success to the mask. He often wondered what would be different if he'd purchased it instead of killed for it. Might its touch bring thoughts of money to his mind instead? Perhaps the obsession with swords was innate to its iron, or perhaps the mask just gave focus to Shichio's hatred of the samurai caste. It was impossible to know for certain.

"You should throw away that demon of yours," Hashiba said. "And throw away thoughts of this northern monk as well. He's no threat to anyone."

"So you *have* heard from the Okuma boy. And not just a wedding announcement."

Hashiba sighed, dropped back among the silken pillows, and surrendered. "Yes."

Shichio only had to think about it for a second. "You received a letter, didn't you? You brought it here? Tonight?"

Hashiba's only answer was to glance in the direction of the door.

Shichio walked saucily to the entryway and found a large, carefully folded page among Hashiba's other things. Smiling, Shichio sauntered back, sitting next to Hashiba again and opening the letter.

As he began to read, Hashiba took hold of Shichio's hand and guided it back down to his crotch. Shichio skipped over the standard salutations and looked for mention of the monk. "*I respectfully recommend against beheading our abbot of Kattō-ji,*" he read. "*He is an old man who does harm to no one, but more than this, he has taken the tonsure. I fear I may bring bad karma upon you by fulfilling your order to execute one such as him, and it is every samurai's sworn duty not to harm his lord.*"

Shichio felt his heart race, but he kept reading. "*Given the choice between obeying and harming the emperor's chosen regent on the one hand and disobeying to protect his interests on the other, I must choose disobedience.* Can you believe the impudence of this boy?"

Hashiba laughed. "I thought him rather clever."

"He disobeys a direct order from his regent!"

"He's the only samurai in the land who vows to protect me even in my future lives. Think of it! A bodyguard for my next reincarnation. Shichio, can you not just laugh this off and let it pass?"

"I tell you, that monk is a threat to you and your house. Kill him."

"The boy has done as much already. Read the next paragraph."

Shichio glanced down at the Okuma brat's scribblings. What he read there made him angry enough to stand up and start pacing. "A garrison? That's all? Just a garrison outside the monastery?"

"It is more than enough. That old man won't leave until he floats out on the smoke rising from his pyre."

Shichio crumpled the letter and flung it at the floor. "He can still talk. He can still teach. He wouldn't be the first monk to turn his order against you."

"That again?" Hashiba dropped his head heavily back on his pillow. "How many times have I told you? The Ikkō sect is no more. Oda and I wiped them out years ago. The only ones to escape the sword did it by swearing their eternal loyalty to me."

"This one is in the north. You never got any loyalty oaths from the north."

"That's because they're all dead. Tokugawa saw to that. He was as scared of them as you are."

Shichio sat heavily and laid his head on Hashiba's belly. His hand wandered back down to Hashiba's cock. "I want his head."

"You can't have it and you'd best get used to it. That old man is worth a lot more to me alive. Killing him would only cost me a future allegiance with this Okuma, and the rest of the Izu daimyo will be harder to get without him."

Shichio's hand quickened its pace. Hashiba's pulse did too. "Are you sure?"

"Oh no, you don't."

"Absolutely certain? No doubt in your mind?"

"Shichio, I'm not killing that old monk for you and that's that."

His heart beating in Shichio's ear told a different story. Shichio resituated himself between Hashiba's knees. The demon mask had two long, sharp fangs that framed either side of his mouth. If he angled his head just so, he could trace the pointed tip of a fang along Hashiba's skin. Done roughly, it could puncture. Done in just the right spot with just the right pressure, it was heavenly.

"Maybe we don't have to kill him," said Shichio, swaying the mask back and forth. "Maybe we can just go and pay him a visit."

Hashiba took in a long quivering breath.

"It's a long way. Lots of time at sea. Hours a day with nothing to do."

Hashiba clenched two silk pillows in his fists.

"Do any of your wives care for sailing? No, they don't, do they?"

Hashiba's fists tightened.

"Maybe I'll just go by myself. You don't want to come, do you?"

"Yes."

"You do? You want to come?"

"Yes, yes, yesss."

"All right, then. You can come."

12

The Okuma compound had received a messenger from To-yotomi Hideyoshi once before. Almost a year had passed since then, and the experience still left an indelible impression on Daigoro's young mind. Shiramatsu Shōzaemon, Hideyoshi's emissary, had come with a battalion at his back to chastise Daigoro's brother, Ichirō, for showing hubris in his duels. It was not far wrong to say Ichirō died because he had failed to heed that advice.

Daigoro had always assumed that Shiramatsu arrived with a show of force in order to cow House Okuma into submission. The daimyo of Izu sometimes rode with an honor guard, but only on special occasions; usually a few bodyguards were protection enough. Shiramatsu Shōzaemon had arrived with an entire battalion as his escort. At the time Daigoro had been duly impressed, but he'd never guessed at what the imperial regent himself might consider to be an appropriate bodyguard.

When Daigoro saw the first junk, he feared the worst. She was twice the size of any Izu fishing vessel. The *kiri* flowers on her enormous sails were as unmistakable as the samurai standing in formation on the deck or their spearheads glinting in the sun. There were dozens of them, and Daigoro had no illusions about whether they came in peace. Surely they've come for the abbot, he thought, and maybe for my head as well.

Little had Daigoro imagined that this was a *small* ship, little more than a sloop. The next ship to appear was one of the famed turtle ships. Daigoro had never seen one before, but there was no mistaking what it was. Scores of interlocking metal shields covered the entire deck in a gleaming shell. The fact that Daigoro could not see the deck only gave his imagination room to wander. How many troops were aboard? A hundred? More?

Izu was a land of high, blocky sea cliffs, stabbing out into the waves like huge black fingers. They made it impossible to see any real distance up or down the coast, and when the surf was high, pale clouds of spray hovered perpetually along the cliffs, further obscuring visibility. As such, a fleet that sailed near the coast appeared out of nowhere. Two turtle ships, then four, then eight. And then came the actual warship.

It was a floating castle. Her hull was like any other ship's, save for its enormous size. But her decks were no decks at all. Instead, sheer wooden walls ascended from the hull, no less than five stories tall. Another two-story donjon towered above the main structure. The ship's oars were like a centipede's legs: spindly, moving in unison, impossible to count. Portholes formed a grid of dark squares on the castle walls, and Daigoro feared every last one of them might harbor one of the southern barbarians' fabled cannons behind it. If so, she bore hundreds upon hundreds of cannon. Daigoro wondered whether there was enough iron in the world to cast that many.

As the castle ship drew nearer, it loomed so large that Daigoro wondered which was bigger, the ship or the entire Okuma compound. It took four anchors to moor her, each one the size of a warhorse. The launch she lowered to take her commander ashore looked like a pea pod compared to the warship herself, yet Daigoro counted no less than thirty-three armored men boarding the launch.

He wondered which one was Hideyoshi. Only one man was clearly visible from Daigoro's vantage high up on the compound's wall: a giant in glittering black *yoroi*, his topknot as white as snow. Too old to be a bodyguard, Daigoro thought. And too big to be the regent; rumor held him to be quite slight. Daigoro wondered whether the giant was one of the regent's generals. He might even be this Shichio that was calling for the abbot's head.

Daigoro watched as his own commanders greeted the landing party. He hadn't gone down himself, for the regent's arrival had come as a surprise. It would have taken Daigoro the better part of the morning to limp all the way down to the beach, and he hadn't the time to gather a palanquin and crew to carry him down there. He'd sent his best officers instead, along with a platoon of spearmen. Even they must have been sweating in their armor after running down the whole way. Daigoro sympathized. The sweat was already running down his back and he hadn't done anything but watch.

His anger felt like a wild animal trapped inside his body. It twitched frenetically in his neck and made it hard to speak. Why had he married his house to the Inoues if not to gain the benefit of their spy network? And how had the ubiquitous eyes and ears of House Inoue failed to notice a ship the size of an island, in the midst of an entire war fleet? Daigoro was going to have a talk with his father-in-law, and soon.

Akiko primped him as he set everyone else about their tasks: the cooks to their fires; the maids to their stations; runners into town to gather food for a welcome feast; still more runners to hire musicians and geisha; manservants to clear every last room in the compound save the audience chamber, in case the regent and his troops decided to spend the night; Tomo to oversee the entire operation. Finally and most importantly, he released Akiko to go and deal with his mother.

Daigoro wished he'd had more time; with a little advance notice he might have sent her to stay with Lord Yasuda or some other neighbor. As it was, the best idea he could come up with was to order Tomo to restrain her using any means shy of lethal force. But Akiko had a better idea. The lady of House Okuma was quite taken with her new daughter-in-law, and Akiko seemed to get on with her quite well. Akiko gave Daigoro a broad smile and kissed him on the cheek. "Don't worry," she told him. "I've got ribbons and balls for *temari*, hairpins and combs, everything two girls need to have fun."

He watched her go, then looked back down to the beach. A second launch had landed with a bevy of palanquins aboard. The white-haired giant stepped into one of them. Two slender men stepped into another. Three more were occupied by quartets of men in varying uniforms, some armored, some not. Daigoro's own commanders were offered the other four. Daigoro's mind boggled at the thought of having four spare palanquins and four extra teams of bearers—and these on To-yotomi's shipboard crew, to say nothing of his palace.

In no time at all the guests had arrived. Every last Okuma samurai had been marshaled into the honor guard. They lined the main courtyard, as still as the walls themselves. Daigoro recognized Shira-matsu Shōzaemon when he emerged from his sedan chair along with three samurai in Toyotomi gold. He wore a silver kimono to match his silver hair, with a thin beard and a thinner mustache. His topknot was immaculate and his movements precise. He approached the center palanquin with short, measured steps, slid its door aside, and said, "You shall bow before the Imperial Regent, His Highness, the Chief Minister and great Lord General Toyotomi no Hideyoshi."

All the Okuma samurai went to their knees, as did the regent's own. Daigoro's leg never allowed him to kneel easily, so instead he bowed deeply at the waist. "You will kneel *now*," he heard Shiramatsu say, and looking up he saw the man's withering glare. This was a very different Shiramatsu from the one who had come a year before. That man was unflappable. This one actually bared his teeth when he repeated his command.

"At ease," said the little goggle-eyed man who hopped out of the palanquin. His armor was black, orange, and gold, and he was so skinny that it hung on him as if on a wooden armor stand. His cheekbones were too high, his chin too long. Against his willing it, Daigoro thought of the macaques one sometimes found in the mountains. It shamed him to liken this man to a monkey, but at least now the nickname Monkey King made sense. This could only be Toyotomi Hideyoshi.

"It's his house," said Hideyoshi. "Let him bow if he likes." He shot Daigoro a conspiratorial smile. His teeth were sharp, misaligned, haphazardly spaced, like a seer's chicken bones tossed on the ground and pointing in all different directions.

"Yes, my lord regent," said Shiramatsu. "Most gracious of you. You may stand, Okuma-san."

Hideyoshi paid Shiramatsu no mind at all. Instead he looked at the assembled Okuma samurai and then around the compound. "Nice place you've got here."

Daigoro's thoughts stumbled over each other like drunks. All his associations and inferences had missed the mark. When Shiramatsu had first come almost a year ago, Daigoro thought him to be a high-ranking emissary, one so important that he warranted a legion of bodyguards. Now he could see the truth, reflected in Hideyoshi's relaxed stance and in his emissary's obsequious gaze toward him. Shiramatsu was nothing more than a lickspittle. Hideyoshi had sent him with a battalion for the same reason he himself had come on the wings of an invasion fleet: to cow the Okumas into submission. And yet Hideyoshi was anything but intimidating. Now Daigoro thought not of mountain monkeys but of his father: approachable, even gentle, but a master at deploying his forces for just the right effect. Psychologically speaking, Hideyoshi had put Daigoro on his heels before he'd even set foot on shore.

Even so, Daigoro immediately understood why the abbot had referred to him as Hideyoshi, not as General Toyotomi. There was nothing lordly about this man. His shoulders were relaxed, his gait bouncy. He'd done a sloppy job of tying his topknot. He couldn't have been much taller than Daigoro, who by anyone's account was a pip-squeak. He was the imperial regent, the highest-ranking military officer in the land, and yet the cording on his *katana* looked as if it had never been touched, to say nothing of having been drawn in battle. His hands were smooth and uncallused. His armor was surely crafted to evoke images of a tiger—orange and black for its stripes, gold for its gleaming, ferocious eyes—but it only called attention to the fact that Hideyoshi was the living antithesis of a tiger. His colors were garish, not subtle, his armor hard, not supple, his movements common, not majestic.

The man behind him was the regal one. He was thin like Hideyoshi, but tall, stately, with handsome features and a graceful air. Even as he stepped out of the palanquin, he preened his hair. He took in his surroundings with the practiced affectation of the highborn, cocking a disdainful eyebrow when his gaze finally fell on Daigoro. In truth he noted Glorious Victory first, studying her as an object of art rather than a weapon. He made a tiny adjustment to his golden kimono before dipping his chin toward Daigoro in an almost imperceptible bow.

He was a peacock, in short, and Daigoro wondered who he was.

The last to emerge from the palanquins was the giant Daigoro had seen in the launch. He was head and shoulders taller than the peacock, and the *katana* sheathed at his hip was almost as long as Glorious Victory. It seemed like a sword of no great length in comparison to his enormous belly. Despite his age he was not balding; it was clear that he still had to shave his pate. His white topknot and little white point of a beard were both well groomed. His black armor was polished to a gleaming sheen, with horse motifs embossed into the leather. He was the very embodiment of nobility and lordliness.

And yet in the company of the giant and the peacock, it was Hideyoshi that the emperor had named regent, Hideyoshi who had brought a thousand daimyo to heel, Hideyoshi who commanded the attention of everyone in the courtyard. Daigoro could not help it: his eyes followed the man wherever he went. He wondered what Hideyoshi's secret was. He and Daigoro were both puny. Both fell short of what it meant to be a man. From birth neither of them was cut out to be samurai—Daigoro because of his disfigurement, Hideyoshi because of his parentage—and yet both had to play the role. And while Daigoro had trouble commanding even the loyalty of his own father-in-law, Hideyoshi had the emperor himself at his back.

The imperial regent walked up to Daigoro and bowed. "Good morning. I'm Toyotomi Hideyoshi. Let's have a seat and chat."

Soldiers and servants scurried like leaves before a typhoon. Soon enough all the required parties were seated in the Okuma audience chamber: Hideyoshi on the dais, the giant on his left, and the peacock on his right, a dozen Toyotomi samurai on either side of them, still as statues. Daigoro was seated before the regent, Katsushima on his right, his lieutenants in a row behind them, the rest of his officers ranked and filed in the back. Shiramatsu, Tomo, and a few other attendants were kneeling at the door, all of them duly submissive and subdued. Sixty men in the room all told, and of all of them only Hideyoshi was relaxed.

"Shichio here tells me we've got a problem," he said, nodding his head toward the peacock. "Something about a monk."

So this is Shichio, Daigoro thought. The man put him on edge. Ever since his arrival, his eyes repeatedly drifted to Glorious Victory Unsought. He seemed drawn to it somehow. Daigoro had seen that obsession before, and he knew it never ended well.

But he could not afford to ruminate on that now. The island's most powerful warlord had asked him a question. "Yes, the abbot of Kattō-ji," Daigoro said. "He is under house arrest. His temple is on the next peak north of here."

"Is he of the Ikkō sect?"

"No, my lord regent. His is a Zen order."

"Was he ever?"

"Of the Ikkō Ikki? No, my lord regent."

"Does he harbor any Ikkō monks? Does he preach insurrection? Does he keep a hidden arsenal in the monastery?"

"No, my lord regent."

Hideyoshi looked over his shoulder to the peacock—no, Daigoro thought, correcting himself: to General Shichio. He could almost hear Katsushima chiding him. Make the slightest misstep and this man will have your head. Best be careful.

"You see?" the regent told Shichio. "The monk is no threat."

"We've come an awfully long way just to take this boy's word for it," Shichio said with a sneer. His voice was so soft that he could barely be heard past the dais, yet Daigoro noticed he used none of the honorifics one would expect in speaking to a man second only to the emperor in rank. Was it because Hideyoshi was so informal that he didn't require such niceties? Or was it the pride of a preening peacock?

Hideyoshi shrugged. "Lord Okuma," he said, "I'm sure you understand my concerns. I've given an execution order. You haven't followed it. Even a common platoon sergeant cannot abide disobedience from his troops. In my office insubordination looms larger still."

"Yes, my lord regent."

"But I respect your title, your name, and your authority. It does me no good to strip a daimyo's sovereignty over his fief. I have no use for your anger; what I want is your loyalty. And there's my problem. The easy solution is to kill you, kill this monk, and sail back home. I've killed disobedient daimyo before. So remind me, Lord Okuma, how is it that you show me loyalty by refusing to carry out my will?"

"My lord regent has no desire for enemies in Izu," Daigoro said, then stopped himself. The abbot's warning about General Shichio echoed in his mind: this was a man who reshaped words like clay. Daigoro's answer could already be reinterpreted as a veiled threat; he chose his next words more carefully.

"The abbot is a very popular man. He presides over the funerals of every family within three days' ride of here. Parents are known to travel twenty *ri* just to have him bless their babies. Killing him is certain to raise the farmers' ire, my lord regent; any daimyo who killed him would have a hard time collecting taxes."

"I see," said Hideyoshi, but Shichio leaned forward and whispered something in his ear.

"Sir, I agree with Lord Okuma," said the giant. He shifted to face his liege lord. "It is no secret that you plan to move against the Hōjōs. Create a disturbance among the northern daimyo and you only create allies for the enemy."

"And yet disobedience is disobedience," said Hideyoshi. Shichio gave a little nod. Daigoro wondered whose words had just come from the regent's mouth.

"Sir," said the giant, "there is disobedience and then there is obeying the spirit of a command without obeying it to the letter."

"Why, General Mio," Shichio said, "I hadn't expected hairsplitting from you."

"And I hadn't expected you to sail the command fleet halfway across the empire to indulge a petty grudge. Someday you'll have to tell me why this monk is so important to you."

The peacock glowered. The giant, Mio, shifted again where he sat, rotating to face Daigoro. "Lord Okuma, we have your word that no one outside this Kattō-ji will ever see the abbot in question again?"

"On my own life, Mio-dono, you have my word."

"He will speak with no one outside his monastery?"

"Yes, Mio-dono."

"And what of visitors to the monastery? Will he speak with them?"

Daigoro bowed low. "My lord regent has only to tell me his preference and I will make it law. Toyotomi-dono, please understand, the abbot had the utmost respect for my departed father. He could have taken the tonsure anywhere, and chose to do it at Kattō-ji in order to be close to my father and learn from him. If I command him to a lifetime of silence, he will obey."

General Mio opened his mouth to ask another question, but Shichio cut him off. Speaking loudly for the first time, he said, "It seems to me that if this man is so beloved by the people, then confining him to his monastery will be no more popular than having him killed. In fact, it may be worse; force him into a vow of silence and he will either violate it or else anger the people further by being present yet refusing to speak to them. So what benefit is it to leave him alive?"

Daigoro's stomach clenched. He had no answer to that. Outfoxed by a peacock, he thought.

But Mio answered for him. "General Shichio speaks directly to my point," said the giant. "For all intents and purposes, the abbot is dead to the world. Lord Okuma was not disobedient. He fulfilled the spirit of the regent's command as fully as anyone could ask of him."

"No," said Shichio. "To carry it out fully would be to deliver a bald head in a box."

"My lord regent," Daigoro said, his heart pounding; he'd never interrupted commanders of this station before. "The abbot himself offered me just that solution. I turned him down."

Hideyoshi fixed his overlarge eyes on Daigoro. "Did you? Well, look at the balls on this one." He laughed and said, "Explain yourself, Lord Okuma."

"My lord regent, my father told me many times that when we are faced with choosing between taking an easy path and taking a hard one, the path of *bushidō* is almost never the easy path."

A knowing smile touched Hideyoshi's lips. "I remember him. I met him only briefly, but I remember thinking, 'Now this one is a samurai.'"

"He was the best," said Daigoro.

"You misunderstand me," said Hideyoshi. "He was an impressive man, your father. The consummate samurai. But this honor of his—this honor of yours—never made the slightest bit of sense to me."

Daigoro was confused. He was sure his ears had deceived him. He could not have heard the regent, a man the emperor himself had raised to the station of samurai, admit he didn't believe in honor. It was impossible. Wasn't it?

Hideyoshi went on. "I'll grant you, I wasn't born into all this honor nonsense, but even if I had been, I'm still not sure I would understand it any better. How did it become fashionable to prefer death to disloyalty? Why not praise self-interest? Why not ambition? Aren't people better suited to pursue their own interests anyhow?"

"I've never thought of it that way," Daigoro said honestly. To him the dictates of honor were as indisputable as the stars in the heavens. They were not something one questioned; they simply *were*. Those who navigated without them did so at their peril. But Hideyoshi had it right as well: left to their own devices, human beings would surely pursue their own selfish interests, wouldn't they?

"Think on it," said Hideyoshi. "I defy you to explain why I should live within the straits of this thing you call honor. Wouldn't your life be easier without it? Here you are, right in the dragon's den, and yet if you had killed that monk as I ordered, you and I would never have met. In fact, if you weren't so damned honor-bound, you could have sent along any old head, *neh*? You could have lied and saved your skin. Yet here you are. I can kill you at whim. Your honor makes you weaker than me, doesn't it?"

Daigoro could almost feel the energy bristling from General Mio—and not just from Mio, but from Katsushima too. Both of them were born samurai and both were too incensed to speak. They gave off heat like a pair of volcanoes. Was Hideyoshi goading them? Was he goading Daigoro? Or was he really so ignorant of what it meant to be samurai?

"My lord, I think I am weaker than you," Daigoro said at last. "But not because of my honor. I am weaker because my influence is smaller. I have a few hundred warriors at my command; you have hundreds of thousands. And yes, I believe you have it right: I think men are naturally inclined not to be honorable but to be selfish. But that is precisely why honor is important; it bids us to transcend ourselves. Without it, we are only clever animals. With it, we can be better than our animal instincts allow us to be."

"Is that what you think of peasants?" said Hideyoshi. "That we're animals?"

"No, my lord, I—"

"Let me ask you this: would you agree that the peasants of our country—the clever little animals—would like to see an end to war?"

"Of course, my lord regent."

"And would you agree that as long as there have been samurai, there has been war?"

"We are born out of war. That is what it means to be a warrior."

"Don't you see what that means? As long as there are warriors, war will never end. What we need is an end to it. When every last province is brought under the reign of one man, that man can stop being a warlord. He can simply be a ruler."

Hideyoshi smiled. It was an ugly thing, his sharp teeth not so different from the sharp rocks jumbled along the coastline. But ugly as it was, there was legitimate kindness in the smile. "Tell me, Lord Okuma, wouldn't your father have preferred to see the end of all wars?"

"Yes, my lord regent. Without a doubt."

"Then what good is this honor of yours if it always leads to more fighting? Would it not be better if all samurai abandoned their honor and started thinking more like peasants?"

"Begging your pardon, my lord regent, but I respect my father above all other men. It was his unfailing adherence to *bushidō* that I admired most. If he were still alive, if he were in this room and you commanded me to behead him, I would do it in a heartbeat and I believe he would be proud of me for doing so. To sacrifice family for one's liege is the hardest path, and it leads to the highest height of honor. But to sacrifice an innocent is the easy path. To sacrifice an innocent to benefit oneself is even worse. And to do so at the expense of one's liege lord is unforgivable."

"Who gave you the right to decide what is unforgivable?" said Shichio, his voice loud and sharp, verging on a snarl. His angry outburst was totally at odds with his genteel appearance. "Are *you* the regent now? Has the emperor given *you* his blessing?"

Daigoro bowed his forehead to the floor. "My most abject apologies, Shichio-dono. I chose my words poorly." And you didn't wait long to capitalize on that, he thought.

Hearing no further objection, Daigoro continued. "My lord regent, you are correct: I could have sent you the head of any bald man. I could have shaved a common criminal. And I could have sent you the head you requested—"

"The imperial regent does not *request* anything," Shichio hissed. "He speaks and his underlings obey."

Again Daigoro's forehead touched the floor. "As you say, Shichio-dono. A thousand apologies, my lords. A thousand times thousand."

"Go on," said Hideyoshi.

"My lord regent, I could have beheaded the abbot as you ordered and all of this business would be over. But to do so would be to kill an innocent for no other reason than to make life easier for my family and myself. Worse yet, I believe it would have been a disservice to you. I believe General Mio is correct, Toyotomi-dono: if I were to kill this abbot, it would strengthen your enemies and drive the northern territories further from your grasp."

"The regent's arm extends everywhere," said Shichio. "Nothing is beyond his grasp. And even if it were, is someone of your station powerful enough to deny him? I think not."

"And I think you talk more than you should," said General Mio. "Shut your mouth and let your superior make his own decision in peace."

Shichio scowled across the dais at Mio but kept his mouth shut. Yet Daigoro noticed a change in Hideyoshi. He sat somewhat taller than before; he'd squared his shoulders and ever so slightly lowered his chin. All this talk of his own power seemed to make him feel more powerful, and in hindsight Daigoro realized that Shichio's words were aimed not just at Daigoro but at Hideyoshi too. It was as if he'd been inflating the man, puffing him up, stiffening his resolve, yet all the while drawing Hideyoshi's position closer toward his own, like iron filings shifting their alignment toward a magnet. Daigoro wondered how many others in the room had even noticed. Mio was oblivious, as was Hideyoshi himself. The peacock truly was a master manipulator.

Hideyoshi was quiet for a long time. "Sir," General Mio said at last, "you must see the logic of the boy's argument."

But Daigoro wasn't so sure. Shichio's hypnotic song still held sway over him. If the regent were to pass judgment now, it could go either way, and Daigoro was certain that once Hideyoshi made a pronouncement, it would stand as fast as Mount Fuji itself. Shichio had overfed his ego; there was no longer any room for backing down.

Would it be so bad? Suppose the abbot were to die, Daigoro thought. Suppose he died on a Toyotomi sword, or even an Okuma sword at Hideyoshi's command. One man would go willingly to his death and the Okumas would escape the regent's wrath. Better still, they would escape the wrath of the regent's right-hand man, who was not only touched by madness but clearly held greater sway than the more reasonable General Mio. Was that such a bad alternative? Be quiet, a voice in his mind told him. Let the regent pass judgment however he likes.

Katsushima's voice spoke in Daigoro's mind too. Patience. Say nothing. You are already poised on the razor's edge; do not compromise your balance.

And there was a third voice too: his father's. There is the easy path and the hard path. You know which one to choose.

"My lord regent," Daigoro said, "there is another way to resolve this dilemma."

Hideyoshi blinked at him as if he'd just snapped out of a dream. "Oh?"

Daigoro swallowed. He felt his heart plunge down a cold, dark well. He willed his hand to remain steady as he withdrew his *waki-zashi* from his waistband and laid it ceremoniously on the floor in front of him. Then he moved to take off his overrobe and bare his chest.

A samurai always had one final method of protest: seppuku. By all accounts there were few deaths more painful than ritual disembowelment, but no one could question the sincerity of a man who was willing to plunge a knife into his own belly. By sacrificing his own life—something he was certain Shichio would never do—Daigoro could prove his cause was right. Seppuku was a time-honored tradition, one that even Hideyoshi could understand.

Daigoro found his arms had frozen. He could only commit seppuku by first removing his robe, and now his very muscles would not let him do it.

"Yes," said Shichio. "There is another solution, isn't there?"

Of course, Daigoro thought. How could he expect Shichio to

make this easier? How could he even expect the man to appreciate the gravity of the situation? He was no samurai. He would relish every moment of Daigoro's suicide. And now Daigoro's own body threatened to taint the solemnity of seppuku. This was not a moment to lose his resolve.

Daigoro closed his eyes and willed life back into his petrified arms. If suicide was his only recourse, he would face it without fear.

13

"Trial by combat," said Shichio.

Daigoro opened his eyes in surprise. Shichio was supposed to relish watching him die. He wasn't supposed to prevent Daigoro from falling on his sword.

"The boy is right," said Shichio. "Men's words are proved by steel. If argument cannot settle this, let it be settled by swords."

"You're joking," said General Mio. "You? Fight?"

"Of course not," said Shichio. "I have no more interest in fighting this child than he has in fighting me. But surely he has a champion. And surely one of our brave samurai will step up to champion our cause."

"*Your* cause," said Mio.

Daigoro's whole body began to quiver. He'd come so close to death. In his mind he'd already willed his death, and now it would not come—or at least not by seppuku. If this trial-by-combat nonsense played itself through, he might still be killed, but in that case the abbot's death would come next. Shichio had anticipated Daigoro's suicide and the effect it would have on Hideyoshi's mind. He'd anticipated it and nipped it in the bud. Once again Daigoro had been outfoxed by a peacock.

And yet Shichio had a point. The duel was first invented to settle questions of honor. The tradition of proving one's word with the sword was as old as the sword itself. If Daigoro refused to duel, it would be tantamount to admitting disloyalty. If refusing to kill the abbot was truly the right course, Daigoro had no choice but to defend it with steel.

But how much blood had been shed needlessly in the name of honor? Daigoro had witnessed his share of duels, including the one that claimed his brother's life. He'd seen men bloodied and maimed and killed, all in the name of a concept that he had always taken for granted, a concept that he'd never examined in any real depth until Hideyoshi called it into question.

And the duels Daigoro had seen were the best of their kind. How many duels ended in a mutual slaying? Half? More? Often as not, two experts would cut each other down. Two neophytes would do the same, out of sheer inexperience rather than skill. Survival itself was often a grim prospect; the samurai caste was full of men who had defended their honor at the cost of a limb. Daigoro had no taste for it.

Even so, a single word of protest would mark him as a traitor and a coward. There was only one path left to him.

"I will not risk one of my men over so trivial a cause," the Okuma whelp said. "I will face your champion myself."

"Trivial?"

Shichio surprised himself with the sharpness of his tone. Did the boy have no shame? There was nothing trivial about this at all. Shichio would have loved nothing more than to watch the boy eviscerate himself, but if that happened, then Hashiba would relent on the monk. From there, Mio's curiosity would only grow, and perhaps the giant oaf would send men to ask questions. If Mio were ever to learn the truth, Hashiba would be the next to learn of it, and that would be the end of everything. No, this was far from trivial.

Even for the boy this was no trifling matter. The regent's own fleet had stormed his lands and filled his home with troops. At any moment Hashiba could have him executed for sheer insolence. Perhaps Shichio should already have done so himself. His thoughts flitted momentarily to his demon mask, and to stabbing this boy through the neck. In his most imperious tone he said, "What part of the regent's business is *trivial* to you?"

"The correct way to handle this matter is clear," said the boy. "I have already placed a permanent garrison at the monastery at my expense. I have already suggested that killing the abbot would unsettle the region and bring bad karma upon the regent. The correct path is clear. All other paths are trivial."

"Sir, I must agree," said Mio, his voice deep and booming. He shifted his hulking, armored body to face Hashiba, making a point of ignoring Shichio completely. "Lord Okuma has your best interests at heart. I believe your best course is to forgive an old man for whatever sins he may once have committed. Please, Hideyoshi-dono, let this go."

Shichio couldn't decide which one he hated more, Mio Yasumasa or the Okuma brat. He was sure of one thing only: he could not allow Hashiba to dismiss the question of the abbot. Shameful acts of the past were like ghosts, growing ever hungrier as time went on. And Hashiba was not known for his forgiveness. Better to deal with a little peasant uprising in Izu than to risk waking the ghosts, and then see how Hashiba would respond to them.

"Give me a garrison here," Shichio said. "Let me show these rubes what good it will do them if they protest the killing of a single backwater monk. Let me show them your power. Let this boy feel the swift stroke of Hideyoshi's justice."

"Justice will weigh in where it sees fit," said Hashiba. "Lord Okuma, we will elect a champion for you to fight. General Mio, assemble the troops."

Mio bowed as low as his enormous belly would let him. "Begging your pardon, sir, but I won't. If the young Lord Okuma will not risk one of his own men for this, then neither will I. I will face him."

Shichio glanced at the boy and wondered if that was a trace of fear in his eyes. Moments earlier Okuma had seemed wholly oblivious to death, speaking his mind as if Hashiba were no loftier than a common maidservant. But Mio was four times the boy's size. He was the veteran of countless battles, and he'd never lost in single combat. The boy might just as well have challenged a tsunami to a sumo bout.

For a fleeting instant Shichio wondered whether Mio was trying to double-cross him. The fat man had agreed with Okuma all along; perhaps he meant to throw the fight. But then Shichio thought better of it. Guile and craft were not in Mio's character. He barged through life like a boulder rolling downhill.

Then an even brighter thought alighted in Shichio's mind: what if the fat man does betray me? He's samurai, after all; it's hardly beyond him to kill himself to prove a point. If Mio means to die on the boy's sword, at least I'm free of him.

The boy's sword. Shichio's eyes had been drawn to it from the moment he stepped out of the palanquin. Apart from his demon mask, it was the finest piece of craftsmanship he'd ever seen. It was rumored to be an Inazuma blade—not an easy rumor to believe of some backwater bumpkin's sword, but one look dismissed all doubts. This was truly a thing of beauty.

And the mask showed a stronger affinity for this sword than any other. He'd had no choice but to leave the mask in the palanquin, because for the first time he could hardly bear to touch it—or rather, touching it inspired a craving so powerful that Shichio actually feared he might lose control of his body. So long as he held the mask, he *needed* that sword. The thought of such a masterpiece being used in battle was anathema to him. What if it were nicked? What if it were stained with blood?

On the other hand, what if it gutted the fat man?

Shichio restrained a grin. Yes, he thought; if Okuma wins, Mio will be out of my life forever. All I'll have to do is find another way to kill the monk. And if the duel goes the other way, I'm free of the Okuma brat and the monk is mine. No matter who loses this fight, victory belongs to me—as will that Inazuma sword, as soon as I can figure out how.

He watched on happily as the brat made one last plea for Hashiba to do the right thing. Then came the fat man's pretensions of grandeur, which were enough to make Shichio giddy; since the boy was unarmored, Mio summoned attendants to remove his armor as well. For a lummox his size it was a three-man job. When they'd finished, Mio and Okuma took their positions in the courtyard, their shadows short and dark under the high noon sun. Mio drew his massive blade, and a tall, gray-haired, shabby-looking man presented Okuma with his sword.

Once again Shichio was struck by the beauty of it. The weapon was nearly as long as the boy was tall, and much too large for him to wield. Were it any other blade, it would have gleamed in the sun, but the Inazuma steel seemed to glow with its own glorious light. Shichio had never been so thankful not to have his mask. With it, he might well have run onto the battlefield to take the sword for his own.

Okuma's steps had become short, shuffling movements under the weight of the sword, and for the first time Shichio noticed the brat must have injured his leg somehow. He limped off the right foot, and though Shichio was no master, he knew enough to understand that the right leg was all-important in swordsmanship. It was the root leg, the primary source of balance, power, and movement. And Okuma's was lame.

So Mio will win this one, he thought. I'll have to rid myself of him some other way. But at least I'll have the pleasure of watching this Okuma brat die, and once he's dead I'll claim that big, beautiful sword of his.

Shichio settled himself next to Hashiba on the veranda overlooking the courtyard. He couldn't wait to see what happened next.

14

Sweat ran down into Daigoro's eyes and he could not afford to wipe it away. Glorious Victory Unsought was far too heavy for him to remove a hand from her grip. His right hand was weak enough already; it was all he could do just to steady the tip of his blade.

It was hot, damnably hot, and though Daigoro's throat was dry he was sure it wasn't from the heat. Mio was a giant. His sword was nearly as long as Daigoro's and his arms were considerably longer. Daigoro's first tactic had always been to rely on Glorious Victory's greater reach, but that would not save him today.

They circled each other and the sun beat down on them like a hammer. More than a hundred people looked on. Daigoro had never dueled in front of so many before. They made him nervous. His sweating, aching hands tightened their grip on his weapon.

He knew he did not want to fight this man, and he knew of Glorious Victory's power to see him through whenever he wanted not to fight, but this time he was not so sure. This was a duel he could have avoided. He could have overruled Shichio's twisting words with one stroke of the sword. If he'd had the courage to plunge his *wakizashi* into his belly, he could have ended all the arguments. And yet here he was, squaring off against a living mountain.

Their blades met. Mio thrust at his throat. Daigoro shoved the thrust aside and chopped down at the wrists. Mio batted Glorious

Victory aside, his parry so powerful that it almost sent Daigoro spinning.

Daigoro pulled Glorious Victory back to center and managed to fend off Mio's next attack. He stumbled but caught himself before he fell.

Daigoro had never faced so powerful a fighter. Yet Mio had more than size in his favor: he was far more experienced. In any other match his age might have counted against him, but the advantages of youth were strength and speed, and because of his leg Daigoro had neither. His brother Ichirō might have made short work of this giant. Katsushima too; he constantly surprised Daigoro with his quickness. But Daigoro had always relied on pacing a fight slowly, taking the measure of his opponent, allowing his adversary to grow frustrated and impatient.

Mio showed no signs of impatience. He advanced, not out of frustration but from sheer dominance. Daigoro moved in, exactly the opposite of what the smaller fighter should do, hoping to catch the big man off his guard. Mio gave him a shove, sword against sword, and Daigoro felt his feet leave the ground.

Horses didn't kick that hard. Daigoro couldn't say how far he flew before landing. He crunched into the gravel, rolled to his feet, and Mio was already on top of him. He showed Daigoro exactly how long his reach was, cutting Daigoro's sleeve while a thrust from Glorious Victory fell well short of Mio's throat. Only sheer luck had spared Daigoro's arm.

Mio pressed the attack. Daigoro dived, rolled, came up behind him. Mio continued his charge, taking himself out of Daigoro's reach. Daigoro had no counterattack, but at least he had a moment's respite.

The fingers ached in Daigoro's right hand. His lips and mouth were as dry as hot sand. His heart pounded in his ears like a *taiko* drum, so loud and so fast that he could hear nothing else. The cold, serene, paralyzing fear of seppuku was long gone. Now it was a burning panic that gripped him, a need to escape this titan and his titanic sword. Swordsmen the size of Mio usually fought demons or *tengu*; they were the warriors of myth, not reality. Daigoro had no desire to be killed by a walking nightmare.

General Mio turned on him and advanced again. Daigoro saw just one hope of victory. Mio was fat enough that he could not see his feet. Men that big usually had poor balance. If Daigoro could make him fall, Mio could not capitalize on his superior strength and speed.

Glorious Victory Unsought was made for mounted combat. It was long enough to cut down foot soldiers from the saddle, long enough to unseat a cavalryman, long enough for the horse-cutting technique Daigoro tried next. Against the legs of a charging warhorse, only the strongest steel was of any use. Mio would be no different.

Mio charged. Daigoro stepped aside, dropped low, and cut for the ankles.

Mio's sword sank to parry, just as Daigoro thought it would.

Parried or not, Glorious Victory was heavy enough to trip him, just as it was heavy enough to fell a horse. But Mio jumped over instead.

He should have fallen. But Mio had the balance of a dancer—no, of a *rikishi*, a sumo wrestler, for sumo required not balance but balance with unthinkable power. Mio landed on one foot, whirled on Daigoro, stomped down hard. Daigoro shrank away. Mio chopped down with terrifying force, a blow that could behead an ox.

Desperately, hopelessly, knowing the fight was over, Daigoro raised his weapon to parry.

Glorious Victory Unsought cut Mio's sword neatly in two.

Against anyone else the fight would have been over. Daigoro was in striking range and Mio's *katana* was useless. But Mio had fought under Oda Nobunaga and Toyotomi Hideyoshi. He'd faced a thousand men in battle before Daigoro was old enough to hold a sword. He threw the butchered sword haft at Daigoro and drew his *wakizashi*.

The haft cut Daigoro across the cheek. The *wakizashi* came next, stabbing at his gut. Daigoro parried, took the sword through fabric instead of flesh. The blade entangled itself in his clothing.

Mio's chest slammed into his face. Daigoro reeled backward. Mio continued his charge, trying to yank his sword free. Daigoro set his feet, pointed Glorious Victory straight at the sky, and put his shoulder into it.

Mio slammed right into the sword.

He toppled backward, dragging Daigoro with him. Daigoro would have landed on him face-first, but at the last instant he stepped up with his flimsy right foot, planting it on Mio's stomach.

A line of blood ran straight up the center of Mio's torso. Yellow fat bubbled forth from his belly, blood mixing with it in scribbling red lines. Mio must have turned his head aside at the last instant, for his left ear was missing but otherwise his face and neck were unharmed.

Only then did Daigoro notice that his sword had stopped just a hairsbreadth from Mio's throat. By luck, by training, by reflex, or by whatever glamer Master Inazuma had hammered into the steel, his sword had stopped just shy of a killing blow.

Daigoro looked to the dais. Hideyoshi was wide-eyed, slack-jawed, with an awed smile playing around the corners of his mouth. Shichio was so furious that Daigoro thought he might draw steel at any moment. Katsushima looked the proud father, chest swelling with pride, hands pressing his thighs as if to restrain himself from leaping to Daigoro's side. Daigoro gave his audience a small bow. Then all eyes turned to General Mio.

Flat on his back, Mio roared with laughter. He touched two fingers to his missing ear, laughed harder, and rolled his head back onto the sand to look at his liege lord. "Now that's a fighter! My lord, find me a hundred men like this and I'll bring those Hōjōs to heel by the end of the week."

Daigoro looked at Mio, at Glorious Victory, and at his own foot, which was still planted on Mio's belly as if the general were a ship's bow and Daigoro were a sea captain. Without meaning to, he'd effectively claimed Mio as a prize.

Hideyoshi clapped and rose to his feet. "Most impressive! Now we see why he's called the Bear Cub of Izu."

Daigoro stepped off his fallen foe, whose laughter now mixed with tiny grunts of pain as his hands prodded his belly wound. "You must understand," Daigoro said softly, "it was not my intention to embarrass you."

"Embarrass me? Master Bear Cub, you've honored me. People will talk about this duel for a hundred years. Think of it! The little cub who knocked down the mountain! Come, help me up. Let's find something to eat."

15

D aigoro awoke with a start. The night was silent—or as silent as it ever was this close to the coast. Frogs chirped; cicadas sang; the surf breathed in and out, in and out. These were his lullabies ever since childhood, but tonight something was amiss.

He slipped out of bed, shivering at the transition from Akiko's warmth under the bedcovers. He found his robe and belt, and automatically tucked his swords into his belt as he looked around for something to tie back his hair. Then he stepped into his sandals and drew the shoji aside to get some fresh air.

A lone figure stood in the middle of the courtyard.

His shadow seemed blue against the white gravel, and his footsteps crunched audibly as he paced slowly toward Daigoro's bedchamber. Another figure approached Daigoro as well: Tomo, running as silently as he could, his stockings making muted thumps against the wooden planks of the veranda. He all but slid to a stop at Daigoro's feet, already kneeling. After a deep bow he looked back up with a worried smile. Out of breath, he said, "Your guest, Okuma-dono. He requests an audience."

Daigoro's bodyguards had not bestirred themselves. They recognized Tomo on sight, and the sword-armed man in the courtyard was still too far away to be any threat. They were right not to have woken Daigoro, but he saw that they'd made that subtle transition from awareness to readiness.

"Stand down," Daigoro told them. "Tomo, tell the rest of our sentries not to interfere."

He limped stiffly down the stairs, sore from the gymnastics in facing Mio, and crossed the courtyard to meet Shichio—for the dark, stalking figure could only be Shichio. His silhouette was tall and thin, his shadow a long needle on the stones, but more than this, only one man in the compound was drawn inexorably to Glorious Victory Unsought.

But as Daigoro drew near, he did not see Shichio's face. His skin went cold at the sight of a demonic visage. Short, wicked horns curled up from Shichio's forehead, and long iron fangs framed his mouth. A row of sharp teeth hid his upper lip, and his expression was unreadable behind a fierce iron scowl.

Daigoro had no idea what to do with this. He'd never faced a madman. His mother teetered on the verge of madness, but even she didn't stalk the house at night wearing swords and masks. Daigoro could measure the reach of Shichio's sword arm with a glance, but he couldn't begin to guess whether Shichio would draw on him. He knew what a sane man would do, but a lunatic? There was no telling what would provoke him.

And do I care? he asked himself. Shichio had given him all the pretext he needed. No one, not even an aide to the regent, had the right to go sneaking through another man's house.

"What are you doing out here?" Daigoro said.

"I wanted to see your sword," Shichio said, his voice distant, even ghostly.

"You might get a closer look than you'd like." Daigoro kept his tone deliberately brusque. If he could tempt the peacock to draw on him, he could cut the man down with impunity. "Take one step closer and I'll take your head."

Shichio seemed not to have heard him. "All this time, I thought I'd understood this mask of mine," he said. "I'd always thought it awakened visions of swords. But they're not, are they? They're visions of *your* sword."

"No. You're wrong."

"I'm not. I felt the change as soon as we set foot on shore. The need . . . it grew stronger, almost like a living creature. I could feel it under my skin. I did not understand it then, but I do now. Your sword and my mask, they are kin somehow. The closer they come together, the greater my need becomes. That sword—what did they say it was called? Glorious Victory Unsought? Yes. It's as if my mask can see it. It needs it. I must have it."

"Your mask has nothing to do with it. This is Inazuma steel. Men have gone mad in pursuit of it. Some have killed for it."

That seemed to snap Shichio out of his reverie. He almost seemed hurt. "Is that how you think of me? A madman come to murder you for your weapon?"

"You're welcome to try. Draw your blade, or else go back to bed. One way or the other, I will not abide a man going masked and armed in my home."

Shichio scoffed. "What do you take me for? A common burglar?"

"An assassin," Daigoro said. "You and your master have accepted my hospitality. A hundred of your clansmen sleep under my roofs. And here you are, skulking around wearing the face of a demon. Do you fancy yourself a *shinobi*? Did you think to pass through walls to kill me in my sleep?"

The eyes behind that mask shifted from Glorious Victory to meet Daigoro's stare. "You are a rude, impudent boy," Shichio said. "You do not deserve to carry such artistry at your hip. I should take it from you and put it in a place of honor, far away from this hovel and its salty air."

"Say it louder," Daigoro said. "Let everyone hear you insult your host and his home. Or else go back to bed. I have no interest in treating with a lunatic."

"Nor I with an insolent cub."

Daigoro felt his temper surging in his veins. Katsushima would have advised patience. Daigoro's father would have reminded him of Glorious Victory's curse. But this arrogant peacock had brought the

regent's own fury to rain down on House Okuma, and he would do
so again if given half a chance. Daigoro was sure of it. He'd given serious thought to murdering an innocent monk just to make this
peacock go away. Why not take the peacock's head instead?

Somehow Glorious Victory Unsought had cleared her scabbard.
Daigoro could not remember unsheathing her. There was no pain in
his right hand. The stiffness in his muscles was gone, though he'd felt
it only moments ago. Shichio looked at the blade and even raised a
hand as if to touch it. "So beautiful," he said.

It was so beautiful. The sight of the boy drawing a weapon on him
should have terrified Shichio—indeed, it *did* terrify him, but his fright
was no match for his desire for the sword. He had never felt such
overwhelming need to have something for his own. Even his beloved
mask paled in comparison. In fact, the mask itself wanted him to take
the sword. His right hand reached out without his even willing it,
desperate to touch the gleaming steel. So beautiful, he thought. He
might even have said it aloud. It was hard to be sure; the sword held
all of his attention.

"If you want it, you can have it," the Bear Cub said. "All you have
to do is take it from me."

He lowered his weapon. Shichio's gaze followed it. The sword could
be his. He needed it. He'd seen it in thousands of visions. His mask
wanted him to take it. The vile boy had left himself exposed. Vulnerable. Shichio reached for his *katana*.

A voice in his mind cried out in protest. This whelp had bested
Mio, and Mio was more than a match for Shichio even if the giant
were only armed with a chopstick. Shichio knew it—hated it, but
knew it. He stood no chance against the Bear Cub, and yet the mask
bent all his will toward that massive, magnificent sword. He was not
one to believe in sorcery, but there was no doubting it now: the mask
held some power over him. It was bewitched, and though Shichio did
not understand the nature of its enchantment, he knew his need for

the Bear Cub's Inazuma blade was irresistible. It might well kill him, and yet he could only obey.

He hurled himself at the sword. The boy anticipated the move and stepped back. Shichio clawed out with both hands, reaching for the sword's hilt but finding only air. The Bear Cub's weapon soared upward, fast as an arrow. Shichio knew his head was soon to leave his shoulders.

But the boy missed. His cut fell short.

It did not strike flesh, but it did find iron. The Inazuma blade sheared off one of the mask's fangs—just the tip of it, but it felt like it cut Shichio's own tooth, right down to the root.

The world began to spin. The Bear Cub lost his balance and stumbled out of reach. Shichio clutched at his face. The mask bit into his palm, just where the Bear Cub's sword had cut. The fang ended in sharp right angles now, its beautiful curves spoiled forever. And through the broken fang, Shichio could feel new power leaking into the mask.

The barest caress of the mask had always made him think of swords. Today was the first time it had ever made him crave a sword so strongly. It hungered for Inazuma steel—and now, because the boy had damaged it, he felt that hunger changing. He could not say how. He knew no more than a wave knows the shape it is destined to take when it hits the shore, but he felt the surging power of transformation.

Still huddled and clutching his face, somehow he could sense the huge Inazuma blade coming toward him. His own sword was still in its scabbard. Even if the mask hadn't distracted him, sheer fright made him forget to draw his weapon. The Bear Cub lunged with a broad, two-handed swipe strong enough to cut a man in half. All Shichio could do was duck and hope.

Daigoro's cut should have chopped Shichio in half. He had the reach. Shichio's blade was still in its sheath. He was defenseless. And once again, Daigoro missed.

His blade sailed over Shichio's head and sent Daigoro spinning. The blade had taken him off balance. *Again.* And he knew why. He wanted Shichio dead. He wanted to claim victory over this cocky son of a bitch and make House Okuma safe once and for all. Hideyoshi could not be angry: Shichio had broken every law of hospitality. If General Mio had anything to say about it, killing Shichio might earn Daigoro a general's rank. Daigoro could outshine even his father, his greatest role model, his hero.

And for that reason, Glorious Victory Unsought would see him dead.

That was his sword's curse: it ensured victory, but only to those who did not seek it. Daigoro had never lost a duel with live steel because he never wanted to fight. The day he wanted to win would be the day his father's sword would make him lose. Daigoro had seen it before. Ichirō died because of it, slain in the snow on a moonlit night just like this one. Now Daigoro, standing under the moon on snow-white gravel, finally understood.

He sheathed Glorious Victory—no small feat, given her length— and it rendered him vulnerable. If Shichio were to draw on him now, Daigoro had no chance to counterstrike. But Shichio did not draw his weapon. He stumbled backward, clutching that sinister mask as if it pained him. Blood dripped from his hands, giving Daigoro the eerie impression that the mask itself was bleeding.

"It was a mistake for you to threaten me in my own home," Daigoro said, wishing to hell that he could just cut this peacock down and be done with it. "I am well within my rights to kill you. But I won't."

Just saying it aloud made his heart sink. This man was a lunatic. Letting him live was dangerous. But he was also cowering and un- armed, and Daigoro had already stretched the bounds of honor by attacking him. Failing to kill him was the worst kind of embar- rassment: every sentry in earshot would have moved to see what trans- pired in the courtyard, and none of them understood the curse and blessing of Glorious Victory Unsought. They would only see a crippled boy try to kill an unarmed man and fail.

"Go back to the safety of your regent," he said. The words were so heavy that he thought they might crush him. "Hide under his wing, and remember the Bear Cub of Izu showed you mercy tonight."

And with that he watched Shichio walk away, knowing full well that this was his family's worst enemy, and that he might never have another chance to kill him.

BOOK THREE

HEISEI ERA, THE YEAR 22

(2010 CE)

16

Mariko jumped just before the oncoming car hit her in the knees.

The screech of tires on blacktop filled the air, overpowered by the stink of burning rubber. Mariko tucked and rolled just like the department's aikido instructor taught her, somersaulting across the hood and coming down in a dead sprint.

Her quarry was ten meters ahead of her and gaining. His name was Nanami, a lanky twenty-two-year-old with frosty blond highlights in his hair, a long history of drug priors, and a distinct height advantage that left Mariko and her shorter legs struggling to keep up with him.

Adrenaline and sheer dumb luck took Nanami through four lanes of traffic without so much as a bump. Mariko's only edge was that his mad dash had panicked oncoming drivers enough to slow them a bit. She skimmed across a taxicab's hood in a feet-first Ichirō Suzuki slide that gained her a precious fraction of a second.

Nine meters now. Nanami cut a diagonal across the flagstone courtyard of a Shinto shrine three hundred years older than the high-rises that flanked it. Mariko cut a sharper angle and closed the gap.

Eight meters. She dogged Nanami into the narrow alley between the shrine and one of the apartment buildings. It was a dead straightaway. In seconds he widened the gap to ten meters, then twelve.

And then Han blindsided him. Just as Nanami cleared the corner of the apartment complex, Han hit him in the knees with a perfect double-leg takedown. The two men hit the ground in a rolling skirmish that saw Han take a flailing haymaker to the jaw before Mariko tackled Nanami and laid him out flat.

"Good morning again," Han said, rubbing his cheek and kneeling on the back of Nanami's neck. "You should have listened the first time, Nanami-san. All we wanted to do was talk."

Mariko cuffed Nanami's wrists behind his back. His highlighted hair sponged up a lingering pool of early morning rainwater. "Sweet double-leg," she said.

"Thanks," said Han. "Sorry I was a few seconds late on the cutoff."

"Don't worry about it. Your jaw okay?"

Han stretched it out a bit. "Yeah," he said, "but I think I chipped a tooth. See, Nanami-san? All you had to do was talk and we wouldn't have to bring you in. But now I need to file an injury report, and that means we have to arrest you."

"Shit," Nanami said, "if I'da known you had all this pincer movement shit, I wouldn'ta lit out like that."

Mariko felt him relax in her grip. It was only the repeat offenders that did that. First-timers always struggled a while, straining in vain against the cuffs. There was a bit of a learning curve before a perp could get comfortable in this situation, but Nanami was an old hand at this.

Mariko wished she could be as calm. The break-in this morning still had her rattled, and the theft of her sensei's sword—her most prized possession—left her feeling bereft. Even her endorphin high wasn't enough to distract her from her worries. All the more reason not to file an official report on the burglary; if Lieutenant Sakakibara thought she was distracted, he could bench her. She blinked hard, wiped the sweat off the back of her neck, and got her head back in the game.

"Speed," she said. "You buy from the Kamaguchi-gumi, *neh?*"

"You know I do." Nanami sighed it as much as said it, his tone sullen. He wasn't wrong. They did know it, and that's why Han had chosen to pay him a visit in the first place. Han had scores of street contacts. Developing a network was inevitable after eight years in Narcotics, but Han was the master: he seemed to have an informant for any given occasion. When they left post that morning, Mariko had said she wanted to talk to someone with Kamaguchi-gumi connections and who also knew where to score top-shelf speed. Han's reply was inevitable: "I know just the guy."

"So how's their product?" Han asked Nanami.

"Kamaguchi? Used to be shit. Now it's good. You wanna get off my head now?"

Han transferred some weight out of the knee on Nanami's neck, but he didn't let him go. "I heard the Kamaguchis have been last in the league," he said. "Are you saying my intel is bullshit?"

Nanami tried to shake his head, but he couldn't do it with his chin pressed into the concrete. "Damn, Han, you gotta treat me right. I'm talking, *neh*? Why you gotta get all police brutality on me?"

Mariko felt her heart rate surge at that—brutality was a serious charge, and it pissed her off when people threw it around like it was nothing—but Han just laughed it off. "You resisted arrest and assaulted an officer. Consider yourself lucky you don't have a face full of pepper spray."

Mariko's phone buzzed in her pocket. She ignored it. "The sooner you talk, the sooner he can let you up," she said.

"Used to be the Kamaguchis were way behind," said Nanami. "In the market, *neh*? Now they're killing it. They got the Daishi. New shit. Kamaguchi's the only ones who got it."

"Daishi?" Mariko had never heard of it. She looked at Han, who shrugged. Evidently he didn't know any more than she did. "Any good?"

"Don't get any better."

Her phone stopped buzzing, only to start anew a couple of seconds later. Mariko guessed it was her mother, the only person she knew who would keep calling until Mariko picked up, so she thumbed a button through the fabric of her pocket to let her voice mail pick it up. She looked to Han and silently—with no more than a glance to Nanami, a slight tilt of the head, and a quick raise of the eyebrows—asked what they should do. Han replied by standing up, letting all the pressure off Nanami's neck. Once again Mariko felt thankful to have a partner whose stream of thought aligned so closely with her own. For one thing, it allowed such acts of near telepathy, which was very handy when neither of them wanted to reveal to a street connection that they'd never heard of this Daishi. For another, thinking like a good narc meant she was a good narc.

She pointed to her jawline and gave Han a querying look, and he replied with a nod and a thumbs-up: in response to her unasked question, he confirmed that his jaw and his tooth were fine, and they wouldn't need to arrest the kid after all. "Next time when we say we just want to talk," she said, unlocking the cuffs, "maybe you should consider the possibility that we just want to talk."

Nanami got to his feet. He knew his part in this unspoken conversation too: he hadn't seen any of Mariko's communication with Han, but the fact that they let him stand of his own accord meant he wasn't going to jail this morning. He gave them a short, contrite, professional bow and left.

Once again the phone buzzed in Mariko's pocket. "Hold on," she told Han. "My mom's having a fit." She answered the call with an exasperated "Yeah?"

"That's not a tone you want to take with me," said a rasping male voice. "You don't want to ignore my calls either."

Mariko looked at the caller ID and couldn't believe her eyes. KA-MAGUCHI HANZŌ, it said. The Bulldog. Son of Kamaguchi Ryusuke, underboss of the Kamaguchi-gumi. Former confederate of Fuchida Shūzō, the yakuza enforcer Mariko had killed in her now-famous swordfight. As the Kamaguchi-gumi's equalizer, the Bulldog had the contract on Mariko's life, and unless Mariko missed her guess, the Bulldog had passed up a chance to kill her this morning. He'd stolen Glorious Victory instead—though the question of why was a mystery that was never far from her thoughts.

She almost put the Kamaguchi on speakerphone, then thought

better of it and just beckoned Han to listen in with her. "Bulldog-san," she said, more for Han's benefit than anything, "you want to tell me how you got this number?"

"Heh. Not by asking politely."

Mariko would not be intimidated by this man—or at least not let *him* know she was scared. "I'm beginning to think you've got the hots for me," she said. "First you break into my apartment. Then you beat up some poor guy to get my phone number. I'm flattered."

"What? Break into—? Ah, fuck it. Where are you at? I'm sending a car for you."

She and Han looked at each other in disbelief. Mariko had to take a second look at her phone, as if to verify that it was still in her hand, that she'd actually dragged herself out of bed, that this whole god-awful morning hadn't been some terrible dream. "And what makes you think I would voluntarily get in a car with you?"

"I got a bargain for you. I think you're going to like it."

She gave the phone another quizzical look. "A bargain?"

"You heard me. You get me something I want and I'll give you something you want."

Mariko couldn't tell which she felt more: confusion or fury. Two seconds ago he seemed to have no idea about her break-in this morning. Now it sounded like he was offering Glorious Victory as a bargaining chip.

In the end, fury won out. "Now listen here, you son of a bitch. I'm not going to be dragged into some kind of bullshit bartering game for my own property. You bring my sword back; then we can talk."

"I got no idea what you're talking about, you loopy—"

"Go to hell," Mariko said. Then she hung up.

Han gawped at her in amazement. "Was that really Kamaguchi Hanzō?"

"Yeah." Her phone rang again. She clicked the call directly to voice mail.

"*The* Kamguchi Hanzō? Like, the Bulldog crazy guy Kamaguchi Hanzō?"

"Yeah."

"And you told him to go to hell?"

"I guess so." Her phone chirped again. She clicked to ignore it again.

"Mariko, this is a golden opportunity. You need to take that call."

"What?" Mariko shot him a you-need-to-go-back-to-the-loony-bin sort of look. "You're kidding me. 'Golden opportunity'?"

Her phone buzzed in her fist again, and Han nodded toward it. "Think about it. What's the one thing a detective needs more than anything else to work narcotics?"

The look on Mariko's face didn't change. "A partner who doesn't want to see her shot dead by a yakuza?"

"Come on. What am I always telling you need to develop?"

"A network of contacts." She answered him as if she were answering a teacher's rhetorical question in grade school.

"Exactly. And who could be a better contact than Kamaguchi Hanzō? This dude's probably got access to everything the Kamaguchi-gumi is running. Dope, guns, extortion, racketeering, you name it." Han was so excited he couldn't stand still. "I'm telling you, Mariko, this is amazing. I've been in this division for eight years and I've *never* had the chance to develop a high-level connection like this."

"I bet you never had any of them put a price on your head either."

"I don't think he wants to shoot you. I really think he wants to talk."

Mariko looked down at her phone, which was vibrating in her hand like a fly trapped in a jar. She was tired of feeling unsafe. She wanted to answer the phone and challenge the Bulldog to a shoot-out at high noon. Clint Eastwood antics weren't her cup of tea, and she still wasn't all that confident in her marksmanship left-handed, but at least a good old-fashioned shoot-'em-up would see her problems resolved once and for all.

And yet Han was right. This was a once-in-a-lifetime opportunity, and every indication said Kamaguchi didn't intend to kill her. First, he seemed to be honestly confused about the sword theft. Second, he wasn't the type to call in advance to schedule a drive-by.

Damn it all, she thought. Then she answered her phone.

"Bitch, you hang up on me again, I'll make you regret it."

Mariko rolled her eyes and almost hung up. Only a panicked gesture from Han made her think twice. She sighed and said, "What do you want?"

"I told you. A bargain. Tell me where to pick you up."

"Metropolitan Police HQ," she said. "Chiyoda-ku."

"Fine. Half an hour." And the line went dead.

The silence made Mariko's heart race. She'd just made a date with the man who was hired to kill her. And he had just agreed to meet the target of his assassination order in front of a high-rise full of cops. More to herself than anyone, she said, "I can't believe I'm going to go through with this."

"You're not going alone," Han said. He gave her shoulder a reassuring squeeze. "I'll be right behind you in an unmarked car, with two others on a rolling tail."

"I'm not scared," she said. It was only a little lie. "It's just . . . the guy's a gangster, Han. He makes a living destroying other people's lives. Do I really want to get into bed with him?"

"This is Narcotics, Mariko. We deal with bad people. It's part of the job."

"Yeah, I get that. It's just . . ."

She didn't know how to finish her own thought. Fortunately she and Han shared a telepathic wavelength. "It's a gamble," he said. "I know. You're on first base and you're thinking of stealing second. That's just one of the risks you take sometimes if you want to win the ball game."

17

The Tokyo Metropolitan Police Department's headquarters looked like a giant concrete book, standing on end and opened slightly, with a three-story drink twizzler for a bookmark. The building's eighteen floors of unadorned, wedge-shaped, postmodern concrete loomed over the heart of Chiyoda City, Tokyo's governmental district, right across the street from the Ministry of Justice and right across the moat from the Imperial Palace gardens. A phallic red-and-white tower stood atop the building, complete with three observation decks full of various antennae, dish-shaped and mini-phallus-shaped, whose arcane purposes Mariko couldn't begin to guess at.

The mere sight of the HQ building still sent a thrill rippling over Mariko's skin. She'd worked so hard to get onto the TMPD, harder still to make detective and sergeant, and seeing the department's headquarters through the windshield of a squad car confirmed for her what still seemed unreal: that at last she'd made her way to her dream assignment in Narcotics. Moreover, HQ's overlook of the Imperial Palace stirred memories heavily laden with happiness and grief. She'd only been in the palace once, and it was the murder of her beloved sensei that had prompted her visit. Thinking of Dr. Yamada was enough to make her want to cry, but since that was something she could never let a coworker see, she had to suppress the urge every time she showed up to work.

And that was on days when no gangsters came calling. Talking to

Kamaguchi on the phone had shaken her to the core, and she hadn't been herself even before she saw his name on the caller ID. If Kamaguchi wasn't responsible for the break-in, who was? And if he didn't have Glorious Victory, what could he possibly offer as a bargaining chip? And what did he want in return?

Han was pretty shaken up too. He tried not to show it, but he was already on his third cigarette, and he paced back and forth in front of the HQ building like a panther in a cage. "Are you sure we shouldn't call Sakakibara in on this? We could have snipers on all these rooftops in ten minutes flat."

"You were the one who said this was a good idea."

"Yeah, but that was before I knew I was going to be waiting on the sidewalk with you. If he shoots at you, he might hit me by mistake."

"You know, Han, you can be a real asshole."

"Just trying to lighten the mood a little." He smiled from behind his cigarette, but Mariko wasn't laughing. "Okay, okay, guilty as charged," he said. "But seriously, shouldn't we call the LT?"

"Come on, you know what he's going to say. 'Frodo, you're a sergeant; think for yourself and do your damn job.'" Mariko caught herself short. "Holy shit."

"What?" said Han, his shoulders suddenly stiff. His eyes darted this way and that, clearly on high alert. "You see Kamaguchi?"

"No. Frodo."

"Huh?"

"The nickname. Frodo. I think I just figured it out. The hobbit part's easy, *neh*? I'm short. But who's the only hobbit who winds up with nine fingers?"

She waved her maimed right hand at him. Han puffed at his cigarette and shook his head. "You're insane. How can you be thinking about that right now?"

Mariko shrugged. "Honestly, I'm just kind of surprised Sakakibara's nerd trivia runs that deep. Didn't figure him for a Tolkien fan."

"Great. Mystery solved. Now all we need to know is—"

Just then a big red Land Rover came to a sudden stop in front of them. Traffic swerved around it like a flock of doves fleeing a hawk. The rear door opened automatically, like a taxi's, and a big man stepped out. It wasn't the Bulldog; this guy was bigger. He obviously spent a lot of time at the gym, and maybe some time with a steroid needle too. Mariko wondered where they ever found enough pin-striped fabric to make a suit that would fit him. Tailoring a suit for a guy with no neck couldn't have been easy in the first place.

He nodded at her. "You Oshiro?"

"Yeah," said Mariko.

"Get in."

Mariko nodded as nonchalantly as she knew how, then sauntered in her summoner's direction. She would *not* be seen to be scared. On cue, Han jogged to the unmarked car idling at the curb. No point in having an invisible tail; they wanted the Kamaguchis to know Mariko was never out of sight.

She waited until Han was in the car before she got within arm's reach of the Land Rover. "Where's Kamaguchi?" she said.

"Waiting for you." The bodybuilder climbed into the backseat, taking up most of it. Under his suit jacket Mariko saw the telltale lines of an antiknifing vest—all the rage in yakuza couture ever since a certain cop got herself all over the news with her samurai showdown. Tokyo had seen a rash of sword and knife attacks since then, mostly among yakuzas who thought it was *gokudō*, extreme, hard-core, to duke it out old-school. Evidently Kamaguchi's errand boy didn't care to become a statistic. "Come on," he said, "get in."

The seat he offered her was on the left side of the vehicle. Mariko didn't know whether this was a calculated tactical choice, but if it was, it was a good one. Most cops wore their holsters on the right hip, and if Mariko had worn hers there, her pistol would have been in easy reach for him. But Mariko shot left-handed now, so when she got into the car, her weapon was safely between her left hip and the door. "Let's go," she said.

The drive seemed to take forever and no time at all. The muscle man had no qualms about discussing business in front of a cop, and so over the course of a couple of phone calls Mariko learned that he went by "Bullet," that one of his errands today was to collect a lot of something, and that the code he and his fellow yakuzas had developed for speaking about their criminal activities left Mariko utterly clueless about whether Bullet was supposed to collect weapons, protection money, or baseball cards. It could have been anything, and it left Mariko wondering whether she'd even pick up on it if he decided to turn the conversation to the subject of where to dump her body after he killed her.

Bullet had a private parking spot in the parking garage under an Ebisu high-rise, and a pass code for the elevator's keypad that admitted him to the penthouse floor. So much for backup. This wasn't good.

The elevator doors opened onto a wide vista of Ebisu and Roppongi, two of Tokyo's wealthier districts. Mariko presumed this was Kamaguchi Hanzō's apartment, since if it were not, she could hardly make sense of the ostentation. Most penthouse apartments would have a foyer with a locked door separating the home from the elevator—the better to keep out riffraff such as, say, police officers, or the pizza boy, or neighbors' kids goofing off in the fire exit stairwell—but if Kamaguchi wanted to overwhelm his guests straightaway, the best way to do it was to flaunt the view. His furniture was too obviously expensive to be elegant. The same went for the carpeting, the paneling, the fireplace ignited by remote control. There was more artwork on the walls than Mariko would have expected from a gangster, but the collection was eclectic, probably selected by price tag more than by taste. It was an observation deck, not a living room, and the intended subject of observation was Kamaguchi's personal wealth. Mariko noted that Glorious Victory Unsought was not in his collection.

Neighboring Roppongi had a nefarious reputation as a haven of the most powerful yakuzas, and Mariko wondered how it felt for a gangster of Kamaguchi's stature to live so close to real power and still be removed from it. Ebisu was gauche by comparison, a Harley parked next to a sleek Ducati, expensive but without the class.

"There she is," said Kamaguchi Hanzō, and as soon as she laid eyes on him she understood why his street name was the Bulldog. His underbite was more pronounced than his father's, even more pronounced than the mug shots let on. His belly was as round as a barrel and his broad shoulders were sloped, as if his skull were so heavy it weighed them down. He had a thick head of jet-black hair, but otherwise he looked older than he really was. His rap sheet—which Mariko read as soon as she'd learned the hit from the Kamaguchi-gumi had fallen to him, and had read umpteen times since then—said he was only thirty-eight, but his wrinkles marked him at least ten years older than that. Just part of the territory, Mariko guessed, for one born into the high-stress life of criminal middle management. She wondered whether his moonlighting as a street enforcer caused him more stress or served as stress relief. As soon as the question struck her, intuition told her it was the latter. Not a comforting thought.

"The hero cop," he said. "The dragon slayer. The girl who doesn't know when she's overstepped her limits." He spoke with a slight rasp, as if he were just getting over laryngitis, or as if he'd been shouting all night the night before.

Mariko felt oddly cold. She'd expected her heart to race at the sight of this man, but instead she only flexed her fingers, calculating the exact distance between them and the grip of her SIG Sauer. She was still scared, but it was a sullen, brooding fear, not nervous jitters. "What do you want?" she said.

"To show you something." He beckoned her over with a meaty hand. "Come on. I'm making kebabs."

Given the sheer pretentiousness of the apartment, Mariko was surprised to learn Kamaguchi cooked for himself, but she had no interest in seeing him in the act—or rather, more pragmatically, no interest in following him into a roomful of knives. But she reminded herself that if he wanted to kill her, his own home would be the last place he'd do it, so she forced a cocky, relaxed deportment and followed him.

The Bulldog's kitchen smelled of onion and peppers. He had a little pile of each heaped on his marble countertop, alongside a few other vegetables and a big steel bowl with chunks of beef marinating in it. He also had a laptop sitting on the counter, on the opposite end from where he was preparing his food, and given the sheer size of the kitchen, the opposite end was pretty far away. His fingers swept up a big chef's knife in a reverse grip, spun it around in a motion that looked like he'd spent a lot of time with a blade in his hands, and gestured at the laptop with it. Mariko hated playing games like this—he was trying to boss her around—so she sat on a stool and waited.

At last Bullet woke the laptop, turned it toward her, and fired up its media player. What followed was a silent video feed from what looked like a closed-circuit security camera. It took Mariko a moment to recognize the room, since she hadn't seen it from the camera's perspective before, but soon enough she identified it as the salesman's office from the packing and shipping company that she and Han had raided the night before.

A cop walked into the frame wearing full SWAT armor, including helmet, goggles, and Nomex mask. No part of his face was visible. He walked with a bit of a limp—not from a recent injury, Mariko guessed. He wasn't hobbling; he just had a rolling gait. He took something off the shelf that Mariko remembered well, the one with the eclectic collection of antiques and trinkets. The feed was just clear enough that Mariko could make out a mask-shaped blob in the SWAT cop's hands.

It was the most brazen theft she'd ever heard of. Stealing from the Kamaguchi-gumi was suicidal, and doing it in the middle of an active crime scene was a whole new level of crazy. Or maybe not, she thought. It was only crazy if you thought anyone was going to see you. If you were a modern-day ninja—the sort of person who could steal a huge sword from a seventeenth-floor apartment, for instance, even with all the doors and windows locked from the inside—then you could probably pull it off. She hit the PLAY button again, and watched a grainy image of the thief who, if her hunch was right, had also stolen Glorious Victory Unsought.

"You let those idiots take my stuff," said Kamaguchi. "Now you're going to get it back."

Mariko ignored him and closed the media player, the better to look at a PDF that Kamaguchi had open in another window. It was an insurance appraisal—a big one, over two hundred pages long, but the page that was displayed showed a familiar antique half mask. Its rust-brown skin was pitted with age, and the blacksmith who forged it clearly had a gift, for the mask was astonishingly expressive, its anger as genuine as any living creature's. Seen up close, its stubby horns looked cruel. Unlike the sketch in Yamada's notebook, Kamaguchi's mask had one broken fang, its tip sheared off in a perfectly straight line. Otherwise Yamada's sketch was a pretty good likeness—though unlike the sketch, the PDF also included the mask's appraised value. It was more than Mariko would make in the next ten years.

She tried to remember what Yamada's notes said about her sword and the mask. They were related somehow. The mask had a connection to Toyotomi Hideyoshi, one of Japan's founding fathers, but Glorious Victory did not. That cold, sullen fear wouldn't let her remember any more than that. It wanted her undistracted.

"Hey!" Kamaguchi said. "Are you listening to me?"

"Sort of." She was provoking him and she knew it. "Who are 'those idiots'?"

"Huh?"

"You said we let 'those idiots' steal your mask. That means you're assuming the guy in the video isn't a cop, *neh*? Why? He doesn't look coplike enough to you?"

Kamaguchi chuckled. "Heh. You guys aren't dumb enough to take *my* shit. No, this was those religious pansies."

"Who?"

"Cult types. Nut jobs. They're the only ones who could have stolen it."

"So why coming whining to me?" Mariko said, feeling her false bravado fade away, gradually being replaced by the real thing. It felt good to stand up to this guy. "Go kick their asses. Get your toy back."

"You don't want me to do that. I lost my patience with these sissies a long time ago. I go after them now, there's going to be blood."

He was bullshitting her and she knew it. Kamaguchi Hanzō wasn't the type to shrink away from a little bloodshed. He was hiding something, but she wasn't sure what yet.

So she took a gamble and headed for the door. "I've got things to do. You want to start talking straight, be my guest. Otherwise I'm—"

"Don't be so touchy," the Bulldog said. "No wonder Fuchida-san felt like killing you. Fucking *women*, *neh*?"

"Yeah. Women. Have a nice day."

"Look, those cult types, they're the ones who wanted to buy the mask. That's what the dope was for. Get it? Last night was all because of the mask."

Mariko came back and sat on her stool. "Keep going."

Kamaguchi's knife dealt the finishing blow to a long, slender zucchini and tore into the next one. "They wanted the mask. Wanted it right fucking now. Offered me way more than it was worth. So I okayed it. But then they told me you assholes were coming to crash the party, so they wanted to hurry things up. I told them to fuck off. But no, they show up anyway, and then everything goes to shit. Heh. I don't need to tell you that, *neh*? You're the ones who made it go to shit. And right after you're done, right in the middle of your cleanup operation, their boy walks right in, takes *my* property, and walks out. Right under your goddamn noses."

"So?"

"So get it back. It's your fault."

Mariko smirked. "Let me get this straight. TMPD's to blame because you went through with a dope deal, didn't pay up, and then your supplier came by to get what you said you'd pay him?"

Kamaguchi chopped into a pineapple, angry enough that his blade banging on the countertop made Mariko's ears hurt. "I don't owe them shit. I told them not to deliver. They delivered anyway, and then you showed up to seize it all. No. I don't owe them a damn thing."

"Yeah," Mariko said, "you're right. Poor you. Nobody ever gives you what you want."

"Heh." Again the knife cut through the pineapple with a bang.

"Look at you, giving me shit in my own place. You think you're pretty *gokudō*, don't you?"

Mariko smirked. She had to admit she was feeling quite the badass at the moment. It made her feel powerful, sparring with this man, getting him to open up about his business dealings. Han had been exactly right in his assessment: if she could figure out a way to make this a regular occurrence, Kamaguchi Hanzō could prove to be one of the most valuable informants she'd ever find. That was assuming he didn't go through with having her killed, but that too was empowering. Better to confront him head-on than to look in every shadow waiting for his hit man to strike.

"Well, maybe I could use some *gokudō*," he said. Again the knife cut through the pineapple with a bang. "Besides, I got an in with you. You get the mask, I call off the hit. Deal?"

Mariko ignored that. She wasn't about to start trusting a contract killer. "What is this mask anyway?"

"Nothing. Some antique. I collect that stuff."

"You shouldn't. You've got shit for taste."

"Heh." Kamaguchi motioned toward the living room/observation deck with the tip of his knife. "In my line of work you want things that'll appreciate in value, *neh*? Art. Real estate. That kind of thing."

"Because it's handy for laundering money?"

"Bingo."

Mariko was begrudgingly impressed. It took guts to talk business so openly with a cop. And the Bulldog wasn't done. "So I got my front companies. A chemical supply place down by the harbor. A couple of travel agencies. That packing company whose door you knocked in."

"Let me guess," said Mariko. "You decorate every office with your art collection."

"Heh. See, Bullet? We got her thinking like a criminal already."

Idiot, she thought. Thinking like a criminal was in her job description. It was how she knew the mask thief was also the one who had stolen her sword. Kamaguchi's mask wasn't the only antique on that shelf. If the thief had been in it for the money, he'd have stolen everything valuable. And since he didn't, the mask had special significance for him.

"There's more going on here. Your friends—what did you call them? Pansies? They wanted the mask for a reason. You bought it for a reason. What was it?"

"Who knows? Sometimes I go on streaks. For a while there I was collecting samurai shit. Armor. Weapons. Your kind of thing, *neh*?"

Mariko didn't care to be reminded of her samurai showdown. "That isn't a *mempo*," she said, pointing at the demon mask glowering back at her from the screen of his laptop.

"Huh?"

"*Mempo*. Face mask. As in armored. The samurai used to wear them. I thought you said you were a collector."

He shrugged. Mariko shrugged back, aping him. She wouldn't have been surprised if he had a wine cellar somewhere with a few hundred bottles whose names he couldn't pronounce and whose nuances he couldn't distinguish from a cheap lager. "This mask you bought is decorative," she said. "Maybe for kabuki or something. It's useless for combat."

Another shrug. "I don't give a shit what it is. I just want to know when you're going to get it back for me."

"Right. Because it was stolen by those mean boys you were playing with after school, *neh*?"

Kamaguchi finished off his pineapple, his hands and blade sticky with the juice. He licked one of his knuckles clean with his too-fat tongue. "Look at the balls on you. I ought to make you drop your pants. Make sure you're a chick."

Mariko hopped off her stool and headed for the door. "Have a nice day, Kamaguchi-san."

"All sass, no patience. You're a chick, all right."

She heard his knife drop on the countertop, felt his heavy footfalls behind her. Without so much as a glance over her shoulder, she stabbed the elevator's down button with the stub that had once been her right forefinger. But her left hand was ready to reach for her gun.

"Okay, fine, you win," the Bulldog said. When he saw her turn away from the elevator, his shoulders sagged in relief. "I ought to put you on my payroll. That way you'd have to listen to me."

Mariko gave him her most insolent smile. "You couldn't afford me. Now, you want me to look into these people, you'll have to give me something."

"I don't *have to* give you shit. This is my house, girl."

"Well, then you're out of luck, because you don't know where these guys are, and neither do I."

"What makes you think I don't—?"

"Please. If you knew where to find the people you're looking for, would you be talking to me? No. So you lost them. So start talking."

Kamaguchi frowned, exaggerating his underbite and making his lower teeth stick out. "You're an annoying little—"

"We can start with why they were so insistent on getting the mask last night. Why did they risk showing up when they knew we were going to launch a raid?"

"Who knows? We're talking religious nuts here, not businessmen."

"What makes you say they're religious?"

"Heh." He shook his head in disgust and licked off another finger. "They call themselves the Divine Wind, for one thing. Sounds pretty *gokudō* at first, naming themselves after kamikaze dive-bombers, but with these guys you get the feeling it's more about the divinity and less about the 'fuck it, let's go down fighting' thing."

"How can you tell?"

"You want to tell me you can't tell the difference between some *guy* ringing your doorbell and some *missionary* ringing it? It's the way they dress, the way they talk—all this 'there is no place the wind cannot reach' horseshit. Why can't they just threaten you like a normal criminal? I swear, this is the last time I'm doing business with a bunch of cultists."

Mariko wasn't a fan of making assessments based on others' gut feelings—especially not people with nicknames like "the Bulldog"—but in this case she guessed he was probably right about the mask thief being religious. For one thing, anyone who deliberately crossed the Kamaguchi-gumi would have to be pretty optimistic about the afterlife. For another, walking through an active crime scene dressed as a SWAT operative took a certain kind of lunatic fearlessness, one Mariko thought she was more likely to find among religious extremists than the dope slinger set.

And then there was the mask itself: an expensive trinket, yes, but the street value of the speed seizure was more than double what Kamaguchi's insurance assessment said the mask was worth. Apart from religious fanaticism, Mariko couldn't imagine what could tempt anyone to pay double its value *and* risk being caught in a police raid. It was a sure bet that the cops wouldn't have seized the mask. It wasn't contraband. The only reason Mariko had noticed it at all was that she'd half remembered that sketch of it in Yamada's notebook.

So why not wait a few days to steal it? Someone could have recognized the perp wasn't SWAT. He might have been masked and armored, but that limping, rolling gait was distinctive. It only made sense for the thief to come for the mask if he had to have it *right then*, at that appointed time for some appointed purpose, and that suggested a very weird belief set. Very weird, very specific, *very* strongly held— all of it pointed to a cult.

It pointed to the break-in at her apartment too. Centuries ago, the mask had some kind of connection to Inazuma steel. Last night, Kamaguchi's mask and Mariko's sword were stolen within hours of each other. It couldn't be coincidence.

Now that Mariko thought about it, she wondered how the perp had stolen authentic SWAT armor too. Apart from the military, only SWAT could legally own fully automatic weapons, and so to say they kept their gear under lock and key was a gross understatement. Better to say it should have been as easy to steal a tank as to steal a bulletproof vest with SWAT's label on it. Yet somehow this perp had the full getup.

Did these Divine Wind guys have an inside man? Was that how they'd known the raid was coming in advance? Or were they really modern-day ninja? Had they stolen the SWAT gear just as they'd stolen her sword? By passing through walls? It was impossible, and Mariko didn't believe in the impossible. She was a detective; she believed what the evidence led her to believe. And faced with evidence of the impossible, a detective's only choice was to reconsider what she meant by "possible." In this case, that might mean a ninja clan operating in twenty-first-century Tokyo.

But that was something she'd have to sort out later. For now, she had a yakuza hit man bullshitting her. "So let's pretend you don't know why they want the mask," she said.

"I'm telling you—"

"Never mind. How did they find out you have it?"

"I don't know."

"Come on. If you were an art collector, then yeah, maybe they'd come looking for you specifically. But you're not. You just like to buy expensive toys that make you feel like you're actually upper class instead of just pretending to be."

"This is my house," he said, slapping his chef's knife down on the counter. "I'm not going to stand here and listen to—"

"Sure you are. You don't know where to find the guys you're looking for. You need me, *neh*? To save face. You lost your little plaything, and you'd better get it back before the street finds out you lost a mountain of speed too. As soon as word gets out that the Bulldog can't protect his own doghouse . . . well, how long have you got before someone puts you to sleep?"

He glared at her with a raw, animalistic fury she'd only seen once before—in the eyes of his enforcer, Fuchida Shūzō, as Fuchida was trying to hack her to pieces. Kamaguchi would have strangled her then and there if he didn't need her. She had no doubt of that. What she did have doubts about was his capacity for anger management. If she pushed him too far, he might kill her and figure out how to fix that little problem afterward. But backing down wasn't a great option either. For bulldogs and yakuzas alike, fighting was all about posturing. To back down was to invite an immediate attack.

So Mariko took a gamble and just glared back at him.

If anything, he got angrier. "You're walking pretty fucking close to the edge, girl."

"You want to be *gokudō*, that's where you walk."

For a moment she thought she pushed him too far. He inhaled noisily, deeply, expanding his broad shoulders—maybe fueling up for a short but deadly fight that would cost Mariko her life. Then hung his head back and laughed. "You got some fire in you, that's for sure. I can't tell if I want to fight you or fuck you."

"I can tell you what happens if you try either one. Now what's it going to be? Are you going to tell me what I need to know?"

18

"They played him," Mariko said. "The light's green, by the way."

"*Who* played him?" said Han. "What the hell happened up there?"

"Green means go," she said.

At last he managed to direct some of his concentration away from her and back to driving. "Mariko, come on."

"I told you already: those cult fanatics. The Divine Wind."

"I thought you said *he* played *them*."

"That's what Kamaguchi thinks. He says a buyer approached him maybe six months ago through one of his front companies, some chemical supply place down in Odaiba. The buyer was a front man for this Divine Wind. The guy's been buying hexamine by the barrel, making payment in Daishi. Kamaguchi says he conned the guy into paying double the volume he should have. But I think the buyer marked him as the owner of the mask from the beginning and wanted to play dumb."

"Wait a minute," Han said. "Did you say hexamine?"

"Yep."

"So our buyer's making MDA?"

"Looks like it," said Mariko, happy to hear Han was thinking along the same lines. A boutique amphetamine like MDA fit in perfectly with Mariko's mental profile of the cultist fanatic clientele. They were more likely to go for stimulants than depressants. MDA was both an upper and a hallucinogen, a religious experience in tablet form. Hexamine might have had a hundred industrial uses Mariko had never heard of, but in narcotics circles it was only known as a key ingredient in MDA.

"So his buyer's got to be a hell of a cook," said Han. "MDA's rare, but this Daishi is something else. It's not just the best speed on the street; it's also cheap enough that these dudes can afford to sling it around by the truckload."

"You're thinking they're *gaijin*?"

"Maybe. Or sourcing their precursor chemicals from out of country, anyway. Someplace cheap; it's obvious they don't need the cash. This mask, is it the only antique they're interested in? Or have they been trading for a lot of stuff like that?"

"Kamaguchi says it was just the mask, just this one time. Otherwise it's always the hexamine. But I think the mask thief and my sword thief are the same guy."

Han's eyebrows popped halfway up his forehead. "Seriously? That's a hell of an inference."

Mariko explained her logic. Han gave her a dubious look. "Twenty-first-century ninja clan, huh? Maybe you need to go back to the drawing board with that one."

"Okay, fine," she said, "the last part might be a little imaginative. But you have to admit it's a hell of a coincidence, these two artifacts being stolen on the same night."

Han agreed, his long hair flopping as he nodded. "Point taken," he said, "but how does that help us make an arrest?"

"Well . . . it doesn't. It's still true, though."

Mariko was embarrassed, but at least she got a sympathetic smile out of Han. "Chalk up a point for Oshiro," he said. "Back to the other thing, I have to tell you I just don't get it. Why are these guys trading speed just to make MDA? Why not just cook the MDA themselves? Cut Kamaguchi out completely?"

Mariko shrugged. "Maybe they can't. Maybe the hexamine's too hard to come by wherever they're from."

"Yeah, maybe." Han went silent, frowning and looking out the windshield for a long time. At length he said, "Something's not adding up. How much product are we talking about here? How much hexamine has Kamaguchi been selling them?"

"A barrel every few weeks," said Mariko.

"So why haven't we seen any arrests? If a new wave of psychedelic speed hit the streets, I'd have heard of it."

"The Daishi got past you."

"Yeah," said Han, "and I'm mighty pissed off about that. My people are letting me down. But in a daily log it wouldn't say 'Daishi'; it would just say 'amphetamine.' We should have seen log entries with 'MDA' on them by now."

"Maybe they're selling it overseas? No. Never mind."

Han shook his head too. Japan was expensive. Dealers here imported from Thailand, North Korea, Cambodia—the cheap markets. Export the other way didn't make sense. Mariko wished she'd reached that conclusion a few seconds earlier, before she'd said the stupid thing she'd said. She supposed she should be glad she caught her mistake before Han had to correct her, but she was embarrassed nonetheless. It was the years of perfectionism that did it, the fear of her male counterparts seeing her as a girl instead of a policewoman. That wasn't a big concern with Han, but still, even the little failures burned, lingering, like droplets of hot oil spat from a frying pan.

"So this Daishi," she said, "what are the chances it's the same stuff we seized from that packing company last night? I mean, it's got to be, *neh*?"

"Got to be," Han said. "We should set up a couple of buy-busts just to be sure, get ourselves a sample to compare it to—but I'm getting sidetracked. Get back to your meeting on the mound with Kamaguchi."

"Okay," Mariko said, "so our buyer marks Kamaguchi, plays to his ego by overpaying for the hexamine, then says he wants the mask and hints that he'll overpay again—"

"So Kamaguchi thinks he's got a live one, because this dumb-ass has been overpaying for months." Han laughed in disbelief. "You'd think a career criminal would have seen that con before."

"Yeah, these guys never made sense to me. Kamaguchi's not a moron. He's not even lazy. You wouldn't believe how much work he puts into keeping his money off the books. If he worked half as hard as a car salesman as he does as a yakuza, he'd still be able to rent a place in Ebisu and none of his clients would ever try to play him the way he just got played."

"Maybe so, but nobody pays for cars in amphetamines."

"Antique masks either."

"Touché." He stopped to think for the space of about half a block—which wasn't long, because he was driving a lot faster than Mariko usually saw him drive. "Wait. Why pay him at all?"

"Who? The Divine Wind?"

"Yeah. I mean, I get why he wants to be paid in Daishi instead of cash. His own product is shit, and it's expensive to boot. The Daishi's better all around. But why should these dudes pay at all? They're obviously willing to steal from him; why not start there? Just waltz in and steal the mask from the get-go?"

"Would *you* piss off the Bulldog if you didn't have to?"

"Well, no, now that you put it that way." Han gunned it through an intersection to make a yellow light. "So you're thinking what? They tried to play it straight at first, but then he strung them along—"

"Longer than they could wait." Mariko nodded. "I think last night is just them running out of time and getting desperate."

They sat in silence for a while, Han driving, Mariko watching the city fly by, both of them mulling over the idea. "All right," Han said at last, "I'll buy it. Still, the whole thing looks too good to be true for Kamaguchi-gumi, doesn't it? They get better product, and more of it, and all they have to part with is a chemical sitting around some warehouse, a precursor chemical for a drug they don't even cook."

"So what? This is breaking news? Dealer tries to get top-quality dope for bargain basement prices? Not much of a headline, Han."

"No, I'm asking, what's in it for the Divine Wind? If a deal's too good to be true on one side, then the other side's getting the shaft, *neh*? And they had *six months* to think about this. They've got to be the dumbest bunch of drug dealers I've ever heard of."

"You're thinking like a narc. The way to solve this is to think like a cultist."

"Huh." Han thought for a second, then shook his head. Laughing at himself, he said, "See, *this* is what we need you for, Mariko. You know how you're riding yourself all the time for being the new recruit in Narcotics? Well, stop. I've been swimming in this pool so long I forget there's such a thing as dry land. We need you. You're amphibious."

"Gee, you really know how to make a girl feel good about herself."

"Come on, you know what I mean."

"Oh, I do. Amphibious. Very sexy. That line's got to kill on the speed dating scene."

At last she got the blush she wanted out of him. "Fine," he said, "so I'm a Neanderthal. Guilty as charged. Will you teach me how to think like a cultist now?"

Mariko indulged in a self-satisfied smile. "The MDA's a hallucinogen, *neh*? Perfect for tripping at, you know, prayer meetings or whatever. So maybe . . . maybe the priest wears the mask to heighten the trip."

"So what are you saying? These guys are devil worshippers? *Please* don't tell me they stole your sword to make human sacrifices."

"I don't know. I'm just spitballing here. But fanatics are willing to risk a lot for their faith, *neh*? It goes a long way toward explaining why they're taking such awful risks to get a mask and a sword. Maybe they need them for some ritual that happens on a certain day—"

"Or when Venus is aligned with Jupiter or whatever." Han thought about it for a moment, then nodded. "Yeah, could be. I guess we'll find out soon enough."

"How do you figure that?"

"We're on our way to Intensive Care. One of our suspects lawyered up."

19

Mariko didn't care for hospitals. She supposed nobody actually *liked* hospitals, especially when, like Mariko, they'd recently been confined to one. She was laid up for a solid week after her sword fight with Fuchida, but that wasn't why she had a hang-up about hospitals. It was her father's death that made her so uneasy.

It wasn't an easy thing to explain. There was no drama to it. She hadn't carried him bleeding into the emergency room. She wasn't in the room for his death rattle. She hadn't been there at all. She'd known he was sick when she went off to school, but her parents hadn't revealed *how* sick. He'd been weak for a long time by then, long enough that the daily fear of death had subsided. It was disturbing how quickly a family could return to business as usual even when one of their number was dying. Get the groceries, do your homework, clean the dishes, Dad's got cancer. So Mariko went off to college with her father's blessing, and then—in her memory it had only been a matter of days—her mom called to tell her he was dead.

For years after that, Mariko had wished she could have been in that hospital room. At a minimum, she wished she'd been the one to make the choice of whether or not to come. At eighteen she hadn't had it in her to make that choice unemotionally; she would have dropped everything, no matter the effect on her GPA, and that was precisely why her parents hadn't called. They knew their daughter well.

All the same, Mariko still thought she should have had the right to make the choice herself. Now and again, even all these years later, she tried to imagine the room where he died. There were no photographs. It wasn't the sort of event you broke out the cameras for. Mariko had never asked her mom to describe it—nor her sister, now that she thought about it, though Saori was younger, so she'd been there until the end. For all Mariko knew, the room where her dad had died looked exactly like the room she was standing in now.

She'd never seen the man in this room before, but she'd seen plenty of battery victims in her time. He seemed to sink into his bed. Both eyes were blacked. A huge swollen dome dominated the right side of his face from eyebrow to hairline, obviously the result of some massive blunt force trauma; it looked like someone had managed to shove a hamburger bun up under one of his eyelids. A neck brace squished wrinkles into his unshaven cheeks. Both lips were punctuated with cuts. His forearms were nothing but knotted, swollen bruises—almost certainly defensive wounds—but neither was broken. In short, by the standards of the Kamaguchi-gumi, he'd gotten off light. He'd stay under observation for a few days, but he wouldn't spend the rest of his life in a wheelchair.

The suspect's mouth moved constantly. At first Mariko thought he was delirious, but after a while she saw he was chanting the same words over and over again. A mantra. His eyes blazed at her, the whites as brilliant as the full moon, unnaturally bright thanks to the red and purple contusions that surrounded them. Mariko could barely hear him, but given the way he stared at her, it seemed he meant to speak directly to her. And that wasn't what she found weird; the weird part was her sneaking suspicion that this man looked at everyone with that same thousand-yard stare. It made her not want to get close enough to hear that mantra of his.

The only other person in the room was SWAT's tactical medic, who was so obviously exhausted that Mariko wasn't sure he'd be safe to drive himself home. "He's been spouting that same line ever since we put him in the ambo," the tac medic said. "Never stops, never sleeps."

"That's speed for you," Han said.

Mariko had reached the same conclusion. Staying up for days on end was probably just another day at the office for a cult that cooked massive quantities of amphetamines. On the other hand, selling that much product probably left a good amount of cash on hand for legal fees.

The lawyer was already reaching into his pocket for his business card as he walked into the room. "Officers," he said, giving Mariko and Han a short bow. His tone was a little too familiar, his dress a little shy of the immaculate benchmark set by the rest of his profession. His shirt was pressed to perfection, but he hadn't quite tucked it all the way in. His suit was of second-best quality, which was to say far more expensive than anything Mariko or even Lieutenant Sakakibara could ever justify putting in their rotation, yet not quite up to snuff in the scrutinizing glare of the courtroom spotlight. If he were a *gaijin* businessman, no one would ever have noticed these details, but in a Japanese defense attorney they bespoke pride, swagger, even gall.

But it was understated swagger, swagger by implication, just like the quality of the business card he proffered with both hands, one to Han and then one to Mariko. The card was not paper but wood, a veneer thinner than cardstock and smoother than silk. HAMAYA JIRŌ, it read, ATTORNEY AT LAW.

It was an implicit request for Mariko and Han to offer their own cards, and to be professional they had no choice but to oblige. Hamaya had already set the terms of their relationship. "I'm sure you'll agree," he said, "that Akahata-san is not yet in any condition to endure a police interrogation."

Mariko eyed the man in the bed, whose eyes still blazed like a madman's. His lips still moved in their playback loop, chanting their mantra. "Akahata, is it? He looks ready to talk to me, Counselor."

Hamaya gave her an insouciant bow. "He speaks, yes, but not to anyone in this room. He prays for Jōkō Daishi to liberate our souls."

Han and Mariko shared a knowing glance. It was the second time they'd across the word *daishi* this morning. Without seeing the kanji, there was no way of knowing what *daishi* meant—with these two characters it meant "nun," with those two, "cardboard"—and so when Nanami had said the Kamaguchi-gumi was slinging Daishi these days, there wasn't much for a narc detective to do with the information. Daishi could have been a nickname, an ingredient, anything. But in context, Jōko Daishi could only be Great Teacher Jōko, the same *daishi* as Kōbō Daishi, whose name was known to everyone. Kōbō Daishi was the sobriquet given to Kūkai, the eighth-century monk who had contributed as much to Buddhism as anyone in Japanese history. No doubt the name Jōko Daishi was meant to evoke images of Kōbō Daishi, earning credibility by association.

"Jōko Daishi, huh?" Mariko eyed the tweaker in the hospital bed. "Let me guess: he's the leader of your Divine Wind?"

"The very same," said Hamaya, bowing, his eyes closing, his voice full of reverence. Akahata's chanting went from a silent mouthing to a barely audible whisper. His lips redoubled their pace.

Not seeing the kanji for Jōko, Mariko couldn't do anything with the name. It would have been nice to have something to plug into a search engine. She'd have liked to wheedle the name the old-fashioned way too, but somehow she didn't think it would fly if she suddenly expressed interest in joining the Divine Wind and asked Hamaya to write down his whack-job leader's name and home address.

The latter might well have been a psychiatric ward. There was no doubt in her mind that this Jōko Daishi was a loony and an extremist. It took an extremist to command such loyalty from Akahata, a brand of loyalty that was almost literally undying: that head trauma might easily have killed him, and if it had, he'd have gone to his grave with Jōko Daishi's name on his lips. Nor did Mariko harbor any doubt that the Daishi pills that Nanami was popping these days were directly connected to the man called Daishi that Akahata prayed to. One glance at Han told her he was thinking the same thing.

"Good to know," Han said. "Now let me take a wild guess and say the way Jōko Daishi liberates our souls is to get us all high."

Hamaya admitted the smallest of smirks. "That would be illegal, Detective."

"Now, what if the thing he was using to do the liberating was MDA?" Mariko said, making Hamaya shift his attention to her. She and Han made a habit of speaking in turns. They had a good rapport that way, each anticipating where the other was going, riffing off each other, always redirecting a suspect's focus, never letting him feel settled. It worked on suspects' lawyers too. "A nice high with some gentle hallucinations—good spiritual stuff, that. Pass enough of that around and you could probably start a cult."

"Maybe so," said Han. "Of course, he'd need a steady supply to make enough MDA for a whole cult to take part."

"But wait," said Mariko, "hasn't your client been making deals with the Kamaguchi-gumi for whole barrels of hexamine?"

"That's right," said Han. "He's been doing that for months, hasn't he? Do you know what you can make with hexamine, Hamaya-san?"

"I'm sure I have no idea."

"Well, your client does," said Mariko. "I mean, he'd have to. He knows how to cook speed, after all. Lots of it. Enough to make himself very rich—rich enough to purchase expensive antiques, for instance. Masks, swords, that kind of thing. If he didn't feel like stealing them, of course."

Han poked Hamaya on the shoulder and whispered, "This is the part where you say, 'Allegedly.'"

"Now, why would a guy who likes to cook amphetamines give a whole bunch of his product away?" said Mariko, laying claim to Hamaya's most obvious legal riposte. She figured they might as well get a good look at it now, before the case went to court. Urano Sōseki, the capo that oversaw the Kamaguchi-gumi's shipping and packing plant, had claimed the same defense right from the outset, just minutes after Mariko had blasted him through that door: there was never any dope deal. No money had changed hands. In court Hamaya could make a mirroring claim on Akahata's behalf: since the speed was in the Kamaguchi-gumi's possession, it clearly belonged to them. A buy wasn't a buy until someone paid for something.

That wouldn't wash for Urano's crew. Just having the speed on the premises was more than enough to convict them. But Akahata was innocent until proven guilty. Unless Mariko and Han could prove he'd been involved in the deal—and holding a big wad of dope money was the usual proof in these cases—Akahata's only criminal activity that night had been as the victim of aggravated battery. She and Han always had the option of getting Urano to dime out Akahata, but Urano's credibility as a witness wouldn't hold up under scrutiny. Mariko could take her turn on the stand, but she'd have a hard time convincing a jury why Akahata would use fifty or sixty kilos of speed to buy an old rusty mask, and an even harder time explaining how she'd discovered that information while hanging out in Kamaguchi Hanzō's kitchen. Unless Akahata admitted to felony possession, Hamaya would see him walk.

But Hamaya ignored that line of defense completely. "No one gives contraband away for free, Officer."

"Oh?" said Han. If Mariko read him right, he, like her, was still waiting for the other shoe to drop.

Hamaya gave them a thin smile. "Please. This little back-and-forth game of yours might work on some poor, hapless purse snatcher you drag into your interrogation room, but we're all professionals here. There's no need to insult my intelligence."

Han was at a loss, literally dumbstruck. His mouth worked, but he couldn't make it say anything.

Mariko jumped in: "Just what are you suggesting, Hamaya-san? Are you admitting your client's guilty of felony possession? Trafficking? Conspiracy? What?"

"I don't wish to be presumptuous, Officers, but allow me to hazard a guess as to your intentions. You expected me to claim my client is innocent. Had no part in the drug transaction, or something like this, at any rate. Since you're utterly lacking in evidence, you've considered trying to get one of your other suspects to testify against him. Being good at your jobs, in all likelihood you'd succeed, and then my client would be sentenced to a very long prison term. Was that your plan, more or less?"

Mariko had never been belittled so politely in all her life. "Uh," she said.

"I guess you think you're pretty smart," said Han, whose tone suggested he didn't take kindly to having his mind read. "Well, two can play this game. You're not really Akahata's lawyer, are you? You're here for his boss, this Jōko Daishi, whatever the hell that means—"

"Great Teacher of the Purging Fire," said Hamaya.

"—who, by the way, we've already got by the balls. We know he's been buying the hexamine, we know he's been cooking, and we know there's a new amphetamine on the street called Daishi that's selling like pointy ears at a Star Trek convention. We also know it's the Kamaguchi-gumi that's slinging the Daishi, and it's only a matter of time before we confirm that your client is their delivery boy. Now we've got your boy and you've got a jabber-mouth tweaker spouting gibberish all day long. The boss-man starts worrying that his disciple might spout something incriminating, so he sends you down here for damage control. How am I doing so far? Is that the plan, more or less?"

Hamaya's laugh chilled Mariko to the bone. An "okay, you got me" laugh would have suited her just fine. She'd even have taken a derisive "you cops are so goddamn stupid" laugh or a haughty "I'm far too big for you to touch me" laugh—*something* to make it clear that Han had him dead to rights. A humorless grin. A little swallow. The tiniest flicker of guilt. Anything. But Hamaya's laugh conveyed an entirely different subtext: *Not only are you not in the ballpark, but you're not even in the right sport. We have even less to fear from you than we thought. You haven't got the slightest clue of what you're dealing with here.*

Han had missed something. Something big. And Mariko couldn't spot it either.

She did what she always did in such circumstances: she started collecting details. She couldn't help it; it was just a habit of mind. And the first datum she caught was a cold light in Han's eyes. He wasn't responding with a detached curiosity like Mariko's. He was furious.

Immediately her detective's mind started seeking connections. She'd seen Han angry before. Losing what should have been a win in court on a trivial technicality. This wasn't like that. Losing what should have been a win because the perp's lawyer was just too damn good at his job. This wasn't like that kind of anger either. Losing big at Lieutenant Sakakibara's Thursday night poker table, getting conned on a hand that should have been a sure thing. That's what this was. Han didn't like it when people got into his head. Or rather, he didn't like it when they got in uninvited. Mariko could read his mind all she liked. They were partners. But when Hamaya did it, he'd violated the most sacred kind of privacy. He'd intruded the sanctum sanctorum. And Han was ready to throw down with him for that.

"Han," Mariko said, interposing herself between her partner and Hamaya, "why don't you step outside for a second?"

"This prick knows his client's guilty."

"I know."

Han's face was getting red. Staring Hamaya right in the eye, he said, "He's going to tell his client to run. He's going to aid and abet a known criminal. I'm not going to stand here and let him do it."

"You don't have a choice," said Hamaya, thoroughly enjoying himself. "I'm afraid Akahata-san hasn't been charged with anything at this point, and until you convince one of your other suspects to attest otherwise, you only have an innocent assault victim and his attorney."

"You'll want to do yourself a favor and shut the hell up," Mariko said, shooting him a quick glare over her shoulder. "Han, you need to take a walk. Outside. Right now."

"Fuck this guy—"

"Please. For me? I'll handle him."

Han paused for a moment, tense, as if coiling to spring. Mariko started thinking about which restraining holds worked best from her current position. Then Han turned and stormed out, slamming the door behind him.

"I daresay that got the nurses' attention," said Hamaya.

"You're an asshole," said Mariko.

"And you, Sergeant, are in over your head. There's nothing you can do to prevent my client from walking out of here—"

"Wheeling out of here."

Hamaya conceded the point with a little tilt of the head. "As you like. He and I will be departing shortly. That leaves you in a position to consider your next move very carefully."

Now it was Mariko's turn to concede the point. She, Han, and Hamaya had all foreseen it: it was illegal to tail Hamaya or Akahata without a warrant. They weren't suspects in a larger conspiracy—yet. That conspiracy, whatever it was, was just starting to take shape in Mariko's mind. Jōko Daishi was connected to the Daishi that dealers were slinging on the street. That much was clear. This lawyer and his lunatic cultist client were connected too. And Akahata wasn't a weak link among the conspirators. That much Han had wrong. Akahata was an asset, not a liability, and he was important enough that Hamaya had to sweep him out from law enforcement's grasp even before it was medically safe to do so.

The best course for Han and Mariko was to follow these two to Jōko Daishi, and Han had foreseen that. That was part of why he was so pissed off: Hamaya had seen his move coming and outmaneuvered him. Given even a few more hours, Mariko and Han might have secured their warrant. With that in hand, tailing Akahata and his Teflon-coated lawyer would have been the easiest thing in the world. And now, because they couldn't do this very simple thing, a dangerous man was going to go free, and he was going to do something very bad very soon.

He wasn't her sword burglar. He'd been in the ICU when the theft took place. But there was no doubt in Mariko's mind that Akahata was dangerous. For as long as she'd been in the room he'd been staring her down, chanting his mantra. This was a man with a mission, and he would not rest until he saw it done. His fanaticism was at least as powerful as the drugs running through his system. He did not sleep.

His every waking breath was devoted to his cause. And whatever his mission was, it was much larger than swelling the ranks of his cult by getting a bunch of people high. That wasn't the kind of "liberating souls" that was on Jōko Daishi's agenda. Mariko had no proof of that, but gut instinct allowed no other conclusion.

People in an altered state were malleable. Akahata and Jōko Daishi were going to manipulate a lot of them, and Mariko wanted to know what for.

In a few minutes she would have a choice to make. She could abandon her duty, blow off the standards of probable cause, and shadow Hamaya and Akahata until they led her to this mysterious Jōko Daishi. Or she could do what she knew was right and let her two best leads walk out into the endless streets of Tokyo, never to be seen again—or worse, not to be seen again until it was too late.

She walked out on Hamaya to look for Han, but there was no sign of him. Mariko would have to make her decision alone. A big part of her wished it was a hard choice, but in her heart she already knew exactly what she was going to do.

BOOK FOUR

MUROMACHI ERA, THE YEAR 198

(1484 CE)

20

Kaida left the surface and returned to the world where she felt most at home.

The water was chilly today, but Kaida didn't mind. She was happy to feel the two cold streams of it worming their way deep into her ears. Underwater, no taunts could reach her. Underwater, everyone was a mute.

Her sandbag pulled at her ankles, dragging her swiftly down to the coral bed. To her right she saw the other three *ama* fluttering down too: Miyoko, as slender and streamlined as a shark; Kiyoko, rounder, more like a puffer fish; Shioko, short and powerful, fanning her arms overhead to accelerate her descent. Shioko was always catching up, always trying to overtake the other two; Miyoko was always the leader; Kiyoko only followed along, always just another dolphin in the pod. At this distance they were no more than naked white blurs against the blue, but for Kaida it was so easy to tell which one was which.

Kaida was happy to see they'd chosen to dive on the Squid's Head, an oblong mound of rock and coral three or four boat-lengths from her. Miyoko's taunts had been especially sharp on the ride over to this part of the reef—hence Kaida's relief to return to the silence of the aquatic world—and when Miyoko was sharp-tongued like this, evil words had a way of becoming evil deeds. The other two weren't vicious like her; if anything, they were scared of Miyoko, maybe even as scared as Kaida was. Not that it mattered. Whether they followed out of loyalty or simply to avoid becoming targets themselves, they still followed.

The fact that Sen was their oarsman today made matters worse. He was a simpleton, born with no more wit than the gods granted a sea turtle. He had just enough sense to row a boat where he was told, and not nearly enough to tell the difference between a wicked smile and a friendly one. When Miyoko's barbs made the other two laugh, Sen understood only that he was to laugh along with them. If Miyoko decided to do more than talk, Kaida could not hope for Sen to intervene, even though he was a grown man and the four girls were all in their teens.

Sand billowed up around Kaida's feet as she reached the long fingers of brain coral that everyone in the village called the Tentacles. Schools of coral fish scattered from her like leaves on a stiff breeze, their whites, blacks, and yellows fluttering like a thousand pennants. A wave of cold rippled over her. She was two or three body-lengths deeper than the Squid's Head, and looking up, she saw the others swimming with long, graceful strokes. They danced like three white dolphins behind the screen of coral fish stripes.

Kaida's own movements felt clumsy in comparison. She hooked the stump of her left arm through the tether on her sandbag, and with her right hand she withdrew her *kaigane* and wedged its metal tip between the coral and the shell of the nearest abalone.

It was a stubborn one, and since she couldn't abide the thought of chipping the beautiful green whorls of coral, it took her some time to coax it free. The other *ama* were already bound for the surface. They'd have more than one lousy abalone in their catch bags. Kaida's lungs burned, but she refused to head back up.

She found a second oyster entrenched even deeper than the first. Passing it by, she found a third one, tiny by comparison. The fourth was worth keeping, so she went to work on it with her *kaigane*.

She couldn't say what it was that made her look up. When she did, the three white dolphins were no longer diving on the Squid's Head.

Kaida looked up at the belly of the boat, hoping to see the other *ama* up there. It was only when she saw Shioko frog-kicking down at her that she knew she was under attack.

Two hands locked fast around her right wrist. They were Kiyoko's, and Kiyoko was the strongest of them all; Kaida knew she couldn't free her hand.

Slender forearms slipped around her midsection from behind like a pair of eels. That would be Miyoko. She always wanted to inflict the worst blows herself. Kaida slammed her head backward, hoping to catch her in time, but Miyoko was ready for it. She must have tucked her head, because Kaida's skull cracked against something hard, not something soft and crunchy like a nose.

Miyoko's squeeze came as fast as a hammer blow. Kaida vomited what little air she had left. Black spots swam like little fish in her vision.

Kaida struggled to free her right arm. She'd show Miyoko how deep a *kaigane* could cut. But Kiyoko's stout hands held fast. By then Shioko was on her, and together the three of them pulled Kaida halfway up to the surface before they let her go.

But only halfway. Kaida couldn't launch herself from the bottom, yet she wasn't close enough to the surface to be certain she'd make it. Black spots were already encroaching on her vision. She had only a split second to decide: dive back down—never the easy choice—or try to reach the surface without the benefit of a push-off.

She swam straight up, kicking like mad. Her lungs heaved mightily, so hard she almost threw up. When she broke the surface her inhalation was a loud, gasping, birdlike cry. It was another five or six breaths before she could hear Miyoko leading the chorus of laughter.

Kaida puked into the boat, inspiring another fit of giggling. Sen, the oarsman, chuckled too; Kaida could feel the vibrations from his deep, dopey voice through the wooden hull. She spat a mouthful of vomit on his foot, regretting it instantly. He didn't deserve it; he was only the closest target. He was too stupid to know any better. And now Kaida had no more vomit to spit at Miyoko or the other two.

She dived back under, as much to silence their laughing as to flush out her mouth. She stayed under for a while, filling her mouth with salt water and spitting it out, over and over until the taste of bile was gone. Then she surfaced, took her deepest breath, and swam down again to recover her *kaigane* and her abalone.

The other three did not follow her this time. Once was enough. No doubt they would content themselves to watch from the surface and comment on how saccadic her movements were. Even the silence of the water was not enough to shut them up in Kaida's imagination. A seal without a flipper. A turtle without a fin. They'd called her as much and worse before. No doubt they hadn't bored of it yet.

Kaida wondered what she could have done wrong to deserve sisters like these.

This time she had plenty of air when she kicked off the bottom, though the whole way up she thought about how far it was and how narrowly she had escaped drowning. Again. The trick of pulling her away from the seabed was Miyoko's newest invention. She really was a virtuoso of cruelty. One of these days Kaida wouldn't make it to the surface, and she wondered whether Miyoko would still be laughing then.

She was certain her other two stepsisters would not. Kiyoko only picked on Kaida to fit in. Like a remora, she attached herself to the shark in order to stay out of harm's way. Shioko wasn't evil so much as competitive. She was the youngest, always catching up, always plagued by the need to prove herself. When she showed genuine malice, Kaida saw it as a sort of emotional karate, practiced out of some vague sense that it might protect her fragile sense of self. Miyoko's cruelty was purer, more hateful. She indulged her malicious urges for the sheer enjoyment of it. Kaida knew about the little animals she trapped sometimes, and what she did to them. Now that Miyoko had an ugly, crippled stepsister, she'd broadened her tastes.

Kaida broke through the crest of a big wave to see the other three already warming themselves around the little fire pit in Sen's boat. By the time Kaida got there, the tea would already be gone—"spilled" overboard, no doubt, if they hadn't actually drunk it all. That was all right. Anger would keep Kaida warm. She did notice, though, that the wind was blowing hard, and the waves were a lot higher than they'd been a few moments before. A storm was brewing, and it was rolling in fast and angry.

21

The moment it sailed into view, Kaida knew the strangers' ship was doomed, yet somehow the sight of it inspired a surge of hopefulness in her. Every time she saw a ship, she dreamed of being aboard. Ama-machi was not a village in her eyes; it was a penitentiary, and the ships were the only way out.

The features that made Ama-machi an ideal place for a settlement were the very features that made it the harshest of prisons. Sheer black cliffs walled in the beach on three sides, protecting it from the worst of the storms and from raiders to boot. The waves rolled in relentlessly, battering down the rock over thousands of years, forming the cove and driving back any who sought to swim beyond it. They'd created the beach, and there the grass shacks of Ama-machi huddled like a bunch of ducklings nestling in close to their mother, the giver of life.

To the southwest, the line of toothy rocks known as Ryūjin's Maw marked the boundary between the cove and the open sea. The sea was the fourth wall to Kaida's prison, pitiless, beckoning eternally yet never offering escape. Out there were the biggest sharks, the strongest riptides, the coldest currents. The jagged, broken wall of the Maw fended off all those threats, but in so doing it fenced in any young woman who dreamed of someday swimming off to the horizon, never to return.

It was only when a ship sailed into view that Kaida felt any hope of escape. Even this new ship, the one that sped under full sails just past Ryūjin's Maw, caused her heart to race, though she knew the strangers and their ship were soon to be swallowed up by the waves. The elders said there was no way to reach another village except by sea. The cliffs surrounding Ama-machi were volcanic rock, sharp and brittle, and even if they were as soft as baby skin they were still vertical where they were not overhung. Kaida had climbed to the top once, back when she still had two hands, for no other reason than to see what there was to see. But there were no other villages up there, nor even a road to reach them; she found only trackless overgrown hills and a down-climb so difficult it had nearly killed her.

Back then she still had reasons to climb back down. Her mother was still alive. Her father still knew she existed, even though he'd have preferred a son to a daughter. Even in those days Kaida found Ama-machi too small for her. The boys were boring and the girls were petty. It was a good thing she was the best *ama* her age—better even than a lot of the women in their twenties and thirties—because the only place she could go to feel sane was underwater. These days she wanted to escape even more than she had back then, but Kaida knew attempting the climb again would do her no good. How could she survive in hill country? There were no coral beds to forage for food, no waterfalls or rain catches for freshwater. She could not imagine how anyone could tell which direction was which; in her memory all those hills looked exactly the same.

No, the only hope of escaping Ama-machi was to sail to another village, and she would not be allowed to do that until she was fifteen. She'd told herself a thousand times to forget about escape, and yet every time a ship sailed into view her heart betrayed her. Every single time it leaped with hope.

This ship had no hope. It was the biggest Kaida had ever seen—far and away the biggest, in fact—and still she had no hope. She was red, the strangers' ship, three-masted, all sails fat with wind as she raced the storm bearing down on her like a school of barracuda. Ribbons of foam whipped off the whitecaps at her prow. The colorful dragon that was her figurehead snarled in defiance as it surged straight for the Claw.

Kaida heard gasps from all around her, and though she could not take her eyes from the dying ship, she knew the whole village must have gathered on the beach to watch. Rain pelted her, and the others too, but the doomed ship was as hypnotic as it was horrifying.

The ship's captain had no more hope of seeing Ryūjin's Claw than his wooden draconic figurehead. It was high tide; the Claw was submerged. And this ship clearly could not have been from anywhere near Ama-machi. Her captain did not know these waters. The elders always said outlanders never valued *ama* wisdom. They never hired locals to guide them, and so this stretch of the coast was dotted with a hundred shipwrecks.

The elders were wrong sometimes, but not tonight.

It was as if the gods conspired to let Kaida watch her hopes founder and drown. The clouds were black almost all the way to the horizon, but between the clouds and the angry sea was a long band of golden sky, and in the center of it, right at the horizon, the sun burned like a round red ember. The strangers' ship sped past the sun. Each tooth of Ryūjin's Maw stood out as black as a shark's eye against her red hull. No doubt the captain had seen the Maw. No doubt his steersman felt a wave of relief at having passed it unscathed. It was a common mistake.

The Claw ripped the belly out of the strangers' ship, stopping her dead despite her bulk and speed. Dozens of tiny human forms tumbled forward, as helpless as baby sand crabs before a rogue breaker. Some of the crewmen disappeared overboard. Others struck the gunwales and clung for dear life.

A huge wave loomed over the port bow, big enough to toss any *ama*'s boat aside. An *ama*'s boat might have been thrown free of the Claw, but the strangers' ship was too heavy, too bulky, impaled too deep. She took the wave broadside and it snapped her in half.

Someone on the beach screamed. Others shouted, but Kaida only heard them say stupid things. Of course those sailors would try to swim this way. Most would die in the attempt. The rain redoubled its assault, hammering Kaida, nearly blinding her. The other villagers on the beach would be holding their hands against their wet foreheads, creating an eave for their eyes. Kaida had but the one hand, but she cupped her eyes with it anyway, the better to see. Hypnotized and horrified, she watched.

The sailors in the water were learning now why the Claw was so dangerous. An invisible riptide tossed them from the Claw onto the jagged teeth of the Maw, just as if Ryūjin was feeding himself. The sea dragon was insatiable. Kaida knew that all too well. He had devoured her mother, and taken Kaida's left hand as a snack. And that had been in calmer seas than this.

Kaida saw the waves pulp one man after the next against the rocks of the Maw, not because she wanted to watch but because she could not pull her gaze away. "Look at her," she heard Miyoko say. "She looks like she's going to cry."

"She does," Kiyoko said, following along as passively as ever.

"Cry your big froggy eyes out," said Shioko. "They're halfway out of your head already anyway. *Neh*, Miyoko? She has eyes like a bug."

Kaida refused to look in her sisters' direction. Men were dying right in front of them, and somehow these three still found the time to pick on her. She debated dragging a boat out into the surf, and maybe recruiting her father and a few of his friends to help her mount a rescue effort. The thought lived only briefly; then she tossed it aside as easily as the sea tossed yet another outland sailor into the Maw. The surf rolled in hard enough to rebuff even the strongest oarsmen in the village, and if they somehow managed to row even halfway out to the Maw, even a hundred oarsmen couldn't keep a boat steady in these seas. For the outlanders, a boat full of rescuers would only be one more weight to crush their skulls against.

And yet Kaida really did want to row out there to save them. She wished she didn't care, or at least that she could keep from letting her care show. As it was, Miyoko had only to read her face to find ammunition for her next attack. "Poor Kaida," she said, mockwhimpering. "Do you want to swim out there and find a husband? Maybe you should. None of Ama-machi's men will have you."

I wouldn't have *them*, Kaida thought, and even if I would, half of them have already had you. Kaida had heard what Miyoko was doing to the boys of the village. She'd even done it to grown men. She'd done it halfway to Sen once with her hand, then run away giggling while he raged and cried. He'd tried to chase her, stumbling with his pants around his ankles and his member sticking straight out from between his legs. The whole village knew about Sen's outburst, but not how Miyoko had started him off. But Kaida knew. She heard it from Miyoko's own mouth, just like she heard all the rest: whispered boasts in the dark after everyone was abed, after Kaida's father had finished rustling and puffing and grunting with Miyoko's mother, after all the girls giggled about it to themselves. None of them knew Kaida could hear them, just as none of them knew Kaida could hear their insults over the drumming rain. Kaida never let it show.

Miyoko repeated her taunt louder. Kiyoko aped her, and Shioko tried to outdo them both. Go fishing for a husband. No, go diving for a husband. They'll all be drowned and still they won't have you. It was all so predictable. They didn't need to shout for Kaida to hear them.

But they knew her every bit as well as she knew them. They knew she wanted to escape. They knew the outlanders' ship embodied hope, and they knew what it meant for Kaida see it smashed to flinders. Yet they'd misunderstood Kaida's hope for the sailors. She wasn't malicious like Miyoko. She didn't want to see these men die. And yet it didn't matter to her if none of them survived. Even if none of them made it to shore, they were too many for their passing to go unnoticed. Someone would come looking for them. Someone whose ship would leave this place, with Kaida on it.

As she watched the last of them cling to the tips of Ryūjin's teeth, battered by the waves, holding on for dear life even though death was certain, Kaida felt a small swell of hope. Realization struck her: regardless of whether anyone expected to find survivors, a rescue ship was certain to come. It wasn't just the sailors who would be missed. Their ship was massive, expensive, and probably laden with cargo. Others would come looking for it after all. And when they came, Kaida meant to leave with them, never to return.

2 2

When at last the outlanders came, they came not by sea but by land.

It was strange. Beyond strange. There was nothing up there: no roads, nor even footpaths; no villages; no food; no water. Yet there they were, a little line of men, black against the sunrise.

They came nine days after the big red ship had foundered, but Kaida knew immediately that they had come for the ship. Outlanders didn't come to Ama-machi. There was nothing for them here— nothing, unless Ryūjin's Claw seized some treasure of theirs. That was why Kaida had been sneaking out every morning to dive on the wreck.

She was treading water over the skeletal hulk when she first spied the strangers. The sun had not yet risen high enough for its light to reach Ama-machi, so the village was still asleep. That meant Kaida was the only one to have spotted the strangers. If only she had already found what they'd come for, she could have delivered it to them before anyone else was even awake. Whatever the outlanders were looking for, Kaida could use it to buy her way out of Ama-machi forever. It did not matter where the outlanders took her, whether they took her back to their home or simply dumped her off as soon as they tired of her. Anywhere was better than Ama-machi.

She took a deep breath and duck-dived straight down. The wreck was below her—the front half of it anyway—purple, not red, at that depth. To her left loomed Ryūjin's Claw, sharp and menacing. A little school of hammerheads circled the Claw, but only five or six of them, not enough to threaten Kaida. Paying them no mind, she swam deeper.

The carrack's bow pointed straight down into the chasm the villagers called the Whore's Cleft, a name Kaida didn't wholly understand. The only thing Kaida knew about whores was that the village didn't have any and that they sometimes did was what Miyoko had been doing to the boys with her hand and her mouth in quiet, secluded places the village. The Cleft was the only rift in the wide, black shelf of rock that formed the belly of this side of the cove. The white sand of the sea floor was much deeper down, all the way at the bottom of the Cleft, deeper than any *ama* had ever dived in Ama-machi's collective memory. Now the snarling dragon that had been the figurehead of the outlander's carrack was buried in that sand, and their ill-fated ship had jammed herself between the sharp black walls of the Cleft.

No one else in the village would dare to dive here. Not since the shipwreck. Usually the hunting was good; the wide rock shelf lay at an easy depth and was pocked with hundreds of holes for abalone to grow in. On flat days one or two boats would risk rowing a little past the Maw and the Claw to anchor out here. This morning the sea as was as calm as a sleeping baby, but Kaida knew she would be the only one to dive here today. Everyone else was worried about the ghosts. Too many dead sailors, they said. Only three had washed up ashore (and of course Miyoko missed no opportunity to ask whether Kaida might beg one of them to mount her, to get her pregnant so she could keep him). Those three burned on a single funeral pyre, but there would be no such satisfaction for the spirits of those who were swallowed up by the waves. That meant dozens of hungry ghosts, so everyone else stayed well clear the great red wreck.

Kaida was more worried about sharks than she was of ghosts, and sharks didn't concern her much. The big ones didn't like the riptide near the Claw, and the little ones that could easily ride the riptide were more dangerous to fish than to people. Besides, the sharks she could see weren't the scary ones. The ones to worry about were the ones she didn't see. An *ama* knew what to watch for, how to tell an aggressive shark from one that just wanted to snatch her catch bag and swim off. But then there were the sharks that hit so hard they knocked you silly, and they disappeared so fast that sometimes an *ama* didn't even know she'd been bitten until there was blood in the water.

So it wasn't the sharks that bothered her. The ones she imagined being out there were scarier than the real ones. What really frightened Kaida was the wreck itself.

It yawned open before her, a blue pit deepening into blackness. Oddly it was the empty parts, the parts that weren't there, that scared her most. The hull of the ship was arguably the most dangerous. Its mouth was a misshapen perimeter of spiky timbers and beams, hundreds of them, any one of them sharp enough to run her through if she didn't judge the riptide right. Snapped spars, equally sharp, hung from tangled lines snagged here and there, swaying in the currents. They too could cut her open, or the lines could catch an ankle, even slip around her neck if the riptide and bad karma went against her. But for all of that, what scared her most were those deep, dark pits that once were holds. Two of them, one stacked on the other, separated by the jagged plain of the deck between them.

Kaida didn't like closed spaces. Her throat grew tight whenever she felt the walls were too close. It was worse when she was underwater, and not because her racing heart burned up more of her body's breath. Her cool, wet, quiet world was her home. She did not like feeling afraid here.

But whatever it was the outlanders had come to find, it would be in those deep blue pits or it would be nowhere at all. Ryūjin's Maw had chewed up the other half of their huge red carrack and spat it back out into the sea. Kaida had looked for it. She'd even risked a swim out to the Maw itself, to get a firm grip on one of the teeth so she could look underwater for as long as her breath would hold out. There were no timbers there, no corpses, only a few lines draped on the coral, undulating back and forth in a rhythm half a beat behind that of the waves.

So if the outlanders had come to find sunken treasure, they would find it in the wreck Kaida was diving on. She hovered over it. It took a lot to convince herself the walls wouldn't close in on her and swallow her up. The tides were strong. The hull was weak. It wouldn't take much to collapse the whole thing.

She dived deeper anyway. Not into where it was dark. Just past the toothy timbers that held siege around the open holds. The sunlight still made it here. She loved the way water caught the light, diffusing it, bending it into areas that should have been shaded. Sunlight didn't work that way up above.

What should have been a bulkhead now lay like a deck beneath her. Ryūjin's Claw had ripped out half of it and the tides had demolished much of the rest, but there was still enough of a ledge for Kaida to hook with her stump and hang from while she inspected the inside of the hold. Just looking inside wasn't so bad.

She saw some coins she hadn't seen on previous dives. For the last eight mornings she'd brought her catch bag out to the wreck, and every time she swam back in to shore to build up her little treasury: a dead sailor's coin purse; a bow case with some kind of pattern worked into the leather, the details of which were swollen and spoiled by the salt water; a jeweled brooch; a collection of hairpins, all contributed by the dead; chopsticks inlaid with mother-of-pearl, kept in a slender golden case; even a short sword, taken from the belt of a drowned man. She kept them all in a little hollow at the base of the cliff behind the village, buried in the sand so her sisters would not find them.

She had a feeling that nothing in her collection was valuable, but she thought that perhaps when the outlanders came, they might see how diligently she'd been collecting and how cleverly she'd chosen what to gather and what to leave behind. The coins, for example, were meaningless. There were probably hundreds more down there, but tens of thousands more in the great cities she'd heard about in the elders' stories. A few more taken from the wreck wouldn't matter. The hairpins, though, or the sword, or the chopsticks in their ornate case, any of them might identify the bearer. Perhaps one of the passengers was important. Or perhaps the outlanders had search parties looking for survivors. If the brooch belonged to some noble lord, Kaida could present it to the outlanders and they would know their lord had been aboard after all.

So Kaida did not bother swimming down to collect the coins. She did not want the outlanders to think her stupid. She swam back up to the surface, filled her lungs again, and dived on a different part of the wreck.

She went on this way for some time, and each time she returned to the surface, she assessed the progress of the outlanders. By the time the sunlight reached down far enough into the bay to strike the beach, the outlanders had dropped long lines from the top of the cliff and several men had descended them. Other men readied large wooden boxes, which Kaida guessed they would lower to the men below. The ones up top had a huge creature with them, its body bigger than a dolphin's, with four tall, spindly legs. Its head was strange too, its neck long and thick, and it had a long tail of seaweed hanging from the back, just like an old turtle. She wondered if this was one of the horses she'd heard about in tales. If so, it was much bigger than she'd imagined.

Kaida dived again, this time gliding down along the starboard side until she reached a rent in the hull. She couldn't guess what had staved it in, but through the gash she could see more dead sailors. One wore a breastplate, and it took her several dives to cut all the cords that fastened it to the body. She used another corpse's knife to do the cutting, which she thought was very resourceful of her, and she tucked the knife into her thin rope belt for future use. She wondered hopefully whether Miyoko would think twice about threatening to drown her now.

She dived again, found the soldier she'd been working on, and pinched the breastplate between her knees to get a good grip on it. With her new knife she cut the last cord free.

The listless corpse lolled to one side, floating out from under the armor. In the next instant the breastplate pulled her right into the dark hold of the carrack. Armor was heavier than she'd expected, much heavier, and now she was in the dark and alone and there were walls on all sides of her. She let the breastplate go. Something massive gave a loud thunk just below her, maybe a big shark trying to bash its way inside. No. It was just the breastplate. The noise gave her a start nonetheless. Her throat tightened; her heart flopped and shuddered like a netted fish drowning on air.

The jagged blue window overhead was the only thing she could see. Everything else was black. She swam toward the blue, but something pushed her away from it. The riptide, making crazy currents over the hollow of the hold. It bounced her into something solid. The wall. It was caving in on her. She screamed a torrent of bubbles and swam like mad.

Then she was bathed in blue light and then she was at the surface again. It took a long time for her to calm down, and when she was calm again she was surprised she still had the knife in hand. She'd have guessed she would have dropped it in her manic scramble out of the hold—which, she realized now, was never in danger of collapsing. She'd bumped into things she couldn't see. That was all. And all too easy to rationalize too, now that she was safely on the open water.

To the best of her knowledge, her sisters didn't know about her fear of tight spaces. Kaida was glad they weren't with her now. If Miyoko ever found out, she'd bury Kaida alive just for fun.

23

Kaida had only her knife to show for this dive, but she swam back to shore anyway. The whole way in she tried to persuade herself that she was returning because she was tired, not because she was still scared. By the time her feet touched down she still wasn't convinced.

She followed her new morning ritual, which was to skirt the village, keeping her catch bag out of sight, until she reached the big camphor tree. Its biggest root was gnarled and arched like a crone's finger, pointing at the sea cliff. Following that root in a straight line, she found her treasure cache, which for the first time she unburied in its entirety. Except for this morning, she'd always returned with a full catch bag, satisfied with the fruits of her labors. But now that she looked at her entire collection, it seemed insignificant. The wreck was so vast, and everything she'd reclaimed she could gather in her own two arms. Why should anyone care about what little treasure a crippled girl could carry? She wondered whether it would be enough to buy the outlanders' favor.

Kaida gathered it up anyway, trapping the bigger items against her belly with her stump, collecting the smaller things in her right hand. She followed the little sandy strip between the sea cliff and the tall grass that filled the back quarter of the cove. She stayed low as she circled around toward the outlanders, lest one of her sisters see her and call the other two.

She saw Sen before she saw the outlanders. He followed a few other men, and Kaida was surprised to see her father at their head. He rarely left his bedroom this early in the morning. His new wife seemed to have fishhooks in him, or else their bed did, because since they'd married a year ago he seemed unable to spend so long as an hour apart from her.

He was a big man, his forearms as broad as the blades of an oar. A lifetime of rowing and rope making tended to shape a man's arms that way. All the men of Ama-machi had muscular arms, and all the women had lithe swimmer's bodies.

"Good morning," her father said, and Kaida peered over the high grass to see him approach one of the outlanders. Her father smiled amiably, not his lady-killer smile but his pacifying smile. The stranger did not smile at all.

"We came to welcome you to our village," her father said, though Kaida could tell he was lying. He had three burly men behind him. That was no welcoming party. And he used the same overly friendly voice he'd used when he'd explained to Kaida that he'd be marrying Miyoko's mother.

There were four of the outlanders, though only one had even recognized the villagers' existence; the others were busy untying the long box that those up above had just lowered down the cliff. Kaida could tell the stranger's silence put her father ill at ease. He did what he could to mask his apprehension. "We wondered if we could help you," he said. "It promises to be a hot morning, and you look like you've got a lot of hard work ahead of you. May we ask what you're doing here?"

"I'm going to break every joint in your arm," said the stranger. His voice was soft and calm, eerily so. Kaida placed him at a little over forty, with a bald head and a neatly trimmed black beard. From the way his jacket flowed in the light breeze, Kaida could tell it was of finer cloth than any in Ama-machi.

"Excuse me?" said her father.

"Starting with the shoulder," the stranger said, "and working my way down. You'll find me to be a man of my word."

"Now listen here—"

One of the other village fishermen took a step toward the stranger. It was a mistake. Suddenly the fisherman was on the ground clutching his knee. Kaida hadn't even seen the stranger move. Her eyes were on her father, fixed with horror.

The outlander's hands were swift and slippery, darting like eels. One shot under her father's armpit, the other over the top. Her father took a swing at him, but the stranger spun away from it easily. Then her father was facedown in the sand. Kaida heard it when his shoulder popped apart.

The elbow came next, louder than the shoulder. The stranger was kneeling on the back of her father's neck, his deadly hands free now, his face impassive. The other three outlanders hadn't even bothered to look up.

The last of the fishermen ran for his life, or perhaps for help, but Sen's mind was too slow to see the sense in that. He lunged for the bearded stranger, who responded with a series of quick two-fingered stabs. One to the inner thigh, one below the ribs, and when Sen bent double the last one took him behind the ear. Sen crumpled as if his bones had turned to sand.

"Wait!" Kaida shouted, just as the stranger prepared to break her father's wrist. She pushed her way through the grass and dumped her entire cache on the sand. "Here," she said, "take it. For him. Let me have him back."

The stranger looked at her with a mix of curiosity and amusement. Under his knee, her father howled like something inhuman, his cries punctuated by coughs and sputtering sandy sounds. His arm was like a rope in the outlander's hands, boneless, jointless.

"*Please,*" Kaida said. She'd never seen violence like this, and with stepsisters like hers, violence was a part of her daily life. But theirs was vindictive, even joyful in its own twisted way. This was brutality at its purest, utterly devoid of emotion. "Please," Kaida said, "let him go."

"What have we here?" said the stranger, eerily calm and soft-spoken even after all he'd just done. "A little girl with half an arm and an armload of gifts. What are these?"

"From your ship," she said. "I've been diving for them."

"Have you, now? And what else have you found?"

Kaida looked at the other three strangers, who were still busily working at their knots. One of them looked over his shoulder, studied her for a moment, and went back to his work.

"This is all," Kaida said. "This and my knife." She put her hand on it, moved to pull it from her rope belt, then thought better of it. It wasn't a good idea to draw a weapon on this man. "You can have it too, if you want. Just let him go."

"Fond of blades, are you? I can see you like that little pigsticker better than all the rest. You keep it." With his thumbnail he scratched his chin just behind his beard. "Who is this fool to you?"

Kaida swallowed. Her throat was growing tight, just as it did back in the dark hold of the ship. The way the stranger looked at her made her want to run away. She wished she could hear some sign of agitation in his voice, the tiniest little hint that the process of tearing another human being's arm apart caused his pulse to quicken. She wanted to run, but she forced herself to stay; she even dug her feet a little deeper into the sand. "He's my father."

"And what is your name, child?"

"Kaida."

"I'm afraid I'll have to break your father's wrist and fingers, Kaida-san. I am a man of my word."

Without so much as a blink he snapped her father's wrist. Another scream erupted from her father's mouth, stifled by sand and a fit of coughing. Every cough jostled his maimed shoulder, which made him grunt and groan, which made him inhale more sand. His whole body trembled with pain. The stranger wrapped his fingers around her father's thumb.

"You said arm," Kaida said, spitting the words out all at once.

"I beg your pardon?"

"You said every joint in his arm. His fingers aren't in his arm, they're in his hand. You don't have to break them."

The outlander cocked his head and raised an eyebrow. "Hm," he said. After a moment's thought, he said, "A fair point," and he stood up, dropping her father's arm.

It flopped to the sand like a boned fish. Her father cried out but did not move. Was it fear or pain that pinned him there? Kaida could not tell. "I am Genzai," said the stranger. "It is a pleasure to meet you, Kaida-san."

Kaida didn't know what else to do. Somehow the words "pleased to meet you" slipped out of her mouth and she found herself giving a little bow.

That made Genzai laugh. His unflappable calm had unnerved her, but his laugh was worse. It was a deep, sinister rumble, barely a laugh at all. "You're a brave little girl," he said. "Why don't you tell me what all these trinkets are for?"

Kaida looked at the ground, where the mother-of-pearl chopsticks in their golden case lay atop all the other treasures she'd collected over the past few mornings. They didn't seem like treasures now. She had imagined the outlanders would be impressed by all she'd gathered for them—clues, she had thought, as to what was in the wreck, or even who. She thought they'd thank her for saving them so much work. She hadn't imagined one person could cripple three big men in the space of as many breaths. These people didn't need her help. They were more than capable on their own. And now all her treasures seemed like a little girl's toys.

"Well?" said Genzai.

"I thought . . . maybe . . ."

"Spit it out, child. Don't tell me your courage has left you already."

"I thought maybe you could take me with you. When you leave."

Her father moved then. With an effort he raised his head to look at her. Half of his face was a white mask, sand clinging to sweat. "Kaida, what are you saying?"

"She's saying your little village is too small," said Genzai. "I should know. I come from a speck of a village like this myself. Little wonder that she wants to escape. Have you been buggering her? Your own daughter?"

He narrowed his eyes at her father, and for a moment Kaida feared he would go back to ripping bones out of sockets. At length he said, "No. She came to your rescue. Maybe she wants to leave because the men in your village need their teenage girls to rescue them. Is that it, Kaida-san? Is this place too small for a girl of such heroic bravery?"

"I'm not brave," she said.

"Kaida, why?" said her father.

"Shut your mouth. We're talking." Genzai's tone was still calm, exactly as it had been just before he destroyed her father's arm. He scratched behind his beard, studying Kaida closely. "What makes you think I want to take a little girl with me when I leave here—a little girl with half an arm, no less?"

"You don't. That's why I brought you the . . . the treasures."

That earned her another smile from Genzai. He laughed like an earthquake would laugh. "Treasures? Indeed. It must have taken you all morning to haul these up, what with that stump of an arm of yours."

"Eight."

"What's that?"

"Eight mornings."

"Oh, ho. Do you mean to tell me eight days ago, you woke up and decided to dive for 'treasures,' just hoping that someone like me would come along to ask you for them?"

"No," Kaida said. Her face flushed and she looked down at the sand. She didn't *hope* they would come. She *knew* they'd come. They had to come, because if they didn't Kaida would be stuck in Ama-machi for two more years. *At least* two more, and even then her best hope of getting out was to marry some boy in another village just like Ama-machi. A bug-eyed, one-armed girl's prospects for marriage were dismal indeed, and Kaida didn't see much she liked in boys anyway. Most of them were mean, and the ones that weren't had no more backbone than a jellyfish. Miyoko got them to pick on Kaida all the time. She enjoyed using her cruelty that way, the same as she enjoyed the baby sparrows she sometimes stole from nests, twisting their little necks to see how far they'd go. So either Kaida would get out with the outlanders, or else she'd stay here to get worn and hollow and brittle like a piece of driftwood.

But she couldn't say any of that. Not with her father listening. Instead she just said, "I knew you'd come."

"Then you have as much foresight as you have courage," said Genzai. "Impressive in one so young. But useless nonetheless—and good luck for you that you are. Tell me, Kaida-san, what is it you imagine strangers would do with a little girl once they took her away?"

"I don't care. Just so long as I get out."

Her father gasped, as pained as she'd ever seen him. Genzai looked at her too, a hint of curiosity on his otherwise impassive face. "You make for interesting reading," he said. "Too smart to be spouting such hopeless naïveté. In another girl, yes, but not you. You really are desperate, aren't you?"

Kaida glared at him. She felt her eyebrows and cheeks scrunch up, heard her breath coming loud through her nose. "Just take me with you," she said.

"I'm sorry, Kaida-san. I don't have any use for little one-armed girls, not here and not where we're going next. You keep your 'treasures.' Tell your father and his friends not to bother us again."

24

I t was everything Kaida could do just to help her father to his feet. His right arm hung from his collarbone as limp as a ribbon, and the slightest movement nearly made him faint from pain. A lifetime of diving made Kaida strong, but not strong enough to carry a grown man by herself.

No one else dared to go back for Haru-san, the fisherman whose knee Genzai had destroyed, or for Sen, who still lay curled in a ball. Kaida would have thought him dead if she hadn't heard him breathing, his voice big and dopey even in unconsciousness. She had to go back for Haru-san alone, serving him as a human crutch, and since Sen was the biggest of them all, there was nothing she could do for him. She tried to talk some of the men in the village into retrieving him, but they would always listen to her father before they listened to her, and what they heard from her father was wails of torment as two of the elder women tried to reset his shoulder. There was no hope for his elbow; it would have to mend on its own.

Kaida overheard the elder women saying as much while she sat outside their hut, watching another long box sliding bit by bit down the sea cliff, lowered from above by the horse, perhaps. Now and again her stepmother, Cho, would walk by. She'd taken to pacing around the hut since she couldn't bear to watch what was happening inside.

"You poor thing," she said as she reached Kaida once again. "How scared you must have been. And bless your heart for bringing him back to me."

"I didn't bring him back for you."

"Oh, of course not. He's your father. I know that." She crouched in the sand and put her hand on Kaida's knee. "And you know it pains me how my girls pester you so. You do know that, don't you? You poor dear."

"Make them stop, then."

Cho gave her a loving, pitying look, like she was trying to smile and frown at the same time. "You know that I would if I could, don't you? It's just in a young girl's nature to be petty sometimes. And their father . . . well, he wasn't kind like your father is. He hurt them in ways a father shouldn't. Do you know that when he died, my girls didn't even cry?"

Kaida remembered that. No one's death was a secret in Amamachi. When it happened, Kiyoko and Shioko seemed more relieved than anything, and Miyoko's grief was so obviously fraudulent that afterward she'd actually *practiced* lying until it was second nature.

"They've been through a lot," Cho said. "And you have too. Poor thing. Being a teenage girl is just hard, isn't it? I was your age too, you know. I know how you feel."

Kaida scowled at her. Cho knew nothing about how she felt. She had two good hands. She had a pretty face. And if the other girls made fun of her when they were young, it would have been for taking too many boys back into the weeds. Some whispered as much about her even now. Kaida knew her father had his dalliance with Cho even before his wife—his *real* wife, Kaida's mother—was killed. It was only natural that they should get married so soon afterward. She was still fertile enough. He was without sons. Cho might provide him a few.

Just then Sen came stumbling groggily into the village. It seemed he'd woken of his own accord, for the outlanders had left that area. Now they were on northernmost end of the beach, closest to where the wreck had sunk. Their long, heavy boxes lay in the sand like a row of sleeping seals.

Two more outlanders were descending the ropes, which made for a total of six down near the village. A few more outlanders remained atop the cliffs. Kaida had heard horses needed caring for, which had always seemed strange to her. Nothing in the sea needed humans to care for it; these horses must have been exceptionally stupid. In any case, the horses were up there, and the outlanders with them reappeared now and then to to toss firewood off the cliff. Their kinsmen below collected it and stacked it by their encampment on the beach. They already had a mountain of it, and they were gathering more.

That meant they were planning to stay for a while. Kaida wondered how much time she had to figure out a way to abscond with them when they left.

Despite the morning's hostilities, there was no good reason not to be diving or fishing. It was a perfectly good day for it, yet even by high noon there were still no boats on the water. The outlanders had everyone spooked.

Kaida didn't fully understand why. She'd never seen violence like Genzai's before, but for all intents and purposes she was the *only* one who had seen it. Haru-san had dropped before the fight even started, and by the time he hit the ground he was already clamping his eyes shut and gritting his teeth, as if he could somehow squeeze the pain out of his body. Kaida's father *felt* all of the violence and all of its lingering ripple effects, but he *saw* very little. Anything Sen had seen was locked in that turtle brain of his and wasn't coming out. The fourth fisherman's memory was wildly fantastical, twisted out of proportion by blind panic. His story changed by the hour; surely no one took him at his word for any of it. So while Kaida was afraid of Genzai and his companions, she didn't see why anyone else in the village had an excuse.

She thought about this for a while as she watched the sunlight play on the ocean. Waves rose and fell, all of them devoid of boats. Dinner in Ama-machi would be sparse tonight. Dinnertime conversation would not. Every tongue would waggle with tales of the outlanders, of preternatural speed and superhuman strength, with talk of portents and *kami*, with frantic speculation about what might have brought demonic outlanders and ghosts from the sea to visit Ama-machi at the same time.

It was stupid, Kaida thought. Embarrassing, even. Her whole village, everyone she'd ever known, cowed by four strangers. For all Kaida knew, only Genzai was dangerous. The other three might have been sand sharks, scary to behold but utterly harmless—unless you were a mollusk. Kaida harrumphed and frowned. She lived in a village of mollusks.

Part of her knew that was unfair. The fate her father had suffered *was* scary. Giving Genzai a wide berth was prudent, not skittish. Once she made that observation, Kaida realized she'd never grasped the difference between being cautious and being afraid. Every morning she'd gone diving on the wreck she'd felt what she thought was fear. Now she identified it as caution. And being cautious while diving on that wreck wasn't weakness; it was . . . what had Genzai called it? Foresight. That was it. Swimming near Ryūjin's Maw was dangerous enough even when there wasn't a wreck lurking out there, ready to swallow her up if the current swept her the wrong way. Being wary of that was no weakness at all. It was wisdom, if someone in her teens could be said to have any of that.

She'd just made her mind up to recruit a rower and go abalone hunting when she heard her stepmother calling for her. "Kaida, you're father's well enough to speak to you now. You poor little thing, you must have been worried sick. Come on inside."

It was much cooler in the house, though it also stank. The elder women must have made a poultice of some kind, and whatever it was, it left a cloying bitterness in Kaida's nostrils. Her father sat on a futon with his back against the wall, naked to the waist, his right arm wrapped up from his collarbone to the tips of his fingers in strips of whatever cloth was ready to hand. His arm reminded her of a sea cucumber, fat and strangely rigid, as if it would have been flexible if only it weren't so swollen.

Cho had been in the doorway to call Kaida inside, but now she sat with her husband, stroking his unbound shoulder. Kaida stopped short when she saw Cho's three daughters kneeling in a row beside her.

"Kaida-chan," her father said. "Come here. Don't be afraid."

"I'm not afraid. How are you feeling?"

"They say my shoulder will probably get better soon."

Typical, Kaida thought. Trying to seem strong in front of his women. "Come in," he said. "Sit with your family."

"Standing is fine," she said, her hand resting on the doorframe. "What do you want to talk about?"

"Kaida-chan, you must get this evil idea out of your head. You cannot run off with those men. Think of what everyone will say."

"I already know what everyone says. If I leave, at least I won't have to overhear them anymore."

"You're thirteen. I will not have people whispering that my daughter is a whore."

Kaida felt the muscles quiver below her right eye. She bit her lip to keep it from quivering too. For the briefest of moments she thought her father was cross because he'd miss her if she left. And perhaps some part of him would. But what he wanted most of her was for her to have been born a boy, and since he couldn't have that, what he wanted now was for her not to malign his good name.

It wasn't so long ago that he hadn't thought that way. When Kaida's mother was alive, he'd still wanted sons, but he'd still treated Kaida with affection. But after her mother was killed, after Kaida lost her hand, he'd never quite looked at her the same way. She felt like scar tissue, a reminder of what had once been whole, and it horrified her to think that her own father thought of her the same way she thought of the ugly, jagged, slick-skinned, distended worms that twisted this way and that on the stump of her left arm. When she looked there she felt anger and loss, and if she didn't want to feel those things she just looked somewhere else.

"A whore?" Kaida said. "The ones who say that about me are sitting right there. I heard Miyoko this morning, saying I'd bought your life with my mouth. She didn't mean *talking* to the outlander, either. Go on, ask her what she said."

Miyoko gasped. "I don't understand what you mean," she said. "Kissing? What is she talking about, Mother?"

"Miyoko never said anything to me," said Shioko. "Did she say anything to you, Kiyoko?" Kiyoko shook her head and shrugged.

Cho clasped her hands in her lap. "Kaida-chan, you're a very sweet girl, but I won't have you putting filthy ideas in my daughter's heads."

"They don't need me for that. The boys put filthier things than ideas in their—"

"Kaida!" Her father winced in pain and bit down on the knuckle of the hand he could still move. Shouting must have shifted something in his arm. With his fist still pressed to his face, he said, "I will not have you speak of your sisters that way."

"They're not my sisters."

"They are. I married their mother. That's all there is to it. Now you will put this nonsense about running off with foreigners out of your head."

He had more to say, but Kaida was distracted by a shout behind her. Over her shoulder she saw two of the outlanders standing by a row of overturned fishing boats. Genzai wasn't one of them. Some of the villagers had gathered there too, forming a makeshift fence between the boats and the outlanders.

At last. Some backbone. Kaida twisted around to see what was going on. Someone shouted that this was his boat. One of the strangers replied, but Kaida couldn't hear him over the protests of other fishermen. There was more shouting, and the fence closed in around the strangers.

The outlanders waited to react until they were wholly surrounded. Kaida could not see what happened first. What happened second was pandemonium. The fence disintegrated; the strongest men of her village scattered like sand crabs fleeing a shadow. Of the five that were left behind, three were bleeding from the mouth and nose and the other two nursed broken bones. The outlanders seemed unscathed. One of them stood at the prow of two boats and picked up one in each hand. The other did the same with the sterns and they walked back toward their little encampment on the north end of the strand.

When they came back for the next two boats, no one offered resistance.

25

Since no one but the outlanders was diving, Kaida had a lot of time to think.

She sat atop the Fin, a high, sharply angled rock in the middle of the beach, watching the waves and running through the conversation with her father—with her "family"—over and over in her mind, wondering how she could have made it go better. When that grew tiresome, which was almost immediately, she recounted the fight on the beach. To see Ama-machi muster its courage had caused such a swell of pride in her. It proved that hers was not a village of mollusks after all, that there were a few vertebrates among them. But then it was all the more heartbreaking to see their backs broken instantly, to see their courage crushed like a paper boat.

It surprised her how much she wanted to root for the people of her awful little village. Perhaps she hoped to see some saving grace, some virtue—*any* virtue—that made it shallow for her to want to leave. But there was no such grace, no such virtue. And in any event, even if she never rooted for the outlanders, she hadn't yet lost her fascination with them, either. If anything, her curiosity bored deeper, pressing on her, demanding her attention. It seemed strange to her that the outlanders waited until they were wholly encircled before they attacked. As handily as they'd defeated the mob of fishermen, it was self-evident that they had risked little by giving their enemy a superior position. But why risk anything at all? The outlanders could have won just as easily by charging straight in.

The moon rose behind her, the sun sank before her, the stars came out one by one, and *still* Kaida could not figure it out. She thought about other things in the interim, to be sure: how Shioko's malice was different than Miyoko's; whether malice in order to fit in, to avoid being left on the losing side, was better or worse than malevolence for its own delights; why Kiyoko seemed to have no voice of her own, wicked or otherwise; why outlanders didn't know how to dive—as, surely, they did not, if Genzai's people were any guide; whether Miyoko had any control over her cruelty, or whether it was the true puppeteer and she the puppet; whether Kiyoko made any moral judgments at all; whether Miyoko was capable of feeling guilt or shame; what the difference was between Miyoko's being amoral and Kiyoko's having no position of her own to call moral or immoral; how the Fin came to be there; whether her father and Cho could go about their rutting with his arm as badly injured as it was; why her father had yet to thank Kaida for sparing all his fingers; whether standing by one's word was an admirable thing if one spoke in Genzai's merciless language. But wherever her thoughts meandered, they always came back to that fight on the beach.

All the ones who had fought—or been injured, anyway; it was hard to say the villagers did much *fighting*—were now in the one house left in the village where fires and lamps still burned brightly. All the elders were in there. Kaida's father, youngest of the village elders, had to be carried there by his wife and stepdaughters. The fathers of all the village families were there, along with all the injured men who could walk or limp their way to attend. They were meeting to discuss how to deal with the outlanders. No one had announced as much, but there was no other explanation for the gathering.

That left the mothers and grandmothers of the village at home, and left the children to do whatever they had a mind to. No sooner did that thought occur to Kaida than she wondered what mischief Miyoko was brewing. That was when she heard footsteps in the sand.

They were nearly inaudible, all but drowned out by the hissing surf, but Kaida had sharp ears. "I'm going to break every joint in your hand," she said loudly, "starting with the thumb and working my way across."

"What?"

It was Miyoko's voice, below and behind her, off to the right. That would put Kiyoko on her left flank, also down on the sand. Shioko, always needing to prove herself, would be climbing the spine of the Fin to push her off.

"Shioko-chan," Kaida said, not turning around, keeping her voice as tranquil as she could, "I'm telling you, if you put your hand on me I will break every joint in it."

"How did she—?" said Kiyoko.

"Never mind," said Miyoko. "She's a freak. Let's go."

"I can still get her, Miyoko."

"You can't," said Kaida. "Climb down now, Shioko, while you still have two good hands to do it."

"*You* don't have two good hands," said Shioko. "You're a freak."

"Follow Miyoko. It's what you're good at."

Kaida forced herself not to turn around and watch them go. Part of her wanted to know what they'd been planning, and whether they'd brought anything with them to play their little game. Miyoko often armed her sisters with sticks and ropes, sometimes with an oar or a spare scrap of net, but this time Kaida wouldn't indulge her own curiosity. Better to savor the moment. Better to let them think she didn't need to turn around to watch their retreat. Better to know that the next time they called her bug-eyes, they'd have to wonder if she really did have bug-eyes in the back of her head.

Once again her mind returned to the puzzle: why did the outlanders allow themselves to be surrounded? Just now, Miyoko and Kiyoko had tried to flank her while Shioko moved in to push her off the Fin. Why wait until they were in position? Surely it was better to strike first, or at least to choose Kaida's path and ward off the attack before her enemies seized the advantage.

At last Kaida could tolerate the riddle no more. She jumped off the

Fin, sinking to her ankles in the cold, wet sand, and walked to the outlanders' camp.

She caught their scent before she heard them. They had a fire going, but she smelled only wood smoke, not fish or rice steam or any other food. A steady breeze pushed at her, weighted down by the scent of salt water as well as the other smells.

As she drew closer the breeze carried a strange guttural chant to her ears. Closer still, she made out muted conversation, and she thought she could pick out a pattern in the chanting. She could see little of the outlanders, as they'd built up a high mound of sand and rock, almost like a dune. The glow of their fire rose from behind it, as if a tiny sunrise were about to happen just on the north end of the beach.

As she made her way around the leeward side of the dune, sand shifted behind her. She whirled, but not in time to keep something from grabbing her hair. She let out a squeal and grabbed whatever was holding her. She'd half expected to find Miyoko's fist there, but it was a big man's fist and for all she could move it, it might as well have been made of iron.

She clung to it anyway, hoping to support at least a little of her body weight with something other than her scalp. "I've caught us a fish," said the one who caught her, and he dragged her by the hair into their camp. Her heels scrabbled for purchase the whole way, but there was nothing but sand to push against, no way to reclaim her balance.

"I seem to remember throwing this fish back into the ocean," said a bemused Genzai. His deep voice unsettled Kaida in a way she could not quite understand, though she did understand that with a big man dragging her around by her head, the fact that she even noticed Genzai's voice indicated full well how scary she found him.

"Let her go, Masa-san." Kaida fell to the sand the instant Genzai spoke. "What are you doing here, little girl?"

Kaida looked up at Masa, who in turn looked down at her. He was surprisingly skinny for one so strong, but Kaida saw his skin was drawn tight across his chest and arms, as if there was nothing soft in his entire body. He wore his hair long and scraggly, and that was what made her remember him: he was one of the two on the beach who let themselves get surrounded. He cocked his head to one side, studying her as if she were an insect he'd never seen before. "She's got ears like a wolf, this one."

"Does she, now?" said Genzai.

"Heard me coming," said Masa. *"Me."*

"I didn't," said Kaida. "You got hold of me before I could get away."

"True, but you started to turn around before I caught you. I must be losing my touch."

Who are these people? Kaida asked herself. Masa was skinny, yes, but not so skinny as to slip between grains of sand. She'd walked right past him on an empty beach and never noticed him. She'd heard travelers' stories of *yuki-onna* who could turn their very bodies into snow, and she wondered whether Masa had a similar ability to turn himself into sand. In the stories the snow was always whipped up by the wind, just as the wind sometimes whipped up sand into whirling spouts. She wondered if snow was some outland kind of sand.

"Well?" Genzai said. "What are you doing here? Has your father hurt your feelings? Do you want me to break his fingers after all?"

"No," said Kaida, taking in the rest of the camp. Four men sat around a little campfire, all like Masa, skinny and strong at the same time, though among all of them Masa was the only one who struck her as friendly. Two of the others busied themselves around a second fire. They'd built a sort of house for their fire, a three-walled house mostly embedded in the little dune they'd piled up. Its walls were flat and straight, more of a wind shelter than anything, and as Kaida could not see the long boxes they'd lowered from atop the cliff anywhere, she guessed the outlanders must have broken down the boxes to build the little house. The floor of the house was a deep ring of stones filled with glowing red embers.

Tending the fire was a one-eyed hunchback close to Genzai's age. The empty socket of his missing eye seemed to stare right at her. The hunchback worked constantly at a bellows, a device Kaida had only seen once before. She was little at the time. An outlander's ship had run afoul of the Maw and they'd unloaded everything to row it ashore. The outlander had told her a bellows was a house for a little birdie, and when Kaida peeked inside he shot a gust of wind right in her face and made her giggle. That outlander hadn't been sweating like this one. This one knelt beside the ember bed, and pumping his bellows seemed like a lot of work.

The one squatting beside him chanted ceaselessly, heedless that his wild, white, wispy hair might well catch fire. At first Kaida thought he was naked and entirely covered in hair, but as her eyes acclimated to the flickering red light, she saw he had clothes—or what passed for them, anyway. He wore nothing but tattered ribbons of threadbare cloth, seemingly colorless except for the orange glow of the fire. Clothes, beard, and hair alike floated on the breeze. He took something out of the fire, banged it with loud, ringing strokes of a hammer, and pushed it back in among the coals.

"I don't remember you being so easily distracted, Kaida-san. Is it past your bedtime?"

"No," she told Genzai. "It's just—I've never—well, what are they making?"

"That's none of your concern. What are you doing here? Have you come to ask to go with us again?"

"Go with us?" Masa said. His scraggly hair rippled when he laughed. "Where?"

"Anywhere," Kaida said. "Anywhere but here."

Masa chuckled again. "And what is it you think you'll be doing once you get there?"

It was the same question Genzai had asked. Kaida thought it was weird that these outlanders all had the same question. "I'll do whatever you want me to do," she said. "Dive. Fish. Whatever you—"

This time Masa laughed so hard she was sure they'd hear it back in the village. Genzai laughed too, just once, a grunt more than a laugh. The hunchback at the bellows scowled and shushed them. "Silence!" he snapped. "We're close now."

Kaida looked at him. He was horribly ugly, and the embers made his wrinkled face as red as a demon's, all crosshatched in black by the wrinkles. He scowled at her too, just for good measure. His missing eye was horrid, but Kaida couldn't help looking right into it.

"Dive!" Masa said, his laughter still more in control of him than he was of it. "That's rich. Is that really the only thing these villagers have learned how to do with girls?"

She looked at Genzai, who had regained his composure and now sat as still as the rocks around the campfire. Masa chuckled, brushed his disheveled hair from his face, and picked his teeth with a sparrow bone.

"You never answered my question," Genzai said, his voice as flat as ever. "Did you come to see what my friends are making in the fire?"

"No."

"Then why are you here, Kaida-san?"

He looked at her silently. The others too. Kaida knew the one-eyed man was the one her stepsisters would find scariest, but they were wrong. The one to be afraid of was Masa. She didn't like the idea of someone that fast, someone she couldn't hear coming. And Genzai frightened her still more, but she forced herself to stammer it out. "I've been thinking about this all day, and I can't figure it out. You let them surround you. The villagers. You and your friend. And then you fought them. But you let them surround you first."

Masa cocked an eyebrow at her.

"How come?" she said.

Masa let out such a guffaw that it knocked him backward onto the sand. Genzai just chuckled, a deep, grating rumble like big plates of rock shifting below the earth. "Silence!" said the one-eyed man, still working his bellows. "We're almost there. No distractions."

"Tadaaki-san has a point," Genzai said softly. Masa gave a little nod and, still sniggering, settled himself back on his rock. "Kaida-san, do you mean to tell us you risked your life just to ask your question?"

Kaida scrunched up her nose. "I didn't risk anything."

"Masa here was ordered to kill or cripple any who approached."

"She was already crippled by the time I got to her," Masa said with a little shrug. "You've got more than sharp ears, little one. You've got heart too."

"I'll go," Kaida said. "I shouldn't have come."

"No," said Genzai, "you shouldn't have. But nor should you leave empty-handed. Tell her why you let them surround you, Masa."

Another little shrug from Masa. "Who was the first one to throw a punch?" he said.

"I don't know," said Kaida.

"And who was the first man I hit?"

"I don't know."

"The one who's missing all his teeth, what did I hit him in the mouth with? A fist? A knee? An elbow?"

"How should I know? I couldn't see anything."

"Because we were surrounded," said Masa. "No one else in your village could see either."

"All they've got is their imagination," Kaida said, to herself as much as to anyone else. "If you don't let them see what you do, and especially if you let them have the advantage *before* you strike . . . the only thing scarier than the shark you can see is the one you can't."

"She's a natural, Genzai."

Genzai scratched the underside of his chin, just behind his beard. "Not bad, little one. Is that really the only reason you came here?"

"Uh-huh."

He laughed that deep, disquieting laugh of his again. "Sleep well, Kaida-san. You can tell your family we don't plan to stay much longer."

Kaida nodded, bowed, and turned to go. As she turned, her eye caught a glimpse of what the wild, wispy, white-haired man held in his tongs. It was a demonic visage, a mask, the tips of its horns and fangs glowing as red as the embers themselves, as red as the setting sun.

26

Kaida hadn't been privy to the previous night's discussion in the elders' hut, but by morning she understood the agreement they'd come to. *Ama* boats were out on the water again, but only in the southern half of the cove. The water was deeper there, and abalone hunting went more slowly, but the south end held the advantage of having no violent outlanders floating about.

Kaida liked the deeper dives. She could go deeper than her sisters—deeper than all the girls her age, in fact—and so she could be alone. A lot of the older women encouraged her diving skills or praised her for the strength of her lungs. A few whispered when they thought Kaida couldn't hear, wondering at how unnatural it was for a thirteen-year-old girl to dive as well as women of thirty-three or forty-three. Everyone knew an *ama* came into her best years as she grew older.

But no one seemed to understand what Kaida thought was obvious: a one-handed *ama* had no choice but to stay at the bottom longer. She could not use her *kaigane* with one hand and pry with her fingers with the other. To catch the same number of abalone, Kaida had to spend twice as long under the surface as her stepsisters.

Pressure on the ears was a different question, but her lovely stepsisters had taught her much about pain tolerance too. And with one good arm, she couldn't swim back to the surface as quickly as the others either. *Of course* she could dive deeper than they could. To Kaida the logic was as obvious as the sun in the sky.

Today the waves rolled in high and broad-shouldered, and down deep they stirred the sand more than usual. It cut down on visibility, so Kaida had a harder time keeping track of Miyoko, Kiyoko, and Shioko. It didn't matter, though. Down deep, the advantage was hers and they knew it. That was another reason to like the south end of the cove; there were three fewer predators to worry about.

She wished she could see the outlanders. Out of caution, not fear, she kept her distance. Like yesterday, their boats floated over the shipwreck. After a whole day of diving on it they hadn't found what they were looking for, which was hardly surprising; even from a hundred boat-lengths away, it was easy to see they had no idea what they were doing. They dived with their pants still on. With no weights to help them sink. Their boats were *ama* boats, but they didn't think to use the braziers to help their divers warm up. Nevertheless, Genzai seemed to think they'd find their quarry today—or so he'd said last night, if Kaida understood him rightly. She guessed his confidence must have had something to do with the demon face that his friends kept putting back in the fire. She thought they seemed to be in an awful hurry to finish it, whatever it was, though Kaida couldn't guess how it could help them find anything underwater. Better for them to learn to swim properly instead. The only other outlanders Kaida had ever met had come from trading vessels, and as near as she could tell, those ones couldn't swim or dive either.

Even so, the thought of diving inside that wreck made the water all around her seem colder. Swimming under a little shelf of coral was one thing. Having it close her in on all sides was something else entirely. There were holes in the shelves sometimes, and sometimes the other girls would swim in through one hole and come out somewhere else. Kaida used to do it too back when she was younger—back when her mother was still alive. But not since. Never since.

Merely imagining it caused her to retch. Foul, burning bile scalded the back of her mouth. Her throat grew tight; she had to kick the sandbag off her ankle and swim for the surface in middive.

"Kaida?" said Haru-san, whose mangled knee prevented him even from rowing, but he liked the sun and the roll of the surf. Sitting in his hut all day didn't suit him, so he'd come out with the divers even though he couldn't do anything but keep Sen company. As Sen found his two oars companions enough, Haru-san busied himself by tending the embers in the boat's little brazier. "Are you all right?" he said.

Kaida nodded, coughed, and swished some water in her mouth until the taste of bile went away. She hooked her stump over the boat's transom and sneezed into her hand. "I'm fine," she said. The tightness in her throat had gone.

"You're usually down much longer than that," said Haru-san.

"I'm going back down."

She scowled down at the water. It was embarrassing, not being able to dive. Diving was the only thing she was any good at. Now she'd put Haru-san to the work of pulling her sandbag all the way up to the surface, and she didn't even have an abalone to show for his effort. She grabbed the line he was hauling in. "Don't," she said. "Let me see if I can get it first."

It was a good test, and a common one—but only in shallower water. The sandbags were almost the same color as the seabed, so retrieving them was a test of vision for little girls learning to dive. The deeper the water, the less light penetrated to the bottom, and the harder it was to discern the sandbag from everything else around it. Villagers had been testing their daughters that way for generations, but never at this depth. Simply following the oarsman's line down to the sandbag defeated the whole point of the exercise, and the deeper a diver had to swim, the more likely she was to miss her mark. "Are you sure?" Haru-san said. "I wouldn't want you to get hurt."

"You don't think I can do it," said Kaida.

"Oh, don't get grumpy with me. No one could find it that deep. Your own mother wouldn't have found it, and she was as strong as they come."

Kaida scowled. She meant this test to be a way to bury her fear, and with it her shame at having been afraid. It was her mother's memory, the memory of her death, that had panicked Kaida in the first place. Bringing it up again wasn't helpful.

"Just let me try," she said.

She filled her lungs and blew them empty, filled and emptied again, filled once more and dived, not straight down like a cormorant but angling like a dolphin. Halfway down she spiraled and cut the reverse angle, trying to track back toward the sandbag. Even at the halfway point, she was deeper than any other girl her age could dive.

She thought about the wreck. At this depth she would have entered the yawning maw of its upper hold. Again, even the thought of being enclosed made her want to vomit. The memory of being dragged down by the breastplate gripped her like Masa's fist. The darkness of the hold was terrifying, even from the opposite end of the bay. The mere thought of what might have been in there—

There it was. The sandbag. Shioko might have called them frog-eyes or bug-eyes, but Kaida's eyes were awfully good at spotting things underwater. She reached the bag and tugged on the line, signaling Haru-san that she'd found it. Then she kicked hard off the bottom and let herself ascend, matching the speed of her bubbles.

Her fear of the dark hold had gone. But where? It vanished as soon as she saw the sandbag. As soon as something else captured her attention. Because what scared her about the hold wasn't the hold. It was what she imagined it to be.

It was just as Masa had told her: imagination could always be relied upon to conjure greater nightmares than the world itself could ever produce. That was why he and Genzai and the others struck such terror in Ama-machi. The villagers contended not with the outlanders but with demons, hungry ghosts, dark sorcery—or so the elders said. And that was why Kaida and the rest were diving on the south end of the cove: imagined fear, nothing else.

Kaida's lungs burned like huge hot coals by the time she broke the surface. She sucked in a deep, loud breath, then latched on to Haru-san's boat and let her body go limp.

"My, my!" he said. "Am I glad to be out on the water today! I can't believe I just saw what I saw."

"Believe it," Kaida said, panting.

"You must be exhausted."

Just then Miyoko appeared, just as if he'd summoned an evil spirit. Her long, pale form fluttered up from under the stern and she too took hold of the little boat's gunwale. "Oh, Kaida-chan, look at you. Are you feeling ill?"

"I'm fine," said Kaida. "Come on, let's go back to the bottom."

Miyoko gave her an evil grimace. Haru-san didn't catch it. Neither did Sen.

"Come on," Kaida said again. "We'll go down there together. Sisters."

"Sisters," Miyoko said bitterly. Usually she regarded Kaida not with hatred but with cruel curiosity, the same fascination she had with the mice she sometimes trapped in little fishnets to see how long they could hold their breath before drowning. Not this time. The hate all but seethed from her now. Haru-san and Sen, bless them, were still blind to it, dutifully hauling in their sandbags. Hand over hand, they steadily drew in the dripping lines, and Miyoko watched on with growing dread. Diving was the only competition she knew Kaida could win. Pride demanded that she compete anyway, and that pride could not abide a loss—not to bug-eyed, one-armed Kaida.

Kaida could almost hear the thoughts wriggling around in Miyoko's mind, seeking some escape, just like the mice she liked to drown. Kaida couldn't let that happen.

"Are you feeling ill, Miyoko-chan? Not too exhausted, are you?"

"I'm fine," she said, her face a squinting, wrinkled mask of hate.

All the while the wet, braided lines hummed against the gunwale of the little rowboat. At last, with a cheery "Here you go," Haru-san passed Kaida a dripping bag. He kept hold of the line while she slipped the tether around her ankle. Sen aped him, handing over Miyoko's bag, and Kaida felt a little thrill of triumph when Miyoko took it.

Miyoko gave her sweet little smile and said, "You know, Kaida-chan, why don't you go ahead and dive, since you're all ready to go, and we'll find something to do together once we're back in the village? You know, something we can do with *all* our sisters."

The veiled threat was not lost on Kaida. The wisest strategy was to deflect and retreat. Go back home, stay alert, and hope that Miyoko lost interest before she got around to mounting a full assault. Kaida's instincts pointed her in exactly that direction, but she was feeling saucy. "You're right," she said. "If we're going to find something we can all do, we can't dive here, can we? Because I'm the only one who can make it all the way down."

Miyoko fumed. Finally Haru-san and Sen took notice. Sen didn't know what to do with it, but Haru-san snapped. "Kaida, that was out of line and you know it. Miyoko's older than you. You ought to show some respect. Go ahead, Miyoko. Tether your sandbag. She opened herself to this. It's your right to show her up."

Miyoko managed a humorless smile. Kaida beamed. "First one to the bottom wins," she said. She let go of the boat and plummeted.

To Miyoko's credit, she made an honest go of it. She made it almost halfway down before she kicked free of her sandbag. Kaida looked up, letting the weight carry her down, watching Miyoko grow smaller and smaller as she kicked hard for the surface.

There would be a price for that. Kaida knew it, but somehow she feared it less than she used to. Perhaps it was because today they'd been diving where she was at her best. Or perhaps it was last night's victory at the Fin. Whatever the reason, Kaida decided she liked not being afraid.

She stayed in the water after most of the other *ama* had grown cold and tired, even though her own teeth were chattering. Her legs were so sore that she was glad they were too cold to feel much. She waited until all three of her stepsisters were sitting in Haru-san's boat, then picked a different boat to ride in on—not because she was afraid, but because she wanted to show them she'd outwitted them again. She made sure they saw her smirking at them too. That would come with a price as well, but in her newfound cockiness she chose to overlook that fact.

For reasons she couldn't fathom, a strange thought floated unbidden through her mind: if Genzai could have seen me today, he'd have been proud.

27

The sand was warm, but Kaida knew she couldn't lounge on the beach long enough to stop shivering. Her stepsisters would come for her soon. So instead of waiting for the sun to do its work, she forced herself to her feet and jogged along the strand to warm herself.

That was what she told herself anyway, though in truth she knew seeing Genzai again was inevitable. It was no girlish, swooning, romantic drivel. The village girls talked that way, sometimes even about men as old as Genzai. Kaida had no thoughts in that direction. If she were ever to love Genzai, it would only be for taking her away from Ama-machi. She did not go to him out of infatuation. She went because she could see the outlanders paddling back in from the wreck, and if they'd found what they were looking for, they would pack up their camp and disappear.

Grown men could row faster than she could run on wet sand, and though she had the shorter distance to travel, they had the surf to aid them. She drew within shouting distance as they beached the first of their rowboats. Their next three boats came in almost in the wake of the first, but Genzai had been in the lead boat and he was already marching toward Kaida, leaving ragged-edged footprints in the sand. Deep creases furrowed his brow and the corners of his mouth turned down.

"Take me with you," Kaida said. *"Please."*

"Go home, little one."

"You found what you were looking for, *neh*?"

"No."

Kaida looked past him. Two men bent down to lift something heavy out of the belly of one of the rowboats. She ran on toward Genzai, drawing close enough now that she could smell the sweat and salt water in his clothing. "You're lying," she said. "Whatever you found, I can see them taking it. Please, you have to—"

Suddenly she was flat on her back. Somehow he'd kicked her feet out from under her, though an instant before she was certain he hadn't been close enough to do that. Now he towered over her.

"I am not one you should accuse of lying," Genzai said, and Kaida found it strange to hear so much emotion in his voice. Up until now she'd only heard implacable calm. Now his words came out thick, tumescent, as if his throat wouldn't let the words pass. "You know this already. I am a man of my word."

"But I saw it," Kaida said, trying to look past him, to get just a peek at whatever his companions were taking from the rowboat.

"You see too little and assume too much." He reached down, grabbed a fistful of her hair, and twisted her head around so she could see full well what she'd been trying to catch a glimpse of a moment before.

His companions were carrying Masa's dead body.

Masa hung loosely, held up by his wrists and ankles, his mouth leaking salt water. His long black hair hung from his head like clumps of seaweed, dribbling shining ribbons of water. When they dumped him on the sand, he landed bonelessly, limp as a rolled-up fishnet.

"There," Genzai said. "Have you seen enough now?"

Kaida's eyes were locked on Masa, whose eyes stared blankly back at her from behind the demon mask—the same one his friends were finishing the night before. Thin ribbons of blood striped his face, matted his eyebrows, trickled in nigh-invisible rivulets down his cheeks. The mask had killed him. Kaida was sure of it.

It was stupid, Kaida thought, diving with a heavy iron mask on; it was as good a way as any to drown yourself. Masa would have known that. Like Kaida, he was a survivor—and unlike Kaida, he was vibrant, full of life. There was no reason for him to kill himself. So had Genzai executed his friend by drowning him? Kaida didn't think so. Genzai was distraught. No, it was the mask that killed Masa, and Genzai knew it too, but Kaida couldn't imagine how a mask by itself could do that to someone. It was as if wearing the mask had caused him to lose his mind.

Now that was a terrifying thought. Kaida wasn't afraid of hungry ghosts haunting the wrecked carrack, but the mask was something she could see, something Genzai's friends had made with their hammers and tongs. She remembered the one-eyed hunchback, the man with the wispy white beard chanting his spells, their faces sinister in the red-hot glow of the mask. What had they done? Channeled some demon into it? Was that why it was demon shaped?

It wasn't so long ago that Kaida had looked down on her fellow villagers for fearing Genzai and Masa as evil magi. Now she found herself fearing the outlanders and their witchcraft. What else could have killed Masa? And what was in that shipwreck that was worth dying for, worth risking a friend's life for, worth provoking the wrath of evil spirits?

"Throw it away," Kaida whispered, only half aware that she'd spoken aloud. "That mask. Melt it down. Let the sea turn it to rust."

"It frightens you?" Genzai said.

"Yes." She was not ashamed to admit it.

"It should. And you are a wise child if you can see how afraid you ought to be. So do not let foolishness escape your lips. That mask is too important to be destroyed. Someone will dive with it again, and may die because of it. And since I have so few of my own men to risk, perhaps the next one to dive will be you."

BOOK FIVE

HEISEI ERA, THE YEAR 22

(2010 CE)

28

Mariko ate her ramen and reflected absently on the nature of her missing finger. She was sitting on her bed, a polystyrene container of Cup Noodles in her right hand and chopsticks in her left, because her right hand couldn't manage the chopsticks anymore. Losing her right forefinger wouldn't have mattered so much if she weren't living in a chopstick culture. Forks and knives worked perfectly well in a four-fingered hand.

No matter where she lived, she would have had to retrain herself to shoot left-handed—assuming she still wanted to be a cop, of course. There were plenty of professions in which a missing finger wouldn't have caused the slightest inconvenience, but Mariko had chosen the one job in which the loss of that particular finger could actually cost her her life. Learning to shoot as a lefty hadn't been any easier than learning to eat as a lefty. She figured she should have logged enough practice by now—a few thousand rounds on the pistol range, three meals a day for a couple of months—but her marksmanship still wasn't where she wanted it to be, and eating still made her feel like a clumsy *gaijin* tourist using chopsticks for the first time.

She supposed that losing a forefinger might have been a particular hassle in the twenty-first century, but Mariko didn't participate much in the trends that would have been a pain in the ass given the state of her hand. She'd been a ham-handed typist even before her fight with Fuchida. She had no interest in Facebook and Twitter, seeing them as two more items on a to-do list already full to bursting. She didn't text more than once or twice a day, and then only to her sister, who was living proof that Mariko wouldn't have needed her forefinger for that: Saori texted at lightning speed using only her thumbs. Mariko had a harder time with old technology: keys, coins, and most importantly, her sword.

She'd skipped her kenjutsu class tonight. It was hard enough to come home and see the empty sword rack where Glorious Victory should have been; its absence would loom all the larger in the dojo, proving more and more distracting with each new drill. And her new sensei, a wizened war veteran named Hosokawa, did not admit distraction in his dojo, least of all from his sole female student. He was of the old guard, the generation that thought it unbecoming to teach swordsmanship to women. His view was hardly unique; for hundreds of years, *everyone* thought that way. But Hosokawa-sensei had earned his belt ranks under Yamada, and as Mariko had the honor of being Yamada's last student, Hosokawa had accepted her as a matter of fealty to his late sword master.

But it didn't follow that he had to be patient with her.

Following along with others wasn't Mariko's forte, and taking a formal class didn't suit her nearly as well as the private lessons she'd started with, alone with Yamada-sensei in his backyard. As that was no longer an option, Mariko trained under Hosokawa for four nights a week, and four nights a week Hosokawa-sensei berated her for her sloppy technique, her wavering focus, and above all for her improper grip.

The right forefinger was of utmost importance in swordsmanship. Highest on the hilt, it was the strongest source of control. Closest to the *tsuba*, it provided the first point of contact, facilitating a fast and fluid draw. Mariko was handicapped on both counts. Of course it was impossible to know whether Hosokawa-sensei was really so obsessed with form or whether he was merely using it as a convenient ruse to mask his overt sexism. Either way, Mariko felt the same kind of pressure at kenjutsu that she felt on the firing range, an incessant drive to outperform her male counterparts just to be recognized for having done anything right at all.

So, sitting on her bed and eating her ramen, Mariko concluded that of all the people who could ever have lost their right forefinger, the one with the most to lose was a Japanese swordswoman in the TMPD.

Because her left hand was clumsy, she spattered tiny flecks of chicken broth on the notebook she was skimming. It was Yamada's, one of the hundreds she kept in her stacked columns of banker's boxes. If there was a system there, Mariko didn't understand it yet. Some boxes were labeled, others not. Sometimes a box would contain exhaustive notes on a single subject, sometimes a chaotic cornucopia with no unifying theme. It had taken her weeks of filtering to set aside all the books that had details on the obvious starting point for her nightly conversations with her departed sensei: Glorious Victory Unsought.

Though she didn't ordinarily believe in that sort of thing, Yamada had convinced her that Master Inazuma had folded the forces of destiny into his steel, and so Mariko's first subject of study was her own sword. It was a subject that appeared in only one library on earth: the one in Mariko's bedroom, piled up in haphazardly labeled boxes. No one but Yamada believed that Inazuma ever existed, and cryptohistory had no place in the history departments of modern academia. That was why all of these notebooks remained notebooks, not published works, and it was also why Mariko accepted that Kamaguchi Hanzō's mask and her own Inazuma blade might have shared a connection that she could only describe as magical. Yamada-sensei had amassed too much evidence to dismiss the supernatural.

But though she accepted her intuition about a connection, she knew nothing about the connection itself. She had that feeling she got when she got up from whatever she was working on and went into the next room to get something she needed, only to forget what it was she was there for in the first place. Tonight was like that, but many times more frustrating, since rooting through boxes upon boxes of notes was far more difficult than remembering she'd gotten up to fetch a pen or a screwdriver or something.

By the time she finished her noodles, she still hadn't run across whatever it was that niggled at her memory. She got to her feet, her thighs and back and shoulders protesting all the way, and traded her current notebook for two new ones. Chasing Nanami through traffic this morning had left a couple of bruises she hadn't noticed at the time. Settling back down on the bed generated a new litany of complaints from her aching muscles. The thought of ibuprofen appealed to her, but inertia proved to be the more powerful motivator.

She flipped through a volume with notes on Okuma Tetsurō and his sons, Ichirō and Daigoro. All were ill fated, but none of them could hold her interest. They might have done so on another night, but at the moment Mariko was feeling tired and she knew she had many more pages to cover.

Two books later she found what she was looking for: a quick note in the margin, scribbled in a wispy hand. *First linkage—Glor Vic to mask?* On the next page, *Mask postdates Glor Vic—how long? 100 years? More?* A few pages later, *Mask-Glor Vic affinity strongest of all.* These were all marginalia, with the majority of the notes being devoted to the puzzle of how best to date Glorious Victory Unsought. He never found the answer in this notebook, but he did answer Mariko's question, one that had been nagging at her ever since that morning, when she woke to find her sword missing. Kamaguchi's mask and Glorious Victory Unsought were somehow connected.

She delved deeper into the notes, and the more she read, the weirder it got. Everyone associated with the mask seemed to share a sword fetish. Some were samurai, some were common criminals, but all were killers. Somehow the mask awakened a destructive hunger in whoever touched it, and the need was especially strong for Glorious Victory. Yamada even hypothesized that the mask was a sort of metal detector for Inazuma steel, coded specifically for Glorious Victory Unsought. Mariko couldn't even imagine how that could be—you couldn't program raw iron the way you'd program a remote control—but she had to take Yamada at his word. For one thing, he was usually right, and for another, she didn't have anything else to go on.

At least Yamada had some evidence to work from. A few salvaged pages from a centuries-old diary suggested that the affinity between the mask and the sword was dependent on distance. On its own, the mask inspired an unnameable yearning, like a caged animal's need to pace, always seeking an exit that wasn't there. But when Glorious Victory was nearby, that yearning magnified into a craving as powerful sexual lust. If the mask could see the sword, it had to have it.

Whatever *that* means, Mariko thought. She wished the diary's author had been a detective; similes of caged animals didn't show up in Mariko's case log.

Things got even more bizarre when Yamada started waxing poetical himself. On one page, she read, *Wind seeks mask? Why?* At the top of the next page, *Wind wants Glor Vic, therefore needs mask?* It made no sense. Figuratively speaking, Mariko could get her head around a winter wind seeking out the gaps in her clothing, but even at her most abstract she couldn't see how wind could be said to *want* anything at all.

His marginal notes developed into paragraphs in the following pages, but the more he developed his thoughts, the more cryptic they became. He developed a bizarre metaphor, likening wind to a *shinobi*, a ninja. No riddles there—wind was invisible—but then his invisible air currents took on human desires. As if wanting and seeking weren't bad enough, the wind started planning, designing, orchestrating. Weather just didn't *do* that.

The only deduction she could draw for certain was that Yamada-sensei knew a lot more about the mask than he bothered to write down. Most of his notes read like someone else's grocery shopping list. Items like "lotion" or "food for Buster" might be on the list, but what kind of lotion? Sunblock? Moisturizer? A medicinal cream? And what was Buster? He could be a dog or a parakeet. There was no way to tell. Mariko could read between the lines all she liked and she'd never figure out everything her sensei knew about the mask.

A couple of notebooks and a couple of hours later, she hadn't clarified much about the mask or the wind, but what little she'd managed to gather had seriously creeped her out. Somewhere along the line, the mask was damaged. Someone had scarred it, and somehow that deformed its enchantment too. Its affinity—or curse, or fetish, or whatever you called it—expanded from swords to all weapons. Yamada even hypothesized about how it might mutate over time, creating a lust for muskets and matchlocks as those came of age, and later semiautomatic pistols, maybe even machine guns. In a modern theater of war, it might have been IEDs. The mask did not discriminate.

Mariko had encountered an artifact like this before: Beautiful Singer, lightest and fastest of all the Inazuma blades. It too infected the wielder's mind, and Mariko knew all too well how deadly that obsession could be. She'd flatlined on Beautiful Singer's edge, the very last in a series of bloody murders stretching back almost a thousand years. Unlike a sword, a mask was benign, but perhaps that was what made it so dangerous: it seemed harmless.

If so, then the Bulldog showed remarkable foresight in separating himself from it. That, or else he shared the sixth sense of the alpha male for any threats to his dominance. Kamaguchi was violent, but only on his terms. If simply holding the mask was enough to awaken a deep-seated need for destruction, then Kamaguchi was right to keep it far away, on a high shelf where no one else would ever have reason to touch it. He didn't even have to know why he did it; alpha male instinct would be enough.

Mariko found the mere thought of it chilling. She wanted to think that the whole story was mere superstition, that while medieval people might have believed in such things, in her world inanimate objects didn't have such power. Yet as soon as the thought struck her, she knew she was wrong. What, other than "obsessive-compulsive," was the right term to describe the average schoolboy's relationship to his video games? Mariko thought of her sister Saori and the four or five thousand texts she sent every month. She thought of her own habits too: feigning kenjutsu strikes while waiting in elevators, oiling her bicycle chain before a ride though she knew full well she'd tuned up the whole bike the day before. How many times had she practiced drawing, aiming, and firing with her left hand? And she'd done the same with her right for years, long before Fuchida had maimed her finger. Was her obsession with marksmanship any less morbid than the hunger to destroy lurking within Yamada's mask?

It *was* different. It had to be, or else Yamada would never have made a note of it. He knew obsession all too well. A man did not collect thirty degrees of black belt without admitting obsession into his life. No, this mask was something unusual, something dangerous, and knowing that made Mariko wish she had something more to go on, some way to track the thing down, some means of predicting the bearer's intentions. But none of the notebooks provided clues.

She looked at the clock. Twelve-oh-eight. She had to work in the morning.

And yet there were two faces she couldn't get out of her head. One was the Bulldog's demon mask, stolen so brazenly from the middle of an active crime scene. The other belonged to that lunatic Akahata, his eyes blazing like twin suns in his bruised and battered face, his broken lips incessantly chanting their mantra. Akahata wasn't the mask thief. He'd been in critical care at the time of the robbery. Mariko remembered the image of the thief, dressed head to toe in SWAT armor, the better to walk through a swarm of cops unnoticed. The feed from the security camera was fairly low fidelity, but now, seeing Yamada-sensei's notes on the mask, Mariko remembered the thief as clearly as if she'd been standing in the room with him.

"Just one more book," she said aloud, to Yamada-sensei as much as to herself. Mariko had never been much of a scholar, and so reading a historian's notes was usually the sort of thing that would put her to sleep, not keep her up. In college she'd majored in journalism, which she defended to this day as the only writing-intensive major that actually left a graduate with legitimate job prospects in her field. She'd always thought of all that "love of learning for its own sake" crap as the lullaby that literature and philosophy majors used to sing themselves to sleep after a tough day of waiting tables. But now she was beginning to understand why Yamada had done what he'd done with his life, pursuing a master's degree, then a PhD, then tenure, then one book project after another until he could hardly see the pen in his hand. Some of this stuff was honestly interesting in its own right—maybe not worth a college degree, but well worth the lost sleep she was inviting by telling herself "just one more."

In fact it was three notebooks later that she struck gold. Yamada had ventured to guess that wind and divine wind might be the same thing. Her first thought was that obviously this couldn't be a reference to the Divine Wind she was investigating, the cult of Akahata and Jōko Daishi. Yamada was a historian: in his context, kamikaze—"divine wind"—was either the suicide pilots of World War Two or their namesake, the great typhoons that swamped the fleets of Kublai Khan, drowned his armies, and saved Japan from being just another province of the Mongol Empire. And since he'd already associated the mask with wind, the two typhoons were a sure bet.

But then came the mother lode. It was a tangential comment about the wind creating the mask, and it sent Mariko shuffling through all the notebooks that now lay scattered like playing cards on her bed. She rubbed her eyes, cursed the clock, and at last she found the book with the weird references to wind. If she reread them to say not "wind" but "the Wind," the most bewildering passages suddenly became clear. The Wind wanted the mask. The Wind sought it out. It all made sense.

And then she reread Yamada's question: was the Wind the same thing as the Divine Wind? If so, then while this Jōko Daishi character was new to the scene, his Divine Wind cult was far older than Mariko could have believed. Whoever Yamada's Wind were, they dated at least as far back as the 1400s, and prior to that it was a stretch to say that Japan was even Japan. More like a rabble of warlords and petty tyrants trying to snap up as much territory as possible. Only the Three Unifiers had brought all of those daimyo to heel and forged a single empire. Mariko had not forgotten the demon mask's connection to

Toyotomi Hideyoshi, the second of the Three Unifiers, though embarrassingly she could not remember when Hideyoshi was alive. Yamadasensei would have known. Mariko ballparked it somewhere around the year 1600. If she was right, then in effect the Wind was older than Japan itself.

And if the Wind and the Divine Wind were the same organization, then two things became immediately clear. First, Yamada's *shinobi* metaphor wasn't a metaphor: the Wind was a ninja clan. Second, Kamaguchi Hanzō had it wrong from the beginning. Jōko Daishi didn't name his cult after the suicidal dive-bombers of World War Two; he was the latest leader of a cult named for the typhoons that saved Japan. These days, calling your cult the Divine Wind was *gokudō*, extreme, badass, like the dive-bombers. But if you went back far enough, calling yourself Divine Wind meant you were the saviors of the country.

Was that what all the "liberating souls" business was about? Again Mariko's thoughts turned to Akahata's bashed-in face and the mantra on his lips. Hamaya, his lawyer, explaining that his client was praying for Jōko Daishi to liberate everyone. There was something sinister there. Mariko was sure of it; "Great Teacher of the Purging Fire" didn't have a nice ring to it. Did these Divine Wind cultists think of themselves as messiahs? If so, they were dangerous. And brazen too. Theft of police evidence carried a much heavier sentence than a simple burglary, but it took a whole new kind of crazy to take it from the heart of an active crime scene. That was the kind of crazy that thought nothing of swindling a powerful yakuza clan on a drug deal. It was also—and Mariko was afraid even to formulate the thought—the kind of crazy that motivated people to wear suicide vests or fill subway cars with sarin gas.

Thus far, Mariko had no evidence that the Divine Wind was a terrorist organization. She certainly couldn't prove the cult was a blood relative of a centuries-old criminal syndicate. She had only a gut feeling that Akahata was unstable and violent, and that anyone who sent a lawyer to defend a person like that was probably even more dangerous.

Han would have pushed for the simplest explanation. Some dope rings stole cars to make extra cash; this cult hocked stolen antiques instead. But instinct told Mariko something else. Stealing the mask suggested a fixation with demons. That fixation, coupled with hallucinogens and religious fanaticism, suggested devil worship—or if not devil worship, then at least a cult of personality centered on whoever was wearing the mask. Jōko Daishi.

Mariko closed her notebooks. Sooner or later she had to sleep. And she had to face it: she wasn't going to figure out anything about Jōko Daishi tonight. Yamada made no mention of him. If the Wind and the Divine Wind were the same group, and if the Wind was originally a ninja clan, then perhaps the Divine Wind had retained some of the ancient secrets—like how to break into a seventeenth-story apartment with all the doors and windows locked from the inside. That squared nicely with her intuition that it was Jōko Daishi who stole Glorious Victory Unsought. But intuition wasn't evidence, and notes on medieval ninja clans wouldn't help her solve yesterday's crimes.

The truth was that she had very little to go on. She didn't have Jōko Daishi's real name, or a description, or past whereabouts—not a damn thing, really. Her only good leads were Akahata and Hamaya, if only it had been legal to follow up on them. But she'd done the right thing: she hadn't tailed them when they'd left the hospital. She'd observed their constitutional rights, and now she cursed herself for having done it. She wanted to know who these people were, who they were pushing their drugs on, what sermons they were delivering to the hallucinating masses, what role the demon mask had to play in any of it.

In short, she wanted to know what kind of storm was coming and when it would strike.

29

Lieutenant Sakakibara liked to hold his morning briefings early, a proclivity that made the top brass admire his diligence and made Mariko wish he'd fall over dead. Ever since she'd made Narcotics, she'd been cutting her hair shorter so it would look less rumpled when she dragged her ass in to post. Her attitude toward makeup was indifferent at best—she'd stopped making a fuss over it in high school, specifically to conserve precious minutes of sleep—and under Sakakibara's command she'd taken to forgoing even a quick dab of mascara.

Orange light streamed in through the briefing room's tall windows, cut into slices by Venetian blinds. One of those slices slashed right across Mariko's face, leaving her half-blind and no doubt looking even more tired than she felt. She knew it was the wrong play, knew she was the newest member of Sakakibara's team, knew she was supposed to make every impression a good one, but at seven o'clock in the damn morning it was hard to care about how she looked. She was well aware of the gossip going around that she was a lesbian, but it was easier to put up with it than to lose ten minutes of sleep every morning to "put her face on."

That was a strange phrase, one she'd learned as a schoolgirl in the States. There was no equivalent slang in Japanese, though there were plenty of sayings about losing face and saving face. Ironically enough, not putting her face on was the very thing that could cause her to lose face. But this morning there was a more pressing concern when it came to losing face: she'd made no progress on the Jōko Daishi case. Her late night reading had been interesting, to be sure, but it hadn't actually given her any leads. Jōko Daishi was an enigma, his lieutenant Akahata was off the leash, and their hexamine was nowhere to be found.

Sakakibara walked into the room, his characteristic long strides clopping like horse's hooves on the linoleum tile. Everyone snapped to attention, including Mariko, who had to do a little more snapping than average, since she'd been slouching in her chair, ready to nod off. "At ease," Sakakibara said, and Mariko redeposited herself in her seat in the back row.

Her LT took his customary place behind his lectern, rapped a couple of manila folders on it to straighten their contents, and said, "All right, people, let's get down to—what the hell, Frodo? Did someone exhume you this morning?"

"Late night, sir."

"Where's your partner?"

"Maybe in the grave next to mine, sir. Haven't seen him yet today."

Sakakibara ran his fingers through his stiff, wire-brush hair. "Oh, I can't wait for this status report. What the hell, why don't we start with you, and we'll just get the embarrassment over with?"

Mariko swallowed. "Not much to report, sir—"

"Except that our investigation is rolling right along," said Han. He pushed through the door in midbow and made repeated apologetic bows on his way to the seat next to Mariko's. Walking while bowing while sitting was a tricky bit of choreography, and it made him look a little like a limping chicken.

"Well, if it isn't the late Detective Han. Sit your ass down."

Han immediately abandoned his course toward Mariko and zipped into the nearest empty seat. "Sorry, sir."

"Well? Status report. Out with it."

Han nodded, his floppy hair catching a little luff with each rise and fall. "Followed up on that supplier from that raid the other night.

Remember him? Akahata? He's the one the Kamaguchi boys tuned up. Easy to see why. Dude's as crazy as they come, wrapped up in some weird-ass cult. So I did some background research on him. He's a sanitation worker for JR, which—well, correct me if I'm wrong, Mariko—I'm thinking probably jibes pretty well with the whack-job cultist angle. Menial position, probably wants to feel like part of something larger than himself, wouldn't even have to be a hundred percent sane to hold down the job, *neh*?"

He looked across the room at Mariko, who nodded and said, "Agreed." She didn't like Han's tone. He was going somewhere with this, and Mariko had a sneaking suspicion where.

"Anyway," Han said, "he lawyered up yesterday—or the cult sent its lawyer, anyway—and we thought he was out of pocket for good. But last night I caught a lucky break: one of my CIs fingered the guy. He's holed up in a place in Kamakura, and right now he's got no idea that we're on him."

Mariko deliberately averted her gaze, looking at the floor lest she accidentally make eye contact with her lieutenant or her partner. Sakakibara would see guilt in her face, and Han would see a bitterness that would rapidly reach a boil. She knew exactly why Han "caught a lucky break." He'd broken the law. He must have tailed Akahata and his lawyer, Hamaya Jirō, from the hospital, even though Hamaya had made it perfectly clear that doing so was illegal. Akahata wasn't officially a suspect. His only direct connection to a crime at this point was as the victim of a host of assault and battery charges. Mariko had considered tailing him anyway, because just like Han, she'd known Akahata was their best lead, and letting him disappear would douse what glimmers of hope they had in their investigation. But unlike Han, Mariko *hadn't* followed him. Now it made her angry just to be in the same room with him.

"Hell of a catch," said Sakakibara, his tone suspicious. Mariko didn't know what to hope for. Did the LT know the same background information Mariko knew? If so, the whole unit was about to see Sakakibara slam Han on his back, grab him by the throat, and show him who was leading the pack around here and whose rules they were going to follow. Sakakibara might have been a prick, but he was good police, and he hated seeing perps slip away because one of his officers took liberties with search and seizure.

But if that happened, questions would come Mariko's way. She'd have no choice but to answer them honestly, and that would sink Han's career. Up until ten seconds ago, Mariko had trusted Han implicitly, unwaveringly. He didn't deserve a torpedo from his own partner.

"You got anything on this guy that'll stick?" said Sakakibara. Mariko tried to read his tone and couldn't. Was it a commanding officer's legitimate question at a morning roll call or was he trying to trick Han into setting himself up for the kill? How much did Sakakibara know about their investigation?

"Still working on that, sir," said Han. "Obviously we've got him at the packing company, and *somebody* over there is guilty of felony possession. All that speed has to belong to someone."

"Akahata?"

"Right now everything we've got on him is circumstantial, but we think we'll find more. Oshiro figures we can connect him to a string of hexamine buys. We're thinking MDA."

That got an approving nod from the LT. "Nice. Both of you, well done. Keep me posted."

And then the meeting went on. Kamaguchi Hanzō's packing company was front and center, and most of the updates had to do with the raid and its various follow-up investigations. Mariko listened to none of them. She kept her gaze studiously on the windows, preferring the sun's glare to glaring at her partner.

But she could only avoid him for so long. Soon enough the meeting adjourned, the troops filed out, and Mariko was left alone in the room with Han. "So," he said, "you want to get a donut or a coffee or something? I didn't eat breakfast."

"Eat shit," she said.

"Huh?"

"You tailed him? What's wrong with you?"

Han looked hurt. "Hey, it's not like that."

"You can't expect me to believe this. You *just so happened* to hear from a CI who *just so happened* to, what, park his car across the street from Akahata?"

Han shrugged and smiled. "Actually, that's pretty close to it."

"And then for no particular reason your CI calls and says, 'Hey, is this guy a person of interest for you, by any chance?' Because I'm sure that happens all the time, Han. Perps who slip through the system suddenly get ID'ed even when no evidence points us back in their direction."

Now Han looked sincerely wounded, and embarrassed besides. "Mariko, will you keep it down? Let me explain—"

Mariko pushed him away. "I trusted you."

"And you're right to. I swear to you, Mariko, I didn't tail him."

It came as a splash of cold water in the face of her burning resentment. He was telling the truth. Mariko prided herself on knowing when people were lying, and Han wasn't. That fact wasn't enough to calm her, but it was enough to make her sit back down. "You've got ten seconds. Start talking."

Han sighed, relieved. "What's the last thing I told you before I walked out of Akahata's hospital room?"

"I think you told the lawyer to go fuck himself."

"Okay, before that."

"I don't know. Something about how Hamaya was aiding and abetting a criminal and you weren't going to stand for it."

"Right."

"So you tailed him? Knowing we didn't have probable cause? Knowing it was illegal?"

Han sighed again. "For *us*. It's illegal for *us* to follow him. But not for one of my CIs. And I've got loads of them. Plenty of them want me to owe them a favor. So I made a couple of calls and I watched Hamaya and his client fly off into the wind. Just like you did. Only I got a phone call a few hours later."

"Han—"

"What? What laws did I break? What regs? An ordinary citizen followed another one. That's not illegal. Hell, if I'd hired a private eye, it would have been a cliché."

Mariko sank back into her chair, heavy with frustration and fatigue. She pressed her palms to her eyes and let her head sag until it hit the top of the backrest. "Do you really want to try explaining the difference between violating civil rights and violating civil rights by proxy?"

"If it helps, I told my guy to stay well away. Keys in the ignition, doors locked, ready to drive off if anything looked fishy. All I wanted was eyes on the target."

"I don't know, Han."

"Think of it like hiring a private investigator. I just did it cheaper than that. And a little faster. And if it was a PI, I wouldn't have had to promise to look the other way on a possession charge or two."

Mariko burst out of her chair, ready to deck him. "Damn it, Han—"

"Joking! Just joking!" Han hopped back and landed in a wrestler's crouch, hands up high to defend against a sudden swing. "Sorry. Maybe not the best comic timing there."

Mariko gave serious thought to kicking him in the crotch. Then she thought better of it. It wouldn't hurt enough. She pulled the stun gun off her belt. "You know, I'm pretty sure I could neuter you with this thing."

Han took an extra step back. "Sorry. Very sorry. I swear." He relaxed his defensive posture, pulled one of the chairs around, and sat opposite Mariko. "So, you know, seriously, are we cool?"

"Han, I don't know. I don't like you cutting it so close to the edge."

"This is narcotics, not beat cop stuff. We work with dirty people. Sometimes we need them to dime each other out, and we have to get out of their way and let them do it."

"And sometimes we need to put them on their way to doing it?"

"Now and then, yeah, we do. Mariko, I know where the lines are.

I might get close to them sometimes, but I promise you, I'm never going to cross them. Not while we're partners. Okay?"

Mariko looked at the floor and took a moment to think. Then, with a weary sigh, she looked back at Han. "Fine. But the coffee and donuts are on you."

"Extra coffee in your case. You look like you could use it."

30

ariko insisted on doing the driving, needing to feel at least
that much control over how things were going. She had to
admit that if Han hadn't strayed so close to the edge, they'd
have no leads at all. Kamaguchi Hanzō had already given her everything he knew. National Health Insurance had an address on Akahata,
but until Mariko could charge him with something, there was nothing
she could do with it. The same went for the address and phone number
on Hamaya Jirō's business card: there would be no wiretaps and no
stakeouts without probable cause. If it weren't for Han's CI, they'd
have nothing.

"Tell me again about this CI of yours?"

"Name's Shino," Han said around a mouthful of danish. "Weird
kid. Totally obsessed with basketball."

"What's weird about that?"

"He's not even your height. The kid couldn't palm this coffee cup.
But man, he sure likes wearing those jerseys. When you meet him, don't
call him Shino. Call him Shaq. Or LeBron. He'll love you for that."

Mariko laughed and shook her head. Her world was full of nicknames. Kamaguchi Hanzō was the Bulldog. Shino was LeBron. Han's
real name wasn't even Han. It was Watanabe, but four or five years ago
Sakakibara saw his floppy hair and long sideburns and called him Han
Solo, and everyone had called him Han ever since. Mariko assumed
she'd be wearing the Frodo badge for at least that long.

She found it strange how important naming a thing could be. It was illegal for her to keep tabs on the house Shino was staking out for them, but she was well within her rights to check up on a CI and make sure he was okay. Han seemed to look at his decision to deploy Shino the same way: perfectly fine if you called it this, against regulations if you called it that, clearly illegal if you called it some other thing.

She didn't like the thought of Shino sitting out there exposed, so she decided to shave some time off their drive by running code. There was no getting to him quickly; as ever, half of the drivers never noticed the lights and siren, and even if they had, the text from Shino said he was all the way out in Kamakura.

"Call him," Mariko said. "Make sure he's all right."

"He said he'd call if—"

Mariko shot him a look that other women might have reserved for a cheating husband who asked for a lift to his floozy's apartment.

"Right," he said. "I'll just go ahead and make that call, then."

"Good idea."

Shino didn't respond to calls or texts. Mariko had half a mind to ask Kamakura PD to send a squad up to check on him, but by the time she got patched through to them and explained her request, she'd almost be at her exit, and from there she'd probably reach her destination before they did. She kept the lights running hot all the way there.

The *there* wasn't what she was expecting. They reached a ritzy neighborhood on a quiet street running the length of a ridge that overlooked Kamakura. In the gaps between houses Mariko could see the ocean, glinting in the morning sun. Some of these backyards would give an overlook on the Great Buddha. The bare fact that they *had* backyards meant that these people made more money than Mariko would ever see in her lifetime. The hot tubs in this neighborhood were bigger than her kitchen.

"Are you sure this is the place?" she said.

"You want see the same text I showed you a minute ago? He's got to be right around—oh, got him. The shitbox."

Mariko looked where Han was pointing, and sure enough, there was a beat-to-hell Toyota Cressida parked along the curb. There was a maxim in police work: shitheads drive shithead cars. Given the choice of two vehicles that were having trouble staying between the lines, you pulled over the beater. That was where a highway patrolman was going to make his lucky drug bust, and that was where a narc was going to put his GPS tracker.

"Hey, LeBron," Han said, getting out of the squad to approach the vehicle, "you were supposed to stay awake, buddy."

Mariko pulled up on the opposite side of the Cressida. It was empty. "Han, what the hell?"

"I don't know. Maybe . . . maybe he got out to take a piss or something."

"Where? Look around you." It was a sunny morning on a beautiful lane bordered by flower gardens, manicured lawns, and trees trimmed by professional gardeners. There was no sign of a public restroom, a Porta Potty, or Han's CI.

"You said he'd be okay. You said you told him to stay away from danger."

"I *did*. Come on, help me look for him."

Canvassing the area houses went quickly. Han rang the doorbells while Mariko circumnavigated the premises, checking windows. It was on the tenth house that she found something suspicious. "Han, did you say this kid likes basketball?"

"Yeah."

"Well, there's a guy in this basement wearing a Lakers jersey."

Mariko knocked on the back door, waited all of two seconds, then kicked it in. With Han she cleared the place room by room until they found the way downstairs. The guy in the yellow jersey lay facedown at the foot of the stairs. His skin was bright red, almost as if he'd been sunburned. He was small, just as Han had described Shino, and he wasn't moving.

Something about the redness of his skin stirred deep in Mariko's memory, but she didn't have time to go fishing for it. She waited only long enough for Han to check Shino's pulse. "Dead," Han said, and he and Mariko moved swiftly through the house, clearing it room by room. If the kid's killer was still on the premises, their first duty was to find him.

The house was weird as hell. Every room said *cult*, though not a single aspect of it matched what Mariko imagined they'd be getting into. A cult that pushed ice on its members to "liberate" them conjured images of a meth den in her mind, but this was no sunless, stinking fleapit. If anything, it was *too* clean, not like a hastily wiped-down crime scene but like an iPod fresh out of the box. Not a speck of dust to be found. OCD clean. Cult clean.

The basement was huge, a wide, open space of white walls and soft white light. Round cushions stacked in the corner were probably for meditation. Judging by the stack and the floor space, thirty people could sit in *seiza* down here. Posters adorned the walls: charts of what looked like yoga poses, an arcane calendar based on planetary cycles, paintings of demons and prints of demon statues. Han took pictures of everything with his phone.

The rooms on the ground floor looked like they belonged to another building entirely. Cute, quaint, lots of floral prints; Mariko's grandmother could have decorated them. They had a model home sort of feel, more to be seen than to be lived in. And the second floor felt completely different again, as if the whole house were schizophrenic— or, more likely, as if the house was a cult headquarters whose owners intended it to seem perfectly normal to anyone peering in through a window. The master bedroom was clearly well used, designed to serve as part-time opium den, part-time sex dungeon. The paraphernalia amassed there suggested orgy-level participation in both activities. The doors fit so well to their frames that Mariko could feel the air pressure shift when Han opened the door to the master bathroom. The room was sealed as if to remain airtight, or perhaps to contain some other gas used in the orgies.

Another bedroom housed a blown-up photo of a good-looking, middle-aged man with long, windblown hair, standing on a seaside cliff and performing yoga or tai chi or something in between. The photo was framed, and below it was an altar with candles surrounding a wide, shallow bowl full of odds and ends: coins, marbles, eights of hearts from a bunch of different decks of cards, a folded pocket schedule of the Yomiuri Giants season, car keys stripped from their key rings. Of particular interest to the narc's eye were the ten or twelve little vials of heroin.

"Jōko Daishi?" said Mariko, nodding at the poster above the bowl.

"Gotta be," said Han. "Kind of looks like John Lennon, *neh*? Except the beard's more like Jerry Garcia."

"Or that Aum Shinrikyō guy," Mariko said. "Remember him?"

"Who could forget?"

Mariko could almost see the shivers running down Han's spine. She'd been all of twelve years old when the Aum Shinrikyō cult released sarin gas in a Tokyo subway. It made the news even in Teutopolis, Illinois, where she'd been in junior high at the time. Mariko could remember the pictures on TV of the cult leader, Asahara Shōkō, with his thick black hair and big, shaggy beard. This Jōko Daishi shared the beard but not the caveman chic; his hair was straight and long, almost feminine, much more in keeping with the obsessive-compulsive cleanliness of his headquarters. Mariko might even have said he was handsome but for the fact that she could imagine him standing over her bed in the middle of the night. Was he the one who stole her sword, or had it been one of his devotees? Either way, this was the man who shattered any sense of privacy in her life.

Mariko took the little folded baseball schedule from the altar, careful to handle it only by the edges, where she couldn't leave a print. The squat, orange, rabbitlike mascot of the Yomiuri Giants smiled up at her from the front cover. She found its grossly oversized eyes creepy instead of cute. Jōko Daishi's eyes blazed with the same kind of inhuman intensity.

She found it strange that it should be the baseball schedule, not the heroin, that captivated her attention so fully that she felt the need to pick it up. Against her better judgment she opened it, pinching only the tips of the corners, hoping now that she wouldn't smear any useful prints. As the little calendar unfolded, she found someone had written a prayer on it with a fat-tipped Sharpie. She couldn't make out much of it—on paper this small the writing was tightly cramped—but she did notice today's date was circled in red. A home game. She wondered what the significance of that might be.

Squinting at the prayer again, she could only identify the characters *jō* and *ko*, Purging Fire. She let the calendar fold itself accordion-style back into its original shape, turning her attention instead to the photo of Jōko Daishi. Leaning in to get a closer look, she noticed the photo frame concealed a wall panel behind it. It didn't open readily, so she started fiddling with it. "Han, we need to talk."

"I know," he said. "I fucked up. Shino's dead and it's my fault." His voice was laden with remorse. "Poor son of a bitch never had a chance. Parking an old beat-to-hell Cressida in this neighborhood; they must have seen him the instant he got here."

"You've got it wrong. It's not your fault he's dead. So far we've only got these guys on theft and felony possession. You didn't know they were going to step it up to homicide."

"Yeah, but I'm the one who sent him up here."

Mariko nodded. "And there's going to be a reckoning for that. It wasn't right, Han, and you should have told me what you were doing before you did it."

She could hear him deflating. "I didn't want to get you involved. This is on me, all right? I'm not going to ask you to back me up on this."

"What do you want, a medal? You broke the rules, Han. You used a proxy to do what you knew we couldn't legally do ourselves. And you think you need to *ask* me not to back you up? You think you were *protecting* me by hiding this crap?"

"Mariko, I'm sorry—"

" 'Sorry' isn't going to cut it. We're partners, Han, and besides that, I'm the ranking officer on this detail. And you say, 'I didn't want to get you involved'? I *am* involved, Han. My job is to be involved. And now you've put my job at risk. Do you have any idea how hard I worked to get here?"

"Mariko, you know I do."

"Then you know how pissed off I am. When we get back to post our whole world is going to turn to shit, and I don't want—uh-oh." The panel behind the photograph popped open with a little click. Mariko didn't like what she saw behind it.

Morose as he was, chastened as he was, Han shifted right back into high gear the instant he heard Mariko's tone. "What have you got?"

"I think I know what killed Shino," she said, "and I think we're going to need a hazmat team right away."

31

ollow-up calls to Hazmat and Lieutenant Sakakibara confirmed they were both due to arrive on scene within minutes of each other. Mariko was well aware that she and Han could have used the interim to get their stories straight about Shino. She knew of cops on the force that would have done exactly that. But whatever his faults, Han had honor enough not to suggest it. The two of them didn't even speak until they could hear the sirens coming.

"Before he gets here," Han said, "can I just tell you one thing?"

"One thing," Mariko said. Her anger was burning at a low simmer. She hoped he had sense enough not to spark off another flare-up.

"I'm really sorry for the 'it's all my fault' and 'I assume full responsibility' shit. I know it was my responsibility to stay within the lines. I never should have suggested otherwise. And you were right: it was Jōko Daishi's people who killed Shino. Claiming responsibility for that is just playing the martyr. I'm sorry for that."

Mariko nodded. After a long, pregnant pause, she said, "That's the tone you want to take with the LT. What you did, you need to own it. Completely. You understand me?"

"Yes, ma'am."

"All right." Again she paused, trying to sort out her emotions. "I'm still pissed at you. Got it? But all the same, I really do hope they don't hang you for this."

Whatever else they might have said would have to wait until later, for the parade of emergency vehicles had arrived. The hazmat team started suiting up and Mariko and Han tracked down Sakakibara and gave him a quick report, starting from the confrontation with Akahata and his lawyer in the hospital. To his credit, Han left out none of the details. Sakakibara sat stone-faced, leaning against the hood of his squad car and taking it all in.

When Han and Mariko were finished, he said, "Explain the cyanide part to me again, Frodo."

"They've got a giant photo of Jōko Daishi on the wall upstairs," Mariko said, "concealing a panel in the wall. Open that panel and you've got two big plastic jugs like the ones you'd find in an office watercooler, screwed together like an hourglass and connected by a valve. The top jug is full of pellets of sodium cyanide."

"Which for some inexplicable reason you recognize on sight?"

"No, sir. Actually, they were kind enough to label it. I guess when you're in the habit of stocking a bunch of dangerous chemicals, you want to keep them straight."

"Right," Sakakibara said. "And this Shino kid, they killed him with the cyanide?"

"Yes, sir. Hard to tell whether they force-fed him or laced it into something else. Not that it matters much."

"Frodo, let me ask you something. Are you trying to make me look bad?"

"Sir?"

"I've trained a hell of a lot of narcs in my day, and not one of them could walk up to a body and identify it on sight as a cyanide killing. Are you trying to show me up?"

"No, sir."

"Why the hell do you even know what death by cyanide looks like?"

Mariko shrugged. "My dad was in plastics manufacturing. Cyanide poisoning is a serious risk in that line of work."

"Which you know because . . . ?"

"He died when I was in college. We didn't know why right away, so I did lots of research on the kinds of things that could kill you at his factory. It wasn't cyanide that got him, but I remember the bit about the red skin. Something about too much oxygen in the blood."

Sakakibara shook his head. "You must be hell to play in Trivial Pursuit. Now do me a favor and apply that weird brain of yours to this case. What can you tell me about this cult?"

"Not as much as I'd like. We know what their leader looks like but not his real name. We know the names of two associates but not where they are. We know they can cook meth, we're assuming they can cook MDA, and we know they've got no troubles acquiring all kinds of dangerous chemicals."

"All right. What do we know about the house?"

"It's rigged to blow," said Han. When he saw a hazmat guy whip his head around, he quickly added, "You know, so to speak. Jug number one is sodium cyanide, *neh*? Jug number two is full of hydrochloric acid. You open the valve connecting them with a little knob in the cult leader's Throne Room of Carnal Pleasures."

"Excuse me?"

"Bedroom, sir. Oshiro's the one who figured it out. Open the valve, let the acid mix with the cyanide, and you get a big cloud of hydrogen cyanide gas."

"Cute." Sakakibara switched his focus to Mariko. "You remembered all of this from your college chemistry notes, I assume?"

"Google, actually. Looked it up on Han's phone while you were en route."

"Aha." Sakakibara scratched the back of his head, making his hair shift on his head as a single unit, as if it were a helmet. "So you're thinking what? Crazy-ass cult leader rigs his headquarters so he can stage a mass suicide if a police raid goes Waco?"

"That's about the size of it, sir," said Mariko.

"How does that explain the dead kid?"

"Obviously they didn't kill him with the gas," Han said, "since we found him in the basement."

"Which your dumb ass sent him to," said Sakakibara.

"Yes, sir." Han tried to stay professional, not morose. "The bedroom's hermetically sealed. The basement isn't. We're guessing only a special chosen few get to die with Jōko Daishi. Everyone else probably commits suicide downstairs."

Sakakibara frowned. "So what, they drag this poor kid into the house and cram a fistful of cyanide down his throat?"

"Probably not," Mariko said. "We think they've got another supply, probably something portable."

Her LT's scowl deepened, forming two deep furrows between his thick black eyebrows. "How's that?"

"Our suspect, the one who calls himself Jōko Daishi, he sees himself in the business of liberating souls. When we first got onto the hexamine, we were thinking MDA, so 'liberating' means getting people high—bringing them into a hallucinatory state, *neh*? But lacing the MDA with cyanide, that's a different story. In that story, 'liberating' means inducing hallucinations and then inducing heart failure."

Sakakibara crossed his long arms in front of his chest and looked at the house. "You find any evidence that they're cooking in there?"

"No, sir," said Han. "The house seems to be a base of operations, kind of spiritual headquarters. We're thinking they must have some other place to cook their meth and MDA."

"And lace it with cyanide."

"Yes, sir."

Sakakibara's frown returned. "So somewhere out there, there's a band of nut jobs with another barrel of cyanide."

Mariko nodded. "We think so, sir."

"And they're not a hey-look-at-the-pretty-lights kind of cult, are they?"

"More like a hey-let's-all-drink-the-Kool-Aid kind of cult, sir."

"Then you two have your work cut out for you," said Sakakibara. "Don't waste your time talking to me; get your asses moving."

Mariko blinked and looked at him. "I'm not sure we can, sir."

Sakakibara squinted at her. "Excuse me?"

"Sir," she said, "we're onto this house because of the Shino tip, and that violated search and seizure. Because of the house we're onto the cyanide, but if we follow that lead, we're still in violation. Anything we find is inadmissible. Isn't it?"

"Yeah," said Han, shamefaced, "and I was kind of thinking you were going to suspend me."

Sakakibara growled, almost like a bear. "Suspend you? I ought to burn you at the stake." He gazed pensively at the ground and ran his fingers through his wire-stiff hair. After a long, tense, uncomfortable silence he said, "Do we know for a fact that your guy Shino didn't walk into this house looking to score?"

"Sir?" Han said.

"He's a junkie, right? That's how you know him? That's why he was useful as a CI?"

"Yes, sir."

"So? Can you say for a fact that he didn't get bored, figure out your suspects were dealing, and walk into that house looking to score?"

"Well, no, not if you put it that way."

"Then I don't have to suspend you. *Yet.*" Sakakibara turned to Mariko. "If you haven't noticed, Sergeant, there's a major case here for you to solve. We've got a bunch of crackpots in this city who want to commit mass murder. So go do your job and *catch them*. We'll sort out the due process questions after you're done. Frankly, I don't give a shit if we don't get a single conviction, so long as we prevent a string of homicides. And you," he said, rounding on Han, "I'll wait until after you've closed this case before I skin you alive."

BOOK SIX

AZUCHI-MOMOYAMA PERIOD, THE YEAR 21

(1588 CE)

32

Daigoro swung his *bokken* and missed. His target was too damned fast.

"Try again," said a smiling Tomo, and Daigoro tightened his grip on the haft. Tomo threw the next ball. Daigoro stepped up and snapped at it with his *bokken*. Another miss.

"I don't understand it," he said. "You hit the damnable thing every time and you've never so much as picked up a sword."

"Sir, perhaps all your kenjutsu has been for naught," Tomo said with a laugh. "At least when it comes to fighting little beanbags. Here, Okuma-sama, switch with me."

Daigoro handed him the *bokken* and went to retrieve the little cloth balls. They were filled with dried azuki beans and they were heavier than they appeared. Now they were dirty too, powdered with fine white dust after having been knocked up and down the gravel courtyard for half the morning. Daigoro took the requisite eight paces back and threw the first toss.

Tomo hacked with a big, wide swing. Were it a sword fight, his opponent would have killed him three times over by the time his blow fell. But unlike Daigoro, Tomo actually hit what he aimed for. The little ball flew from the tip of the *bokken* as swift as an arrow, striking Daigoro squarely in the chest.

"A thousand pardons," Tomo said, but his boyish laughter betrayed his true feelings.

Daigoro laughed too. "I swear to you, I might actually find some useful sword technique in this game if only I could get the hang of it. Here, let me try again."

"Not so fast. You owe me two more tosses, sir."

Tomo hit them both, one in the dirt at Daigoro's feet, one into Daigoro's breastbone with a loud smack. He giggled again and they traded weapons, or playthings, or whatever the proper name was for these frustrating contraptions. "What did you say this game was called?"

"Cutting Swallows," Tomo said. "I can't believe you've never played before. Every boy in the village knows it."

Yes, but I'm not a villager, Daigoro thought. He did understand the swallow-cutting reference, though. Tsutsui Kosuke, a minor cousin of the Shimojo clan, was renowned for his draw. In addition to his blinding speed, he had a preternatural accuracy the likes of which no one had seen before or since. It was said he'd practiced as a boy by cutting down moths at twilight. By the time he came of age, rumors held that he could cut the wings off a swallow in midflight. That launched him into the firmament. He was a local hero for years, until Tsutsui squared off against Daigoro's father in the Battle of Mikatagahara. Middle-aged men still sang a drinking song whose refrain ran "Bravely fought the Swallow Cutter, but the Red Bear of Izu was the Swallow Cutter cutter." Even so, it was Tsutsui who had the children's game named for him.

Daigoro tried Tomo's sloppy swinging method, and though he missed the first two balls he clipped the third. "Ha!"

"Well done, sir! You're getting the knack of it."

As Daigoro bent to pick up the little bean-filled swallows, he saw Akiko approaching along the shady veranda. "Aki-chan," he called, "you've got to try this."

"Oh, I don't know. . . ."

"Come on, you don't have to be a swordswoman to play—though I must say, anyone who could couple precision like this with proper form would be a dangerous opponent."

She stood in the shade with her hands folded over her belly. "It's hot."

"So we'll go down for a swim later. Have mercy on me, Aki. For once there isn't a political crisis on my lap. Let's have a bit of fun."

She unfolded her hands and clapped them back down on her belly. "I'd say you've had your share of fun already, lover."

It took a moment for her meaning to sink in. Daigoro looked at her hands, her belly, and then up to her face. Her smile seemed to be held in check, straining to hold back a flashflood of joy. "Do you mean it?" he said.

"Yes."

"You're . . . ?"

The smile broadened. "Yes."

"Tomo!" Daigoro seized him by the shoulders. "I'm going to be a father!"

Tomo giggled and Akiko joined in. Daigoro rushed over and lifted her off the veranda. Miraculously—or because all his sword training had toughened it, or maybe because sheer exhilaration infused it with strength—his lame leg held their weight. Even when he twirled her around, it did not buckle. "Easy, now," she said, clutching his head to her chest, "easy on your baby's bedroom."

"Oh, right. Sorry."

He set her down but held her close. Somehow it had never occurred to him that with all the time they spent in bed she might get pregnant. Now he wondered which surprised him more, the fact that she was with child or the fact that he was happy about it. By all rights fatherhood should have been terrifying. He had a family to govern, a province to stabilize, and a mortal enemy whispering in the imperial regent's ear. His life was a maelstrom, no place to bring a child, and yet he was so giddy his face was actually tingling.

Katsushima came running around the corner of the house, sweat on his brow. As he drew near, Daigoro opened his arms wide. "Katsushima, have you heard? She's with child!"

"You've got visitors, Okuma-sama."

"Don't sama me. I'm going to be a father!"

"Yes. How nice. You've got visitors."

"Good, good, *everything's* good. Show them in. We'll pass the sake all around."

"They're already in your courtyard. Armed."

Only then did Daigoro notice how stern Katsushima's face was. His jaw muscles stood out in his cheeks, and a cold light seemed to glow in his eyes. Out of habit his thumb flicked his *katana* loose in its sheath, drawing it back in only to loosen it once more.

"Armed? Who?"

"Guess."

Daigoro nodded and picked up his own swords, which had been lying on the veranda while he was playing games. One day of peace, he thought. Is that too much to ask? And to think I'd been planning on swimming later.

As he rounded the corner, Tomo and Katsushima in tow, he saw a horde of dusty, armored men sweating in the hot sun. They looked as though they'd endured many a forced march to come here. Daigoro put them at no less than half a hundred strong, all wearing twin swords and topknots. Every tenth man wore a tall red banner bearing the *kiri* flower of Toyotomi Hideyoshi. With the sunlight streaming through them, the banners cast a red glow on the faces of the men in their shadows.

The company stood in formation just inside the front gate. It was not lost on Daigoro that he could not leave his own home except by going through them. Nor was it lost on him that there was only one reason why a guest would enter uninvited and armed. The laws of hospitality were clear. Even the most boorish of brutes knew to announce himself at the door if he did not want to be thought an enemy.

"Patience and caution," Katsushima said quietly. Hideyoshi's company was still fifty paces offs, but he kept his voice low all the same. "We're one wrong word away from a bloodbath."

"I know," said Daigoro. He took a deep breath and shortened his strides. There was no blood on these men, so either they hadn't killed his gate guards or there was a second company outside that had done the fighting. Now that he thought on it, he was certain he'd have heard swordplay even if he was wrapped up in Cutting Swallows or rejoicing with Aki. So there had been no fighting. Whatever this was, the situation was not yet so bad that diplomacy was impossible.

Yet.

And he had a baby on the way. It was a fine day to fend off an invasion.

"Commander," he said, forcing as much cheer into his voice as possible, "to what do we owe the pleasure of your visit?"

The company commander had thick eyebrows and a weak chin. His mouth wore a slight but permanent frown thanks to the chin, and between that and his eyebrows he had a perpetually scowling look. He pulled a roll of paper from a bamboo scroll case tethered to his sword belt, keeping his eyes on Daigoro the whole time. "His Eminence the lord regent Toyotomi no Hideyoshi presents you with an edict, sir."

Sir, Daigoro thought. That was good. This man held him in some esteem. He wasn't thinking of Daigoro as a target—or at least not solely as a target. Then again, Daigoro supposed, if these were assassins, he would have known by now. They'd have started the killing already.

He looked over the edict, which was not addressed to him or even to the daimyo of Izu, but rather to all of Japan. It was a new Sword Hunt, and in substance it was not much different than the one declared by Oda Nobunaga some years before. That one had been effective in disarming the peasantry, and like the last one, this one banned pole arms and firearms as well as swords. This one would no doubt be as effective as its predecessor; peasant revolts were much harder to stage if no one but samurai went armed. Hideyoshi's own success was itself a peasant revolt, a fact he would not soon forget. Evidently he had no desire to be supplanted by some upstart with ambitions similar to his own.

Like the last one, this Sword Hunt applied countrywide too, but this one also specified three mountains by name: Kōya, Tōnomine, and Sōshitake. Though Daigoro had never seen either of them, he knew Mount Kōya and Mount Tōnomine by reputation. They were monastic havens far off in the Kansai; Kōya lay not far from Sakai, and Tōnomine was quite close to Nara. Strategically, economically, and politically, Sakai and Nara were nearly as important as Kyoto itself. If the neighboring monks kept arsenals, it was reasonable for the regent to see them as a threat.

But Sōshitake was nowhere near the Kansai. Daigoro's own home sat on it. So did Kattō-ji, home to the abbot who inspired such hate and fear in Hideyoshi's peacock, Shichio.

So that's what this is about, he thought. A new Sword Hunt as a masquerade for attacking the abbot—and me too, I suppose. He read the rest quickly. Accompanying this hunt was an order for national census, a ban on relocating during the term of the census, an expulsion edict against the southern barbarians, and a promise to melt down all weapons seized in the Sword Hunt into bolts and nails for a massive statue of the Buddha. True to form, Hideyoshi was nothing if not grandiose. But Daigoro saw an easy escape from this extravagant trap.

"Commander," he said, "I'm sure you've noticed that my home sits on Sōshitake. But the regent's Sword Hunt is a ban on *peasants* owning weapons. You'll find no armed peasants in this house."

"My orders were most specific, sir." The commander's tone was stiff without being gruff. Daigoro sensed some hesitation in him. "Most specific. We are to disarm all residents on Sōshitake."

Daigoro forced a smile and did his best to include some warmth in it. "Surely the regent can't have ordered you to disarm samurai. A samurai without his swords is no samurai at all."

"Understood, sir. But the edict stands."

"Of course it does. Come, won't you sit down? You and your men have marched a long way. And I've learned just this morning that I'm to be a father. Let us open a few casks of sake for your men and we officers can sit in the shade for a while."

"No, sir. My orders were most specific. Most specific. We're to move from here to the next compound as quickly as may be, sir."

The next compound. So they hadn't been to Kattō-ji yet; they'd marched right past it to come here. And there wasn't a second company deployed there either; this one was tasked with disarming both compounds. What was Hideyoshi thinking? Or, closer to it, what was Shichio thinking? Daigoro had no doubt it was Shichio whose orders were "most specific." The man had an ax to grind, plain and simple. But his motivation wasn't yet clear. These men could easily have overwhelmed the tiny garrison Daigoro had stationed at Kattō-ji. They could have been marching back home with the abbot's head in a sack before Daigoro could ever have marshaled his troops to stop them.

Shichio couldn't possibly expect Daigoro and all his men to simply hand over their weapons. Better to ask them all to commit suicide; at least there would be some honor in that. So, Daigoro wondered, if he was never really after our swords, what did he want?

Only two answers were possible. One: he hoped Daigoro would resist. He hadn't sent enough men to overwhelm House Okuma. In fact, Daigoro had no doubt that his own commanders had already reached the same conclusion, and deployed their troops in every room facing the courtyard. Daigoro had only to give the order and scores of samurai would burst out from every building. The company arrayed before him would be dead in minutes—taking some of Daigoro's own men with them, to be sure, but if Shichio's goal was Toyotomi blood on Okuma blades, he had certainly set the stage for it. And if Daigoro's current predicament degenerated into combat, Shichio could convince Hideyoshi to wage war on the Okumas.

Two: he wanted not the Okumas' swords but *Daigoro's* sword. A sudden vision flashed in Daigoro's mind: Shichio's demonic mask, its angry scowl cut with deep shadows in the moonlight, and Daigoro's own shadow running parallel to Shichio's across the snow-white stones of the Okuma family courtyard. Then came another vision: his brother facedown in the snow, slain in a duel after claiming Glorious Victory for his own. It was Ichirō's unrelenting desire for the sword that had killed him. Shichio felt the same hunger. He believed it was his sinister mask that made him need the blade; Daigoro thought otherwise, but he supposed the truth didn't matter. One way or the other, that haughty peacock was willing to destroy House Okuma to acquire Glorious Victory, and Daigoro wasn't sure how much more punishment his family could take.

Yet there he was with fifty hostile samurai in his own home. They were all trained killers, and no doubt they'd all seen more combat than Daigoro's own men. These warriors had come up from the west country, where the fighting was hardest. Yes, the Okumas outnumbered these men, and yes, the Okumas would carry the day, but not without bitter losses.

But Daigoro could not give up his sword—the sword his father had bequeathed to him as his last act in life—and he certainly couldn't disarm his entire clan. He read the edict once more.

"See here," he told Hideyoshi's commander, "your orders are to disarm the residents of Sōshi-*take*, not Sōshi-*san*. *San* means mountain, as in Kōya-san. *Take* means peak. And Mount Sōshi has two peaks. You just came up the saddle between them. Kattō-ji, that monastery you passed on the way here, sits on Zensōshi-take. My home is on Gosōshi-take. So which of the two Sōshitakes are you to disarm?"

"My orders were most specific," the commander said, but now doubt crept into his voice.

"Not specific enough, I'm afraid." Daigoro motioned toward his sitting room. "Come, let's have a seat and I'll have Tomo here fetch us a map. Your men look weary; let's give them a bit of a rest, shall we?"

As soon as Daigoro saw the commander's shoulders relax, he knew he'd won. He'd given the man a way to keep his honor, fulfill his orders to the letter, and not disgrace a samurai family by asking them to give up the unthinkable. In short, he'd given the commander a way out. The man wasn't stupid, and clearly he was uncomfortable with the orders foisted upon him. Did he know of Shichio's madness? If Daigoro had noticed it, surely an officer under Shichio's command must have seen it. The commander's permanent frown had not left his face, but up until a few seconds ago he'd been visibly on edge. Daigoro felt his own muscles loosen too, and a cool wave of relief washed over him. "Tomo," he said, "send a few girls for sake, and then bring my chest of maps."

Then a Toyotomi soldier drew his *katana* and leveled it at Tomo's throat. "This boy isn't going to fetch any maps," the swordsman said. "He's not going anywhere."

33

"Sir, we have our orders," the soldier said, the tip of his sword a handsbreadth from Tomo's jugular. "We're to disarm this house."

Armor clattered like a thousand metal birds taking flight. All the Toyotomi samurai sprang to the ready. None drew swords, but all were tensed, crouching, ready to attack. Their commander rounded on Tomo's captor, furious. "You'll sheathe your weapon this instant," he said. "Stand down or I'll have your head."

"No, sir," said the samurai. He had a lean, quick, runner's body and a face like a mouse. He was just out of striking range; if the commander drew on him, Tomo would die.

Daigoro's feeling of relief evaporated instantly. He studied Tomo's face, which had gone utterly white. He studied the commander and the rest of his troops, their hands on their hilts, knees bent to pounce. No eyes were on Daigoro.

Tomo and his captor were out of reach for the commander, but not for Glorious Victory. "Patience," Katsushima whispered.

Had he read Daigoro's mind? Glorious Victory was long and heavy, very slow on the draw. But with no eyes on him yet, he might be able to draw and cut and save Tomo's life. Maybe.

It was bad enough to draw a weapon in another man's home. That by itself violated every convention of civility and honor, and Daigoro was well within his rights to kill this boor. But worse yet, the man had threatened one of his own. Daigoro could not let that stand.

Then again, neither could Hideyoshi's commander. Tomo's captor had disobeyed a direct order. Under no circumstances would he leave the courtyard alive. His commander would strike him down, and all Daigoro had to do was watch him kill Tomo.

Or he could strike. Save Tomo and take his chances on what happened next.

That was assuming his draw was fast enough. It assumed he'd judged rightly in reading the commander's intentions. If any of his estimations were even slightly off—of his speed, of his reach, of the commander's mind—then by trying to save Tomo he would only draw Toyotomi blood, guaranteeing a fight.

All this flashed through Daigoro's mind in the space of a single breath. His pulse pounded hard and fast. Apart from that the courtyard was deathly quiet.

Daigoro's mind raced with a thousand calculations. Had he misjudged Glorious Victory's reach? How long would it take to clear her from her scabbard? It should have been so simple. Daigoro felt a flash of anger at himself: all he had to do to prevent a bloodbath was sacrifice a servant. For other lords this would have been easy. Others would never have befriended a lowborn peasant like Tomo.

But now that he thought about it, he realized he'd have to exact vengeance for Tomo one way or the other. If he let this commander report back that his men had killed an Okuma without reprisal, Shichio would know he could abuse the Okumas however he liked. Daigoro had no choice but to defend his own. And yet if he drew Toyotomi blood, that would invite retaliation from Shichio too.

The best solution was to order Hideyoshi's commander to kill Tomo's assailant. But that should have been obvious to the commander already. In fact, the man should already have bloodied his blade. Daigoro could hardly issue orders to an officer from the regent's own house.

He was trapped, plain and simple. There was no reaction that would not invite further aggression. And yet the right reaction might still save Tomo's life.

Hideyoshi's commander shifted his fingers on the grip of his *katana*. Was he preparing to draw? If so, Tomo was dead. Daigoro needed more time to think.

"Whom do you serve?" he asked the mousy man with the sword to Tomo's throat.

"Shut up!"

"You're Shichio's lackey, *neh*?"

"I said shut up!" The man started shaking.

"Stand down," the commander said, saying each word as if it were its own sentence.

Eyes flicked between Daigoro, the commander, and Tomo's captor. Sand shifted underfoot. Armor plates clacked like bamboo. Daigoro's heart hammered at his ribs like the hooves of a galloping racehorse.

Tomo's captor took a deep breath and released it. He stopped shaking. Daigoro knew that look. He'd felt it himself. It was the look of a man who had given himself up for dead—a man who no longer had anything left to lose.

Daigoro pulled hard and fast, clearing Glorious Victory from her scabbard. Tomo recoiled as the blade at his throat drew back to strike. Hideyoshi's commander drew his blade.

Glorious Victory fell. She took a sword with her, a fist still closed around it. Daigoro still had but one hand on her grip. She was too heavy; he stumbled forward.

The commander whirled, chopping at Daigoro's extended arm. His stroke went wide; a kick from Katsushima caught him in the kidney and sent him rolling. Fifty Toyotomi swords flashed from their scabbards. Three of them hacked at Daigoro.

Glorious Victory was long enough to parry them all. His left hand finally found Glorious Victory's grip. He turned the blades aside and cut low. Three men fell in a torrent of blood.

Daigoro couldn't say how he found his way to the heart of the

Toyotomi formation. His mind was reeling; he'd never fought like this before. Single combat was nothing at all like a swirling melee. It was as if his mind had no relation to his arms. He cut, blocked, deflected, counterstruck, all on raw instinct. By the time he figured out what was happening, he and Katsushima were standing back to back in the middle of the courtyard, surrounded by Toyotomi samurai.

The enemy formed an impenetrable hedgerow of red armor, gold plating, and shimmering steel. Surrounding them was another circle, this one russet and black and silver: over a hundred samurai adorned with the Okuma bear paw.

Somehow amid the chaos there came a lull, a standoff, and Daigoro found he could hear and see with amazing clarity. Every sword and spearhead shone as distinctly as stars on a moonless night. Katsushima was breathing heavily; his broad shoulders pressed against Daigoro's back, hot and heaving and stinking the coppery reek of blood. A wry laugh made Katsushima's body quake. He said, "What did I tell you about patience?"

Daigoro twisted his fists tighter on Glorious Victory's cloth-bound grip. The circle of enemies drew tighter.

"It's been an honor," said Katsushima.

"Likewise," said Daigoro, suddenly thinking of Akiko and the baby in her belly. Today of all days, it seemed a terrible shame to leave her.

Again the circle tightened. Daigoro readied himself to strike. Then a voice broke the eerie silence, bellowing "*Stand down!*" There came a clicking, clanking commotion through the ranks of samurai, and then the Toyotomi commander muscled his way to the center of the circle.

"Hold," he yelled, sensing his men's uneasiness. "Lord Okuma! What is the meaning of this?"

"Your man started it," Daigoro said. As soon as the words left his mouth they sounded childish. It took him a moment to regain his breath before he could speak again, and only because his words failed him did he notice that he was panting hard enough to make his lungs burn.

"Not your man," he said finally. "General Shichio's. He was planted in your ranks. I'm sure of it. Shichio wants a fight with me, whatever the cost."

"And you certainly obliged him, didn't you?" said the commander. "You tell me how I'm to leave your head on your shoulders."

Daigoro tried to slow his breath before he answered. "If I die, you die. And your men too. We outnumber you two to one."

"We've been outnumbered a lot worse than that."

"You've been used, Commander. You were sent here on false pretenses."

"That's as may be. Orders are orders."

"Your orders are no more than a screen of fog. They only cloud what hides behind them, and indeed I believe that to be their purpose. What honor is there in dying on orders like these? Spare your men. Let them die a more glorious death, in a battle worthy of their birthright."

The commander closed his eyes. He returned his *katana* to his hip, ready to sheathe it—or, if he was a crafty fighter, ready to attack the moment Daigoro let down his guard. His lips moved almost imperceptibly; Daigoro wondered if it might have been a prayer. If so, Glorious Victory's work was not yet done.

The commander looked at him again, his eyes utterly emotionless. His gaze did not waver; his sword hand did not shake. He had no fear of dying where he stood. "If you grant me leave to go, I can come back in force," he said. "I can push this whole mountain into the sea."

"Yes, you can," said Daigoro. "And I can send riders and ships to the regent, telling him of how your men barged into my home to pick a fight. Do not forget: my family holds a treaty with the regent. When your reinforcements arrive, it might be your head they come for."

The commander's right forefinger was tapping his sword's *tsuba*. It was a tell, a nervous tic, and Daigoro desperately wished he knew what it meant.

"*Bushidō* demands forbearance," he said quickly. "Commander, you must see that by now. It was one of your men who instigated the fight. All I did was finish it. How can you start the fighting anew and still retain your honor?"

The two of them met each other's gaze. A long, tense, electric silence passed between them. Then the commander sheathed his blade.

Just like that, the danger vanished. The storm cloud hanging over the courtyard dispersed on the wind. Swords went back into scabbards; muscles relaxed; Okumas and Toyotomis found their way into two facing formations of ranks and files, taking care not to bump shoulders with each other as they passed. Daigoro found it surreal. Had Hideyoshi's commander chosen to strike instead, dozens of these samurai would already be dead.

As it was, Daigoro still thought too many had died needlessly. Making his way back to the veranda, he stepped over four corpses and one bleeding samurai who hadn't yet succumbed but only had strength enough to blink. Daigoro stopped, took a step back, and looked at the dying man again. His face was a sticky red mask, but nevertheless Daigoro made out his mousy features. This was the lean one with the runner's body, the one who had started it all. Daigoro resisted the urge to cut his throat and hasten his passing.

He looked up from the instigator only to find Tomo sitting with his back against one of the porch posts. He was staring at his feet, his jaw slack. Then Daigoro saw the little cut just above his collarbone. It was no wider than the tip of his thumb, but it was enough.

Daigoro fell to his knees beside him. Tomo's palms were red with blood, but otherwise the external bleeding was minimal. By clutching his throat he'd probably been able to keep himself from bleeding to death, Daigoro guessed, but unable to keep the blood from gushing inward. More than likely he'd drowned in his own blood.

It was no way for a fifteen-year-old boy to die. Daigoro wanted to order his men to attack. He wanted to start the slaughter all over again. He wanted to chop and hack and slash until there was nobody left to kill.

Instead he took a silent moment for himself over Tomo's body, then struggled to his feet. His legs were weak, the right one even weaker than usual. "Commander," he said sullenly, "I see no need to send word of today's events to General Toyotomi. The only one who conducted himself dishonorably lies dead. Do you agree?"

The Toyotomi commander looked down at the scrawny, mouse-faced corpse. It did not bleed anymore; it only seeped. "I do," he said.

Daigoro's thoughts turned inevitably back to Tomo. It took a while to muster enough energy to speak again. Without looking up at the Toyotomi commander he said, "You may tell your troops to sit if you'd like. I'll see to it that they have something to eat and drink before you take them on the march again."

"That would be most gracious of you," said the commander, and his permanent frown seemed to lessen somewhat. "And lest I forget," he added, "congratulations on your baby."

Daigoro's shoulders sank. He'd forgotten all about that. He'd have to hunt down Akiko and he'd have to do it soon. She had never seen bloodshed in her own home before. She would need consoling—and so do I, he realized. He felt like a dying campfire in the rain, as if what little spirit he had left was soon to sputter out, never to return.

Daigoro looked around for Tomo, who would have understood what provisions he wanted prepared with no more than a nod. Then his conscious mind took the reins from instinct; he remembered, and then his gaze found the body. The cherubic face was bloodless now, the ever-present smile erased.

How had it come to this? He'd done the right thing, hadn't he? How could it have been wrong to try to save Tomo's life? And yet more bodies lay in his courtyard than he cared to count. It could have been just two: Tomo and Tomo's killer. Now he and Hideyoshi had both lost men—good, brave men who'd spent their entire lives in servitude, and who had surrendered their lives without hesitation.

Daigoro had been so sure he'd done the right thing. Glorious Victory Unsought agreed with him; had he been seeking glory, she would have seen to it that he too lay among the dead. But *he* was the one to draw first blood. Not Tomo's captor; Daigoro himself. He was the one who initiated combat, even if he wasn't the one who instigated it. And now his friend was dead, and others too.

Why? he wondered. Why is it always so costly for me to do the right thing? And why can *I* not be the one to bear the brunt of it? It should be me sitting there. I should have been the one to drown in my own blood.

It was no way for a fifteen-year-old servant boy to die. It was no better a death for a sixteen-year-old newlywed expecting his first child. Nonetheless, Daigoro wished he'd been the one to fall.

34

Much later, when the regent's company was long gone and the stars had blossomed in their millions, Daigoro led Katsushima down to the hot spring tucked away in a grotto on Okuma lands. There was a little house built around the spring, not for privacy so much as protection from assassins' arrows. The Okumas had held this land for a long time, including days when Izu was not so stable as it was now.

As Daigoro lowered his aching body into the pool, he looked up at the stout wooden rafters, wondering which of his forefathers had ordered them hewn. Perhaps his ancestor had hewn them himself, back in the days when the Okumas did not have flocks of servants and laborers at their command. Those old beams had weathered so much, and still they showed no signs of weakness.

Daigoro thought about that while he stretched, bending his neck this way and that, rolling his stiff shoulders under the waterline. He wondered how many years he had left in him. At sixteen he already felt like an old man.

"You were clever," Katsushima said. He'd let his topknot down and his long gray hair hung wet and limp on his shoulders.

"Choosing the hot spring?"

"No. Seeing to it that the Toyotomi commander would not tell Hideyoshi what happened today. That was your goal in promising not to send riders of your own, wasn't it?"

Daigoro nodded. "I can only hope it works."

"It should. You've got him thinking defensively. It was his man who started the fiasco, after all."

"We'll know soon enough," said Daigoro. He could only imagine how bad Hideyoshi's reaction might be if word ever reached him that Daigoro drew Toyotomi blood *after* receiving the edict to disarm. The grim-faced commander had threatened to push Sōshitake's twin peaks into the sea, but for an angry Hideyoshi that would be no empty boast. The lord regent was congenial enough in person, but his whims were fickle and his acts of vengeance were well known. Any daimyo could order his generals to commit suicide, but Hideyoshi was known to eliminate even their families. Daigoro thought of Akiko, of how she chose not to join them in the bath lest the water overheat their baby's little bedroom. As bitter as Tomo's loss had been, what made his heart race was the thought of how easily Aki might have been slain too.

But what was done was done. Daigoro could not afford to linger on the past. "What now?" he said.

Katsushima shrugged. "Hard to say. Do you think Shichio will move against you again?"

"Yes. He is like Ichirō. He is compelled."

"I cannot understand him. I don't wish to cause offense, but he is much too big a fish to be hunting a little minnow like you. If you were down in Kyoto, yes, perhaps you would be of some consequence. Down there the allegiance of every last family has political implications. But as far as Kyoto politics are concerned, House Okuma might as well be on the moon. Why does he even care that you exist?"

Daigoro winced as he rolled his neck. "My father. Shichio has a grudge against him. On top of that, he fancies Glorious Victory."

"So give it to him."

"I can't."

"Why not? It's too big for you anyway."

Daigoro shook his head. "It may not be in the nature of a *rōnin* to understand. My father wrote his will on his deathbed with a musket ball in his spine. In it he made it clear that I was to have his sword. Not his eldest son. Me. I cannot disregard his final wish."

"If you say so," said Katsushima, but Daigoro could tell by his flippant tone that he didn't fully grasp what was at stake. That was the difference, Daigoro supposed—the difference between a samurai with a name to uphold and a *rōnin* who had forsaken all other relationships when he wedded himself to his sword.

"We can be thankful for small mercies, at least," said Katsushima, who submerged himself until the waterline was just at his lower lip. The very picture of contentment, he said, "At least your mother chose not to fly from her birdcage today."

"Damn you," Daigoro said, his anger suddenly spiking. He pounded the rim of the bath with his palm. "Must you speak that way?"

His fatigue was to blame. The entire day had taxed him emotionally, and now his temper was like a willful horse, stronger than him and too hard to control. But like it or not, there he was in the saddle. He did his best to rein his feelings in. "I beg your pardon, Goemon. That was unkind. But it is unseemly to speak of her that way. She is no house pet. She's my mother."

Katsushima closed his eyes. "That she is."

"Is it not bad enough that I have to sedate her day and night? Is it not bad enough that I'm likely to empty the last of my coffers buying all those poppies for Yagyū to milk? You are the only friend I have left. I will not have you berating my own mother. I cannot bear it."

"How did I berate her? I said she had a good day. She didn't run off foaming at the mouth."

Again Daigoro felt that spike of anger. It hit him like a physical thing, stabbing through his veins. He was not certain that the volcano heated the water; his own rage was more than hot enough to make it steam. "First she's a bird in a cage, and now she's a rabid animal. What would you have me do, Katsushima? Cull her to spare the rest of the herd?"

"Your words, not mine." Unlike Daigoro, he kept his voice low and calm.

"Now you're provoking me on purpose."

"Am I?" Katsushima gave Daigoro a stern stare. "Or are you finally giving voice to the thoughts you've kept to yourself in the darkest of nights? You are not blind, Daigoro: you must see your family would be better off without her."

"So what do you suggest? That I murder my own mother?"

"I do not *suggest* anything. I *say* your family would be better off without her."

"And what would you have me do? Expel her from her own home? Banish her from the compound? Would that satisfy you?"

"I would be satisfied if you put an end to your temper tantrum and examined your decisions honestly. You are unwilling to sacrifice your sword, unwilling to sacrifice your mother, unwilling to sacrifice your monk, and now you and your family have become quarry. And, as you may have noticed, so have I. I've stood by you every step of the way. Have I not earned the right to speak my mind?"

"She is my mother."

"This has nothing to do with your mother. It's to do with your refusal to make hard decisions."

"I drew my blade against the most powerful man in the empire today, and I did it just to save a peasant boy that any other daimyo would sacrifice as easily as he'd part with a piss pot. You tell me that wasn't a hard decision."

"You did it because you were afraid of losing your friend. That's not hard; it's not even noble. Any common thief would have done the same."

Daigoro wanted to punch him. He wanted to jump out of the water, grab Glorious Victory, and call him out then and there. And it wasn't because Katsushima had compared him to a thief; it was because he wasn't sure Katsushima was wrong.

Until now Daigoro thought of himself as noble for risking his life to save a lowborn servant like Tomo. Now he had his doubts. Katsushima had spoken the truth: even bandits would murder to save their friends. Was defending Tomo a selfless act or a selfish one? Hindsight was never perfect; how could he know for certain?

The fact that he couldn't be sure of his own motivations made Daigoro even angrier. He slammed his fist down like a hammer on the rim of the pool. The black lava rock was sharp enough to cut the fleshy part of his hand, but Daigoro didn't care. "Damn it, Katsushima, what need was there for him to die? And why does she have to be pregnant? And why can none of this be easy? Just for one day, why can it not be easy?"

Katsushima rose from the bath. "You've never understood me. My choices. How I could stomach the thought of going *rōnin*. I think you've just gotten your first glimpse."

Daigoro dropped his bleeding hand back into the water. As it plopped through the surface it made a little wave—a fleeting phenomenon, a manifestation so ephemeral that it could hardly be said to have happened. It made Daigoro think of the word *rōnin*, "wave man." A samurai without his liege lord was said to be as free as a wave on the ocean, owing nothing to anyone, dependent on no one. But Daigoro's classical education had something very different to say about waves.

He remembered discussing the *Tao Te Ching* with his father when he was very young. He'd been confused by the idea that the wave and the ocean were just two faces of one thing, so his father had taken him down to the beach. "Tell me where the ocean ends and the wave begins," his father had said. "Which drops belong to the wave but not to the ocean?"

It was impossible to answer, of course. There were no oceanless waves, nor were there waveless oceans. And if no boundary could be found between those two, how could there be a boundary between the wave named Daigoro and the ocean called House Okuma? How could Daigoro be himself without being an Okuma? Son of Tetsurō and Yumiko. Brother to Ichirō, husband to Akiko, father to the next little wave on the Okuma sea. There was no Daigoro except Okuma Daigoro.

Was a *rōnin* any less dependent? If so, then why had Katsushima stood back-to-back with him, with fifty swords pointed at their throats? Wouldn't he have expressed true independence by simply standing back and observing?

Katsushima began the long, moonlit walk back to the compound, and Daigoro punched the surface of the water again. He almost wished he'd gone through with his attempted seppuku. There was no point in doing it now—as an act of protest, it had to be done in full view of the regent—but if his courage hadn't failed him then, he could have solved his two greatest problems: how to protect his family and how to fulfill his father's dying wish. By committing the ultimate sacrifice, he would have convinced the regent of the abbot's innocence. In addition, once Daigoro was dead there would be no disgrace in parting with Glorious Victory Unsought. His father had bequeathed her to Daigoro, and Daigoro would have kept her until the end. If Shichio wanted her after his death, so be it. If he still wanted to kill the abbot, so be it. No one could say Daigoro hadn't done his utmost to fulfill his duty.

A chill ran over his body, in spite of the heat of the bath. It came not on the midnight breeze, but with the realization that seppuku was still an option. He had only to ride to Kyoto. Hideyoshi had a palace there. Daigoro could request an audience, carry out his ritual disembowelment, and see his family protected once and for all. Better yet, perhaps he could find a way to make a bid for Shichio's neck. Suicide was far more honorable than execution, but Daigoro would gladly suffer the shame of a death sentence if he earned it by driving Glorious Victory through Shichio's heart.

Either way, he had no choice but to ride to Kyoto. The road would be long and hot, and he knew death awaited him at the end. It was inevitable. So long as Okuma Daigoro lived, all of the Okumas would be under threat.

So unless he could conjure some third option before he reached

Hideyoshi's palace, his fate would be to commit seppuku or to be executed for the murder of one of the regent's top aides. He hoped Katsushima would still be willing to ride with him. If it came to seppuku, Daigoro would need a second, and if it were execution, he would need someone to deliver his head to his family.

Whatever the outcome, he hoped Katsushima would acknowledge his willingness to make the difficult choice.

35

Daigoro had been as far as Hakone before, the last time to disastrous results: Ichirō was killed—brutally, predictably, needlessly—right before his eyes. That had been in the winter, when Hakone was cloaked in heavy snow and there was little of the town to see. The north road had been nothing more than a thin track of mud and slush, but now, in the height of summer, Daigoro found it had become an entirely different entity.

It seemed Hideyoshi's military exploits had been good for business; the dusty streets around the Mishima checkpoint were bustling with activity. Horse trains and baggage carriers marched in their lines; hawkers proclaimed the virtues of their products while farmers and peddlers sold their wares more quietly; palanquin bearers jogged here and there, slithering between packhorses and jugglers and white-faced geisha.

"There's a good brothel just up here," Katsushima said as they reached the heart of town. "It'll be a good place to bed down for the night."

"No," said Daigoro.

"Why not?"

"I have no interest in those women."

"So ask them to bring you a boy."

"No!"

Katsushima gave him a quizzical frown. "I did not think you to be a prude in such matters. Perhaps it's your . . . well, your upbringing in the hinterlands, if you'll pardon my saying so. Among city folk there is no shame in saying boys and girls both have their uses in a pleasure house."

"You misunderstand me." Daigoro reined his mare in closer so he didn't have to speak up. "Have you no eyes? I'm a cripple."

"What of it? You got Akiko pregnant, didn't you?"

"Yes."

"So your cock works."

"Yes."

"All right, then. Which will it be: a boy or a girl?"

Daigoro kept himself from blushing, from rolling his eyes, from giving Katsushima a good backhand. "Do you still not see? My leg is *unsightly*. I don't care to disrobe in the company of others."

"If it's a woman with discretion you're concerned about, believe me, there's no need to worry—"

"No," Daigoro said with finality. "I have no taste for consorts. My Akiko is more than enough for me."

"Spoken like a true newlywed." Katsushima sighed, sincerely heartbroken. "Very well, then. As you like. I must tell you, though, *my* chances of finding a sporting woman fall dramatically once we pass beyond city limits. And one of these nights we'll have to stay at a brothel, even if you only want to pay to sleep there."

"Why?"

"Are you joking? They're the traveling man's greatest asset! Where else can you gather reliable information about the road? Pubs? Inns? No one there is *paid* to give you small talk."

Daigoro hadn't thought of it that way. And Katsushima wasn't through. "Never forget the value of a whore's discretion, Daigoro. It's their livelihood. A good madam will never reveal who stays under her roof. If you're a hunted man, there's no better refuge than a high-class whorehouse."

"Spoken like a hunted man," said Daigoro.

Katsushima shrugged. "It's a *rōnin's* lot. But even those who never run afoul of the law can still acquire enemies—a fact you of all people ought not to forget."

Daigoro shifted the shoulder straps of his Sora *yoroi*, which he'd worn ever since leaving the Okuma compound. His father had died at the hands of a paid assassin, and a breastplate like this one might have saved his life. Now that he thought about it, Ichirō had died on the road too. Was that to be Daigoro's fate as well? Did Okuma men live under a curse?

"All right," he said with a resigned sigh. "We visit your brothels. But not every night. And not tonight."

The next nine days held sights Daigoro had never seen before. Mount Fuji peeking out from its ever-present cloak of clouds. Huge square fields of white along the coast, dotted with salt farmers collecting their crop. A thousand fishing boats on a single beach, arrayed before the sunset like troops standing for inspection. Mountains so sheer and so variegated that they looked like they could exist only in woodblock prints. Rivers wider than any in Izu. Lanterns bobbing on the water like foxfires, suspended from the bowsprits of cormorant boats. Bridges as steeply arched as rainbows; bridges with tollhouses and armed guards; missing bridges whose absence was only told by the line of spindly trestles crossing the water.

He passed rice farmers clutching their broad *sugegasa* to their heads in a driving rainstorm. He saw towering temples boxed in by tall bamboo frames, with workers clambering about the frames like monkeys as they replaced roof tiles and patched crumbling walls. He watched the wind batter gnarled pine trees, the trees themselves already permanently bowed over like old crones. He rode under tall orange *torii*, under pines and maples and bamboo and ginkgo, under fog so dense that he could not even see Katsushima beside him. He crossed paths with armed companies from a dozen major houses and was thankful that none of them stopped him, lest one of them have an alliance with Shichio.

At the Arai checkpoint they tethered their horses on a ferry and sailed across the placid waters of Lake Hamana. Once again Daigoro gave thought to the Sora breastplate he'd worn ever since leaving the Okuma compound. It was heavy, and with his mare's every step its weight had plowed furrows into his flesh, each sore the exact width of a shoulder strap. He did his best not to scratch at them by night in the hopes that the skin would callus, but now the breastplate posed an entirely different threat. What if the ferry should capsize? Daigoro knew how to swim—he'd grown up in Izu, after all—but in the water his breastplate was not armor but an anchor.

But the ferry did not keel over, and once he was on dry land again he found nagging fears still plagued him. When they rode before dawn or after dusk, he imagined how he might fall if his beautiful chestnut mare should falter and break a leg. By night he had horrible dreams of waking to find someone had stolen their horses, or even just their tack and harness. Daigoro's saddle was one of a kind. Old Yagyū, the Okumas' healer, had designed it to brace Daigoro's right leg so he could ride. This was the largest of the saddles, but Daigoro still owned the smallest and all those in between, racked on a shelf in the stable. They charted Daigoro's growth over the years, as well as Old Yagyū's growing understanding of Daigoro's affliction. Apart from his sword, Daigoro's saddle was the most precious thing in the world. He could not ride without it, and he did not know what he would do if it were stolen.

At length he could contain himself no more, and at the inn in Okazaki he finally asked Katsushima about his fears. "It's natural," Katsushima said through a mouthful of grilled squid. "It's nothing to do with horses and armor. You fear what happens once we get to Kyoto."

"Do you think so?"

"I know so. You talk about it in your sleep."

Daigoro frowned. "I don't talk in my sleep."

"Oh no? Then how do I know about your plans to become a monk?"

Daigoro's frown deepened. "What?"

"It took me a few nights to put it together. The greatest threat to House Okuma isn't Shichio. It's you, *neh*? If there were no Okuma Daigoro, there would be no vendetta. If you take on the tonsure, you give up your name and all your worldly possessions. Glorious Victory could go to Shichio. Any duty you ever felt to protect that abbot would be lifted. You could even stay in Kattō-ji and watch your child grow up, if only from afar. I congratulate you. It's an elegant solution."

Daigoro looked at him in shock. "I said that in my sleep?"

"Not *just* like that, no. I told you, it took me a few nights to sort it all out." He chuckled when he saw Daigoro's jaw drop. "You don't like it? Just think: if we'd slept in brothels every night, we'd never have shared a room, and then I'd never hear you talk in your sleep."

Daigoro rolled his eyes. "I wonder if Akiko hears me talking too."

"Ask her when we get back. Do tell me you've put this seppuku nonsense out of your mind. In your heart you know it's not the right way."

Or else I wouldn't be fretting about it in my sleep, Daigoro thought. But there would be no returning home. Even if Daigoro survived Kyoto, the Okuma compound could never be home to him again. He would have abandoned his name and his birthright—and not in the way Katsushima thought, either. Obviously he'd gathered all the clues he needed, but he'd reached the wrong conclusion.

"You're very clever," Daigoro said, "but not as clever as you think. I've no intention of becoming a monk."

"Oh no?"

"Have you forgotten? The Buddha may say you erase your past karma when you take on the cloth, but Shichio doesn't forgive so easily. If he did, he'd have no cause to kill the abbot, and you and I would still be in Izu."

Katsushima nodded sagely, conceding the point. "Are you going to eat that?"

Daigoro looked down at his dinner, which he'd scarcely touched. "I suppose not."

Katsushima's chopsticks snatched a nicely grilled tentacle and a slice of pickled daikon. "There is another way, you know. We're only a few days' ride from the Kansai. That's *shinobi* country."

"Are you serious? Magic men?"

"It's not magic. They don't pass through walls; they climb over them, or slip through windows. But they do it so invisibly that people start spinning tall tales. They tell stories of masked men dressed head to toe in black, but only because they do not want to believe that death may hide in plain sight."

"What are you getting at, Goemon?"

"Shichio cannot stay on his guard against every cook and steward and scribe that crosses his path. A good *shinobi* can become any one of them. Put a few coins in the right hand and we can ride home tomorrow."

He was right. Daigoro knew it. Given the choice of committing seppuku, facing execution for Shichio's murder, or placing a hired knife in Shichio's bedchamber, the easiest road was clear. All Daigoro had to do was compromise his honor and he could ride back home to his wife.

But the easy path was not the path of *bushidō*. "No," he said. "I cannot pay some unknown mercenary to fight my battles for me. My father would never have done such a thing."

"Your father died at the hands of 'some unknown mercenary.'"

Katsushima waited to see whether that hit a sore spot. A pang of grief stabbed Daigoro in the heart, but he did not allow it to show in his face. "The Iga are renowned for their spies and assassins," Katsushima said. "The greatest houses of Kyoto employ them all the time."

"All the more reason not to hire them. If a man is willing to sell his sword, what keeps him from selling his secrets?"

"The Wind, then. Have you heard of them?"

"No."

"Then they've done their job well. They make clans like the Iga and the Rokkaku look like amateurs. I used to know people who can find them; we can find them again."

Daigoro looked down at his rice. The cooks he'd grown up with cooked it better. All he had to do was ride north instead of south and he could have that rice again, in a familiar bowl, under a friendly roof. It was true that to hire an assassin was to abandon his father's path. But if he strayed from the path just this once, just for a little while, he could keep his father's name. Protect his father's house. Raise his father's grandchild and heir.

And be unworthy of that heritage himself.

"I cannot do it," he said. "What if my *shinobi* should fail? Then I'll have sullied my honor for nothing."

"It always comes back to that, doesn't it?" Katsushima stole another piece of octopus from his bowl. "You know I'm proud of you, *neh?*"

That made Daigoro look up. It was the sort of thing a father would say, and as such, it was the sort of thing Daigoro hadn't heard in a long time. "Why?" he said. "You thought this was a bad idea from the outset."

"All the more reason to admire you. You stood up to me—and not just to me. To Hideyoshi, to that idiot Shichio, to the whipping boy he sent to your house, even to that abbot of yours. You haven't taken so much as a single step from your original position. If I could make your kenjutsu stance as firm as you keep your moral stance, you'd be a fearsome swordsman."

Daigoro thanked him, but only halfheartedly. He knew he would never be father's equal in swordsmanship. That much had been fated in the womb, where some curse had emaciated his right leg before he was even born. If he could not match his father's stature as a warrior, at least he could have done it as a statesman, but he'd botched that too. The only way left to him was to hold fast to his father's moral principles, but he could not deny that Katsushima had it right from the first: killing the abbot would have spared Daigoro and his family no end of trouble.

Now Daigoro knew of just one solution left to him, and the mere fact that it had entered his mind inspired guilt so strong that he felt it viscerally, like a little sharp-clawed demon crawling around in his gut. His solution would solve all his family's problems, but he was certain that neither his mother nor his wife would ever forgive him for it.

36

They met the crowds of the big city when they were still thirty *ri* from the city itself. One afternoon, still three days' ride from Kyoto, the population of the Tokaidō suddenly quintupled. By sunset the following day, the foot traffic was so steady that the road itself resembled a tiger, striped with the long shadows of scores upon scores of peasants. By the time they reached Kusatsu the Tokaidō was hardly a road anymore, but rather a long and crowded open-air market. Potters and knife sharpeners, greengrocers and fishmongers, singing clowns surrounded by mobs of giggling children; the travelers lacked for nothing—except, Daigoro thought, the scent of the sea, replaced by dust and wood smoke and the musk of oxen. Patrols of Toyotomi samurai were as ubiquitous as the mangy dogs hovering on the edges of every crowd, though of course the samurai were not so thin that Daigoro could count their ribs, and the dogs carried no spears to announce their presence from a hundred paces away.

Not only were the Toyotomi men not looking for Daigoro; they recognized neither his colors nor even the Okuma bear paw, though both were prominently displayed on his breastplate, his *haori*, and his horse's tack and harness. That was good, Daigoro supposed; it proved his earlier fear of Shichio's roving assassins was unfounded. Now he wondered whether that too was merely symptomatic of a greater fear, just like his worries about drowning in his *yoroi*.

Never in his life had Daigoro been made to feel so provincial. To be born samurai was to be born into high station—not quite noble born, far short of being born into the Imperial Court, but nevertheless even a newborn samurai inherited a certain aristocracy unknown to the farmers, artisans, and merchants. As such, despite his relief at being unrecognized, Daigoro also felt somewhat insulted. He had always thought of himself as a man of world—or a boy of the world, at the very least. Now, after ten days on the road, he felt like a rube.

And that was before he crossed the bridge into Kyoto itself. He'd always heard Kyoto was cold, and to his embarrassment he'd even packed a quilted jacket among his things. Now he wondered how it could ever get cold here, given the sheer press of human bodies. The Sanjō Ōhashi was hardly the longest bridge he and Katsushima had crossed during their ride, but traffic in and out of the city was so dense that Daigoro thought he might just as well make his mare ford the river as wait to cross the bridge like a civilized person. Katsushima only clucked his tongue and said, "Patience."

Never before had Daigoro seen so many buildings. They were built so close to each other that the monkeys simply hopped from roof to roof. "Can you believe how many temples they have?" said Daigoro. "You could hardly throw a rock without hitting one."

"Brothels too," Katsushima said wistfully.

Not ten paces later Daigoro spotted his first southern barbarians. A group of twelve men walked in a block, hands folded and strange round eyes downcast, wearing simple orange robes. Daigoro could not help staring at their sickly pale skin. Their eyes were bizarre, too big, showing too much white. They did not shave their heads properly, but only the pate, like a samurai without his topknot. One of them had hair the same color as Katsushima's blood bay gelding. Another had curly hair like a sheep.

Fully half the city seemed to be newly built. Homes were packed in cheek by jowl, the shops packed in tighter still. In the space of a single block Daigoro saw three tailors, a cooper, a farrier, a furrier, a cobbler, a carpenter, a papermaker, a signmaker, a cloth dyer, two taverns, two sushi restaurants, four noodle shops, and three inns whose common rooms served food as well. Daigoro wondered what these people did all day to require so much to eat.

There was a whole district for buying produce, still another for buying crabs, lobsters, and other fruit of the sea. Now and then a wheelbarrow would pass, stacked so high with caged poultry or bags of rice that it was impossible to see the man doing the pushing. There were geisha and there were low-class whores. There were leather-workers, blacksmiths, goldsmiths, silversmiths. There seemed to be no imaginable service Daigoro might ever need that could not be pro-vided for within ten minutes' walk of where he stood.

At the heart of the commotion was Toyotomi Hideyoshi's home, the newly built Jurakudai. It wasn't hard to find; one had only to look for the golden roofs. Daigoro could not begin to guess how many buildings lay within the whitewashed wall that ran the perimeter of the complex. Every one of them was crowned in gold. Even the wall had a little roof of its own, its thousands of curved roof tiles gilded at unthinkable expense. Their circular endcaps shimmered like little suns on the green surface of the moat.

Daigoro had to circumnavigate the complex to find the front door—no short distance, to be sure; the palace was a city quarter unto itself. From every angle he could see the towering three-story keep, whose gabled roofs also shone like solid gold. Daigoro found it garish, but he also found himself second-guessing his every instinct. If riding a hundred-and-some-odd *ri* on the Tokaidō hadn't done the job thor-oughly enough, the clamor and alarum of Kyoto had fully impressed on him the fact that he knew nothing of the world beyond his own front door.

Now, dwarfed by the gleaming golden palace before him, he won-dered if he'd taken leave of his senses entirely. Was he really so gullible as to think that gaining an audience with the imperial regent was no harder than paying a visit to a family friend? He blushed at his own naïveté. He'd ridden half the length of the empire and now he hadn't the slightest inkling of what to do next.

And then, impossibly, Mio Yasumasa came out to greet him.

There was no mistaking him. If his snow-white topknot were not enough to identify him, his glittering black breastplate was so big it could almost serve to bard a horse. Mio's shadow stretched out broad and long behind him as he lumbered through the visitor's gate. "Young master Okuma! What a strange day this is. That viper Shichio told me I would find you here, and here you are!"

Daigoro looked to the tower standing high atop the keep. It was a viewing deck, not a defensive structure—the walls were no more than lattice—and so Daigoro should have been able to see any observers. The tower was empty.

"How did he know I was here?"

"Eh? You'll have to speak up, son. Some northern upstart had the gall to cut my ear off."

Mio made a flourish of cupping a hand to the scar on the left side of his head, and just as Daigoro was about to apologize, the giant let loose a thunderous laugh. Daigoro smiled with him, but he was not in a joking mood. "Please, General, tell me: does Shichio have spies watching for me? How does he know I'm here?"

"It's that mask of his. Pure devilry, if you ask me." Mio sneered and spat. "He says it 'felt you coming'—no, felt your *sword* coming, he said, and if you can make any sense of that, I'll conscript you on the spot and make you my personal soothsayer. By the Buddha, I could use a clearer view of the future."

"What do you mean?"

"Shichio. He's changed. Leave him to his maps and numbers and he can do your army some good, but I campaigned with him for years and never saw him draw a blade. He's got no stomach for it. But all of a sudden he's taken to wearing swords. Why? Why now?"

Mio led them into the palace as he spoke, and Daigoro made a careful note of every guardpost, every building, every intersection of lanes. When he and Katsushima tethered their horses, Daigoro memorized every door and window facing the hitching posts. If they needed to make a hasty retreat, he'd need an accurate mental map.

Katsushima was equally on edge. "Is that why you go armored?" he said. "Because you can't foretell what Shichio might do with his swords?"

Mio looked down at Katsushima—he was that tall—and snorted a laugh through his nose. "Say what's on your mind, *rōnin*."

"Very well." Katsushima's left hand fell to his hip, and with a flick of the thumb he loosened his *katana* in its sheath. "I think a man dressed for battle usually intends to go to battle. So unless fashions have changed since I was last in Kyoto, you're prepared for a fight."

Mio noted Katsushima's hand but made no move for his own weapon. "Maybe I am," he said, his tone darker than before. "Maybe I always am." Then he slapped a big hand on his armored belly. "Or maybe I need it to keep my innards from spilling out. Ever since your little friend put his sword in my gut, it hurts every time I bump it into something—and at my size, that happens quite a lot!"

He slapped his breastplate again, laughing mightily at his own joke, then bade Daigoro and Katsushima to follow him past a teahouse and into the garden on the opposite side.

Hideyoshi sat on a stone bench at the edge of a tranquil little pond. The grass surrounding him was lush and green, punctuated by flat white stepping-stones tracing a winding path to the water. High walls surrounded the garden, largely invisible behind the sprays of bamboo that whispered to each other in the light breeze. Carp swam in the pond, their colors ranging from white to orange to black. Now and then came a sucking sound as one of their gaping round mouths breached the surface.

General Shichio sat by the pond as well, petting the demon mask that rested in his lap as if it were a cat. He wore a *katana* at his hip, just as Mio had said, but it did not suit him. It was too short for him, and too clean; no sweating hand had ever touched it. He wore it at an awkward angle, like a sandal stuck between the wrong toes. And yet he had an eye for Glorious Victory that bordered on the lascivious. Daigoro had seen murder in the eyes of a rival swordsman before, and this wasn't it; this was closer to rape.

"Well, now," said Hideyoshi, "here's a guest we didn't expect."

Somehow Daigoro's memory hadn't fully retained how ugly Hideyoshi was. It was a shame; Daigoro found him quite likable, and he thought fate unusually cruel to make such a personable man so simian in appearance. Then again, maybe the regent's charisma was born from his unfortunate looks; perhaps it was a defense mechanism, born of necessity in a needlessly superficial society. Daigoro wondered why he himself had never thought to practice being charming; perhaps he could have deflected some of the bashing he'd endured all his life thanks to his lame leg.

"Sit, sit," Hideyoshi said, gesturing to another stone bench on the opposite side of the pond. At the raising of an eyebrow, servants sprang noiselessly into motion. Daigoro had a little cup of sake in his hand from the very moment he sat down, and Katsushima had a little cup of southern barbarian whiskey. To Mio they gave the entire flask of whiskey, along with a cup that all but vanished in his enormous hand. Then, just like that, the servants vanished back into the woodwork. Hideyoshi clapped his hands on his knees. "So, what occasions this visit?"

"Assassins," said Daigoro. "I just turned fifty of them out of my house."

Hideyoshi laughed, baring sharp teeth that pointed every which way. "Well done! Fifty, you say. That must have been quite a fight."

"I tried to avoid fighting, my lord regent. I nearly succeeded too, but my efforts were sabotaged."

"Were they, now? By whom?"

"By the one who sent the assassins, my lord regent."

The regent smoothed his wispy mustache. "Ah. Some local trouble, is it? Well, you came to the right place. I like you, Okuma-san. You've impressed me. Tell me who the rabble-rouser is and I'll set him straight."

The clacking of armor plates reminded Daigoro that Mio sat just to his left, opposite the pond from Hideyoshi and Shichio. Why was Mio sitting with him and not with his own people? Perhaps Katsushima's earlier suspicions were right on the mark. Had Mio armored himself for a fight? Had he positioned himself to be ready to strike, or was he implicitly siding against Shichio by sitting with Daigoro? It was impossible to tell, and impossible for Daigoro to know how to answer the regent's question. If Mio had not allied himself with Daigoro but was merely flanking him, accusing Shichio might be the last thing Daigoro ever did.

He steeled himself, gulped down his sake, and said, "General Shichio sent the assassins, my lord." Then he waited for Mio's sword to clear its scabbard.

It didn't. Mio continued to sip his whiskey. For his part, Hideyoshi grinned, as friendly as ever. "I told you before," he said, "you've impressed me, Okuma-san. Would you like to know how you can tell that I like you?"

"Because you said so, my lord regent?"

"Because I didn't burn your house down."

All warmth vanished from Hideyoshi's face. The smile stayed, though, an eerie, empty, hideous mask. "You've got some fire in you, kid. Coming all the way here with only this haggard bodyguard as your retinue? Impressive. But impressing me is one thing. Getting me to turn against one of my own top men is something else entirely."

"Sir," Mio blurted, "surely he didn't mean to—"

"Oh yes, he did. Isn't that so, Okuma-san? You meant to suggest that General Shichio sent assassins against my will. You thought a show of bravery against overwhelming odds would be enough to talk me into killing him. Isn't that why you rode all the way here? Alone? Right into the dragon's den?"

"No, my lord regent," said Daigoro. "I come to make a truce."

That brought an honest smile back to Hideyoshi's face—the smile of a bully, to be sure, but no longer a reptilian facade. "Do you, now?" he said. "And why should I treat with a gnat like you?"

"Because you treated with my father. Because honor demands it."

"Back to honor!" Hideyoshi laughed and slapped his knee. "You never tire of it, do you? Let me ask you something, Okuma. Why haven't you killed General Shichio?"

"My lord?"

"You've had opportunity. You've served us food in your home; your cooks could have poisoned him, *neh*? Or if that offends your sense of honor, why not kill him here and now? You're armed. You're a fine swordsman. If this man is such a threat to your house, why haven't you separated his head from his shoulders?"

"Because he is your man."

"So what? Honor is honor, *neh*? What does it matter who offended you? What does it matter who his friends are? You're bound to defend your honor anyway, *neh*? So do it. Cut him down."

"I'm afraid my lord regent may not understand honor the way I do. When you treated with the united lords of Izu, you treated with my father. That means I am to regard you as my ally. Honor forbids me from crossing an ally."

"Is that so?"

"Yes."

"Even if the ally sends assassins to your house?"

"They were his, not yours, my lord regent. Dismiss General Shichio and I will cut him down on the spot. Otherwise he is your man and the treaty between our houses remains."

Hideyoshi laughed. Shichio most pointedly did not. He narrowed his eyes at Daigoro and said, "Did I just hear you threaten to kill me?"

"It was no threat. If your master gives me the order, I will cut you in half. If he does not, then I have no course left but to parley."

"You? Parley with *me*?" Shichio sneered. "Do tell! Just what would a worm like you have to offer the likes of me?"

"It was you who wrote Sōshitake into the Sword Hunt, *neh*? Kōyasan and Tōnomine I understood; the regent has enemies there. But you were the one who slipped a third mountain into the edict, *neh*? In fact, I should not be surprised if the edict delivered to my family's compound were the only copy to list Sōshitake by name."

It was a guess, an arrow loosed in the dark, but Daigoro could see from the way Shichio's jaw hardened that his arrow struck the mark dead center. "Little Bear Cub," Shichio said stiffly, "you will address me with respect or I'll have your head."

"You can claim my head whenever you wish. You have no honor; any pretended slight is warrant enough for you. And since there is nothing I can do to change that, I might as well say my piece. You tried to disarm my family, General. But in truth I think you want less than that. House Okuma owns a sword you want—one sword in particular. Is that not so?"

"What if it is?"

"Then in exchange for a written declaration that neither you nor the lord regent will make war against my clan, House Okuma will surrender its Inazuma blade."

Over his left shoulder Daigoro heard a gasp from General Mio. "No," Mio whispered. "That sword was your father's."

"Whose side are you on?" snapped Shichio.

Mio ignored him. "Think carefully on this, my boy. There must be another way."

"I stand by my word." Daigoro said it quickly, decisively. He could not afford to think it over as Mio advised. He had already taken the plunge; there was no room for hesitation.

A sly smile crept across Shichio's face. "The sword and the monk."

"The monk is already dead to the world," Daigoro said. "He will never leave his monastery again. When he dies, I hope his spirit haunts you for the rest of your days, but in this life he is no threat to anyone. And the Inazuma is a onetime offer. Take it now or show me to the door."

"You presume a great deal, little cub."

He was right and Daigoro knew it. Shichio could have him killed with no more than a word. He wouldn't even have to do it here, where fortune might turn against him long enough to see Glorious Victory's razor-sharp edge find his throat. Shichio had only to wait until Daigoro and Katsushima were safely outside the palace, then order an entire regiment to run them down.

Daigoro had only two things in his favor. The first was greed. He'd seen it before in his brother, whose lust for the Inazuma had killed him. If Shichio were as mad for the blade as Daigoro suspected he was, his need for it would blind him. Even now Shichio's eyes were fixated on it; perhaps his thoughts were equally fixed, equally immune to distraction.

The second factor in Daigoro's favor was no more than a gamble, about a man he'd met only once before. Daigoro studied Hideyoshi, trying to read his thoughts, but the regent's apelike face revealed nothing.

"Done," Shichio said, distracting Daigoro from his attempt at reading Hideyoshi's mind. "Jun! Fetch your writing tools."

A reedy young man appeared in an instant, a tiny table under one arm and a wooden box under the other. In no time at all he deployed his paper, ink block, inkstone, and brush. The reedy man wore neither topknot nor sword, so he was not military, but the fact that Shichio knew his name told Daigoro that he must have ranked highly among the servants. The thought of such a servant brought Tomo's smiling face to mind. Daigoro wondered how deep the silt layer was on the bottom of the pond. Was it stable enough to support his weight? If so, he could reach Shichio in two steps and remove his head from his skinny peacock neck.

No. Through force of will he pressed his palms into his lap so he would not draw his sword. "On behalf of the Okuma clan," Daigoro said, and he proceeded to dictate the terms of the truce. The man-servant quickly inscribed two copies.

"There," Shichio said after signing them and affixing his seal. "Give me the sword."

"I haven't signed yet," said Daigoro. "Nor will I, unless the lord regent and General Mio also sign."

Shichio's face soured as if he were suddenly seasick. His dark eyes glared at the imposing form of General Mio. No doubt Shichio had been planning betrayal, but as soon as Mio signed the treaty, Daigoro knew his family was safe. Any treachery on Shichio's part would now malign Mio as well, and Mio was born to the code. He took his honor seriously, and he was in a position to hold Shichio to his word.

The regent's signature was necessary too, for it was not enough for Daigoro to shield his family against Shichio's troops. Shichio wielded a mysterious power over Hideyoshi, and though Daigoro could not explain it, his intuition insisted that it would not be hard for Shichio to orchestrate a Toyotomi attack on any target he chose. With his regal seal and a few brushstrokes, Hideyoshi himself rendered that possibility both illegal and—far more importantly—dishonorable.

"Very well," Shichio said impatiently, passing the little writing tablet to Hideyoshi, who, having signed, had the manservant pass it to Mio. "Does that satisfy you?" Shichio asked. "Would you like anyone else to sign? The emperor, perhaps? Or would you like to see if the gods are busy this afternoon?"

"No," Daigoro said, "this is quite enough, General." He brushed the characters on each page, not Okuma Izu-no-kami Daigoro but simply Daigoro. It was the first time he'd ever signed that way.

He handed Shichio a copy of the signed treaty along with a second scroll. He did not hand over Glorious Victory Unsought.

"What is this?" Shichio snatched both documents from Daigoro like a dog stealing food from a table. Tossing aside the truce he'd just signed, he hunched over the second scroll and read it with a frown that deepened with every passing line.

"Damn you, Okuma, what is the meaning of this?"

"My name isn't Okuma anymore," Daigoro said. "I have formally relinquished both name and title."

"No," Mio said, aghast. "Okuma-san, what have you done?"

"I could not retain my father's name and my father's sword. General Shichio saw to that. As I am honor-bound to protect both, I can only keep his sword by relinquishing his name. And now, thanks to you three noble men, my family is protected too. I thank you all."

"Pah!" Shichio threw the scroll into the pond. Carp scattered away as if it were a pouncing cat, and the ink from it sent little black snakes swimming through the water. "What do I care what you call yourself? The Inazuma is mine."

"The Okumas' Inazuma is yours," said Daigoro. "I am no longer an Okuma."

Shichio rose to his feet. "A technicality! Give me your sword!"

"If you care to wet your feet, General, you may yet be able to make out the date on that scroll. I delivered a copy to my family at the same time I signed this one—three days ago. The decree you've fed to your master's carp takes precedence over the treaty you signed with me."

Shichio was fuming. General Mio gave a little snort. Hideyoshi laughed so hard he nearly fell off his bench.

His laughter only angered Shichio further. His carefully preened hair released a few rogue strands to stray across his face, and when he pushed them away from his sweating forehead he knocked loose even more. "No!" he shrieked. "*You* signed the truce. Only an Okuma can sign for the Okumas!"

"An Okuma," Daigoro said, "or their duly appointed representative. You there—Jun, isn't it?—read the first sentence of our treaty."

Already on his knees, the gaunt young man scrambled across the grass for the truce. " 'On behalf of the Okuma clan—' "

"There," said Daigoro, "do you see?"

"Ha!" Hideyoshi's laugh came with the force of a musket ball. "He's got you there, Shichio. Clever, isn't he?"

"Very," Mio said solemnly. "Daigoro-san, what have you done?"

"He's outfoxed the fox," said Hideyoshi, still enjoying himself immensely. "Signing on behalf of his family instead of as one of them! I like this little bastard."

"He is insolent," said Shichio, his voice warmer that it should have been—warm as a serpent's, whispering in Hideyoshi's ear. "You ought to reprimand him. He disrespects you."

"Maybe so," said Hideyoshi, "but he sure is good for a laugh. Okuma-san—or Daigoro, or whatever the hell you're calling yourself—I swear, if I had a thousand officers like you, I'd have conquered China by now."

Daigoro bowed deeply. The regent just shook his head and snickered. "I'd offer you room and board for the night, you and your bodyguard too, but even I couldn't vouch for your safety. Shichio wouldn't sleep until someone put a knife in you."

"A knife!" Katsushima said the word with disdain; it was a child's toy, better suited for whittling than for a fight between grown men. "Let him go and fetch one. I'll wait."

"Mind the laws of hospitality," General Mio said in a warning tone. "If guests provoke a fight in another man's home, the penalty for the instigator is death."

"I'm happy to pay the price," said Katsushima. "If he wants to pretend at wearing a sword, let him draw it. If not, let him go and get his knife."

"Easy, now," said Hideyoshi, suddenly as cold as an ice storm. "Don't go spoiling things now that you're ahead."

"My lord regent," Daigoro said, "the treaty—"

"Yes, yes, the treaty. Don't worry, boy; it's as good as my word—and I know you don't think much of a peasant's word, but trust me, I've no plans to wipe out your family. Hell, just keeping the treaty in force will be enough to entertain me for years. You have no idea what fits of madness I can expect to see from Shichio over this."

And just like that, Hideyoshi was warm and sunny again. Suddenly Daigoro understood why the man was so dangerous. With a hundred thousand troops at his back, a mind like his could tear down the world—and Hideyoshi could muster a million if he had a mind to.

But capricious as he was, the regent was still a keen judge of character. Just as he'd said, Shichio was apoplectic. The peacock tried to speak, maybe even tried to scream, but his anger choked him. The sight of it made Hideyoshi snort and snigger.

"I daresay it's best for you to take your leave," said General Mio. He eyed Shichio as if he were not a peacock but a rabid dog. "Sooner would be better than later." Rising noisily to his feet, Mio led Daigoro and Katsushima out of the garden.

37

When they reached the stables, Mio said, "Do you have any idea what trouble you've caused?"

"General, my most heartfelt apologies," Daigoro said. "You must understand, I needed one who lives by the code to sign with him—"

"Oh, I understand well enough. But I did not speak of the troubles you've caused for me—though you've released a flock of them, damn you. I was speaking of the troubles you've caused for yourself. You are no longer lord protector of Izu. You've no title to protect you anymore."

Daigoro nodded. The full weight of his decision had not yet settled on him, and now he wasn't sure he could bear it once it fell. "What other choice was left to me?" he said.

"None," Mio said with a shrug. "But have no fear; I'll keep an eye on Shichio for you. Even so, it is in his nature to look for a way out of the treaty. I cannot promise he won't find one."

"He won't. I thought it through."

Mio laughed his deep, booming laugh. "That you did. The regent wasn't wrong, you know. With a thousand officers who think like you, we could conquer the world. It's a shame you surrendered your troops when you surrendered your title."

"They're safer without me at their head."

"And yet there's not a one of them who wouldn't die for you. You're a good leader, son. They won't forgive you easily for leaving them."

Daigoro swallowed. "I hadn't thought about that."

"Few leaders do. But a commander can abandon his troops just as well as a soldier can abandon his post. They'll be adrift for a while. Your family will be vulnerable."

"But Shichio—"

"Yes. Shichio." A frown soured Mio's face. "He cannot touch your family. You've seen to that, and I will see to the rest. By this time tomorrow, all of the regent's high command will know your family is untouchable. But have no doubt, Master Bear Cub: he will send people for *you*. Bounty hunters. *Shinobi*. You'd best be careful."

"You too."

"Me? He doesn't have the balls to come after me. He never was one for bloodshed. No, our Shichio is no swordsman. He did all his generalship with an ink brush."

Daigoro nodded. "I'll take your word for it. You know him better than I do."

"More's the pity."

The three of them exchanged bows and farewells; then Daigoro and Katsushima mounted up and were on their way.

Their horses trotted across the bridge into the light of the setting sun. Behind them the Jurakudai gleamed so brightly that they could see their own shadows cast before them. The noises and smells of the city returned: sweat and horse droppings, hawkers hawking and prostitutes cooing, sandalwood incense from a nearby temple, hoofbeats on cobblestone.

The low angle of the sun cast deep shadows too, these ones pointing in the right direction, pooling behind every barrel and handcart. Daigoro thought of Mio and his warning about *shinobi*. As a child he'd always imagined black-clad ninja warriors hiding in the shadows, but now that he understood more about tactics, he knew it was better to hide in plain sight. Shichio's *shinobi* would not come to Daigoro in black masks; they would come in the guise of an innkeep, a beggar, a farmhand. Daigoro looked down the street that stretched before him and could not tell if he saw a thousand people or five thousand. He had no acquaintance with people in such masses. He knew only that it was impossible to keep an eye on every one of them, and any one of them might be an assassin.

"By the buddhas," Daigoro said, "Katsushima, what are we going to do?"

"You hadn't given thought to that already?"

Daigoro realized he hadn't. He'd thought as far ahead as keeping his family safe and staying alive himself, to protect them if need be. He had no plan for getting back to Izu, nor any idea of where else to go or what he might do when he got there.

He was glad his mother was tucked safely away in some corner of the Okuma compound. He was relieved to know Aki was safe too, though he could not imagine how he could ever earn her forgiveness. The news that he'd renounced his name would reach home before the week was out. He realized now that he'd given too little thought to how his mother and wife would take it. Would they see how much he'd sacrificed, or would they focus only on how he'd abandoned them? Would they understand that he'd saved their lives? Would Akiko think he'd fled as soon as he learned he was to become a father? They hadn't known each other long; could she guess how sorely he longed to be with her, to meet his child?

He wanted to book passage on the fastest ship bound north and east. He wanted to put his heels to his mare and ride all night. And he knew that Shichio would expect exactly this reaction. He would have people watching the ports, and every entrance to the city as well. Daigoro had already seen him place his own agents within Hideyoshi's troops, and Hideyoshi's troops patrolled every road in the Kansai.

There would be covert threats too. Assassins would come. Daigoro did not doubt Mio's word on that. For the time being, Daigoro had to be unpredictable. He had to vanish—for a while, he told himself. Until Shichio finds someone else to fixate on. Soon enough someone else will anger him, he thought. Soon he will find some other treasure he wants, maybe even another Inazuma blade. Glorious Victory is not the only one. Yes, Daigoro told himself, soon there would be someone else to hate, something else to need, and then Daigoro could go back and reclaim his rightful place at the head of his clan.

He envisioned that day, riding past the kudzu-covered peaks of Izu on his triumphant return home. Then he remembered the abbot of Kattō-ji, whose temple sat on one of those peaks—the abbot of Kattō-ji, who remained the object of Shichio's petty, vindictive spite even after all these years. Suddenly Daigoro's dreams of returning home became nightmares.

There was only one solution. Until he brought it to fruition, he had no choice but to remain hidden. But sooner or later, he would ride back home—right after testing Glorious Victory's steel on Shichio's throat.

38

"General Mio! I can't tell you how glad I am to see you awake."

Shichio watched the fat man's eyelids flutter. Mio tried to sit up, but only succeeded in causing the rope across his forehead to pull tighter. His skin went white where his skull pressed against the rough hempen rope, then flushed again when he relaxed.

Shichio watched the arms next, which, with all the coils of rope digging into them, looked like stacked balls of *mochi*. The fat bulged up between the tight coils, and as Mio's entire body was enrobed in a layer of fat, the bulges stood out everywhere, like massive worms lying in rows. The candles in their wall sconces cast a hundred dark valleys of shadow across Mio's body, making the bonds seem tighter and the bulges seem larger. The biggest rolls stood up between the ropes across the belly; the smallest curved across the tops of the feet and the backs of the hands.

The table he lay on was specially constructed for this purpose. It was vaguely human in shape, sloping downward at the head, its armlike protrusions pointing at the molding where the ceiling met the wall. Each hand was bound to the table with a single coil, making the back of the hand look like two puffy loaves of bread.

The eyes rolled wide and white in Mio's head. Shichio followed their gaze to the stout rafters, the white plaster between them, the elegant golden wood grain of the walls. "Ah," Shichio said, "wondering where you are, *neh*? Shall I give you a hint? This is the least beautiful room of the Jurakudai—and I say that even considering Hashiba's hideous taste in decorating."

Shichio gently ran his fingertips over Mio's swollen right hand. "I must confess my ignorance," he said. "I never knew a man could grow so large that his feet and hands were fat. But then I took another look at the *rikishi* painting that Hashiba commissioned from Kanō Eitoku. Do you know Kanō?"

Mio strained against his bonds, causing his skin to go white in a hundred places. "Shichio?"

"At your service." Shichio smiled, causing the iron mask to push against his cheeks. "You're slurring your words, General. Best to wait until the sleeping poison wears off, don't you think?"

Mio's eyes rolled this way and that, reddening as he strained to turn his head. "What is this?"

"I'll be asking the questions tonight," Shichio said, stuffing a wad of silk into Mio's mouth. "Now, Kanō: do you know his work? He's quite the fashion in the Imperial Court. And do you know what? In Hashiba's painting, the *rikishi*'s hands and feet *are* fat. Isn't that something? It takes a Kanō to devote that much attention to detail, *neh*? I swear to you, I never noticed it before tonight."

Mio managed to spit out the silk. "Have you stripped me naked? Damn you, untie me this instant!"

Shichio would not be yelled at like a little boy. He whipped out his knife and sliced off one of the fat rolls on the back of Mio's hand. The giant roared like a bull.

"Oh, that is a shame," Shichio said. "And to think all this time I'd planned on making the first cut with *your* sword."

The bright red wound on Mio's hand looked like a mouth. The sight of it made Shichio want to retch, but the mask wanted him to take off another slice. Yet its power was not so complete that it over-whelmed his moral sensibilities. Once a man was tied down and helpless, even to threaten him was morally despicable. Shichio knew that in his bones. That was what made the samurai caste so tyrannical:

the peasantry lived in fear of them, every hour of every day, with no hope of defense or reprisal. Shichio had lived his entire life in fear, until Hashiba showed him a higher path. If the Toyotomi flag flew over every last province and territory, if everyone bowed to one man, then there would be no more need for samurai. It was war that necessitated warriors, and it was the existence of the warrior caste—a caste with exclusive rights to arms and armor and vengeance—that made every commoner live in terror.

And yet here he was, behaving like a samurai, exerting his might over a defenseless man.

No. Not a defenseless man. A defenseless *samurai*. Mio deserved this. All of them did.

"Let me show you the one I'd planned to be the first cut," Shichio said. He walked away from the table, and from the bleeding, cursing, struggling giant. He took up Mio's enormous *katana*, drew it, and tossed the scabbard aside. Mio strained against the ropes, furious. Shichio could not help but laugh. Only a born samurai could be bound to a table, naked and bleeding, and still be angry that someone had disrespected his scabbard.

"Release me! I'm Mio Yasumasa, damn you! I demand that you release me this instant!"

"Oh, you're not in a position to demand anything, are you? No. No, you're not."

Shichio laid the base of the blade gingerly on the roll of flesh just above Mio's left knee. He drew the blade slowly across, penetrating deeper just a hairsbreadth at a time, so that only when the very tip of the sword passed through did he sever the last ribbon of skin. The roll of flesh flopped to the floor like a butchered fish. Mio roared louder than ever.

"You see?" said Shichio. "*That's* what I was looking for."

The blood streamed toward Mio's groin, for Shichio's table sloped downward at a slight angle and Mio's head was lowermost. "You don't think much of me as a fighter, do you, Mio? No, I think not. But unlike you, I appreciate martial art as *art*. Precision. Patience. Exactitude. Hallmarks of my brand of swordsmanship, though not so much of yours, I think."

Through gritted teeth Mio said, "Cut my bonds and we'll see who's the better swordsman."

This time Shichio laid the blade on Mio's shoulder, drawing it across the skin slowly and deliberately. Mio growled like a rabid animal. "You would expect more blood from a cut this large, *neh*? It's the ropes; they slow the bleeding considerably."

Shichio lifted the blade and whipped it past Mio's face. Warm red droplets flew from the steel, spattering the fat man's cheeks and eyes like rain. "Ah," Shichio said. "Figured out to stop talking, have you? That's all right. This was always meant to be a one-sided conversation anyway, wasn't it? Yes, it was. Yes, it was."

This time he laid the *katana*'s razor edge against two rolls of flesh, these on the top of Mio's left foot. "I suppose you're wondering now whether you should have sided with the Okuma boy, *neh*? Maybe you're also wondering whether Hideyoshi will allow me to kill the boy once you're no longer at court."

Mio twitched and cursed and struggled. "Oh, now look what you've done," Shichio said. I nicked the rope, you fat oaf; you've gone and spoiled my cut."

A mighty kick from the fat man freed his left leg, but only from the shin down. Shichio shuddered at the sight of it. "Idiot! You'll only bleed faster now. It's a good thing I didn't tie you with your head upward, *neh*? You'd lose consciousness in no time. And where would be the justice in that?"

Mio bellowed so loud that it shook the walls. Shichio lost patience with him and stuffed a silken scarf in Mio's mouth. "You've already spoiled my chance to kill the boy," he said. "You and Hashiba both. And I can't punish Hashiba, can I? No. But you? You deserve it. All samurai deserve it." And with that he sliced off a nipple.

The fat man writhed and raged, but he only succeeded in chafing himself on the ropes. "Isn't it ironic?" Shichio said. "From the very beginning, my mask awakened thoughts of swords in me—but only thoughts. I always found bloodshed repugnant, but then the boy marred my beautiful mask. Now I find it's not enough merely to think of blades; I must put them to use. Your bleeding still sickens me. Yes, it does. I despise it, and yet the mask awakens this *need* in me. Do you see the irony? It's because of the boy that I'm going to kill you, and you were the boy's last remaining defender."

At last Mio managed to spit out the silk. "You forget your precious 'Hashiba,'" he said. "Let him take his cock out of your mouth long enough to think straight and he'll remember that treaty you signed. Then you'll be the next one strapped to this table."

"I am growing tired of that tongue of yours," he said. "To tell you the truth, I tired of it a long time ago. I had all but convinced Hashiba to push the Okumas into the sea, and you talked him out of it, didn't you? Yes, you did. Well, how much longer did you think I was going to put up with that?"

"If you kill me, he'll kill you next."

"I think not. Oh, but I've forgotten to tell you, haven't I? I've made you an enemy of the throne."

"What?"

"They will find the first evidence of your treason in the morning. You've been corresponding with Tokugawa Ieyasu, I'm afraid, conspiring to unseat the lord regent. I don't know all the details. It's Jun who wrote the letters on your behalf—at my command, of course, but I allowed him a free hand when it came to their actual content. It wouldn't do for me to accidentally implicate myself, would it? Not when I'm so close to ridding myself of you and the Bear Cub."

"You son of a whore! I'm no traitor!" Mio pulled so hard against the ropes that Shichio could hear the fibers stetching. "You're deranged! I'll see you burned at the stake for this."

"Now what did I tell you about that tongue?" Shichio tied another bond, this one across Mio's lower jaw, pulling Mio's chin back so he could not bite down. Then Shichio tossed Mio's huge *katana* aside, drew his knife, and stuck it in Mio's mouth.

"You see? Look what good struggling does you. I didn't mean to cut your lip, did I? I didn't mean to cut the roof of your mouth. But you won't take your punishment, will you? No, you won't."

The tongue was warm and sticky in his fingers, utterly repulsive. Shichio flicked it on the floor. "Now, how am I going to destroy the Okumas if I can't attack them? Hm? Answer me that. And how long do I have until Hashiba starts getting serious about the monk? Thus far I've been able to distract him, but if he ever presses for the truth in earnest, I am not long for this world. And we can't have that, can we? No. No, we can't."

Shichio ran his hand over his iron brow. "The monk vexes me," he said. "His very existence makes me want to scream." Then he laid his knife against the largest roll on Mio's belly and drew it across with exquisite languor.

"How?" Shichio said, ignoring Mio's gurgling, wordless moans. "The Okumas are the key to reaching the monk, but how can I put an end to the Okumas? No doubt the boy is already plotting to kill me. And can I kill him? No. Hashiba even denied me the use of his assassins. Can you believe it? He favors the boy over me. He said the little Bear Cub has big bear balls. Those were his exact words. How could he say such a thing?"

He looked back at Mio, who spat up a mouthful of blood. "You agree with me, don't you? I can hardly let the boy live. No doubt the monk told him my secret. And what of his family? The monk is under their protection. How can I allow them to live? You'd do the same, wouldn't you? If you were in my position, you'd kill them all. Yes, you would."

He pushed the knife through one of the fat rolls on Mio's thigh and left it there. The hilt quivered every time the fat man twitched. "I'm going to finish this with my own sword, I think. It seems the more appropriate choice." He stood over Mio and drew his blade. "It will be no challenge when I decide to take your head, you know. I'll just chop it off, won't I? Yes, I will. But how do I decapitate a clan whose head has simply decided to leave it?"

His sword dropped idly toward Mio's neck. It was more than sharp enough to kill even with only its own weight behind it, but Shichio's intent was only to nick Mio's remaining ear. But that wretched Okuma boy had unsettled him even more than he'd thought, for he missed the ear completely. Instead he cut the rope binding Mio's neck to the table.

The fat man took a deep gulping breath. He made a strangled, gurgling noise, then a horrid red geyser erupted out of his mouth, followed by a desperate gasp. His sputtering sent flecks of blood everywhere. Shichio didn't dare think of what a mess it made of his kimono.

"Do you see?" he said. "You samurai are no different from the rest of us. You claim to be fearless of death, but when you're choking on your own blood, you cough it up just like anyone else, *neh*? Yes. Yes, you do. Samurai, peasants, nobles, outcasts; we're all the same. Even the Bear Cub will die the same as anyone else, and to hell with all his vaunted nobility."

Shichio paced around the table, willfully ignoring the blood on the floor. It reeked. Somehow Mio's blood overwhelmed even the fetid stink of the slaughterhouse, which was just next door. "How to decapitate a clan that has no head? It's almost a *kōan*, isn't it? Beheading the headless."

He looked at his sword. "Who commands the Okumas now? The cub's deranged mother, I suppose. The poor creature. She lost her husband and her eldest in the space of a year, didn't she? Yes, she did, and now her youngest son has forsaken her too."

Like a bolt of lightning, a plan suddenly flashed before Shichio's eyes. He only caught a glimpse, but the vision of it lingered in his mind. "That's it, isn't it, Mio? Yes, it is. She's unmarried."

He sliced off another flopping fish, this one from just under Mio's armpit. "Do you see the brilliance of it? I needn't decapitate the Okumas; I need only to give them a new head. If I marry the dowager, *I* become head of the clan."

The thought of it sent chills down Shichio's spine. "But do I dare? If I marry her, I become one of you. Samurai. The caste I want most to extinguish. And yet . . . ."

He laid his blade carefully along the length of Mio's right thigh, poised to cut not one but three of the bulging rolls of flesh. "If I were to do this thing"—he craned his head to meet Mio's gaze—"I remove that little cub from his house forever. I earn myself name, station, and land. Oh! And when I take the Okuma estate, I also acquire that old traitor's monastery, and then I can kill him whenever I like. Even you can see the beauty in that, *neh*? I win three prizes in one stroke."

With that he let lashed out with his *katana*, slicing off three fat gobbets in one blow.

Suddenly the table crashed sideways. A fat foot struck Shichio in the chin. Fragments of rope flew through the air, and ribbons of blood too. The back of Shichio's head bounced hard off the wall, and when he could see through the stars Mio Yasumasa was gone.

There was a huge, blood-streaked hole where the fat man had crashed through the *shoji*. Some way off there came a wooden, splintering crash—Mio, probably bashing his way through another sliding wall, far enough now that he posed no immediate threat.

Shichio stood. His gore-stained clothes clung to him, making him want to retch. He stepped outside into the cool night air, seeking respite from the coppery stench of the table. Footprints, elephantine and bloody, described a stomping path toward the slaughterhouse. Fitting, Shichio thought. Let him die with the rest of the swine.

It took him a long moment to sort out what had happened. His final cut must have bitten deeper than he'd intended, slicing through rope as well as flesh. He'd inadvertently freed Mio's right leg.

It was an understandable mistake. Shichio had never been a practiced hand at torture. Up until tonight he'd never been able to stomach it beyond the first few cuts. Somehow the Bear Cub's blade had changed that: it released some demonic bloodlust latent in the mask, a thirst so intense that it could overwhelm Shichio's revulsion. And even if Shichio had been an expert, Mio was so bloated that it was impossible to see all of the ropes. Still, it amazed Shichio to think of how much strength the fat man had. Even after losing all that blood, he still had the strength to tip the table, to aim a kick Shichio's head, to brace his legs firmly enough to burst his remaining bonds.

Shichio stroked the sharp corner of his mask's broken fang, the one the Bear Cub had nicked. He wondered what to do next. The fat man wouldn't make it far. He was naked, unarmed, and bleeding horribly. There was nowhere for him to hide; he was simply too noticeable in his current state.

On the other hand, Shichio had indulged his habit of thinking out loud. The fat man had heard everything. If he somehow managed to reach the Bear Cub . . .

No. He had no tongue.

Shichio laughed out loud. It was unthinkable that Mio would find the boy—for that matter, it was hardly imaginable that he hadn't collapsed already—but if karma allowed Daigoro to find the fat man before Shichio did, it wouldn't matter; Mio could relay no secrets.

In any case, Daigoro would certainly have to find him before sunrise. No one—not even a mammoth of Mio's size—could survive more than a few hours with such hideous wounds. What was more, Daigoro had left the Jurakudai three days ago, and he was mounted while Mio was on foot. And of course Mio would not think to run to Daigoro. He would run to Hashiba, where his wounds would be recognized on sight. Hashiba knew the fruits of his table all too well; he'd sentenced dozens of men to this fate.

And that meant Mio would have recognized the table too. Shichio hadn't thought of that: unlike anyone else who had ever been lashed down to the table, Mio had seen its results before. He must have known what was coming from the moment he came to, yet all he'd shown Shichio was vitriol and spite. Not the slightest trace of fear.

Shichio could not help but marvel at that. Nor did the poetry of the moment escape him. How many times had the samurai been compared to the cherry blossom, beautiful precisely because it died at the height of its beauty? It was worthy of a song: Mio, the most honored of samurai, and Shichio, gaining his first shred of respect for Mio only after he'd killed him.

Hashiba felt otherwise. He'd honored Mio from the start, and that meant his initial reaction would be harsh. There was no way of guessing whether it would be sharp words or sharper swords; Hashiba was nothing if not capricious. Shichio knew he would have to be swift in presenting the evidence he'd fabricated of Mio's treason, or else risk facing execution himself. But he was a practiced hand at making others believe what he wanted them to believe, and it was not as if Mio Yasumasa could speak in his own defense.

No, there was little to worry about. "But," Shichio said, alone in the moonlit garden, "you are nothing if not thorough. It wouldn't do to leave things to chance, would it?" Shichio cleaned the blood from his blade and sheathed it. "No. No, it wouldn't."

He sent for Jun and began composing the orders in his mind. Riders would be sent to every gate and bridge in the city, looking for the fat man. And—why not?—for the now-nameless Bear Cub as well. If the boy hadn't left the city, and if Mio somehow found him . . .

Shichio smiled. "Why, that would be the best of all, wouldn't it? Yes, it would. Execute the boy for collaborating with a known traitor."

Suddenly Shichio wished he'd let Mio go on purpose. He couldn't have laid a better trap, and he was a little disappointed in himself that he hadn't planned it that way from the start.

39

The Kamo River gurgled at Daigoro's feet, though he could hardly see the water. Across the river a fierce red glow loomed over the rolling line of the horizon: the sun's last light above the hilltops, lingering in spite of the stars that had already begun to multiply. They would overwhelm her soon enough. Here and there a bush warbler whistled its melancholic song. To Daigoro they were singing an elegy for the day.

He'd come down to the riverbank three nights in a row, relishing the relative cool after sweltering days, hoping to find beauty somewhere in the world and finding only emptiness. Katsushima had described him as forlorn. And well I should be, Daigoro thought, watching the sun's last light die out. I haven't the faintest clue how to draw Shichio out without angering Hideyoshi. If I kill Shichio without Hideyoshi's leave, I make myself an enemy of the mightiest, most capricious warlord in the empire—and worse yet, Hideyoshi might well extend his vengeance to Akiko, my mother, and the rest of my family. We made our truce over Glorious Victory Unsought, not over me decapitating the regent's favorite peacock.

Daigoro knew he could not return home until Shichio was dead, but neither could he stay on the outskirts of Kyoto. Katsushima had been right to suggest that they could burrow themselves in the city—there were so many people to hide behind, so many out-of-the-way places—but that ruse would only last for so long. Shichio had hun-

dreds of men at his command, and even if he did not, he had only to
offer a few coins for any word of the crippled boy with the enormous
ōdachi. Sooner or later, news of Daigoro's whereabouts would reach
him, and once that happened, the hunt was on.

Daigoro's only chance was to draw Shichio out somehow, but shel-
tered as he was in the regent's shadow, Shichio might as well have been
hiding in an iron fortress. Daigoro could not imagine how he might
strike Hideyoshi's top adviser without striking Hideyoshi himself.
Katsushima had suggested calling on the Wind, but Daigoro wasn't
desperate enough to resort to that yet.

Footsteps approached through the tall grass behind him and
Daigoro whirled around to see who was coming.

"Good news," Katsushima said. He held up two large sacks, flat on
the bottom with rigid, bowl-shaped lumps inside.

"Our armor?" said Daigoro.

"Yes. He finished early."

Katsushima set one of the sacks right next to Daigoro, then sat
down on the other side of it. "Nice night."

Daigoro grunted something noncommittal and opened the draw-
strings. Inside the sack was his Sora breastplate, its russet Okuma
lacing removed and replaced with white, the color of death. In fact,
everything replaceable had been replaced in white: the silk cording,
the leather straps, the padded damask, all of it. Even the steel plating
had been relacquered in white. Daigoro's helmet was in the sack too,
nestled inside the breastplate with the *sune-ate*, the *kote*, and the rest
of the smaller pieces.

"It hardly feels like mine anymore."

"It's yours, Daigoro. And it's far easier to dye if it's white. We may
need to disguise ourselves again."

Daigoro started laying the pieces out on the grass. "I know," he
said. "And in the meantime, I guess it's appropriate enough that we're
dressing ourselves in funeral colors."

"You need to lighten up. I'm telling you, a good sporting woman
will have you in fine fettle in no time at all."

Daigoro shook his head and began to bind his *sune-ate* to his shins.

"What are you doing?" said Katsushima.

"Standing by my word. I told you already: as long as Shichio lives, I am at war. I may as well dress for the occasion."

Katsushima smirked. "Fair enough. But armoring yourself *now* is overmuch, is it not? Tonight we go only to our beds. Do you intend to sleep in your armor?"

"I would if I could."

"Daigoro—"

"We're *targets*, Katsushima. For us the whole countryside is a battlefield."

"All right, all right. But we're only going down the road—"

"My father was killed only riding along the road. And he had no enemy so powerful as Shichio. Going unarmored is a luxury I can no longer afford."

Daigoro slipped his right arm into its *kote* and tied it fast, examining it as he did so. The ruddy damask padding that lined the inside had been replaced with white, but where the original had silken bears pacing across its surface, the replacement was a simple, unadorned basket weave. That made sense, he supposed; Kyoto's weavers might take days just to learn the bear pattern, a pattern that Okuma weavers knew from memory. Even so, Daigoro regretted the change. Even in the waning light he could feel the difference, and the problem was not that this coarse fabric was suited for common stock; rather, it was the thought of his family's bear crest heaped in the rubbish bin of some Nishijin weaving-house.

He donned the second *kote*, lamenting the fact that even his Sora armor couldn't protect him as much as he'd like. Wearing his full *ōyoroi* wouldn't do—it would only serve to call attention to himself—but he had resolved to wear every piece he could reasonably hide under his clothing. That ruled out all the large pieces save the Sora breastplate. It felt strange to be armored only partially, but then everything about his new situation felt strange. He was Daigoro but not Okuma Daigoro. He was married and yet he might never see his wife again.

Some not-so-distant day he would become a father, but in all like-lihood he would never know when it happened.

Daigoro slipped between the clamshell pieces of his Sora *yoroi* and pulled the straps until the heavy steel pressed firmly on his chest and his back. Last came his new *haori*, the overrobe he'd purchased the day before, right after he and Katsushima had left their *yoroi* with the ar-morer. With its wide, white, pointed shoulders, the *haori* made Daigoro feel as if he had wings, and between the *haori* and the added girth of his armor, he thought perhaps he no longer looked like a little boy. For the first time in his life he actually looked like a samurai. And it would not last long. He'd scarcely gotten used to shaving the top of his head, and now he would have to stop. It was the samurai's birthright to maintain the caste's traditional topknot and shaven pate, but Daigoro had given up his birthright when he'd renounced his name. For a few months Okuma Daigoro had been samurai, a man of age, the lord of his house. Now he did not know what he was.

"What do you think?" he said. "How do I look?"

Katsushima inspected him. "You look like a lordly man who will sleep alone tonight."

"Be serious."

Katsushima laughed and said, "By the buddhas, the world is not only shadow; there is sunlight too." Seeing Daigoro's reaction, he forced a straight face. "Very well. In all seriousness, you do not appear to be armored, and in all seriousness I think you will go to bed tonight without a woman to play your flute."

Daigoro slung Glorious Victory over his back, thrust his *wakizashi* back through his belt, and led Katsushima back to their shelter for the evening.

Three nights earlier, when they'd left the Jurakudai, Daigoro had found himself at a loss. He'd never had to hide from anyone before. In fact, in his whole life thus far he'd always been able to get what he wanted simply by announcing his name. To go abroad without an-nouncing himself was awkward, and to actively deceive people about his identity came as naturally to him as riding horseback came to a fish. He remembered all too well saying, "Goemon, I have no idea what to do or where to go."

And he remembered all too well the wry smile Katushima had given him in return. "At last," Katsushima had said, "we come to my territory."

Hence the brothel.

It embarrassed Daigoro even to cross the threshold. Jasmine perfume and opium smoke had worked their way into the very woodwork, so that Daigoro was overcome by the smell of the place. Girlish giggling was constantly in the background, punctuated now and then by the whistle of a *shakuhachi*, the humming harmony of a *shamisen*, or the staccato rhythm of some unseen man grunting like a pig.

Daigoro did not think of himself as a prude. Back when he was at home he'd been well aware that he could have visited any pleasure house in Izu on any night he wished, and the only difference in being married was that as manager of the household finances, Akiko would have been the one who paid the bill. She would have understood as any wife would have understood—and she'd be all the more understanding, Daigoro reminded himself, if he availed himself of the women here, so many *ri* from home. But the smells and sounds of this house reminded him all too vividly of the pleasure house Ichirō had taken him to visit when they were boys. His cheeks burned as he remembered the embarrassment, the woman's cold hand slipping down into his *hakama*, her fingertips finding the wasted tissues of his thigh on their way to what they sought. Her face had been so close to his that he could feel her breath, smell it, taste it. Had she been any farther away, he might not have noticed her wince when her fingers touched his thigh. It was a vanishingly small expression, and she'd recovered instantly, but still he'd noticed. That same embarrassment was reborn in his face even now.

The girls that eyed him now misinterpreted it as boyish hesitation. He was small, and had a young-looking face even for a sixteen-year-old. Two of the girls tittered at him and pranced up on tiptoes. They were wispy and delicate, and when they whispered in his ears their breath made the skin on his forearms tingle. The things they said would have made their own madam blush. He knew his ears and cheeks turned red, because the girls exploded in a fit of giggles and went flitting off like a couple of butterflies.

"Ladies, be polite," the madam told them. She was stately, statuesque, with a husky voice and sly, knowing eyes. She wore a green brocade kimono with silver threads that matched the silver streak in the middle of her long, flowing hair.

"Gentlemen," she said, her voice low and smoky, "so pleased to see you again. I've got something special in store for you if you'll follow me."

"No, thank you," said Daigoro. "I'll just need a bath and a bed."

The madam arched a black eyebrow at him. "You'll forgive me, my young lord, if I suggest a woman of my maturity knows what you need more than you do. Trust me: come this way and you won't regret it."

Daigoro felt his cheeks flush. She held his gaze much longer than she should have, and Daigoro thought it might have been a silent offer to service him herself. Her eyes flashed at him, and he realized what he saw in them was not desire at all. It was fear.

"All right," he said, and the madam's eyes flashed again. What was she afraid of? It certainly wasn't Daigoro. She stood head and shoulders taller than him, but apart from that, she had the air of one who had survived everything a man could imagine. She needed only a glance to know Daigoro had no intention to kill her, and none of his other intentions could threaten her in the least.

He followed her upstairs, where the lanterns burned low and the scent of incense was stronger than ever. Katsushima followed, along with the two butterflies that had whispered in Daigoro's ear when he'd first come in. "Your man should wait in there," the madam said, and her graceful hand gestured snakelike at a door. Instantly one of the butterflies knelt beside it and opened it. The other flitted to Katsushima, tucked a finger under his belt, and beckoned him inside.

Katsushima's hungry eyes appraised her; then he looked back to Daigoro. "I, uh—"

"You won't be needing him where you're going," the madam told Daigoro. The second of the butterflies took Katsushima by the arm, and the two of them tugged him into the room and closed the *shoji*.

Daigoro studied the madam. She looked back at him coolly, as if she'd contained her earlier fear. Daigoro didn't know what to expect when she led him to the next door. His best guess was an assassin. Why else would she have been afraid? And why else should she feel relief to have separated Daigoro from his bodyguard?

Whatever her reasons, Daigoro was glad to be wearing his armor. "I'm warning you," he said, but before he could finish his sentence she slid the door open.

Inside lay General Mio—or what was left of him, at any rate. Huge sores had opened all over his body, every last one festering with maggots. His mouth was swollen and purple, livid with infection. Loops of purple and black bruises coursed around every part of his body, almost as if he'd been tattooed to look like he was wrapped in cords. Despite the efforts of the three girls tending to him, he stank like a corpse. But they were whores, not healers, and the putrid stench of him was enough to make their eyes water. One of them laid a folded wet cloth across his sweating forehead, holding another over her own nose and mouth.

"Get inside," the madam whispered. "I beg you, *quickly*."

Daigoro stepped into the room and the madam hurriedly shut the door behind them. Mio's head lolled in the direction of the noise, and the folded cloth slipped off. "He was feverish when he barged in this morning," the madam said, keeping her voice low. "Several times he started shaking, and I was sure he would die. But he just kept moaning your name."

"I never told you my name."

"There are only so many boys here, and of them, only one I thought to be a lord." She unrolled a small scroll and showed it to Daigoro; on it someone had used brown ink and a clumsy hand to scrawl the characters for *boy* and *lord*.

Her relief was as obvious as a mask on her face. Now Daigoro understood: Mio terrified her. And why wouldn't he? The man was a giant, and his wounds should have killed a horse. Judging by the stench, they'd been rotting for days, and yet Mio still mustered the strength to force his way in.

"How did he find me here?"

"How did he even take the first step on that path?" said the madam. "Some demon drives him—or else some higher purpose. Either way, 'relentless' does not begin to describe him. He should have been dead days ago."

"He wanted to see me alone, did he?"

"That's what he said. Or wrote, rather."

That explained the rest. Mio doubted Katsushima's loyalty—a reasonable reaction from one who had just been betrayed by one of his own allies. These wounds could only be Shichio's work.

Daigoro knelt next to Mio, who groaned something unintelligible. His jaws were locked tight and he sounded drunk—sounded like his tongue was missing, in fact, or like his fever had caused him to forget how to speak.

Mio gestured feebly at the madam and Daigoro saw someone had mutilated the general's hand. Two oblong wounds gaped like mouths, extending from the knuckles all the way down to the wrist. Similar wounds stood out on his legs, his belly, his chest, as if a wild animal had taken bites out of him.

Daigoro noticed the madam drew a tiny breath through her mouth, as if she needed to brace herself against the stench of decay before approaching. She unrolled the scroll along the tatami next to Mio's hand, then quickly retreated. For his part, Mio pushed his fingertip into his swollen mouth, and it came away bloody to serve as his writing brush.

The least talented schoolchild had better penmanship. Then again, the least of Mio's wounds would have killed the child outright. Mio's finger was slow and sloppy, and it was a triumph of will every time he mustered the strength to raise his finger back to his mouth. As he traced one bright red character after another, Daigoro inspected the rest of the scroll. The first characters he'd traced were *boy Daigoro*, followed by *doctor*, *lord Daigoro*, *here*, *water*, *fetch boy*, and *boy danger*. Things became less clear after that. A waggling smudge here and there hinted at the moments Mio lost consciousness. The characters followed no uniform lines and no cohesive train of thought. It was clear Mio's fever was baking his brain.

Wed, Mio wrote. *Mother*.

"He's fading away again," said one of the nursing girls, peering over Daigoro's shoulder. "His spells last longer and longer each time."

Mio slapped the paper—a childish and feeble gesture for one so strong. His bloody fingertip stabbed at the scroll, poking tiny crescent-shaped holes and leaving red prints.

"General, I don't understand," Daigoro said. "Please, help me."

Again Mio wetted his finger and traced it on the paper. The first character was *nana*, seven. The second was illegible.

Wed. Mother. Seven. It made no sense. Daigoro tried again to read the character after *seven*, but it was just a mess of red. "Seven what?" he said. It could have been anything.

Mio desperately slapped the paper again, his face a red, bunched, pain-stricken grimace. Daigoro looked hopelessly at the scroll once more. There were no more clues now than there had been a moment before, and Mio was fading quickly.

And then it clicked. *Nana*, the character for seven, could also be read *shichi*. "Shichio?" he said. "You mean Shichio?"

Mio grunted. It sounded affirmative, but Daigoro could only guess.

Wed. Mother. Shichio. He tried to think of other readings for the characters *wed* and *mother*. No insights there. Mio tried to lift his finger to his mouth and failed. Daigoro took his arm gingerly by the wrist and helped him. Together they succeeded in bloodying the finger, but Mio could manage to write no more. Somehow he still clung to consciousness, but his body had failed him. Daigoro knew he would not regain control of himself again; the giant man was dying, and dying quickly.

Desperately, Daigoro scanned the other characters on the page. *Water* and *medicine* were of no help. *Where* was probably an inquiry about Daigoro. *Boy* and *lord* were obvious. *Dai* became shorthand for those two somewhere along the way.

On one line he found *mother* again, this time paired with *dai*. *Daigoro's mother.* He paired that in his mind with *wed* and *Shichio* and came up with the unthinkable.

"Shichio intends to marry my mother?"

Mio moaned through lips so swollen he could no longer part them.

"General Mio, please. One more word. Please. Does he plan to marry my mother?"

A last groan from General Mio. Then the breath leaked out of him.

A burst of noise and splinters exploded behind Daigoro. He turned to see Katsushima, naked, kicking his way through the *shoji* with sword in hand. The steel held an orange glow in the dim light of the lanterns. "Daigoro!" he said. "Are you—?"

He choked on his words when he saw Mio's body. "What is this?"

The madam rounded on him, and if she had them she would have bared claws. The smell of incense flooded the room—which, Daigoro thought, could only mean that the reek of the enormous corpse was flooding out of the room. The madam looked angry enough to burst into flame.

Before she could say anything, Daigoro spoke. "Make yourself decent, Katsushima. We need to lay plans."

40

By the time Daigoro had a minute's respite to think, he was utterly exhausted. Their only reason for staying at the brothel was that it was supposed to be the sort of place a man could go discreetly. They needed to lie low; smashing through walls and stinking up the place was hardly the way to do that. Every man in the house must have heard the racket; rumors would spread, and Daigoro's height and limp were distinctive. Word would reach Shichio in no time. Yet he and Katsushima could hardly flee; they needed to help the madam set her rooms back in order, or else it was all but guaranteed that she would betray them to Shichio herself.

So they had a corpulent, putrefying corpse to get rid of, and since it was Mio's, Daigoro felt obligated to see him laid to rest properly. They could not give the general the stately funeral he deserved, but neither could they simply roll him off a bridge into the Kamo. Then there were repairs to see to, and silence to be paid for, and all the rest. It was sunrise before Daigoro had a moment's peace.

"We must be away," Katsushima said, though he too looked as exhausted as Daigoro felt. His unkempt hair seemed grayer than ever. Neither of them was in any condition to ride. Even so, Daigoro managed to sling himself into his saddle, Glorious Victory clattering on his back. Her weight threatened to pull him to the ground. Even at this hour the Kyoto streets were growing crowded, and Daigoro worried about how many eyes lingered on his chestnut mare and Katsushima's blood bay gelding.

They rode back to the Sanjō Ōhashi under Daigoro's lead. More than once he drifted off in the saddle, and every time the feeling of falling jarred him awake. He never fell off his horse, but each time he gripped his saddle horn tighter and did not easily let go.

It was late into the hour of the dragon by the time the road had cleared enough that they could speak without being overheard. It was hot and Daigoro was sweating in his armor. Exhausted as he was, he knew he had to explain everything Mio had told him.

"It's damned clever," Katsushima said when Daigoro had finished. "Assuming it's true."

"I cannot make sense of it," said Daigoro. His eyes felt sandy and he found it difficult to link two thoughts together. "Why should he suddenly want to marry my mother?"

"To weaken you. Think about it. Any Okuma samurai who remained loyal to you would be guilty of treason. Shichio would be the rightful head of the clan."

"No. Shichio? The next Lord Okuma? He'd be taking on his wife's name, Goemon. No man could bear the shame."

"No *samurai* could bear the shame. But what of a farmer's son?"

Daigoro hadn't thought of it that way. Shichio had no name of his own. He had no estate, no station, and no respect at court. Hideyoshi had once been in the same stead, until the emperor himself raised him up. Shichio would never receive such favors. There could only be one regent.

Of course Hideyoshi had the power to give Shichio nearly anything he wanted, but he also owed a great many favors. He was renowned for his battlefield cunning, but known better for his skill at parley. He'd conquered whole territories with nothing more than promises, granting this or that to every daimyo that would oppose him. Rumor had it that he paid his newly conquered enemies better than he paid those who were already close to him—as well he should, if his purpose was to buy allegiance. Hideyoshi had secured everything west of the Nobi plain, but even *he* could not grant land endlessly.

And there were those things even Hideyoshi could not grant. Glorious Victory Unsought. The esteem of others. A samurai's birthright. An estate acquired through conquest, not granted as a gift. A surname and a house of his own. Shichio thought himself superior to the likes of Mio Yasumasa, the consummate samurai. It only spoke to his delusion—a peacock was a peacock—but at least he could play make-believe by taking on the name of Okuma and having warriors of his own to order about.

"You may be right," Daigoro said at last. "He probably thinks even Glorious Victory would be his, as the rightful property of the Okuma clan."

"He might," said Katsushima. "But the more pressing question is what you will do to stop him. You're no longer the head of the Okumas. You have no say in whether your mother marries."

"And she hardly has a say herself. . . ."

Daigoro could already see it in his mind's eye. Shichio the honey-tongued. Shichio the pretty, preening songbird. In all likelihood he was already composing a serenade to the fair Lady Yumiko. In her current state she had no defense against him. He would insinuate himself in her mind until she could not help but say yes to him.

And worse yet, Hideyoshi no longer had a sober voice to counsel him. If anyone could have talked Hideyoshi into forbidding the marriage, it was General Mio. He had promised to keep an eye on Shichio—and, now that Daigoro thought of it, he'd also promised that Shichio would find a way to worm his way out of the truce. This was it. Marrying Daigoro's mother was the most complete victory imaginable. Far worse than simply razing House Okuma to the ground, this would see House Okuma rise to prominence with its worst enemy seated at its head. The Okumas would become Shichio's slaves. He could even order them to hunt down Daigoro and Katsushima. Daigoro's family would become a monster, a hideous ghoul of its former self.

"Maybe you were right," Daigoro said. "Calling on the Wind seemed desperate to me before, but now—"

Katsushima shook his head. "I've thought on that too. *Shinobi* were never the best option. For one thing, I'm no longer sure you can afford them. For another, we cannot be certain they would take your coin. The Wind are the best in the world, but they will not have forgotten what happens when they take aim at people in high office and miss."

"What do you mean?"

"Oda Nobunaga. Toyotomi's predecessor. His enemies tried sending *shinobi* against him. When they failed, Oda did not stop at killing the assassins, nor even the enemies who hired them; he destroyed the conspirators' families, and the families of the assassins too. Whole clans vanished overnight."

"But Shichio is just a general—and a lowborn one at that. He's no Oda Nobunaga."

Katsushima shrugged. "He doesn't need to be. Hideyoshi has risen higher than Oda ever did, and Shichio stands in Hideyoshi's shadow."

Daigoro hung his head, and with his gaze downcast he saw his hands armored in their white *kote*. Now that the plates on the backs of the hands had been lacquered white, he could hardly make out the bear paws worked into the steel. "The Wind! I can hardly believe I've uttered the thought aloud. Who am I, Goemon? What am I doing?"

"You know perfectly well what you do. You strive to keep to your father's road."

"Do I?" Suddenly Daigoro felt weighed down by his armor. Glorious Victory pulled at him more heavily still, threatening to pull him right out of the saddle. "I walked that road once. But do I still? Or have I wandered off onto some other path?"

Katsushima was silent for a while. At length he said, "There was a time when I knew, Daigoro. No longer."

"I've surrendered my name. I've surrendered my family. I am an enemy of the throne. I've even surrendered the right to wear the topknot. How can I say my life has anything at all to do with *bushidō*?"

"Perhaps you shouldn't."

Daigoro had hoped Katsushima would say something like that, but now that he heard it, it made his heart feel colder and heavier than ever. He'd hoped to feel some solace in the thought of giving up. It should have comforted him. At any rate, that's what the abbot of Kattō-ji would have said: give up everything, and when you have nothing more to lose, you will lose all fear of loss. But if I surrender *bushidō*, Daigoro thought, will I even know who I am?

"The life of the *rōnin* is not without riches of its own," Katsushima said. "Sake, women, freedom; they're much warmer companions than duty."

"Is that why you followed me all this way? Hoping to recruit me?"

Katsushima chuckled. "If I wanted to recruit you as a *rōnin*, I wouldn't have let you get married."

Daigoro wished he could smile too, but he couldn't muster the energy. "Tell me the truth, Goemon: why do you still follow me?"

Katsushima swallowed. "We should discuss that another time."

"I cannot say how much more time we have."

"We'll talk after we've rested."

Daigoro shook his head. "I cannot say how much rest we're likely to get, either. We are quarry. The arrows bound for us are already in flight. And apart from all that, if we do not keep our tongues waggling, I'm apt to doze off and fall out of my saddle. Tell me, Goemon, why do you still ride with me?"

Katsushima's face grew stern. "You're drowning, Daigoro. You need someone to help you keep your head above water."

"What do you mean?"

"You're trying to carry your family and your father's image and all the rest of it. It's too much for a drowning man to bear, Daigoro. You need to let them go."

Exhausted as he was, Daigoro had trouble following the metaphor. He actually felt as if his armor were pulling him off his horse; it was not hard to imagine it dragging him underwater. "Speak plainly," he said. "I do not understand."

Katsushima's face grew sterner still. "I speak in circles because I don't wish to give offense. We approach a crossroads, you and I. You have a problem in Shichio and a problem in your family. There is a single solution for both problems, one I've hinted at before. I can solve both problems for you with one stroke of my sword, but you bar me from doing so. You can solve it too, but you bar even yourself. A man can hold up his drowning friend, Daigoro, but only for so long. Sooner or later he must let him go or drown with him."

"I'm too tired for this, Goemon. Just tell me what you mean."

"No. You need to reach this conclusion yourself. Shichio means to marry your mother. In so doing he will destroy your clan forever. You cannot kill him; he is out of your reach. So what do you need to do?"

"I don't understand—"

"Yes, you do. All it takes is one stroke of your sword to save your family name."

"Who—?"

"You tell me, Daigoro. Who must die to save your family?"

Daigoro's pulse pounded in his ears. His breath came short and quick. He had to press against his saddle horn to keep himself upright. "My mother," he said. "You're telling me to kill my mother?"

"Of course."

Daigoro stammered. A hundred objections bubbled up, but the only word he could make intelligible was "Why?"

"Is it not clear? You should have put her out of her misery months ago." Katsushima scowled, his voice harsh and low. He was losing his patience. Daigoro wished he could think faster, but he was just too tired, and Katsushima's suggestion was too enormous for him to grasp.

"No. I cannot—"

"She is a constant distraction. Were it not for her, your negotiations with the Soras would have been a success, Inoue Shigekazu would be your ally instead of your father-in-law, Izu would be stable, and your house would be the stronger for it. Now she is the key that will unlock the Okuma clan. You cannot allow Shichio to take that key, Daigoro. If you don't destroy it, he'll use it to destroy you."

"No." Daigoro's heart pounded so hard he thought it might burst.

He was scared and angry—angry not at Katsushima but at himself. Why could he not think faster? Everything Katsushima had said was true, but still, was there no counterargument?

"There must be another way," Daigoro said, but even to his own ears his voice sounded feeble.

"Perhaps there is," said Katsushima, "but that is why we stand at a crossroads. To me the right path is obvious. If you want to look for a different path, then here is where we part company. I cannot watch you destroy yourself, Daigoro. Standing up to Shichio and Hideyoshi was noble. Throwing yourself on Shichio's sword is stupidity. And that is what you do if you allow him to marry your mother. He'll turn your own men against you. It is more than foolish; it's appalling, and I will not stand by and watch you do it."

"I'm so tired," Daigoro said. "I can't think. . . ."

"What need is there for thinking? You need only to act. Ride with me, north and east, as fast as we can. Put your mother out of her misery. Save the rest of your clan."

"No. I can't kill her, Goemon. I just can't. And neither can I allow you to do it."

Katsushima frowned. "I will not kill her without your permission," he said, "but I will not watch her sink you either. She is ballast, Daigoro. She will pull you under unless you ship her overboard."

With that Katsushima put his heels to his horse. Daigoro's chestnut mare ambled to a halt, bending her head to eat a tussock of grass growing along the edge of the Tokaidō. Daigoro was too tired to make her change her mind.

He watched as the white dust settled in Katsushima's wake. Now more than ever, he felt utterly alone.

BOOK SEVEN

HEISEI ERA, THE YEAR 22

(2010 CE)

41

"Do I have to call him?"

"Yeah, pretty much."

Mariko looked down at the phone in her hand, then looked back at her partner. She and Han sat at their desks in Narcotics, canned coffee at their beck and call. Phones rang, keyboards clicked, desk fans hummed, all background music to the ever-present murmur of a dozen different conversations. In short, the unit was abuzz, as well it should have been given the case Mariko was running. Cultist fanatics were at large in her city, well supplied with drugs, cyanide, and the willingness to distribute them liberally.

Mariko's sole advantage was a hard-nosed lieutenant who was willing to go to the mat with any commanding officer, anytime, to get what he wanted. Sakakibara reassigned every cop in his unit and commandeered another six or seven detectives besides, handing out orders like a blackjack dealer dealing cards. Back when Sakakibara first gave her this case, Mariko thought she was investigating the Kamaguchi-gumi on a simple trafficking ring. Now she lived under the cold, dark, looming shadow of a potential mass murder. She had two officers in the field trying to track down Akahata. Two others were working on Urano Sōseki, the Kamaguchi-gumi's capo, pressuring him to testify that Akahata was the one who delivered the Daishi. She paired another detective with a lab tech to sort out how much speed they'd seized in the packing plant raid and how to find a line on who cooked it. All of them reported to Mariko.

But there was one lead on the Kamaguchi-gumi that Mariko had to follow herself. She took a deep breath to steel herself, poised her finger over her phone's keypad, then thought better of it. "Han, you know I hate this guy."

Han blew his hair away from his face and took a sip of coffee. "Think of it as cultivating a contact," he said. "This is police work, not a social call."

And you've been coloring outside the lines, thought Mariko. As far as she was concerned, Han's judgment about good police work was suspect. But in this case he was right. She sighed and dialed the number.

"Well, well, well," said Kamaguchi Hanzō. "My hot little *gokudō* cop. I been wondering when I was going to hear from you."

Mariko already wanted to hang up. "I need you to tell me about your chemical supply company," she said.

"Fuck that. When are you going to give me my mask?"

Mariko squeezed the phone; the plastic crackled in her grip. "We're working on it. Tell me what you sold the Divine Wind."

"Hexa-something. Why ask me? Don't you detectives keep a notepad or something?"

"Just the hexamine? Nothing else?"

"Nothing else."

"Don't hold out on me, Kamaguchi. This is important."

"Look at the balls on you! What, you want me to sell them something else? I got girls, I got guns, I got whatever. Tell me where these cocksuckers are holed up and I promise I'll deliver something they won't forget."

Mariko rolled her eyes. "Did you sell them sodium cyanide?"

"Hell, no."

"You sound pretty sure for a guy who only runs a front company. You can't tell me you memorized every item in your inventory."

"You're irritating as hell, you know that?"

"The feeling's mutual."

Kamaguchi snorted. "I remember the cyanide because they asked me about it, okay? And I'll tell you what I told them: I don't deal in that shit."

"Why not?"

"Prohibited substances list. There's no money in it."

"Why not?"

"*Prohibited substances list.* You buy that stuff, they watch you. You sell it, they watch you. You use it for anything dodgy, they watch you. Who's got the time for it? I just sell other shit."

She cupped the phone against her shoulder. Whispering, she said, "Han, can I please hang up on this asshole now?"

Han gave her a wink and a thumbs-up.

"Good-bye, Kamaguchi-san."

She resisted the urge to hurl the phone at the wall. Instead she crushed it like a stress ball, squeezing more little crackling noises out of the plastic. "Tell me you got something good on the house," she said.

Han grinned. "Grand slam. Turns out it belonged to a cult member. She willed it to the Church of the Divine Wind right before she died."

"Not to Jōko Daishi?"

"If only. At least that way we'd have the dude's real name in the will. But get this: the family got pissed that they didn't get the house—"

"Figures," Mariko said. "It's a nice house."

"It's a damn expensive house. So one of the sons gets uppity and demands an autopsy. The rest of the family doesn't go for it, but they okay some blood work. Guess what? The old bird tested positive for amphetamine."

A little thrill rippled down Mariko's spine. "MDA?"

"Can't say. Can't say on cyanide either—they didn't test for it—but she was a geezer; it wouldn't be that hard to induce a heart attack with a little speed."

That thrill chased itself up and down Mariko's spine again. She felt a little guilty too; it was macabre to take pleasure in a hunch when that hunch was confirmed by a homicide. Nevertheless, she couldn't help feeling encouraged; this murder reinforced her suspicion that the Divine Wind was willing to use cyanide-laced amphetamines to kill. "What else have you got?"

"On the house? Let's see." Han reopened a window on his computer and drained the last of his coffee. "Five hookahs, thirty-eight jabs of heroin, big thing of cyanide. Everything says these guys split in a hurry, *neh*? I mean, there's a ton of admissible evidence they could have stashed or destroyed or whatever."

Mariko nodded. Perps didn't leave evidence behind if they could help it, and they almost never left expensive evidence behind. Whoever had been in that house, they'd left immediately after killing Shino. The only part Han had wrong was that it was admissible evidence; she and Han had gotten onto the house in violation of Akahata's civil rights. She was glad they had evidence to draw inferences from, but nothing on Han's list was worth a damn thing in court.

"How about you?" he said. "You get anything?"

"Pulled a couple of good prints from this," she said, and she produced a carefully folded Ziploc bag from her back pocket. In it was the little fold-up Giants schedule she'd found next to the heroin on Jōko Daishi's altar.

"Nice grab," he said, clearly surprised to see the thing. "Where'd you get the Ziploc, by the way? Please don't tell me you walk around with one in your pocket all day. If you're going to go all TV cop on me, at least make it an evidence bag and carry a pair of tweezers."

"You're a smart-ass."

"Guilty as charged."

"I swiped it from her kitchen," she said. "And by the way, if anyone asks, *you're* the one who swiped it from her kitchen. As long as you're breaking regs, you can take the hit for stealing private property from dead little old ladies."

"*Ouch.*"

"Pull that schedule out and tell me what you make of it."

He did as he was told, and crinkled his eyebrows just as Mariko did when she tried to make sense of the scribbles written on it. "What is this, some kind of prayer?"

"That was my guess too."

"Look, today's game is circled. I'll bet somebody's got tickets—and hey, if that prayer is for the Giants to win, maybe I'll start praying to Jōko Daishi too. They could use any help they can get."

"Go back a second," Mariko said. "Tickets? For today's game?"

"Yeah, but if you're thinking we might pull a lead out of that, you'll have to tell me how we're going to identify one nut job in a crowd of forty-two thousand."

Mariko's fist renewed its stranglehold on her phone. She willed her fist to loosen, then took back the schedule and made a point of folding it slowly and precisely before bagging it again. She hoped it might calm her a bit. It didn't work.

Neither did angrily jamming it back into her pocket. "Han, I'll be honest: I'm nervous. My gut tells me these guys are dangerous—a lot more dangerous than they're letting on. And we have nothing. Aka-hata's in the wind, and we haven't so much as laid eyes on Jōko Daishi, whoever the hell he is."

"So what's our next move?"

Mariko shrugged, wishing she had more to go on, wishing the caffeine she'd been slamming would hurry up and give her brain the kick-start it needed. "Kamaguchi tells me cyanide is too heavily monitored for him to trade in it."

"Do you believe him?"

"Can't see why not."

"Then let's hope the fact that it's restricted means we won't have too many distributors to run down."

They didn't. Not for the first time, Mariko wondered how detectives had ever gotten along without the Internet. It would have taken days to make the headway she and Han made in twenty minutes. Han was the faster typist, and not because he had ten fingers to Mariko's nine; even before her injury she'd always clunked along with two fingers on the keys. His keyboard sounded like little galloping horses; hers clicked and clacked sporadically, like a bag of microwave popcorn right before the *ding*. She'd always done better with the paperwork you had to fill out by hand.

It was a funny word, *paperwork*, now that it rarely involved paper anymore. *Screenwork* was more apropos, or *keyboardwork*, or something like that. She wondered what Yamada-sensei would have had to say on the matter.

Thinking of him made her think about all those yellowing handwritten notebooks sitting in stacks in her bedroom, and that gave her second thoughts about the cyanide lead. According to Yamada, anyone wearing the mask became obsessed with weapons. Maybe cyanide pills could count as weapons, but they seemed a bit tame compared to cutting someone down with a sword. Mariko suspected Jōko Daishi had grander, bloodier visions than that.

"Huh," Han said, interrupting her reverie. "How about that? Apparently you can use sodium cyanide to mine gold."

"Yeah, I saw that," Mariko said.

"Seems like a better use for it than murdering people."

Mariko chuckled weakly. She'd followed the gold mining trail too. Han was better on the computer, but Mariko had a stronger sense of what might lead where. She supposed it came from putting in time as a detective outside of Narcotics. Han knew exactly where to follow drug leads, but Mariko was better at seeing the overarching patterns, the counterintuitive connections. What seemed like random trivia for Han seemed like dots to connect for Mariko.

And she'd already connected a few. "We're not exactly mineral-rich as a country, *neh*? I mean, where do you think the nearest gold mine is?"

Han scrunched his brow and thought about it for a second. "Beats me. Could be California for all I know."

"Exactly. And we know sodium cyanide is on the prohibited substances list, so you'd need something like a mining license to buy it, *neh*?"

"That or some other license, maybe for some other kind of industry."

"Right," said Mariko. "So I tracked down how many companies are authorized to sell it—"

"Nice."

"—and the answer is two."

"Nice!" Han made a fist-pump. "So we just need to figure out who they've been selling to—"

"Or who they've been selling to under the counter."

"Exactly. Because these guys have already shown they're willing to go black market for their dangerous chemicals."

Mariko used to love the fact that she and Han thought the same way. Now she wasn't so sure. It made communication a whole lot easier, and it hadn't been so long ago that she'd also considered it a badge of honor. Han was a good narc, or so she'd been inclined to think, and so if her mind worked like his, she must have been a good narc too. But that was before he'd stepped out of bounds, before he'd sent his CI to do what he couldn't legally do himself. A vision flashed in her mind: Shino sprawled facedown on the floor, his skin sunburn red against the bright yellow of his Lakers jersey. If Mariko thought like Han, and if Han was capable of getting an innocent person killed, then what did that say about Mariko?

She elected to avoid that question for the present, choosing instead to let the moral questions take a backseat to practicality. With no small amount of trepidation, she called her CO. Sakakibara answered with a growl.

"Good morning, sir."

"This better be good," he said.

"Bad morning, sir?"

"Hell, no. It's not like I've been wringing favors out of every last lieutenant in this department to get you the manpower you need. Do you have any idea what this is going to do to my Thursday nights?"

"Sir?"

"Poker, Frodo. Lieutenant Tortoise in Violent Crimes takes for-fucking-ever deciding whether to call or fold. Like we all don't know what's coming. It would be easier on everyone if I could just knock him over the head with a baton and take his wallet. But no, the stupid bastard wants in, and thanks to this Divine Wind of yours, I needed to wangle two more detectives to your detail. So you've got them, damn you, but it's going to ruin my Thursdays until I take enough of his money that he needs to start working a night job."

"You're a hero and a public servant, sir."

"How nice for me. Now what the hell are you calling me for?"

Mariko swallowed. "You sound like you could use a way to take out some aggression, sir."

"Get to the point, Frodo."

"How would you feel about jumping in the ring with a circuit court judge?"

Sakakibara grumbled. "What do you need?"

"Search warrants, sir. We've got two chemical distributors licensed to sell sodium cyanide. And since you just got me two more detectives—"

"Fine. What do you need? Inventory?"

"And shipping manifests. Personnel records. Employee absence reports. Phone and e-mail records if you can get them."

Sakakibara's breath came loud through his nose, roaring low like a jet engine flying past his phone's receiver. "Anything else? Maybe the phone numbers of the companies' most eligible bachelors?"

"Why not? No workaholics, and if he can cook, that would be a plus."

"Don't push me, Frodo."

"Sorry, sir."

More growling and grumbling from Sakakibara. At last he said, "Start typing up the paperwork. I'll have a judge in the unit to sign them within the hour. But I swear to you right now, I'll smother that son of a bitch with a pillow before I put one more chair around my poker table."

In the end he only needed half an hour. He stormed out of the elevator with his jaw clenched, the veins bulging in his temples, and a worried-looking judge in tow. Mariko wondered what Sakakibara had told him to put that look on his face. The judge scribbled his signature on everything Mariko put in front of him, taking only a few seconds each to skim the pages. Yet again her thoughts returned to Han, and what a corrupt commanding officer might have been able to get a hurried judge to sign off on. Backdated paperwork okaying Shino to tail the Divine Wind? It wasn't hard to imagine.

But once again, ruminating about morality and civil rights had to give way to practicality. Mariko had two new detectives and two chemical supply companies to investigate. She reassigned four others to join them, making a total of three detectives per company, and detailed two patrolmen to raid the nearest coffee shop and bring up as much caffeine as the store would sell them.

Part of her hoped her detail wouldn't find anything until tomorrow. She hadn't forgotten how hard it had been to drag herself into post this morning, how Sakakibara said she looked like hell. A long, stressful day full of moral conundrums couldn't possibly have improved her condition. What she really needed was a good meal, a hot shower, and ten or twelve hours of sleep. She didn't exactly want her team to fail, but she would have been thrilled if they didn't succeed until noon tomorrow.

Which, given her luck, meant they got a hit on one of her search warrants before she could finish digesting her lunch. She'd tasked one of her detectives with checking calls from Anatole Organics against activity in area cellular towers. He found a number of one-to-one matches on the time stamps, which was inevitable—there would be pizza deliveries, salesmen calling in from the road, corporate reps who got lost on the way to an on-site meeting—but a string of them corresponded with calls from the cell phone of an Akahata Daisuke. Always wary of coincidence, Mariko followed up on it, and sure enough, it was the same Akahata she'd met in the hospital, the fanatic who never stopped chanting his mantra.

As soon as she confirmed the match, her heart began to race. A growing dread had been swelling in her gut like a tumor, ever since they'd discovered the cyanide. There might have been some who argued that anyone crazy enough to join the Divine Wind deserved whatever fate Jōko Daishi would lead them to, but Mariko didn't fall in that camp. Mass murder was mass murder, regardless of whether the victim was willing to swallow the poisoned pill. With Akahata out of pocket and Jōko Daishi still a ghost, each passing hour amplified her queasy sense of foreboding. Every time she looked at the clock, she wondered how much time she had before the fateful bell would toll.

And since Han was better on the keyboard, Mariko could only stand by and wait as he executed the very same searches she would have done. Once again their likemindedness struck her. There was no point in hunting and pecking her own way through; whatever she might have learned through the computer, Han would learn it first. So Mariko made what phone calls she could, but her concentration never strayed far from Han.

"Got it!" he said. "Rented storefront in Bunkyō. Tax-exempt status, leased to the Church of the Divine Wind." He released a sigh he seemed to have been bottling up for some time; evidently he was every bit as nervous as Mariko was. "I figured we were going to get a front company, you know? But I guess the regs on prohibited substances are too strict for that. This isn't a front; it's the real deal."

"Let's move," said Mariko.

42

She'd never commanded a raid before. The decision didn't come easily, either. The biggest part of her wanted to wait for Lieutenant Sakakibara, but he was busy unruffling the feathers of all the circuit court judges he'd pissed off in railroading his warrants through the system, and Mariko's growing sense of dread wouldn't accept unnecessary delays. She might have asked SWAT to take command, but their reputation in Narcotics was that they were too slow to respond. The SWAT guys would have cast it in a different light, to be sure: you couldn't prep an assault on a target in a matter of minutes, and barging in without a plan was a good way to get people killed. Asking them to launch a raid in less than an hour would be like asking a drunk surgeon to operate before sobering up. The right thing to do—the professional thing to do—was to say no.

So, since Sakakibara had already assigned a small army to report directly to Mariko, she decided to deploy it. Borrowing heavily from SWAT's playbook, she found electronic maps of the Divine Wind's rented storefront-become-church and studied the layout carefully. She chose a staging ground in a parking lot half a kilometer away from the target building, where she could convene everyone in her command. And now she stood in a circle with them, with all of them looking expectantly at her. It was discomfiting, having twenty cops glued to her every word. She couldn't help noticing that, as usual, she was by far the smallest one in the group.

"Listen up," she said, too quietly if she wanted to command as much authority as Sakakibara would have done. That was a lot easier at his size than at hers, and until she'd worked with them long enough to earn their respect, most guys in the department treated her not as a cop but a girl cop. She wasn't off to a great start, but she had no choice but to raise her voice and soldier on. "I'm not going to try to stage this like the SWAT guys would. We're just going to do good old-fashioned police work. Treat this like you did it back in academy, when you focused on the fundamentals. Watch your corners, clear your doorways, nobody enters a room by himself. Got it?"

"Yes, ma'am," her twenty officers said, much louder than she'd anticipated. She entertained the thought that maybe this wasn't going as poorly as she thought—or maybe her nervousness just made everything bad seem worse and everything good seem as thin as Han's cigarette smoke.

"Consider our targets to be armed and dangerous," she said. She meant the chemicals, not guns and knives, and now she wished she'd remembered to requisition gas masks for everyone. SWAT wouldn't have forgotten that. "Remember, on paper this place qualifies as a church. That means we might be seeing parishioners in there, not just bad guys. But we know our bad guys have killed at least once using cyanide, maybe using a laced pill, and we suspect they're willing to kill a lot more. If you see civilians trying to pop pills, do what you can to stop them—but don't let that compromise officer safety, understand?"

Her chorus boomed, "Yes, ma'am!"

"All right. Let's hit it."

When they breached the building, it was nothing like the SWAT raid of Kamaguchi's shipping company. There, four teams had hit four sides of the target in the same instant. Here, Mariko heard shouts from inside before she even reached the front door. She, Han, and the four cops with them broke into a dead sprint.

The target used to be a discount mattress retailer, which meant it was *big*. The commotion was coming from somewhere to Mariko's left—what SWAT would have called the B-side of the target—but she repressed the urge to head that way. One of the officers with her did not. She didn't bother to call after him; she'd have words with him later about breaking ranks, but for now she only had eyes for her own objective.

Han reached the door before she did and put his boot into it. It burst open and Mariko was through. She'd expected to see what was happening on the B-side, but to her left was a flat wall. The room she was in—probably the showroom floor at one time—was now empty and dimly lit. B-team must have hit offices or a stockroom, something on the opposite side of that wall. She couldn't help them. She could only clear the area in front of her.

An exit sign glowed green on the back wall, with a steel door beneath it. On the other side of that door, a motorcycle engine roared to life, followed by another. Mariko's team declared the vacant showroom clear. Mariko couldn't even remember any details of the area; she knew only that wherever she pointed her SIG, there was nothing dangerous to be found.

Mariko charged the steel door and kicked it with everything she had. It burst open and she breached the next room. Sunlight blinded her. The room was a cavernous expanse, the sun streaming in from the truck-sized door scrolling itself open on the far wall. Han was right on Mariko's heels, shouting "down, down, down!" at someone off to her right, someone Mariko hadn't even seen. Her eyes were fixed on the two motorcyclists in front of her.

They were big bikes, maybe fourteen hundred cc's, and Mariko instantly recognized one of the riders as Akahata. His face, still purple and livid, was too bruised for him to wear a helmet. The man astride the second bike had long black hair and wore an iron demon mask instead of a helmet. He could only be Jōko Daishi.

He cut a sharp turn in front of her, filling the air with the stink of scorched rubber. Akahata had already made the same turn, and now he rocketed away. He raced for the loading dock on the far side of the room, where that scrolling door rolled ever higher. Mariko saw five cops—her C-team—converging on the opening door, pistols drawn.

Akahata cranked the throttle, jumped the loading dock, and blew past her officers before they could react. Jōko Daishi whipped his bike around and gunned it.

Mariko put her front sight on him but hesitated before she took her shot, doubting her aim with her left hand. C-team advanced on the door, closing Jōko Daishi's line of escape.

He put the bike down in a hard spin, forcing a howl out of the back tire and leaving a wide black slash on the concrete floor. His engine roared louder than gunfire. He made for the emergency exit on the B-side, where Mariko's officers were already embroiled in a fistfight with three or four men in white. Mariko could only assume they were Divine Wind cultists, but whoever they were, their free-for-all blocked the fire exit.

Two of her B-side cops spotted the bike, broke free of the fight, and brought their weapons to bear. Jōko Daishi whirled again, leaning so low his knee touched the floor. It was the same squealing spinout as before, only this time he used it as a leg sweep. His back tire arced wide, breaking bones, reaping both cops to the ground. He rammed the throttle again and bore down on Mariko like a charging warhorse.

She didn't know what happened to the rest of her element. Han was gone. The cops with them were gone. The door behind her was still open; she didn't know why, didn't care. For Mariko the whole world was herself and Jōko Daishi.

She put her front sight right on that iron demon mask but she couldn't pull the trigger. It would be the first time she'd ever fired her weapon in the line of duty. She was shooting left-handed and rattled. And she had five cops behind her target. Her training took over; she simply couldn't risk the shot.

He was nearly on top of her. Her body weight wouldn't be enough to slow him. He'd blast her right through the open doorway and keep accelerating. There was no one else behind her; she was literally the last line of defense. And she stepped out of the way.

The technique that her TMPD aikido class called *irimi-nage* looked a lot like the one American pro wrestlers called a clothesline. She caught Jōko Daishi with it right under the chin. If she were an American wrestler, it probably would have torn her arm clean off, but she didn't match her target power to power. She just redirected his momentum upward and backward, absorbing none of it herself. The world went into slow motion. The motorcycle roared past her, loud as machine gun fire. Mariko turned her *irimi-nage* downward. Jōko Daishi hit the floor like a meteor.

43

In the aftermath, coming down from her adrenaline high, Mariko took stock of her surroundings. The giant storeroom—and in a mattress shop the store room was truly gigantic—wasn't as empty as she'd first thought, though obviously there was room enough to ride a motorcycle. Once there must have been racks or bins big enough to contain mattresses, but those had gone. A couple of forklifts still remained, abandoned in a corner. The right-hand wall was dominated by a production line of sorts, a long string of collapsible tables blocking both fire doors on that side. D-team hadn't even managed to breach the building; their entries were blocked, locked from the inside, useless.

Near the tables, black steel barrels and plastic drums of a similar size stood like troops in rank and file, festooned with warning labels instead of insignia. At first glance, Mariko had expected to see an assembly line for cyanide-laced MDA. She'd seen enough stash houses to recognize a meth lab for what it was, and this wasn't that. This room smelled more like motor oil than ammonia. In a quick scan of the folding tables Mariko saw pipe cutters, spools of wire, a cardboard box full of outmoded cell phones, a smaller box full of SIM cards—nothing useful for a meth cook. The only items that made sense to her were the hexamine and sodium cyanide labels on the barrels and drums.

Even in retrospect it took some concentration to string together the chain of events. B-team had been the first to enter, and Jōko Daishi's cultists had mobbed them. It must have been at about that time that someone hit the button to open the big loading dock doors. That might have been Jōko Daishi, who would then have gone for his bike.

However that went down, another mob of cultists had been heading to cut off Mariko's element at the very instant she booted the door to the storeroom. Even in the heat of the moment, she'd thought the door had given way more easily than it should have. It seemed to have exploded away from her foot. But what probably happened was that one of the cultists was opening the door just as she kicked it in. It must have struck him full in the face, knocking him unconscious. Mariko shot right past him, but the rest of her team had run smack into his cohort of cultists. Han and the others on A-team were mobbed, but they handled their fight better than B-team, which was why Jōko Daishi made his run at the A-side door. Mariko just had the bad luck to be the only one left standing in front of it.

The final tally was sixteen Divine Wind cultists, plus their leader and prophet, plus one more unexpected treasure: Glorious Victory Unsought. Mariko spotted the empty scabbard first, lying empty on one of the collapsible plastic tables, and imagined the worst: the cult had sold the sword for drug money. When one of her officers announced he'd found a giant sword, relief surged through Mariko's veins like morphine. Then she asked where it was, and when he pointed her toward what was left of Jōko Daishi's motorcycle, she thought she might throw up on her shoes. The reason her sword wasn't in its scabbard was that the cultists had mounted a sheath for it on the bike, and now the bike was a debris field twenty meters long, ending in a crumpled heap wadded up against the wall and suppurating oil.

Emotionally, Glorious Victory Unsought ranked with the few existing pictures of Mariko's father, who, because he'd always been the family photographer, rarely appeared in their photo albums himself. Sometimes Mariko wondered whether her family would be offended by how much sentimental value she found in Glorious Victory Unsought. She'd only known Yamada-sensei for a matter of weeks, yet somehow he'd become a grandfather to her, a mentor and role model. What did it mean that she held her sensei's last gift on par with precious family photos? Mariko didn't even know how she felt about that herself. She only knew that it was true, and that she'd never forgive herself if her Inazuma blade was reduced to a steel ribbon entangled in the remains of the bike.

But she was lucky, or else Master Inazuma's masterpiece was bound to a different fate. The bike had fallen on its left side and Glorious Victory's scratch-built scabbard was mounted on the right. Three different colors of fluid leaked from the wreckage, and the air above it shimmered with heat, but the sword sat on top unharmed.

The only other material items in the win column were a couple of mostly empty barrels of hexamine and sodium cyanide. No MDA, no speed, no other drugs. In the loss column she had two cops from B-team nursing leg injuries bad enough to leave them in the fetal position gritting their teeth and awaiting an ambulance. She had no ID on Jōko Daishi and he wouldn't offer any other name. There was no sign of his lieutenant, Akahata, though Mariko had placed an APB on his motorcycle. But her most significant loss was her composure.

She hadn't backed up her partner in a fistfight, which, technically, was all to the good, since of her element she was the only one able to keep a weapon trained on Jōko Daishi. She hadn't been able to bring herself to shoot, which was also good, since Jōko Daishi had— miraculously—survived being snagged by the chin off the back of a speeding motorcycle, and so they now had their prime suspect alive to interrogate. She'd hastily orchestrated a raid that could have gone much worse but didn't. Her officers were outnumbered because a quarter of their force never actually made it into the building. They were uncoordinated in their movements. It was only because they all performed admirably that no one got shot. In other words, with the lone exception of her perfectly executed *irimi-nage*, Mariko had fucked up everything she could possibly have fucked up, and yet somehow everything had worked out for the best—or if not for the best, then pretty damn well, all things considered.

Self-confidence didn't come easily to Mariko. She knew she was good at her job, but the job was relentless. Tiny errors could have major ramifications, and overshadowing that was the constant threat of being seen as incompetent just because she was a woman. Losing her right forefinger had set her at least a year behind on the pistol range, a fact that wouldn't have mattered much in any other outfit in the country. Most beat cops went from academy to retirement without ever drawing a weapon, because most police work was reactive. Apart from traffic violations, most cops rarely witnessed a crime; the calls always came after the fact. But Narcotics didn't just react; it initiated action too, and that meant Mariko was might have to draw down on people now and again. How was she going to do that if she couldn't trust her aim?

She should have taken the shot. Jōko Daishi had come within a millisecond of killing her. She could have changed her angle; even crouching down and firing upward would have been enough to take C-team out of harm's way. That should have been her instinctual response, but instead she'd committed an egregious mistake: she thought about it.

She remembered Yamada-sensei's term for that. Paralysis through analysis. Han would say the same thing about baseball that Yamada said of swordsmanship: hitting a moving target had to be done automatically or not at all. Deliberate concentration could only screw it up. Marksmanship was no different. Yamada-sensei once told her it was better to drop the weapon than to get tangled up in thinking. At least that way no one would get hurt.

That meant the next best alternative was to quit Narcotics and start working a beat instead. Go the rest of her career without any real risk of shooting or being shot at. Her mother would have loved it. And Mariko would have given up everything she'd worked so hard for, for so many years.

She could have missed with her *irimi-nage*. She could have broken every bone in her arm. She could have killed Jōko Daishi, just the same as if she'd shot him, but with a lot more risk to herself and her fellow officers. So much had been at stake, and Mariko's nerve had failed. Paralysis through analysis. She wasn't sure she'd ever forgive herself.

"Hey," said Han, "you okay?"

"What?" Mariko paid only enough attention to know he was there. "Yeah," she said distantly, "I'm fine."

Han clapped her on the shoulder. "This was a win, Mariko. Come on, we've got a crazy-ass cult leader to interrogate."

That snapped her out of her reverie. "He's conscious?"

"Conscious? Hell, he's walking around."

It was impossible. Jōko Daishi must have hit a hundred kilometers an hour by the time she ripped him off the bike. So when she saw him walking, a cop pushing him by his handcuffed wrists, the demon mask pushed up onto the top of his head, all she could say was, "You should be dead."

He laughed—a good-natured laugh, amiable, not forced. "You cannot kill me. It is not yet my time."

Han aped his laugh right back at him. "If you'd have landed on your head instead of your shoulders, it would have been your time, all right. We've got a couple of murders to pin on you—a kid named Shino and the little old lady whose house you killed him in—but when it comes time to charge you, I'll make sure riding without a helmet makes the list."

"I have seen the hour of my death," said Jōko Daishi, "and also the manner. I shall die by the sword."

Mariko didn't care if that was a biblical reference, a deliberate jab at her famed samurai showdown, or just the ramblings of a grade-one concussion. One way or the other, the guy was a nutcase.

He was smaller than she'd thought. He'd been downright terrifying on that motorcycle, his beard and hair streaming from his devil's face as if his head were ablaze and trailing black smoke. He did not look at them when he spoke, but rather stared off into the distance, his tone reverent, as if there were a god in the room for him to talk to. Again Mariko reached the same conclusion: nutcase.

Something about him was familiar, but she couldn't put her finger on it until they'd walked him all the way to the wall. They put his shoulder blades against the dusty cinder blocks and made him sit, hands cuffed behind his back, and every last movement should have hurt like hell. He was lucky to be alive. He wore white clothes, loose but otherwise nondescript, certainly not padded like motorcycle leathers. Given how he'd landed off the bike, his entire back should have been in spasms.

Mariko could explain that away easily enough: his cult gave him easy access to kilos upon kilos of speed. He'd feel pain when he came down off his high, but not until. Yet he limped, an odd, rolling gait that couldn't have come from Mariko's high-speed takedown. If it wasn't from pain, it must have been from a pre-existing injury, and Mariko would have sworn she'd seen that limp before.

Sudden insight flashed. She *had* seen it before, only a grainy image of it, on a low-fidelity security camera feed. "You're the one who stole the mask," she said.

"He is?" Han blurted.

"I saw him on the Bulldog's security camera tape. He walked right past us to steal that mask from Kamaguchi Hanzō. Dressed head to toe in SWAT armor, remember?" She rounded on Jōko Daishi. "That was a nice touch."

"There is no place the Wind cannot reach," he said.

"And I'm guessing you're the same son of a bitch who broke into my apartment and stole my sword."

He responded with an eerie, peeping-through-the-window kind of smile that gave Mariko the creeps. She'd been eyed up and down like a piece of meat before. Guys did that all the time, responding with an "I'd hit that" smile when they liked what they saw. This wasn't like that. This was the smile of a serial rapist, one who was willing to kidnap and batter and bury alive because he didn't really understand that other human beings were real. The "I'd hit that" guys viewed women as sex toys; Jōko Daishi saw people as children's toys: fascinating in their own way, but hollow, incapable of pain or fear, worth only as much as he valued them. And he had watched Mariko in her sleep.

Chills washed over Mariko like an icy wave, raising goose bumps all over her body. A vision flashed in her mind: Jōko Daishi looming over her bed, silent, ghostly, masked behind the iron face of a demon. He had the sinister patience of a stalker, an invisible, disquieting, perpetual presence. It was every woman's deepest dread: the ex-boyfriend who would never relent, never disappear, never let her go.

"Is that true?" Han demanded, snapping Mariko out of her nightmare. "Did you break into my partner's apartment?"

There was that smile again. "There is no place the Wind cannot reach."

"The same goes for the Kamaguchi-gumi," Mariko said, feigning a cocksure confidence she did not feel. "Remember that sword you saw yourself dying on? The Bulldog's going to be the one who rams it through your chest."

"Kamaguchi did not respond quickly enough for our needs. The New Year approaches. The appointed hour is at hand. Securing the mask was necessary to usher in the Year of the Demon."

Mariko and Han shared a glance. He could see in her what she saw in him: this man scared the hell out of both of them. But rather than revealing that fact, Han said, "Is this dude turning you on?"

"Big-time."

Turning to their suspect, Han said, "See how that big loading dock door is open and we're not freezing our balls off? That's because it's summer out there. We've got a few months until New Year's, buddy."

Mariko remembered the calendars in the basement where they found Shino. She wasn't able to make much sense of them at the time, but she did remember that they seemed to be based on planetary cycles, not the Chinese or Western calendars. Not that it mattered. For all she cared, he could hang his pretty calendars in his rubber room in the asylum. In any case, she had bigger fish to fry. "I want you to tell me where the MDA is," she said.

He blinked. Frowning, confused, he said, "I cannot help you."

"MDA," Han said. "Psychedelic amphetamines. You know how to cook them—or your people do anyway. Maybe your boy Akahata, *neh*?"

"Akahata-san is a servant of the Purging Fire," said Jōko Daishi. "He carries out his divine duty."

"Right now?" Mariko felt something cramp up in her as she said it. Had she executed her sting more professionally, Akahata wouldn't have escaped. C-team hadn't been in position. Mariko wondered if she should have waited for SWAT after all.

"You cannot stop him," Jōko Daishi said. "He is bound on his holy errand."

"And what might that be?" said Mariko.

"Purging society of its impurities."

His serenity gave Mariko chills. "With MDA or with cyanide?" she said. "It's both, isn't it? How many people worship the great Jōko Daishi? How many did you talk into following your path?"

"Do you even have the stones to follow it yourself?" said Han. "No. When we came, you tried to run. You're not the type to go down with the ship, are you? You're going to let all your people kill themselves and then you're going to go recruit another batch."

Jōko Daishi cackled, not like a cartoon evil genius but like a little boy watching the cartoon. "You understand nothing. But soon you will. The Wind is coming. There is no place it cannot reach."

Mariko inspected the table next to him. She saw nuts, bolts, rubber bands, all in little piles; sheets of foil, boxes of stainless steel BBs; duct tape, wire strippers, lengths of copper pipe. None of it was standard fare for making speed or Ecstasy. All in all it seemed less like a meth lab and more like the back room of a small appliance repair shop. And above it all, hanging on the wall, was another copy of that weird planetary calendar, just like the one from the house where they found Shino's body. The calendar was all off—twenty-four months instead of twelve, ellipsoid instead of linear, festooned with astrological markers—but only one day was circled on it, and Mariko had a good guess about what that day might be: New Year's Day of the Year of the Demon.

You understand nothing. That's what Jōko Daishi had said. It made

Mariko think of the knowing laugh she'd heard from the lawyer, Hamaya Jirō, right before Han stormed out of that hospital room, right before Akahata slipped out of the TMPD's grasp. She remembered with perfect clarity how that laugh had chilled her. That was the moment she realized the Divine Wind were dangerous. The cyanide cinched it. Coupled with her MDA theory, everything pointed to poisoned pills. A Jim Jones–style mass homicide, masked as a mass suicide. But Jōko Daishi seemed sure that she and Han had it all wrong.

Mariko looked at the table again, then at the madman sitting beside it, then at the barrels of hazardous chemicals arrayed at the end of the line of tables. That motor oil smell permeated her nostrils and seeped into her mouth. She remembered what Jōko Daishi said about his lieutenant, Akahata: *he is bound on his holy errand.* She remembered what Yamada-sensei had written about the mask too, and about the weapon fetish attached to it.

"Han," she said, "take a walk with me." When they were well out of their suspect's hearing, she said, "What do we know about hexamine?"

"Big barrels like those ones make a whole lot of MDA."

"No, I mean what do we *know*? What if we don't assume he's cooking?"

Han shook his head. "We know he cooks. How else do you explain Akahata carrying fifty kilos of speed?"

"They could be unrelated, *neh*?"

"What about the Daishi? The drug, not the dude. Word on the street says it's outselling cigarettes. And we never heard of it until we heard of this idiot."

"I know," said Mariko. "Just bear with me. I'm not saying he's not cooking; I'm just saying he's not cooking *here*. Does this place feel like a meth lab to you?"

Han looked around. "Honestly? No."

"*Neh*? That's been bugging me since the minute we kicked down the door."

"So what are you getting at?"

"Han, what if he's using the hexamine for something else? What else is it good for?"

He shrugged. "What am I, a pharmacist? I barely passed high school chemistry."

"But you've got a smartphone, *neh*?"

Han nodded and opened his Web browser, and Mariko headed back toward their suspect. "Jōko Daishi," she said. "Great Teacher of the Purging Fire. Teach me. Tell me what needs cleansing."

"The mind is in fetters," he said. Even now he looked past her, up into the distance. "Property. Family. Hope for the future. The people cling to them as if they are lifelines, but in fact they are shackles. The mind is bound by them, constricted, weighed down. You are bound too, drowning, but I can set you free."

It was clear he'd given this little homily before. Mariko wasn't interested. "Swell. You do that."

"You belittle because you do not understand. You dream of stability, order, immortality. It is in the nature of what you do, who you are, but you are living a lie."

"So enlighten me. Tell me how you rescue all these drowning minds. And don't waste my time on the pretty speeches; that crap might work on your little Wind cult, but not on me."

"*Divine* Wind," he said. "Born of the Wind and yet not of the Wind." He seemed to find this funny; it made him giggle like a little boy. "And I *am* divine," he said. "My mother is the future and my father is the past. I am come to shatter the fetters, to burst the bonds, to explode the barriers. I am the light, the brightest fire. Stability, permanence, order, belonging, harmony, they are but shadows. Before my light shall they disperse, never to return."

"Now we're getting somewhere," Mariko said. She could see the excitement rising in him, swelling his chest, raising his gaze higher. It got her heart racing as well, but not out of some twisted sympathy inspired by his charisma. She was afraid. He was a zealot, all right, and he was dangerous. "Tell me," she said. "You want to do away with order and harmony? Tell me how."

"Still you cling to your fetters. You shy away from the light when in truth the light will set you free. Nothing you can do will stop the Purging Fire."

"Then you might as well tell me your plan. Your deadline's coming right up, *neh*? What did you call it? The hour of the demon?"

"The Year of the Demon," Jōko Daishi said ecstatically. "The appointed hour is at hand."

"Of course it is." Mariko tried to remember what else he'd said. "Your friend, Akahata-san, he's out to do some purifying right now, is he?"

"Soon. Very soon."

"Right. Because the wind is coming."

"There is no place the Wind cannot reach." He said it as if singing a hymn.

"Mariko!" Han shouted. She turned to see him running toward her with his phone outstretched. She ignored the phone, her attention captured by the look on his face. He was terrified.

He forced the phone into her hand and see saw the screen. "Holy shit," she said.

"Bombs," Han said, panting. "The hexamine. You can use it to make high explosives."

"There is no place the Wind cannot reach," Jōko Daishi said joyfully. "The appointed hour is at hand."

Mariko grabbed him by the beard and jerked him to his feet. "Where's Akahata? Where are the bombs, you crazy son of a bitch?"

As she lifted him up, the demon mask slid down over his face. He locked eyes with her, his nose not a millimeter away from hers, looking at her from behind the crazed iron visage of the mask. "The Year of the Demon," he whispered. "The appointed hour is at hand."

BOOK EIGHT

MUROMACHI ERA, THE YEAR 198

(1533 CE)

44

The waves roared so loud that Kaida could hardly hear the thunder.

Lightning ripped another gaping rent through the dark gray underbelly of the sky. It was just after midday, and yet the lightning's claws stood out clearly against the clouds. Kaida had never seen a storm so angry.

If anything, the sea was angrier still. Another huge, rolling wave tossed the rowboat as easily as Kaida could skip a stone. Her mother held her close with both arms, her knees and feet pressed hard into the sidewalls of the boat to keep herself and Kaida stable. She sang in Kaida's ear, and though Kaida could scarcely hear her she knew which song it was. No other girls' mothers ever sang this one. It was the song about the Kaida-fish, a little lullaby about a make-believe creature, which she'd been singing for as long as Kaida could remember.

Her father was the very opposite of calm. He clenched his teeth so hard that the tendons in his neck stood out. He back-paddled like mad, trying to keep their bow pointed into the waves. The muscles of his arms stood out like braided cords. He snarled and cursed and battled with the sea, a samurai armed with twin oars.

The boat lurched again, and for a fleeting moment Kaida was atop a mountain of water instead of falling down into a valley. She looked toward Ama-machi and saw nothing but flinders. Her mother told her the village would be destroyed and that they'd build it anew, but

Kaida hadn't understood what that meant until now. There was no home. Nothing to re-build, nothing there to repair. Just a beach and the rolling walls of water that pounded it, grinding down what little remained of Ama-machi.

This was the way, her had mother said. The *ama* had always lived like this. Kaida had taken comfort in it when the storm was still on the horizon, but now she saw it as an empty promise. She could not see a future for her village, for her family.

Kaida's stomach dropped, the boat falling with it. For an instant she could see Ryūjin's Claw. It ripped the guts out of a rogue breaker and then vanished, swallowed by the water. The teeth of the Maw were always visible above the waterline, but the Claw was in deeper water. Kaida realized these waves were far bigger than she'd suspected if the troughs were so deep as to expose the Claw.

But her mother would protect her. Even in the face of this hell-spawned storm, she sang the song of the little Kaida-fish.

Thunder clapped again. A wave moving in the wrong direction smacked the stern and spun the boat like a little child throwing a stick. Kaida's father lost his grip on one of the oars. Her mother's hand darted out faster than Kaida thought possible. She snatched the oar's grip in midair and thrust it back toward her husband, who damned the wind and the waves and his spent, wet hands.

Kaida felt her mother's arms wrap around her once more. She would be all right. All of them would be. Storms are stronger than men, her mother always said, but they have no patience. We only need to outlast them. That's what she always said, and already Kaida could tell the thunderheads had blown out most of their anger. She could hear her mother's lullaby a little better now.

Her father never saw the other boat coming.

It caught them broadside, flung by a rogue wave. Wood screeched louder than thunder. Then it burst apart, shooting splinters every-where. Kaida caught a volley full in the chest. Only afterward did she realize her mother took as many in the arm, protecting Kaida's face.

Kaida watched her family's boat crumple like *washi* paper. The other family's boat plunged on, shearing itself in half like a giant barracuda opening its mouth wide, bearing down to bite Kaida's boat in two. The sidewalls split down the middle, the bottom half submerging with the keel, the top half exploding into a hail of splinters as big as the bones in Kaida's forearm. The bottom half of the boat dragged its occupants down with it. Still the two boats plunged on, ripping each other apart. Huddling against her mother, Kaida watched the other family go under. She could feel it through the soles of her bare feet when one by one the keel crushed their heads to pulp. It was merciful; at least they would not drown.

Drowning was every *ama*'s worst fear, and Kaida knew she and her parents were likely to face it soon. Their boat wasn't taking on water; the water was taking *it*. The starboard side was no more than a jumble of ragged timbers. Kaida felt her guts heave up into her throat. The boat crested high above the sea, carried by the biggest wave Kaida had ever seen. For a terrifying moment she could see Ryūjin's Maw. Its black teeth dripped with white foam.

Then the sea dashed her family right into the Maw.

The world was nothing but darkness and noise. Kaida thought drowning would be quiet. She did not expect it to thunder so loud that it drowned out her other senses.

She tried to clap her palms over her ears, but she could only move her right arm.

Just for an instant, the noise abated. Just for an instant, there was light. Kaida saw her mother huddled over her, hugging her close. She saw her father too, his back against sheer black rock, holding on to the inside of their rowboat as if some crazed mob were trying to pull it away from the other side. Then she understood. Somehow they'd landed between two of Ryūjin's fangs, and the weight of the water wrapped their little boat around them, trapping them as snugly as a turtle in his shell. But a turtle had flesh and bones to keep its shell attached. Kaida had only her father, fighting the sea with a tenacity found only in wild animals and madmen.

Kaida tried to help. It was stupid—she was a little girl, without a tenth of her father's strength—but she tried to grab the boat anyway. She couldn't reach with her right hand; her mother was in the way, so she tried with her left. Once again her left arm would not move. She looked down to see why.

Her hand looked like a stomped-on crab.

It was almost next to her nose when she turned to look at it, so she could see all the details clearly. Part of the boat pinned it to the black, bloody rock. Some of her fingers were still intact. The hand itself was nothing but jagged bones. They stuck out in crazed directions, all a-jumble.

The world went black again, the water pressing their turtle shell back down with deafening fury. When the noise relented the light came back, and Kaida got a good look at her dead mother.

Kaida sat bolt upright under her covers. She didn't scream—not with her stepsisters around; she knew better than that—but she remembered screaming back then. She remembered the echoes of her cries within the wreckage of the boat, the intermittent fits of blackness and noise, the hope in every black moment that perhaps when the light came again she'd see she was mistaken about her mother. But the dark had been worse than the light. In the light she could see what was. Once the dark closed in around her, she could only imagine, and imagining made it worse.

She pressed her stump to her chest, trying in vain to slow her panicked heart. The house seemed smaller when she was afraid; the ceiling felt too close, as if it might collapse at any moment. She couldn't stay inside. She couldn't stay inside.

As silently as she could, she slipped out of bed. She tried to think of Masa, how quiet he could be, how he had melded into the sand the night she met him. Then she thought of how his dead body slumped when his friends dropped him in the shorebreak.

A moment's inattention was enough. She didn't crouch low enough when she passed by the window. She'd exposed her silhouette, and she should have guessed her father's injuries would make it hard for him to sleep.

"Kaida? What are you doing awake?"

"I'm sorry, Father. I just have to go outside."

She tried to make it sound like she just had to pee, but her heart was still racing; she couldn't keep the tremor out of her voice.

"Kaida-chan, what's the matter?" said Cho, her voice raspy and sleepy. Even now, after all these nights, Kaida still forgot Cho slept with him. Hearing Cho's voice coming from her father's bedroll startled Kaida every time.

"It's all right," her father said. "She just gets frightened sometimes."

"Father, no—"

He didn't hear her, but Kaida couldn't risk raising her voice, couldn't risk waking her stepsisters. They couldn't hear what was going to come next. They just couldn't. It would be the end of her.

"Father—"

"She was right next to her mother when she died," he said, oblivious. "Dark, close spaces have troubled her ever since."

Kaida froze. She held her breath, the better to hear whether anyone else was awake. If even one of the other girls overheard him, Kaida's life would descend into a kind of misery that made everything she'd suffered so far feel like a mild sunburn.

But no one stirred. No one's breath changed its pace. Kaida lingered for a moment just outside the door, listening, but she was safe. Her stepsisters were all asleep.

All the same, she stayed outside until she could make herself pee, close enough to the hut that Cho would hear her. Better for Cho to be confused in the morning. She was still groggy from sleep; maybe she'd remember the peeing and not the rest.

Kaida crouched outside and hugged her knees. It was cold, but she forced herself to count to a hundred before she went back inside. If the disturbance has jostled any of her stepsisters even halfway out of sleep, Kaida would allow them plenty of time to sink back into their dreams.

At last she crept back inside. Wiping the sand from her feet first, she padded over to her little bedroll. Just as she reached it, skinny, cold fingers tightened around her ankle.

"To think," Miyoko whispered, "all the things we've contrived to torture you, and all we really needed was to put a sack on your head."

Kaida's guts went cold. She wanted to cry. She wanted to stomp on Miyoko's hand, maybe break some bones. But that would only make things worse. Her father and Cho would hear. Then Kaida would be the villain, not Miyoko.

"Or maybe flip over a boat, *neh*, Kaida-chan? Sit on it with you under there. Maybe even bury it. What would you think about that?"

Kaida could almost hear Miyoko's triumphant smile.

45

Ama-machi was just waking when the outlanders invaded. Kaida was the first in her house to hear them; her father lived close to the center of the village, and screaming from somewhere on the outskirts roused Kaida from a fitful sleep.

She felt like she hadn't slept at all. First the nightmare, then thinking of Miyoko's new weapon all night; it was enough to make anyone exhausted, and an *ama*'s life was exhausting to begin with—especially an *ama* with only one good arm. Nonetheless, Kaida pushed herself out of bed, shivering at the transition between the warmth under her covers and the cool dawn air. She knew she had to move quickly, just as she knew it was the outlanders who had caused the screaming.

A loud shriek from next door woke everyone else in the hut. Her father sat up in bed. In his dreams he'd forgotten his injuries; instantly he was flat on his back again, favoring his ruined arm and wincing. Kaida could see his teeth clamping down, oddly bright in the twilight. She wished she could stop for him, tend to him, do *something* for him. But she also knew that Miyoko might well kill her today—and if not today, someday soon. Miyoko already had no sense of when to quit. She could not begin to guess how terrified Kaida was of close spaces, and that meant every word of protest would goad her on. Even Kiyoko and Shioko wouldn't be able to talk her down.

And that meant Kaida had to escalate weaponry too. She'd figured

that out last night, lying in her bed and staring up at the thatch, listening intently to Miyoko's breathing and wondering what would
happen if she just smothered Miyoko and got it over with. In many
ways that was the easier course. She'd do more than free herself of
Miyoko; she'd be exiled from Ama-machi for life. It wasn't much of a
punishment for someone who wanted to leave anyway. But Kaida
wasn't like Miyoko. She didn't delight in causing pain. And as much
as she hated Kiyoko and Shioko, as much as she wished her father had
never met Cho in the first place, she knew Miyoko's death would hurt
them so deeply that they'd never recover. Kaida knew what it meant
to lose family. She wouldn't resort to anything so extreme unless she
had no other choice.

And since Miyoko had no such compunctions, Kaida knew she
might have to resort to extreme measures soon. She slipped through
the doorway and immediately saw one of the outlanders moving in her
direction. His back was turned—he was talking to someone just out
of sight—and Kaida threw herself behind her family's hut before he
turned back around.

She pressed herself to the wall, heart pounding, and heard him
barge into the hut. There were shouts, protests, the sound of ripping
cloth. "You get out there or I'll kill you in here," the outlander said,
and everyone inside had wisdom enough to see he meant it.

Kaida froze, listening to them make their way outside. It sounded
like Cho wasn't alone in getting her father to his feet; Kiyoko might
have been helping, but it was hard to be certain. "Get out," her father
said. "What right do you have to threaten my family?"

"Is one broken arm not enough for you?" There was a grunt from
the outlander, a slapping sound, a cry of pain. "I'll break the other and
send you out for a swim. Move!"

A small part of Kaida wanted to have sympathy for her father. He
certainly wanted for it. But the greater part of her was bitter and hurt.
"My family," he'd said. He could have asked the outlander what they'd
done with his trueborn daughter, but no: his first concern was for Cho
and her evil offspring.

It was not hard for Kaida to wait in silence as the outlanders dragged her "family" away. She heard her father groaning in pain, but she could do little to help him even if she wanted to, and at the moment that urge was unusually easy to suppress. She didn't move a muscle until everyone was well clear; then she sprinted toward the sea cliff behind the village.

She found the old camphor tree with its big gnarled root pointing at the foot of the cliff. When she dropped to her knees, she was still panting so hard that she could see each breath hit the sand. A flat rock the size of a rice bowl lay nearby; she picked it up and started digging.

When she was elbow deep she wondered if she was digging in the wrong spot. Then the edge of the rock rasped on something hard, and with a little more digging with her fingers she found her knife.

Yesterday she'd given thought about keeping it under her pillow, but that was far too risky. Nowhere in the village was safe enough; there were too many eyes, too many people wandering about, too many little children playing games in all the good hiding spots. The knife didn't do her much good this far away, but she didn't want to just throw it back in the ocean either. And now she was glad she hadn't; if Miyoko wanted to take their little war to deeper and more dangerous depths, now Kaida could go deeper too.

It took a little work to hide the knife properly, but for once her stump worked to her advantage: her *yukata* never fit right—the left sleeve was always much too long—and with her teeth and her right hand she found a way to tie the scabbard tightly enough to her stump that she could hide the knife up her empty sleeve.

By the time Kaida got back to the village, everyone she'd ever known was huddled together on the beach, a dark, whispering mass not far from the Fin. Kneeling and sitting as they were, they looked like a shoal of big, docile birds. The outlanders surrounded them—but only if *surround* was the right word to use for six people corralling a hundred. As soon as she thought of it that way, Kaida marveled at it. How could six men imprison a whole village? And how could the people she'd grown up with be so utterly cowed by only a handful of outlanders? She had no love for life in Ama-machi, but she did respect many of her neighbors. That respect was ebbing away even as she looked at them.

She moved cautiously, remembering all too well how easily Genzai and Masa had disabled her, fearing what the outlanders might do if they found her armed. Genzai might believe her if she said the knife was for her stepsisters, not for outlanders, but none of the other outlanders would care. Flitting from the shadow of one house to the next, she got as close as she could to the beach without being seen. In the end she had to sneak into one of the elders' huts—a grave transgression; she could hardly believe she was bold enough to do it—and peer out the window.

Genzai marched up to the base of the Fin, holding one end of a long, bulging, rolled-up tarpaulin. The one-eyed hunchback held the other, and Kaida wouldn't have been surprised if they had a full-grown seal rolled up in there, because it looked unbearably heavy. Genzai was as strong as any man in the village, and the muscles in his arms stood out as if they were about to tear free.

"We come with an offer," Genzai announced. As ever, his voice was deep but soft, emotionless but utterly riveting. The villagers strained their necks forward to hear him.

"There is a shipwreck in the bay, and somewhere deep in the wreckage there is a sword. Its name is Glorious Victory Unsought. No doubt that name means nothing to you. In a place like this its power is meaningless. This is a sword capable of carving out an empire, while your village is no more than a barnacle clinging to the edge of the empire, so far away from anything that matters that you're not even aware it's an empire you're clinging to."

He said it without the slightest hint of derision. For him it was a simple observation, and if any villagers took offense to it, Genzai showed no sign of noticing. He spoke to them just as he might have spoken to a cluster of barnacles, Kaida thought.

Genzai still held his end of the heavy, rolled-up tarpaulin; the tendons in his arm quivered, taut as an anchor line, but he still spoke as if he were sitting calmly on the beach. "Even the dullest of you will already have guessed we have taken our turn at diving on the wreck," he said. "The brightest of you have already guessed that we have not yet found the sword. I have decided that one of you will find it for us."

"Why should we?" said Kaida's father. Even with a ruined arm, even though his every breath pained him, he was always the first one to defend Ama-machi's interests. Even though she still felt hurt, Kaida found herself feeling proud of him too. "The Maw is treacherous. Why should we risk our lives for a sword that's no concern of ours?"

"Because you'll be amply rewarded," said Genzai, and without ceremony he dropped his end of the rolled-up tarpaulin. Gold spilled out like water. And not just gold; jewelry, jade, treasures of every sort Kaida had found and then some. Miyoko gasped with delight. Shioko did too, and a beat later Kiyoko followed suit. Their mother, Cho, had a similar reaction, and she was not alone; at least half of the adults rose halfway to their feet, the better to see the riches gleaming before them.

Kaida thought it was stupid. What could they buy with all that pretty gold? The sea provided everything needed for life in Ama-machi, and to the best of her knowledge, Kaida was the only one who wanted a life elsewhere.

"Name your price and you shall have it," Genzai said, "if you are the one to retrieve the sword."

A wave of chittering swelled up among the villagers, but the loudest voice belonged to Kaida's father. "What price is so great that we can enjoy it in the afterlife? Show us what else you took from the sea yesterday. We saw your friend's body."

That caused chittering of a different tone. "You said it yourself," Kaida's father went on. "That sword of yours means nothing to us. We have no intention of risking our daughters for it, and neither will we risk them for you."

"A commendable position," Genzai said. "I salute you." He scratched behind his beard. "You put me in a difficult position. I told my men any *ama* village worthy of the name would provide us with good divers, and as you well know, I am a man of my word. So if none of your daughters will dive for us . . . hm. I'll have broken my word. That won't do."

He folded his legs and sat in the sand beside Kaida's father. As if speaking to a co-conspirator, his voice so low that Kaida could scarcely hear him, he said, "But I think there may be a way out. If I were to kill every last one of your women, down to the newborn girls, it would no longer be an *ama* village worthy of the name, would it?"

Seated as he was, he was vulnerable. The villagers outnumbered the outlanders more than ten to one. And Genzai had just threatened every family among them.

Kaida felt a crushing surge of shame. Not one of the villagers reacted. They would never have greater provocation to kill this man, the leader of the outlanders. Nor would they ever have a better opportunity. Yet they sat and did nothing. Some even had the temerity to glance at the heap of riches Genzai and his one-eyed henchman had dumped so indifferently at their feet. Now more than ever, Kaida wanted to get away from this place. She could never look her neighbors in the eye again. They were no fiercer than a shoal of sticklebacks: skittish, flighty, impotent even when traveling in huge schools.

And yet she was proud of her father. He alone stood up to Genzai, and he was the one with the best reason not to. He knew exactly what kind of violence this man was capable of. If she'd ever felt certain about leaving Ama-machi, about leaving her father to his new family, that certainty was crumbling now. Her father would stand up for the whole village, but who would stand up for him?

She took a deep, tremulous breath and told herself it was her long run, not fear, that made the breath flutter in her throat. Then she stepped out of the elders' hut and made a straight path toward Genzai. She had never felt so exposed.

His eyes caught her first. Then he turned to face her, arms folded, the corners of his mouth turned up ever so slightly. She wanted it to be a smile of paternal pride. More likely it was the thrill of anticipation in seeing wounded prey.

"I will get your sword," she said, wishing her voice wouldn't quiver.

46

"It's too heavy," Cho said, adjusting the demon mask on her face. Genzai watched as the one-eyed outlander—Kaida remembered his name was Tadaaki—gave a last tug on the leather ties, undoing the little adjustment Cho had just made to the mask. Tadaaki had bound it to her head tightly, with twice as many ties as were necessary. "What does it do?" Kaida asked.

She was ignored. "I cannot dive with this," Cho said. "We put our weights on our feet, not our faces."

"Weight is weight," said Genzai, rocking easily in the prow of the boat. "Diving is diving. Just get the sword."

He and Cho weren't in Kaida's boat. Their boat was abeam of Kaida's, in a whole fleet of *ama* rowboats. All the village women were out, and all the girls of diving age too. They were clothed in light *yukata*, not naked as they usually went, because usually they spent their time in the water, not cooking in the hot sun in their boats. The outlanders would only allow them to dive one at a time, for they had only one mask.

The *ama* boats floated in close company like so much flotsam, rising and falling each in their turn as the waves rolled in. There were not enough outlanders to go around, so Genzai could only man one boat in four with one of his own people. Once again Kaida's village embarrassed her. In every boat the outlanders were outnumbered, and spread out as they were, none could come to another's aid—not immediately, anyway, and it didn't take long to brain someone with an oar.

Genzai shared his boat with two other outlanders: Tadaaki and the other one she'd seen sitting by the fire two nights ago, the one with the wild, white, wispy mane and the ragged clothing not so different from his hair. He stank of days-old sweat, and his cloth was so tattered that Kaida wondered why he wore it at all; it certainly did nothing in the name of modesty. He made a ceremony of handling the mask, caressing it almost like a lover until Tadaaki took it from him to tie to the next *ama*. Kaida thought she heard him chanting under his breath, but his hair and beard conspired to cover his mouth and the wind was coming in too strong for her to hear clearly.

But she could hear Cho well enough. "It is the mask that prevents us from finding your sword," she told Genzai. "Our way is to let our sandbags carry us down, then let our rowers pull the bags back up. We never swim back up with anything heavier than a catch bag."

"Not today. Dive."

Cho sighed in defeat. She was the tenth diver of the morning, and the other nine had worked themselves to exhaustion, all with nothing to show for it but a series of failed experiments on how best to dive under these conditions. They'd fastened an anchor line from the prow of Genzai's rowboat to the widest hole in the carrack's hull, so that no effort need be spent steering the course of their descent. And they dived with extra sandbags too; the faster the extra weight could bring them down, the more bottom time they'd have for searching. Yet none of them had so much as laid eyes on their quarry.

"At least let me dive without this silly tether tied to my ankle," Cho said.

"No. That mask is one of a kind. We need to be able to pull you back up if you should drown."

Cho's face blanched. Until that moment, Kaida had been a little proud of her—begrudgingly so, to be sure, but she was the first to speak up to Genzai. It was obvious to all of them why these outlanders hadn't found their sword; they knew nothing about diving. But only Cho had said so, and Kaida thought that bespoke courage.

But Genzai cowed her with a stare. Cho got in the water and did as she was told, and to no one's surprise she did not find the sunken sword. She dived again and again came up empty-handed. Kaida watched her as she went down. Cho was as pale and lithe as her eldest daughter, and like Miyoko she swam as gracefully as any creature of the sea—but much deeper, staying down much longer. An *ama*'s lungs tended to get stronger with age, and wisdom and experience gave insights into diving that none of the younger girls understood. The oldest *ama* didn't move at all on their descent, and when they swam it was only little flicks, like a sea turtle's: small, strong, precise. Every movement, every flexion or tension of the muscles consumed the body's breath. Kaida understood the principle better than any girl her age, since with her handicap she needed to make the most of every movement. On most days, she tried to let the principle direct her dives, but on this particular morning she could not help but resent it. At this rate, one of the older women was certain to retrieve the sword before she could get to it herself.

She already knew the reward she'd ask of Genzai. She just needed to get to the sword before anyone else. But the *ama* had decided among themselves that the oldest would dive first. They were the strongest, and it was better for the village not to risk girls of marrigeable age. Diving on the wreck was precarious enough by itself, they said, even without the hungry ghosts that must be circling it like sharks. But Kaida wasn't afraid of ghosts. She was only afraid that someone would find the sword before she had her turn. At thirteen, she was close to the bottom of the list.

Her mind raced. She had to think of a way to make Genzai choose her, and more difficult yet, she had to think of a way to find his precious sword. She'd already scoured every corner of the wreck; she'd pulled up every treasure she thought outlanders might want. There weren't any swords down there.

Not in the open, anyway.

But then there were the dark spaces, the holds that were still intact, still locked up tight. She'd never mustered the courage to get into those.

As if to mock her, Cho's pale silhouette wriggled into the gaping dark maw of the carrack. From the surface, it looked exactly like the wreckage had gobbled her up.

"Scary, *neh*?" said Miyoko. Kaida looked up to see her stepsisters riding abreast of her. Sen was their oarsman again, gazing blankly from under the shadow of his broad *sugegasa*. Kaida wondered what lies Miyoko had conjured to coax him into rowing his boat closer to Kaida, within tormenting range. Her thoughts strayed to the knife she'd bound to her stump, still concealed by the loose sleeve of her *yukata*. It was of no use to her at the moment, but she was glad to have it nonetheless.

"*Neh*, Kaida?" Miyoko said it as sweetly as if she were talking to a newborn. "What a fright it must be, swimming inside that dark shipwreck. It must feel like the walls are closing in."

"Not such a difficult problem to fix," Kaida said. "Don't dive."

"Oh, but if we don't dive, how can we win the treasure? You do want the treasure, don't you?"

Kaida didn't feel like exercising patience today. She jumped headfirst over the gunwale, thankful for the cold water rushing past her ears. Genzai's boat was close, but she chose to swim under it and surface on the far side, out of sight of her sisters.

"Why is that sword so important to you?"

Genzai looked down at her, frowning. "That is no concern of yours." He turned away, redirecting his attention to the wreck and the *ama* within.

"I can tell you how to get it," Kaida said. "Tell me what it's for."

He gave no hint that he'd even heard her speaking, and Kaida had almost resigned to swim back to her boat when finally he broke his silence. "The man who tames Glorious Victory cannot be defeated in battle. In the right hands, that blade can change the fortune of an empire."

"And you want to be emperor? Is that why you're here? You're a warlord?"

"A broker." He smirked. "Battlefields are for fools. Those who prefer their heads attached to their shoulders find other ways than war."

Kaida thought about that for a moment. "Is there a battle coming? There is, isn't there? And you want to choose who wins. Is your plan to give the sword to some other warlord? To tip the balance in his favor?"

A laugh rumbled in Genzai's throat. "You are no fool, Kaida-san. Shortsighted, but not a fool. There are *many* battles to come, and we do not leave their outcomes to chance. Now tell me, what is your secret for retrieving the sword?"

"If I tell you, will you choose me next?"

Genzai gave her a grunt of disappointment. "So you can be the one to claim the sword? So you can demand that I take you with us when we go? No, Kaida-san. If a little ribbing from three little girls is too much for you, you'll not fare well with us when we leave."

"You were listening?"

"That *is* what you want, *neh*? For me to take you away from those sisters of yours?"

"You said whoever gets the sword gets whatever she wants. You said she could name her reward."

"I did." He glanced down, prompting Kaida to do the same. Cho was just emerging from the wreck. "Tell me your secrets, Kaida-san. How would you reclaim Glorious Victory?"

"I will say nothing until you agree to take me with you."

He scratched behind his beard. "Very well. If you tell me how to make these women retrieve the sword, we will bring you with us when we take our leave."

Kaida felt a thrill of triumph. "One more thing: promise you'll let me dive next. Before the rest of the older *ama*."

"Because you're so sure someone else can use your secret to find the sword?" He gave her a studious frown, as if she were some new breed of seal no one had ever seen before. At last he grumbled his consent. "As you like. Reveal this secret art of yours and you will dive before any of these grown women."

Kaida all but floated with glee. "We cannot swim with that tether tied to our ankles. Tie it to your mask instead. That way you won't lose your mask if I get into trouble, and I can dive deeper because I won't have to make my ascent with that big iron weight pulling me down."

Genzai looked at Tadaaki, then at the other one, the outlander with the hair and beard like clouds on a stiff wind. "The mask must be worn to serve its purpose," said the wild-haired one. It was the first time she'd ever heard him speak a coherent word.

"Bind it to me if you like," Kaida said. "Just not as you've been doing. Tie it so I can take it off."

Genzai looked to the old man again, who frowned as he thought about it. At last he gave a curt nod.

Another thrill of triumph ran down Kaida's spine. Her skin bloomed with goose bumps not born of the chilly water. "You, girl, get in the boat," Genzai said.

Kaida started to get in, but Genzai told her, "Not you. The tall one."

He pointed, and Kaida followed his finger to Miyoko, whose broadening grin bespoke victory and malice and joy all at once. She looked at Kaida as a flame might look at dry kindling.

"No," Kaida shouted. "Genzai-sama, *please*, you swore you'd let me go with you—"

"*If* you found the sword," Genzai said. "I will stand by my word: no grown woman will dive before you. But I have no desire to drag a crippled peasant girl in tow. If you should retrieve the Inazuma blade, I will carry you along with the rest of our luggage. But I intend to give every one of your sisters the chance to find it first."

47

Kaida was heartbroken. All she could do was sit dripping in her wet *yukata*. She'd sealed her own fate.

On any other morning, she would have no fear that Miyoko would claim the sword. The water was just too deep. But between the anchor line and the extra weight of the mask, Miyoko could reach the carrack with no effort at all. Worse yet, all the *ama* who dived before had worked out a sort of verbal map of the ship's innards. Kaida's best advantage had been her knowledge of the wreck. She'd dived on it dozens of times, while everyone else came to it for the first time. Now Miyoko had detailed instructions about which holds had already been combed over, which way to turn after swimming through this hatch or that one.

On top of that, Miyoko had the mask. Every *ama* who wore it said she felt it pulling her toward the sword. Kaida didn't quite understand how that worked; all of them admitted they hadn't seen the sword, and Kaida could not grasp how they knew they were being pulled toward something none of them could see. But that hardly mattered. Miyoko had one unsurpassable advantage over Kaida: she wasn't scared of closed spaces.

Miyoko positively glowed as Tadaaki fixed the mask to her pretty face. "Take care not to snag the line," he told her, just as he'd told every *ama* before her. "Should you lose the mask, we will send your corpse down to join it. Understand?"

He'd said that to all of other divers too. Miyoko nodded and promised and did everything else a good little girl was supposed to do. Then she flashed Kaida a sinister smile and made her first dive.

Kaida hoped she'd drown. Then she saw Cho's face.

Cho knew perfectly well that none of her daughters had ever been as deep as the wreck. Kaida's aptitude for deep diving was freakish for girls her age. Cho couldn't hide her apprehension: she bit her lower lip; her hands clasped tightly to each other; she held her breath.

Only when a slender white form slipped out of the battered hull did she allow herself to breathe normally. Kaida saw the tension pour out of her shoulders, and she realized then that she couldn't wish any of her stepsisters dead. Not really. She imagined her father with the same anxiety, and then with the same relief. He would have been a more attentive father if Kaida were a boy, and that was wrong of him. The death of a son would have hit him harder than the death of a daughter. But whatever his failings, a father should not have to bury his child, and the same was true of a mother like Cho. Kaida could wish her stepsisters would disappear, but she couldn't wish them dead.

"Too deep," Miyoko gasped when she surfaced. "It's too— I can't—"

"I can do it," said Shioko, exactly in time with their mother's saying, "It's all right, sweetheart, they can send someone else."

"Get back down there," Genzai said, as deadly calm as ever.

"I can't," said Miyoko, still panting. "It's too deep."

"Not for me," Kaida said. "Give me the mask, Genzai-sama. I've been down there. You know I can do this."

For once Shioko ignored her. "Did you see the sword, Miyoko? I can do it. Just give me the mask."

"No," said Genzai. "This one goes next." And he pointed his finger at Kiyoko.

Ever the follower, Kiyoko agreed. But she trembled as Miyoko removed the mask and actually broke down crying when she donned it herself. She did not shed tears so much as squirt them. Fear gripped her entire body; she looked as if she was about to faint.

"You don't have to do this," said Cho. "Please, Kiyoko-chan. . . ."

As it happened, Genzai and Cho both got their way. Kiyoko dived, but she only made it halfway down to the wreck before she lost her nerve and flailed for the surface.

"I can do it," said Shioko. At last she had the chance to outdo both of her sisters. All she had to do was touch the hull and she'd have surpassed Kiyoko. Surpassing Miyoko had been her goal for as long as she'd been alive. Her whole life she'd been catching up. Now, at long last, she had her chance to excel. And Kaida wasn't sure she'd survive the attempt.

"Shioko, this is foolish at best," she said. "Suicide at worst. You've never been that deep. You only stand to get yourself hurt."

"Shut your mouth!" Shioko said. "I'm a better swimmer than Kaida. Just look at her. Please, Genzai-sama, let me go next. I can do it."

Genzai looked at Kaida, then at Cho. If there was even a trace of compassion in him, Kaida could not see it. "This one goes next," he said, and he summoned Shioko into his boat to don the mask.

She rushed her first dive, paddling with her arms to hasten her descent; by the time she reached the wreck, she had to come right back up. With coaching from Miyoko she made the second dive in fine form. Kaida started counting when Shioko disappeared within the wreck, beating time with her thumb against the haft of her hidden knife, which she'd been concealing by crossing her arms and sitting hunched—no doubt seeming sullen to everyone else. Now she forgot herself, counting forty-nine raps of the thumb before Shioko emerged again. It was a good dive. At this depth Kaida herself didn't always stay down that long.

Shioko came up gasping, swallowing as much air as she could. Cho's relief was almost palpable; Kaida imagined waves of it rippling through the air. "Well?" said Miyoko.

"I saw it," Shioko said when she could manage to speak. "With the mask I saw it. It's just as you said, far forward, almost at the bow. It's so dark in there. You can only see with the mask."

Kaida couldn't make sense of that. The mask had eyeholes, not eyes. But Miyoko and Cho nodded as if Shioko made sense, and in any case Kaida had other worries. As Shioko described it, the sword was in the deepest, darkest, narrowest part of the wreck. The mere thought of such a place made Kaida's throat grow tight.

A sudden splash broke her out of her reverie. Miyoko was back in the water. She swam over to Shioko and gave her a hug. Then, softly enough that their mother couldn't hear, she said, "You have to get it, Shioko-chan. She can go deeper than either of us. We can't let her have it."

"You're a fool," Kaida said. "Better to cut her throat than to kill her this way."

Genzai shot her a sharp glare; he must have thought Kaida was talking to him, and clearly he wasn't fond of peasant girls calling him names. Cho made a face at her too; she'd heard none of her daughter's conversation and she must have thought Kaida was talking to ghosts.

"Cho-san," Kaida said, "you must get your girls out of the water. Do it now, before—"

"Enough," Genzai said, as angry as Kaida had ever heard him. "You, girl, get back in your boat. And you, the mask stays on, you stay in the water. You will dive. Now."

"Shioko, you must," Miyoko said. Then she did as she was told, returning to Sen's rowboat.

Shioko dived again, and again Kaida beat time with her thumb as soon as her stepsister entered the broken hull.

She reached fifty-nine and there was still no sign of Shioko. Kaida told herself that was to be expected; she was going a little deeper this time. At seventy-nine Kaida feared the worst. At eighty-nine, everyone but Cho understood what had happened, and at a hundred there was open weeping in every boat but Genzai's.

Tadaaki tugged at the thick, taut tether. When it suddenly gave way, it was obvious he'd snapped the mask from Shioko's corpse. Nothing floated to the surface.

"You dive next," Genzai told Kaida, before Tadaaki had even finished reeling in the mask.

48

"It's *her* fault," Miyoko screeched. "She was the one who told us how to dive deeper. If it weren't for her, Shioko never would have stayed down that long."

Kaida didn't bother to defend herself. The truth was plain for anyone who wanted to see it: it was Miyoko who killed her sister. In fact, it had been a joint effort, Shioko's sheer competitiveness weighed down by Miyoko's prodding. Kaida had seen it coming before it happened. She'd warned them all. No one listened.

Cho sat dumbstruck in her boat, so stunned by her Shioko's death that she couldn't do anything but stare at the water. The tears ran down her face but she couldn't even cry out loud. Kiyoko was at her side, hugging her close, Cho returning the embrace. But more importantly—to Kaida's eye, at least—was that Cho made no effort to console her eldest daughter. Apart from Kaida, Cho might have been the only one who grasped the whole, horrifying truth.

Guilt and shame tugged at Kaida like sandbags, pulling her mind into deep, cold places. She should have said something more convincing. She should have argued more forcefully with Genzai. But her better judgment said none of that would have mattered. No one would have listened. No one ever listened.

But they were listening to Miyoko. "She killed my sister! Kaida killed my sister!" It was a litany, a mantra, maybe even a magical spell. If she said it often enough, perhaps she could beguile herself into forgetting her own part in her little sister's suicide. A part of Kaida hoped it would actually work. Make yourself happy, Kaida thought, so long as I can get away from you first.

She swam to Genzai's boat and clambered in. "Someone shut that girl up," she heard Genzai say, "or I'll send her down to join the other one."

"Don't," Kaida said. "Her mother has lost enough."

Genzai snorted. "So says the one who means to abandon her own father. Since when did you start listening to conscience, Kaida-san?"

"Shioko wasn't the evil one. She was only trying to keep pace."

"And you? How evil are you?"

Kaida didn't know how to answer that. Not long ago she thought she wanted her stepsisters dead. Now she thought that was wrong. Not long ago she'd been certain she wanted to leave Ama-machi behind her. This morning, having seen her father take a stand for the whole village, she'd felt qualms about abandoning him. But Shioko's death would drive Miyoko to new depths of cruelty. Leaving Ama-machi was no longer just a dream. She'd be killed if she stayed. And it would break her father's heart if his stepdaughter murdered his only trueborn child. So Kaida's only answer to Genzai's question was "I'm not evil. I just do what it takes to survive until tomorrow."

That earned her an approving grunt from Tadaaki. "Spoken like a true *shinobi*," he said. "You may be one of us after all."

Kaida felt a strange sense of satisfaction in hearing that. She didn't know why. These men felt nothing at having just sent a young girl to her death. For Kaida to throw in with them now was almost suicidal. Of course, staying in the same village with Miyoko was suicide as well, so Kaida supposed she might just as well have the admiration of her potential killers, rather than their scorn.

Kaida stripped off her *yukata* and was now naked but for the knife strapped to her left arm. Genzai narrowed his eyes at it and gave a little harrumph. Kaida took it as a sign of approval. The strangest of the outsiders, the one with the streaming white hair, stared at her, and she felt his gaze as surely as she felt the sun. He muttered guttural

chants as he caressed the demonic half mask. When Tadaaki took it
from him, the old man seemed reluctant to give it up. Something in
the way they handled it made Kaida suddenly afraid of it. They held
it as one might hold a sleeping venomous animal.

Tadaaki leaned in toward her, and being so close, she could see into
the bottom of his hollow eye socket. It was awful, all filled with scars.
She supposed everyone must have looked at her stump the same way.
She hated the way their eyes lingered on her scars, then darted away
as if they'd never seen a thing. Now she condemned herself for doing
the very same thing to Tadaaki. She looked away from his missing eye,
focusing on the iron mask she'd inexplicably come to dread. Tadaaki
cupped the back of her head in one hand, and with the other he
pressed the demon mask to her face.

The metal was coarse, pointy in places, and the instant it made
contact with her skin she felt a strange hunger she'd never known
before. *Hunger* wasn't even the right word for it. Hunger could be
patient. Hunger could be sated. This was like a new set of muscles
under her skin, writhing with need. It made her want to move, to go
and take hold of something she simply had to have, but she could not
figure out what that thing was. Suddenly she understood why the
wild-haired one never stopped moving his hands over the mask. The
same force that moved her was moving in him.

She felt Tadaaki's fingers move to and fro around her head, around
her mask, but paid them little attention. Even when he pulled the
bonds tight, mashing the coarsest part of the mask against her
forehead, she paid him no heed. Such trivial concerns were nothing in
the face of this new craving.

The strangest thought occurred to her, one that distracted her from
her fear, if only for a moment: was this the way Miyoko felt? Was she
driven by some deep-seated hunger? One like the mask's, a nameless,
formless, all-compelling need? Perhaps some demon possessed her, one
with a face like the mask, one that spawned a visceral urge to dom-
inate and subjugate and hurt. If so, then Kaida could understand why
Miyoko took such pleasure in it: the greatest hunger promised the

greatest satisfaction. She knew what she needed. She had only to dive down and get it. Without the mask, impossible. With it, inevitable, even if it killed her.

"You know what must be done," Genzai told her. "You understand the price of failure."

Kaida barely heard him. She got in the water and fixed two sandbags to her feet. Tadaaki handed her a modified *kaigane*, its scoop curled like a bird's talon so Kaida could hitch it to the anchor line leading down to the wreck. Everyone else could do that with one hand while holding on to the prow with the other. Kaida could not, so as soon as she hooked the line she was already plunging toward the bottom.

She'd never gone down this fast. Equalizing the pressure in her ears was impossible without a free hand. She felt like someone was pushing chopsticks into her ears.

But soon enough her toes touched down on the broken, silt-covered carrack. When she freed herself from her sandbags, one of them slipped into the hole in the hull and instantly vanished. The sight of it terrified her. In her eyes the wreck had just devoured the sandbag, and now its mouth was open and waiting for her.

Even the mask's strange hunger did little to quell her fear. Her throat grew tight. Her heart started pounding; she knew it would consume her body's breath too quickly. The sheer length of the mask's tether frightened her too. She'd only used a third of its length in getting down this far. She had a *long* way to go yet, and all inside the gutted wreckage.

Steeling herself, she drew her little knife from its sheath on her stump, and in one deft stroke she snipped the tether linking Tadaaki to the mask. The outlanders wouldn't be happy with her for that, but she'd planned on doing it long before it was her turn to dive. The thought of being snagged by the face while trapped in the wreck was too frightening to contemplate. Freeing herself of the tether was the only way she could make herself go in.

She let the mask's weight pull her inside. Its craving had a direction now. She could not yet put a name to that hunger, but its object was directly below her. And the hold was not as dark as she thought. Remembering what Genzai had taught her about imagination and fear, she let herself fall deeper.

An open hatch lay before her. She swam through it face-first, pulled downward by the mask. The light was lower in here; what little she could see was purple, not blue, except for the yawning black mouth of another open hatch. She avoided that one. Others had gone down there. It was a dead end. But there was supposed to be a second hatch here, right next to the first. Was she in the wrong hold? Had she gotten lost already?

She looked up to find the sun and find her bearings. Shioko looked back down at her.

It was her stepsister's last ambush, but it gave Kaida such a fright that she thought her heart might jump out of her chest. Shioko's pale face almost glowed in the twilight of the wrecked ship's bowels. Her eyes stared blankly; her mouth hung open. Her arms and legs dangled like braids of seaweed from a mooring line.

Recoiling in horror, Kaida accidentally found the second hatch. It must have fallen shut somehow, and in the low light it was indistinguishable from the rest of the bulkhead. She'd only found it by backing into it. Now she wondered: had it fallen shut on Shioko, trapping her? Had she spent her last breaths pushing it back up? How hard she must have fought to free herself, only to see daylight just as the water filled her lungs?

More than anything, Kaida wanted to retreat. Push off hard and kick for the surface. Get her panic under control and dive again. But she knew she could never make herself enter the ship's corpse again. Not after seeing Shioko. Not after seeing where her own body would come to rest.

Kaida hefted the closed hatchway and fell through it. It was the hardest, bravest, most foolhardy thing she'd ever done. Drawing her knife again, she stabbed it into the swollen wood, jamming it so that the hatch could not close. It would still be heavy, held down by all that water, but at least Kaida would be able to see its outline when she came back up. *If* she came back up.

And now she had no choice but to surrender herself to the mask. She could sense the object of its desire quite clearly now. It still lay deep below her, calling to her somehow. A long, graceful curve, glowing in the darkness the way sunlight glowed through closed eyelids. It could only be a sword.

The mask pulled her straight down. Kaida couldn't see a thing. Something clubbed her in the shoulder. Kaida tried not to imagine what it might be. She tried to focus more on the craving of the mask than the demons conjured by her imagination. Her throat was as tight as if Miyoko were choking her.

She fell headlong, cold water flowing over her skin, and soon collided with a wall of soft, waterlogged wood. She hit face-first; tiny pinpoints in the mask bit into her forehead. She pushed the pain out of her mind. In so doing, she became aware of her body's other pains. Those chopsticks were back in her ears, pushed in deep by all the water overhead. Worse, her lungs burned as they'd never burned before. Now Kaida understood how Masa had died. It was the mask that killed him after all. The demonic hunger of the mask erased the pains of the body, and those pains were the only voices telling Kaida to go back up for air. The closer she got to the sword, the less she feared drowning, and that lack of fear was more dangerous than anything else in the ocean.

Her fingers probed this way and that until she found the lip of another hatch. It wasn't heavy like the last one. As soon as she opened it, she saw the welcome glow of purple light. Ryūjin's Claw had raked open the keel, and through those gashes she could see coral. These were the wounds that condemned the outlanders' ship. This was the sea dragon's deathblow.

And trapped in a mashed, splintered corner was the sword. The mask let her see nothing else. She dived for it. It was a good way down, four or five body-lengths at least. As soon as her fingers wrapped around it, her desire for it vanished, and all of a sudden she felt the wild heaving of her diaphragm. She'd all but expended her body's breath. And she was twice as deep as she'd ever gone before.

She looked down at the coral and up at the hatch she'd come through. The shortest route to the surface went straight up through the wreck. But there was no straight line there, only a dark and circuitous path. The clearest route lay outside in the open water, but she had to swim farther down to get free of the carrack. She was already far too deep. And the sword was as heavy as an anchor.

It was never the easy choice, swimming down instead of up. But obviously Shioko had tried swimming upward. Kaida was the stronger swimmer, up or down, but Shioko hadn't shared Kaida's fear of being trapped in the wreck. And Kaida had already spent too much time choosing. Black spots formed drifting schools in her vision.

Up, down, both options were probably fatal. There was no doubting it. Kaida gave herself over to the mask and the sword. They pulled her downward, out of the wreckage.

Escaping its innards was such a relief that it gave her newfound hope. She even had a flash of insight: she knew she lacked the strength to drag her two anchors all the way to the surface, but perhaps she could use the hull as a sort of ladder, launching herself one push at a time, just like kicking off the sea floor. Suddenly the broken carrack became the most beautiful thing she'd ever seen.

Then she looked up. As soon as she realized just how deep she was, she knew she'd never make it.

49

The black spots in her vision pressed in, multiplied, reeled drunkenly. She saw more darkness than light. Being the strongest diver of her generation meant less than the fact that, unburdened, her body would float to the surface even if she were dead. At least her father would have the chance to give her a proper funeral. Shioko's mother could not say the same.

Kaida's lungs had long since stopped hurting. Even her diaphragm had given up its death throes. Kaida pushed off the wreckage one last time, then let her body's buoyancy do what it could for her. She didn't think it would count for much.

She blacked out entirely. She could no longer sense the water moving around her, and because of that she was no longer sure she was even floating upward. She vomited into her mouth. Pushing the filth out let seawater in. Kaida knew it was the first taste of drowning.

And then she broke the surface. Her gasps of breath didn't even sound human. Still seeing black, she nearly slipped below the surface again, but sheer animal instinct forced her legs to kick.

Soon enough daylight pressed its way into her vision. Genzai's boat was not far away. It bobbed crazily on the waves—or was it Kaida's mind lurching, throwing everything off-kilter? He was saying something, but she had to get her breath under control before she could hear him.

"Where is the mask?" he bellowed. It was the first time she'd ever heard him raise his voice.

"Down," she said, gasping, paddling toward his boat like a wounded animal. "Down there."

"The tether is broken," he said. She saw Tadaaki beside him, holding the dripping, limp end of it. "And broken *cleanly*. You cut it?"

"Had to." Kaida's breath still came raggedly. "Can't—can't dive with it."

"You cut the cord to the mask," said Genzai. He'd regained control of his temper. "If you've lost it for us, I will kill you. You know this."

"Anchor line," Kaida said. At last she reached Genzai's rowboat. She didn't want to swim to him, but his was the closest boat, and her body swam to it instinctually, without her willing it.

"Make sense, girl."

"Anchor line," she said, hooking the gunwale in her feeble grip. "Haul it in."

"I felt it the moment you cut it," said Genzai, his fury so hot she thought she could see it rising from him like the sun shimmering on sand. But that too might have been a trick of her staggering air-starved mind. "I can only assume you cut the anchor line for spite. That will not be the offense I kill you for. Tadaaki, pull in that line. And you, girl, tell me about my sword and mask."

At first Kaida could not answer. Her relief at having something sturdy to hold, some reason to think she might escape drowning, left her incapable of anything other than a weak, exhausted smile.

"Well? Speak! I will have you tell me where you left the mask before I send your body back down to join it."

"It was too heavy," Kaida said. "The sword too. I couldn't swim back up with them. So I tied them to the anchor line."

Even as she said it, the demon mask rose toward the surface. Trailing it was a broken wooden spar, the anchor point that had connected Genzai's little boat to the wreck until Kaida kicked it loose, her last conscious act before ascending to the surface. Trailing the spar and the mask was the sword known as Glorious Victory Unsought.

Kaida watched the light play on them as they came up. They were the strangest school of fish she'd ever seen.

Genzai rumbled like distant thunder, and his anger seemed to lessen somewhat. His breath was less audible, at any rate, and his shoulders and jaws relaxed. Perhaps it was relief at seeing the sword, and no abatement in his anger at all. Kaida wondered if he still meant to kill her.

At length, begrudgingly, he said, "I suppose you'll be wanting me to make good on my word."

"And then some," Kaida said.

He grunted again. "You press your luck too far, little girl."

"You said whoever got the sword could name her reward. *And* you promised to take me with you if I told you how we could dive better. So I did. I told you to tether the mask, not our ankles."

"What of it?"

The strange fish were almost to the surface now, close enough that she could make out the fangs and horns of the mask. "So you were sworn to take me with you even if the sword remained at the bottom until the ocean dries up. Now you owe me my reward as well."

He grunted again, almost growling. She didn't look up, but she could hear him scratching behind his beard. "This one's too clever by half," Tadaaki said.

"She is. And damn it all, I'm a man of my word. Name your price, Kaida-san."

"Not here," she whispered. "There are too many people listening."

She wasn't wrong. Every last villager fixated on her, agape, stunned into silence. Not only had Kaida spared the village from Genzai's wrath, but she'd also pulled off the impossible, diving deeper and longer than the best *ama* in the village. She did not meet their stares, and did not speak again until all the other boats had turned in to shore. She waited until the wild-haired grandfather had his iron mask back in hand and Tadaaki had bound the Inazuma blade to his own body, so that even if he were killed it would not sink out of reach again. All the while Genzai scowled at her wordlessly.

At last she asked him, "You're *shinobi*, *neh*? Men of magic?"

"There are no magic men. The only place you'll find *shinobi* is in fairy tales."

"Fairy tales and in this boat. You said it earlier. 'Spoken like a true *shinobi*.' That's what you said."

"Too clever by half," he muttered, frowning at her. "If I were any other man, I'd drown you here and now."

"But you're not. You're a man of your word."

His grimace became a squint-eyed scowl. "Name your price, then."

"I want to be one of you. A *shinobi*. I want you to train me."

He scratched behind his beard. "You do not know what you ask."

"What need is there to know? I know I cannot stay here. I know my father would do better to see me go than to see me killed by his own stepdaughter's hand. And I know if I go with you, you'll sell me off as a whore at your first opportunity. *Neh*?"

"The thought had crossed my mind."

"Then I need you to make me one of your own. I cannot dive and fish for the rest of my life. Now I see how much more is possible. I don't want to be pushed around ever again. Nobody pushes you around. You overpowered my whole village with six men. I want to learn how to do that."

Genzai scowled. A guttural growl rumbled out of him.

The wild-haired one finally broke the silence. "She has her uses," he said, caressing the mask in his hands. "She has proven her fortitude. And cripples pose no threat. We can put her close to targets we could not otherwise approach."

"Nonsense," said Genzai. "There is no place the Wind cannot reach."

Kaida had no idea what that meant. They didn't give her time to puzzle it out. "She did retrieve the sword for us," said Tadaaki, seeming to meet Kaida's gaze with his missing eye.

"And you would speak to me of what? Debt? Morality?" Genzai

scoffed. "The Wind recognizes neither. We have the sword in hand. What is past is irrelevant."

"Your word isn't," said Kaida. All this talk of wind made little sense to her, but she understood moral obligation well enough. "Your word may be in the past, but it matters in the present. You said I could name my reward. Do you stand by that or not?"

"Watch your mouth or I'll sew it shut," said Genzai. "Do *not* take that tone with me again."

There was an uneasy silence, broken at last by the old man with the wild white hair. "There is another consideration. We have achieved our ends, yes. With or without the girl, we can deliver the Inazuma to whomever we wish. But when that man falls, or when his ambitions no longer coincide with our own, we must place the sword in new hands."

"What of it?" said Genzai.

"For that we may require the mask again. The other divers did not succeed with it. Can we say with certainty that we know why? Perhaps this cripple was the stronger swimmer, or perhaps her spirit has an accord with the mask, one we do not yet understand. This girl may be a tool for us, just as the sword and the mask are tools."

"Then we will forge another tool. I will not be a wet nurse."

"Masa spoke highly of her," said Tadaaki, seeming to study her again with that empty pit that should have been an eye. "Sharp ears and a strong heart, that's what he said."

"He did," said Genzai.

An image flashed in Kaida's mind: Masa's drowned body falling lifelessly to the sand. Then came another image: Masa falling to the sand in a fit of laughter. She'd felt embarrassment at the time, but now she understood that he hadn't been mocking her; he'd merely been taken aback by her naïveté. If he was mocking anyone, it was Ama-machi.

Hearing he'd spoken up for her gave Kaida a little surge of pride. It also gave her hope. Masa had perceived Ama-machi's true nature;

he understood why it could never be Kaida's home. His vote of confidence in her said she *could* find a home among these men. And Masa and Genzai had been good friends. Kaida was sure of it: she'd seen Genzai's distress when Masa died. Genzai would take Masa's word seriously. He just *had* to take Kaida in. She had no other prospects for survival.

"No," Genzai said. "I cannot. I will not." Kaida thought he meant to speak with finality, but she also thought she heard a hint of doubt in his deep, grating voice.

"Consider it this way," Tadaaki said. "You may get lucky. Like as not she'll die in the training."

That got an appreciative nod out of Genzai. "What do you say to that, little girl? He has it right: you may not become one of us. You're far more likely to become a corpse."

"Better than dying in Ama-machi."

"Is it?" He scratched behind his beard. "I suppose it may be at that." Then he shook his head, as if snapping out of a bad dream. "No. You will find no place among us."

"Then you lose nothing by taking me in," Kaida said.

"We have no soft futon for you, only a dirt floor. We would sooner serve you shoe leather than fish. Do you think your sisters torment you? Our sensei are worse. Do you think it was difficult, diving for Glorious Victory Unsought? We will push you into the depths of hell. Do not underestimate the comforts of home."

"A crippled girl is not at home anywhere. My mother is gone and my father has turned his back on me. My village is a prison and my house is a cage of predators. If a cold corner on your dirt floor is all the home you can offer me, it is still more than this crippled orphan can expect."

"You may live to regret those words."

"Then make me regret them. Take me with you."

The two of them studied each other a long time. Kaida could not put her finger on what it was—a slight relaxing of the shoulders, perhaps, a hint of resignation in his breath—but she knew it the moment he changed his mind.

"You cannot kill me willfully," Kaida said. "You must swear to do your best to train me. If I die anyway . . . well, that's the fate I get."

"We shall see soon enough. Welcome to the Wind."

BOOK NINE

AZUCHI-MOMOYAMA PERIOD, THE YEAR 21

(1588 CE)

50

The brothel in Minakuchi was called the Bridge to the Other Shore and it was true to its name. The broad reception room was in fact a bridge: a narrow brook bisected its floor, burbling pleasantly and giving the building an unusually cool atmosphere. The brothel itself was unusually long and unusually narrow, extending from the road over the brook and deep into the bamboo grove flanking the road. The interior walls were reminiscent of a covered bridge in their construction, just substantial enough to contain the milder air within them.

After a long day of hot late summer riding, Daigoro knew he should have found the Bridge to the Other Shore refreshing. Instead, he felt no less embarrassed than the first time he'd entered a pleasure house. Evidently these things grew no easier with time.

Nevertheless, he knew Katsushima had advised him rightly: he could only afford to stay with those who would not betray his presence. He had even hoped to find Katsushima here, though that was all but hopeless. The brothels along the Tokaidō were countless, Katsushima could have chosen any one of them, and none of them would disclose the fact that he was there. That was precisely why wanted *rōnin* took their lodging in a house that knew the value of discretion.

As Katsushima did not happen to be dangling his feet in the brook, Daigoro had no way of knowing whether his friend was under the same roof. He saw only the girls, so delicate that they almost seemed weightless. One of them bowed as he entered and escorted him across the zigzagging slate bridge in the center of the room. "Welcome to the Other Shore," she said.

Daigoro endured the standard conversational gymnastics, deflecting her flirtations and bandying about food and comfort as an indirect way of discussing the price of a room. Katsushima had always found the game exhilarating, but as Daigoro had no intention of laying claim to one of the girls in the end, he only found it tiresome. He was scarcely a day's ride out of Kyoto, he'd already gone two days without sleeping, and there was yet more to do before bedding down tonight.

But his rooms were comfortable, the food was warm and filling, and the very walls were redolent with perfume and incense and spice. He almost nodded off while drinking his tea.

It was the sensation of slipping into sleep that caused him to snap back, wakeful and wary. He'd escaped the sprawling capital, but Minakuchi and the Other Shore were still in the heart of the Kansai, and visions of General Mio's mutilated body left Daigoro feeling cold. He would not feel safe until he was well clear of Shichio's hunting grounds.

He called for the madam and asked for a girl who was skilled in conversation. It was one of the geisha arts, and an expensive one at that. Daigoro wasn't sure what he'd do when his money ran out—he'd never been paid to work in his entire life, and hadn't the slightest idea of how to go about seeking employment—but he needed to gather information and he remembered Katsushima mentioning on their long ride from Izu that this was the best way to do that. Daigoro wished he had Katsushima with him now.

The girl's name was Hanako and her kimono was of the palest blue silk, tastefully embroidered with parasols the color of cherry blossoms. She was tiny, not as pretty as Aki but shapely enough to make Daigoro remember how long he'd been away from home. They talked about trivia first, but only long enough for Daigoro to steer the conversation toward politics. "I hear the regent has been beset by something of a storm," he said. "One of his chief advisers retired or was sent away, I'm told."

"Oh yes, quite the to-do," said Hanako. "Only the adviser did not take his leave; Toyotomi-sama executed his adviser on grounds of treason. Can you believe it? It was one of his generals as I recall, a man called Mio."

"Is that so?"

"*Neh?*" Hanako clearly found the whole affair terribly scandalous, and all the more delicious for that. "They say Mio-sama was caught with letters to Tokugawa Ieyasu. You know who he is, of course. Well, the regent couldn't very well have the likes of Tokugawa killed, *neh?* Think of the message that would send to all the other great houses! So he ordered Mio-sama to open his belly." She giggled. "And it was quite a belly. As I heard it, this General Mio could have swallowed a whale."

"I heard something similar." Daigoro forced a smile, but his mind recalled images of Mio's terrible, gaping wounds.

"Can you imagine the mess, Daigoro-sama? A big, disgusting man like that. Not like you, my lord."

So it's back to bantering, Daigoro thought. He said just enough to keep the conversation going. His mind was elsewhere, trying to get the measure of Shichio. The man was as comfortable with deceit as Daigoro was with breathing. He used his lies as deftly as a sword, cutting down his enemies while defending himself. Katsushima's suggestion of resorting to *shinobi* no longer seemed desperate at all. Shichio was a foe unlike any Daigoro had ever faced. Squaring off against an enemy with a sword was simple—terrifying, yes, but simple. But Shichio didn't square off with his enemies; he maneuvered and manipulated, always from the shadows, and if a steadfast retainer was sometimes killed in the process, so be it.

Daigoro didn't know how to fight an enemy who wouldn't come out of the shadows. The only recourse he could see was to hire shadow warriors to fight in his stead. It shamed him even to think of it—his father would never have allowed someone else to do his fighting for him—but Daigoro didn't see what else he could do.

"Tell me, Hanako, have you ever heard of the Wind?"

She giggled. "Have I ever heard the wind? Silly man. What kind of question is that?"

"Magic men. *Shinobi*. You've heard of them?"

More giggling. "Of course. And *tengu* and *kappa* and snow-women too. What do bedtime stories have to do with hearing the wind?"

"*Shinobi* are more than bedtime stories. Many daimyo hire them, especially in the Kansai."

Now Hanako laughed out loud. "Ah! And now I understand. You aren't from around here, are you? I knew it! It's your accent."

"Be serious."

"How can I, with you toying with me like this?" She giggled, or at least pretended to in order to take the focus away from Daigoro's hinterland gullibility. "You've heard about our local legends and you're trying to scare me. The wind! Honestly, Daigoro-sama, you're too much."

Daigoro swallowed his frustration along with the last of the sake. Pointless, he thought; it's all pointless. Maybe back in Izu he might have known which ears he ought to whisper to if he wanted to hire *shinobi*, but finding them here was like finding a snowflake in a waterfall.

He dismissed Hanako and doused the lantern. As tired as he was, he found he couldn't sleep, which only added to his frustration. It was shameful enough that he'd resorted to hiring someone else to fight his battles for him. Simply attempting it already betrayed his father's principles. Worse still was the fact that he'd betrayed his principles and hadn't accomplished anything by it. He'd compromised his conscience, and his reward was exactly what his father would have said it would be: nothing. Nothing but guilt and disappointment.

He lay in bed for an eternity before the weight of his shame lifted enough that he could sleep.

When he woke he saw a man sitting at the foot of his bed.

Daigoro recoiled, his heart a ball of ice. The man did not react. He was barely visible, a presence felt as much as seen, for although the moon was three-quarters full, she shed little light through the room's only window. The door had not opened. Daigoro was certain of that. And the window was nothing more than a long, narrow transom running along the top of the back wall; nothing bigger than a finch could get through it. Yet there the man sat, cross-legged, looking at him.

Daigoro reached for Glorious Victory and could not find her. His *wakizashi* was missing as well. He carried no knife and his armor was bundled in the corner. He was naked, defenseless, and alone.

"You seek the Wind," the man said.

His voice was low and gravelly, the voice a boulder might have. Daigoro found it eerie that even when he spoke his body did not move at all. Daigoro could not even see him breathing.

"I do," Daigoro said, and the pleading tone in his voice shamed him.

"For what purpose?"

"I have an enemy. I want him dead."

"Then kill him."

Daigoro swallowed. "He is beyond my reach."

"Name him."

"Shichio."

Daigoro's eyes were beginning to adjust to the darkness. He could just make out the whites of his visitor's eyes, though he could discern no other features. The man did not blink. Ever.

He stared at Daigoro, silent for so long that Daigoro wondered whether he'd actually managed to say Shichio's name, or whether he'd heard himself in his mind but hadn't mustered enough self-control to voice it aloud. "General Shichio," he said. "He is Toyotomi Hideyoshi's man."

"He is known to us."

"Us?"

Those eyes shifted to a point beyond Daigoro's right shoulder. Daigoro twisted where he sat, straining in the dark to see what his visitor might have been looking at.

More eyes stared back at him.

Daigoro all but leaped out of his skin. Three more figures sat behind him, silent as statues. He could only make out their eyes. A chill washed over him, goose bumps too, despite the heat of the night. He scrambled away from his futon, crab-walking until his shoulder blades struck a wall panel. Not one of the four figures moved. Only their eyes followed him.

"Expensive," said the only one who had spoken.

"But you can do it?"

"There is no place the Wind cannot reach."

Daigoro's eyes strained against the dark, trying to make out something, anything, of his interlocutor's face. It was not lost on him that there were four *shinobi*, and that four was the number of death. It was a symbol; these men had brought death to Daigoro's bedchamber.

"Name your price," said Daigoro.

"Too high," said the boulder-voiced man.

"My family can pay. I guarantee it."

"You are without family."

It was a statement of fact, not a guess. Daigoro could tell by his tone. "You don't even know who I am," he said.

"Daigoro. Once Okuma Daigoro of Izu."

"How do you—?"

"There is no place the Wind cannot reach."

Daigoro swallowed. The noise seemed terribly loud to him in the dark.

"Then you know my reputation," said Daigoro. "The clans of Izu will stake me. Name your price and you shall have it."

"Gold is one thing. Blood is another. We will not spill our own in killing this man."

Daigoro braced himself against the wall. "Then why have you come? To kill me?"

"Our designs are our own. But we will help you if you wish."

"I want him dead. You already said you will not do it."

"Kill, no. Help, yes. Meditate again on what you need."

Daigoro's mother leaped to his mind. Katsushima's suggestion to kill her leaped to mind next. "Has my man Katsushima spoken to you?"

"He is known to us."

"I will not have her come to harm. Do you understand me? My mother is not to be touched."

The boulder-voice snorted. "Limited thinking. Limited vision. You know not what you need."

"I know perfectly well what I need."

Daigoro realized he'd spoken too loudly—to say nothing of too harshly, given the fact that he was unarmed with four *shinobi* in his rooms. "I know what I need," he said again, quiet and calm this time. "My mother cannot marry that madman. I need to stop their wedding."

"Still you see as if from the bottom of a well."

"How else am I supposed to see things?" It was an effort for Daigoro to keep his voice down. After a long day of frustrations, he had no patience for word games.

"Two are to marry. You will not kill her. We will not kill him. Broaden your vision."

"Explain yourself, damn you. Why did you even come to me if you only plan to speak in riddles?"

"We are of the Wind. Our designs are our own."

Daigoro's breath came loud and angry through his nose. Some strange metamorphosis had transformed his fear into exasperation. Neither emotion was worthy of his birthright. In his mind his father's voice chided him: the samurai makes every decision in the space of seven breaths—and not angry breaths, either.

He tried to calm himself. He had a wedding to stop, and he could touch neither the bride nor the groom. His thoughts ran to his own forced marriage. Akiko had many sisters; could he somehow force Shichio to marry one of them? House Inoue was of samurai lineage; that would satisfy that preening peacock's need to pretend at nobility. But no. Even if he could persuade his father-in-law to marry off another one of his daughters, nothing would prevent Shichio from taking Daigoro's mother as a concubine.

But the reverse wasn't true, was it? If his mother was married, she would be out of Shichio's reach.

It was a dark thought. Daigoro did not care to think of his mother as a playing piece. Neither did he care to speculate what the lords protector of Izu would think of him for marrying off his own mother as a political ploy. But he didn't see that he had a choice. Outside of Izu, he didn't have a single ally—apart from Katsushima, anyway, but Daigoro had no better hope of reaching him than of reaching the rabbit in the moon. In any case, this was a better prospect than Katsushima's plan of matricide.

"I know how to stop the wedding without bloodshed," Daigoro said. "I have no need for your assassins. I only need you to deliver a package."

"This package, it will prevent this wedding?"

"If it reaches its destination in time, yes."

The silhouette gave the smallest of nods. "Where?"

"Izu."

"Expensive," said the silhouette, in that voice one might expect an earthquake to have. "Far from here. Many eyes to avoid."

"You said there was nowhere the Wind cannot reach. Do you stand by that or not?"

The silhouette looked at him, and though Daigoro could make out none of its facial features, somehow he was sure it was frowning. "There is no place the Wind cannot reach," it said.

"Then you'll do it?"

"Difficult now. Many troops in Izu. Many *shinobi* here in the Kansai."

It took Daigoro a moment to grasp his meaning. "You mean Shichio, *neh*? He's hired ninja to kill me?"

"Stupid question. Obvious."

His tone was even more ominous, if that was possible. Daigoro tightened his grip on his *wakizashi*. "Did he hire *you* to kill me?"

"Our designs are our own."

It was hardly an encouraging answer. For all Daigoro knew, their designs included extinguishing House Okuma. Or perhaps Daigoro was being deployed as a weapon against Shichio. He imagined himself as an arrow, and thought of how little the archer would care if the arrow splintered after felling the target.

He supposed he'd never learn the truth. Not from inscrutable replies like these, anyway. But he also decided the answers didn't matter. Shichio was his target. The Wind was the bow that could launch him there. What did the arrow care why the bowstring was drawn? It cared only about the target.

"This package you would have us deliver," the boulder-voice asked him, "is it large or small?"

Daigoro smirked. "That depends on what you mean by small."

The *shinobi* looked at him sternly—a notable accomplishment for one with no discernible face.

"It's me," said Daigoro. "The package is me."

51

Shichio had birds of prey on his mind.

His mask glared down at him from the shelf where he'd sequestered it. He could feel its empty eyes following him as if it were a hawk perched on a high branch, patient and deadly. He was spending another late night in his study, and the oil lamps cast fluttering shadows behind the mask that made it appear to have wings.

At the same time he imagined himself as an eagle. A map of Izu lay splayed across his writing table, and Shichio imagined himself circling over the peninsula, searching the landscape for his prey. Somewhere down there, a lone bear cub was crawling home. Shichio wanted to find it and kill it before it burrowed into some den he could not see.

The image of the eagle was fitting: a hunter, a carrion feeder, a creature that could not live except on death. Shichio had come to think of the mask in the same way. He wanted nothing more than to touch it, yet the thought of its touch repulsed him. It was making him more and more like itself. Before, it inspired a lust for swords in him. After the Bear Cub scarred the mask, that lust had become hunger, and one who could hunger could also starve. The mask's need had become deadly.

And bloody. He'd purchased thirty swords, some of them massive *ōdachi* like the Bear Cub's, and had sword racks installed in his bedchamber, his study, even his bathhouse, so that no matter where he went, he would be surrounded by blades. His people had scoured the

Kansai in search of an Inazuma blade for him to buy. There were none, and even if there had been, Shichio knew it would not help him. There was a time when Inazuma steel would have satisfied the mask, but now it hungered for blood.

He'd hoped Mio's death would sate it, but he wasn't so lucky. If anything, it made matters worse. So long as he wore the mask, its hunger drowned out his moral sensibilities, but as soon as he took it off—to bathe, to sleep, or simply because the mask had come to frighten him—the memories came flooding back. Wearing the mask, he imagined tying the Bear Cub to his table; taking it off, he shuddered at the same vision.

One way or the other, he would see the Bear Cub dead. That much had nothing to do with the mask—a fact the boy should have known by now, if he had any sense. But if he'd had any sense, the boy would have recognized Shichio as a threat from the moment he learned who the abbot was and why Shichio wanted his head. Shichio's grudge against the abbot was probably older than the Bear Cub himself. The whelp should have seen it from the outset: to make an enemy of Shichio was to make an enemy for life.

But foresight wasn't a virtue of the warrior. No, the Bear Cub venerated that savage naïveté known as *bushidō*. All samurai were alike: they believed savagery could be bound by rules, and that their enemies would handicap themselves with the same set of rules. Their honor code would only be—could only ever have been—their undoing.

That was why Shichio would always have the advantage over them, and it was why the Bear Cub was doomed to fail. From the moment the boy left the Jurakudai, he had but two tactics available to him: he could face Shichio head-to-head, or he could admit he was outnumbered and outclassed. The boy was smart enough to choose the latter, and perhaps he was even desperate enough to overcome his pretended nobility. Falling in with the ninja clans was the only intelligent choice left to him. But Shichio had foreseen the *shinobi* threat years ago, and he'd established informants within all the major houses save one. The Wind would not sell him their own secrets, not for any price. Shichio didn't care for such peevishness from his underlings, but when he'd attempted to infiltrate their ranks with a *shinobi* of his own, he'd woken one morning to find his agent in his antechamber, waiting with the patience of the dead. They had flayed all the skin from his face. The message was crystal clear: there is no mask we cannot see through, and no place the Wind cannot reach.

The sight was so horrifying that Shichio never tried to make contact with the Wind again—until now. As soon as the Bear Cub left the Jurakudai, Shichio had reached out to them with a new contract: not for an informant within their halls indefinitely, but rather for a contingency plan to inform him if the Bear Cub should ever come calling. It came at enormous expense, but the gamble was worth it: he'd received a message before the week was out, confirming that the Bear Cub had made contact.

And, since he did not subscribe to the samurai's savage naïveté, he immediately made the next move. *Bushidō* forbade the Bear Cub from paying another man to do his fighting for him, but Shichio had no such compunctions. He did not even balk at the price—which, in this case, was extortionate. Shichio suspected they doubled their fee just for him, for no other reason than that they knew he was desperate enough to pay anything they asked. They weren't wrong; he would empty Hashiba's treasury if that was the price to put an end to the Bear Cub.

In fact, he'd already gone to enormous expense. Even before he'd made contact with the Wind, Shichio had foreseen the possibility that the Bear Cub would slink back home. He'd deployed ships, riders, carrier pigeons, everything he had at his disposal. He had even bullied two Portuguese sea captains into devoting their galleons to the cause. That was likely to cost Hashiba in the future—those southern barbarians were touchy, especially when it came to their ships—but Shichio could see no faster way to deploy troops to Izu in sufficient numbers. Patrols on every road, guards at every crossroads, crews in every port and harbor; nothing less would suffice. Every friend and ally to the Okumas had to be under watch. Hashiba would never have approved the expense, but as the regent's chief logistics officer, Shichio was the only one who could give himself away.

No. There was one other, but he did not have the backbone to speak for himself.

"Jun!" Shichio cocked his head, listening for movement from the corridor, but heard nothing. "Where is that confounded man?"

He dismissed one of his door guards to hunt him down, then returned his attention to the map. It was a seafaring chart, not detailed enough for him to judge the distances between House Okuma and its neighbors by horseback. They were all insignificant houses—Shichio had heard of none of them at court—but even ignoble allies were allies. Any one of them might offer a burrow where the Bear Cub could go to ground.

None of them were likely. If Shichio's informant in the Wind was correct, the whelp was heading straight for home. It seemed he had a mind to forestall his mother's marriage—and if that were true, then Shichio had underestimated Mio Yasumasa. What a staggering feat of endurance that must have been, to track down the Bear Cub even after Shichio had lavished such attention on him. Those wounds should have killed an elephant, but somehow Mio must have survived long enough to reveal Shichio's wedding plans to the boy.

Now that was a pleasant thought. Since Shichio was now Hashiba's top adviser, revealing Shichio's secrets was tantamount to treason. And since colluding with a traitor was itself a treasonous act, a rendezvous with Mio was all the pretext Shichio needed to name the Bear Cub an enemy of the state. It would be a pleasure to write the order for his execution.

There came a series of squeaks and chirps from the nightingale floors in the hall. The bobbing foxfire glow of handheld lamps drew closer, and at long last the *shoji* slid aside. There was Jun, bowing so low that his forehead touched the floor. "My lord?"

"It's about damned time. What took you so long?"

"A messenger came, my lord. It's—"

"Did I send you to dally with messengers? No." Shichio extracted a little stack of lists from under his map and slid them along the floor toward his adjutant. "Now look at this. It says here that I've deployed a double garrison at some 'green cliff,' wherever that is, and but a single platoon at the compound of Inoue Shigekazu—at *your* behest. Why?"

"Sir, the Green Cliff is the name of House Yasuda's most fortified compound."

"Speak up, damn you. Explain yourself to me, not the floor."

Jun raised himself into a less sluglike pose. "My lord, the message, it's quite important—"

"*I'll* be the one to tell *you* what's important, Jun, and at the moment what I deem important is for you to stop your prattling. Now tell me, why should I care about these Yasudas?"

"Lord Yasuda's wedding gift was most generous, my lord. Nine prized horses from excellent stables."

"And yet he did not attend the wedding."

That had been one of Hashiba's better ideas, requiring all lords to keep records of who married whom, who died when, what dowries and tokens of respect were exchanged. In truth Hashiba had stolen the idea from his predecessor, Oda Nobunaga, who saw dowries as convenient cover for his enemies to amass an army. A gift of horses might have been a pretext for building cavalry; a gift of land today could easily become rice for feeding soldiers tomorrow. To Oda's devious mind, any gathering of the powerful represented a possible conspiracy.

Shichio had never met the man personally, but as near as he could tell, Oda had been a brute and a bully—a samurai if ever there was one. But in this case, Shichio was glad Oda had ruled with an iron fist. It was through wedding and funerary records that Shichio could see his adjutant was even more incompetent than expected. "Read it," he said, stabbing a finger at the stack of lists in Jun's quivering hands. "Did the Bear Cub wed himself to the Yasudas? No. He wedded himself to the Inoues. So why are my troops stationed as if it were the other way around?"

"House Yasuda is thought to be the closer ally."

"*Thought* to be? Come, now, Jun, you're a bright man. You wouldn't invite me to cut your tongue out, would you?"

Jun swallowed. "No, my lord."

"No, you wouldn't. So is this an idle guess of yours, or do you have what we might call evidence?"

Jun shuffled through the lists, found the one he was looking for, and passed it to Shichio, all without lifting his head more than a handsbreadth from the floor. "If you'll read here, sir, Lord Yasuda attended both the father's and the elder brother's funerals, and the Yasuda retainers were more numerous at both funerals than any other clan's. It is believed that Lord Okuma—er, the Bear Cub, that is— well, that he married the Inoue girl under duress."

"It is *believed*," Shichio said. Jun shivered, but Shichio would not be so harsh on him this time. He'd made his case. "Send a pigeon. Double the guard on House Inoue, but leave the garrison at this Green Cliff right where it is. Now, then, what other news from the north? Has there been a reply to my marriage proposals?"

"Not yet, my lord."

"Why not? This messenger tonight had no word? What's taking so long?"

Jun shrank into himself as if hoping to become invisible. "I'm certain my lord remembers that the Lady Okuma is quite mad. Who can say what errands she'll attend to and when?"

"Have another proposal written up, and send it with the same pigeon. And tell the captain of the guard at the House Okuma garrison that he will return a reply from Lady Okuma or I'll have him buried alive."

"Yes, my lord."

Shichio gave a satisfied sigh. "Very good, Jun. Now, what's so important that you'd risk me cutting out your tongue?"

Jun looked up from his brush and paper, his eyes wide with fear. "My lord?"

"The *messenger*, you dolt. The one whose ramblings sent you running here all in a lather."

"Ah." Jun swallowed and cleared his throat. "My lord, the Bear Cub is dead."

"What?" Shichio rose to his feet so fast he knocked the table over. "Where? How?"

Jun produced a small slip of paper from the pocket of his sleeve, pressed it on the floor with both hands, and slid it forward. Shichio snatched it up. In a tight, neat hand it read BEAR STRIPPED OF PELT TONIGHT. THERE IS NO MAN THE WIND CANNOT REACH.

Shichio gave a triumphant cry, crushing the note in his fist. Images flashed in his mind: the whelp's throat cut open; the whelp disemboweled; the whelp dead with an arrow in his eye. He couldn't decide which method he liked best. It hardly mattered. He'd receive another note from the assassin soon enough, chronicling the details. In the meantime, though, he'd relish the moment.

Before he knew it, the mask was in his hands. He couldn't say how it got there. "Be gone," he said to Jun. Even the most incompetent aide had his uses. It would be a shame to kill him for no better reason than to celebrate the Bear Cub's demise.

52

ightning struck like Raijin's own fist, so close that the thunderclap shuddered every timber of the inn. The bolt threw a rhombus of white light through the open *shoji*, causing Daigoro's bloody form to glow like a foxfire where it lay on the floor.

In the next instant all was black, darker than it should have been even for an inn nestled deep in the pines in the dead of night. That instant of brightness made the ensuing darkness impenetrable.

A lone figure stepped over the prostrated body. It opened Daigoro's unresponsive mouth and forced a vile, poisonous liquid down his throat. Then, with fingertips striking as hard as hammers, it drove penetrating blows into vital nerve centers and pressure points. Each strike landed expertly, in precisely the right sequence, to ensure that the task was finished.

It was the last blow that forced Daigoro to vomit. His body twitched and heaved, splattering the rain-slicked floorboards with poison and blood and counterpoison. Pain bent him into a fetal position. With one arm he clutched his aching belly, and with the other hand he pressed down on the seeping wound in his neck.

Lightning flashed again, illuminating the little glass bottle that the figure astride him had emptied into his gullet. "What was that?" Daigoro groaned, his reeling eyes trying to focus on the bottle.

"Antivenom," said the *shinobi* crouching above him. "An old formula. We carry it often. Too easy to be cut on one's own blade."

"No. I mean, what—what poisoned me?"

His *shinobi* did not deign to answer, leaving Daigoro to piece things together himself. He recalled collapsing to the floor. That explained his throbbing forehead, but not the sharp pain in his throat bones. Something hard and thin had struck him there.

A knife-hand strike. He remembered now. It was meant to crush his windpipe, to keep him from vomiting. And there was the vile taste a moment before, burning his tongue like fire. He'd been asleep, and he'd opened his eyes to see a shadow-clad figure above him.

They'd struggled. Daigoro could still feel it: the panic of being entangled in his bedclothes. Pain rupturing through his right hand as he landed a punch. Poison raging through his guts like wildfire. He remembered the world slowing to a crawl. His senses took on the preternatural clarity of the dying. A hissing noise like an arrow in flight, audible even over the wind and the rain. A glimmer of steel flashing past his face. A tiny *thunk* when it caught his assailant behind the ear.

The *shuriken* wasn't fatal. It had only driven the assassin back. Daigoro had finished the rest, grabbing the *shuriken* with his good hand and ripping it across his assailant's throat. The wounds went numb where he'd cut his fingers on the *shuriken*. Venom. He remembered stumbling toward his cabin door, delirious. Then nothing.

"You," Daigoro said, his throat still burning with bile, "you saved my life."

"Yes," said the *shinobi*. "Most uncautious. Should learn not to sleep so soundly."

Daigoro looked at the dead man sprawled at the foot of his bed. He recognized his face: another ninja, one of six he'd hired from the Wind. This one had been masquerading as Daigoro's palanquin bearer. For three days Daigoro had traveled with him, even shared meals with him, and tonight he'd killed him.

Daigoro struggled to his feet. The wind knocked him over twice before he managed it, and when he stiff-armed the doorjamb to steady himself, his right hand recoiled in pain. His fingers were broken again, the same ones Sora Samanosuke had broken in their duel. Hot lines of pain burned in his left hand too, across the palm and the pads of the fingers, everywhere the *shuriken* had left its mark.

"What's the time?" he said.

"Time to flee," said the *shinobi*. "This inn, no longer safe."

"No," Daigoro said, frustrated with his inability to communicate. The attack, the poison, the *shinobi*'s violent curative, they'd conspired to beat his brain into something approaching drunkenness. "What I mean to say is, why were you in my rooms at this hour? How did you know to look for an assassin?"

The *shinobi* grunted. "Sent message to Shichio. Confirmed assassination of Bear Cub. He responded with pleasure, not confusion. Only one explanation."

Daigoro stepped out on the veranda, hoping the cold rain whipping his face might also whip the fogginess from his mind. "How did you know?"

"Didn't. Shichio's reaction proved it. From there, only a matter of waiting."

Daigoro tried to make out the *shinobi*'s face, but it was too dark. He was certain this was the *shinobi* he'd first spoken to—that lupine voice was unmistakable—but somehow he'd still never gotten a clear look at the man's features. They'd traveled together for three days and three nights, but this one had always ridden ahead as a scout until sundown, and from sunrise onward Daigoro had always been confined to his palanquin. The Wind had chosen to disguise him as a junior emissary of Tokugawa Ieyasu, on the assumption that no one would molest even the lowliest lickspittle of such a powerful lord. Daigoro could not begin to guess how they'd stolen a palanquin bearing the triple hollyhock leaves of the Tokugawa, with uniforms and weapons to match. It was enough that the emblems were authentic, and that the six ninja in his employ were utterly fearless, even of the most powerful warlords in the empire.

"What's your name?" he said.

"Stupid question."

"I just wanted to thank you."

"The Wind is without name. I am of the Wind."

"Well, thank you anyway," Daigoro said, choosing not to add, *you stubborn son of a bitch*. "For saving my life."

"Too early to be thankful. Now matters are worse."

"Why?"

The *shinobi* looked at him as if Daigoro were holding his sword backward. "Well?" Daigoro said. "Am I wrong to think I'm better off now that my assassin is dead? Does that make me an idiot?"

"We do not know how many Shichio has in our company. We do not know whether this one prearranged a second message to Shichio. We know nothing."

"Second message?"

Even over the storm, Daigoro heard the ninja grumble. "No fool, your assassin. Must have anticipated a false report to Shichio. True confirmation of your death would be followed by a second message, verifying the authenticity of the first. A code phrase, something no one else could guess. I could have extracted it from him. You killed him too soon."

Daigoro didn't like the way he said *extracted*. He didn't like being blamed for defending himself either. What was he supposed to do, lie back and let his assassin go about his business?

Even as these irritations crossed his mind, he also felt ashamed. Not only had he killed their only source of intelligence on the enemy, but he'd even managed to poison himself while doing it. He squeezed his left hand into a fist, mashing the open cuts in his palm. Let this be a reminder, he thought. You're alone now. Self-pity and impetuous action are luxuries you can no longer afford.

In his mind he could hear the same warning, the same lesson, summed up in a single word: *patience*. He missed Katsushima more than ever.

"So what now?" he said.

"You already know."

There was that look again, as if Daigoro were a wayward schoolboy. "All right," Daigoro said, "I'll work that one out for myself. You said

Shichio was happy to hear I'm dead. That means the one you sent to confirm my death must have reported back to you already. When?"

"Last night."

A rush of righteous anger hit Daigoro like a slap. This man—his *hireling*, bought and paid for—had let an entire day slip by with no mention of the threat on his master's life. No samurai should brook such an offense; Daigoro had the right to behead a servant just for spilling his tea.

But Daigoro had given up his station. His highborn instincts would not serve him anymore, and in any case, this *shinobi* had taken heroic efforts to keep Daigoro alive. Had the man slept last night, or had he kept a vigil just like tonight, waiting for the assassin to strike? Daigoro assumed the latter—and if he was right, then this hireling of his was forged out of pure steel. As the company's outrider he would have covered twice the distance of the palanquin bearers he scouted for. He'd been riding hard for three days in a row, he hadn't slept in two nights, and not only did he show no sign of tiring, but he was the one saving Daigoro's life, not the other way around.

"Last night," Daigoro muttered absently, working out the logistics in his head. Traveling by palanquin was cumbersome. As of last night they'd been two days on the road—less than a day's ride on a fast horse. If the *shinobi*'s messenger could report from Kyoto in that time, then Shichio's second message, the one confirming Daigoro's death, could have reached him in the same time. That meant the second message was already at least a day overdue, and maybe two. "Oh, hell," Daigoro said. "Shichio already knows his assassin failed."

A mute nod.

"And that means more assassins are already on our heels."

"Amateurs. The Wind would already have killed you."

Daigoro found it hard to take comfort in that. He was a novice at this game himself. Shichio wasn't. If he knew his newest henchmen were not up to the task, he had only to send them in greater numbers.

"We'll have to abandon the palanquin," Daigoro said. It was too slow, and even if it were not, Shichio's informants might have told him of it already. Shichio was no simpleton; as soon as he learned Daigoro rode not a horse but a sedan chair, he would understand why. It wasn't enough for Daigoro to travel disguised; he needed complete invisibility. He was a runt who walked with a distinctive limp. His *ōdachi* was famous, and even those who knew nothing of swords could see it was too big for him. His tack alone was enough to give him away: Daigoro could not ride without the special saddle crafted by Old Yagyū, the one that accommodated his lame, wasted leg.

The only way for Daigoro to conceal his size, his leg, his saddle, and his father's sword was to box them up and keep them out of sight. A sedan chair was the perfect solution, and traveling under Tokugawa insignia afforded an extra degree of protection. To leave it behind was to abandon his best chance for speed and secrecy, but Daigoro could see no other choice.

"To hell with it," he said, trying to sound confident. "It was hot enough in that palanquin to boil noodles. And my mare never cared for you anyway; she'll be happy to have me back in the saddle."

He beckoned the *shinobi* into his rooms and closed the *shoji* behind them. It did nothing to silence the raging storm, but at least they wouldn't get any wetter. They sat in the center of the bedchamber, farthest from the walls, where prying ears couldn't hear them over the weather. "I wanted us to sail from the beginning. You overruled me. Why?"

The *shinobi* said nothing; he only nodded toward the dead man lying on the floor.

"You knew Shichio had an agent in your ranks?"

"Knew it was possible. That was enough."

Daigoro looked at the body and shuddered. He'd contracted six men to deliver him to Izu in secret. At present he only could trust two of them. One had just saved his life. The other lay staring at the ceiling, his throat ripped open, proof positive that the other four could also be Shichio's. Daigoro's savior had anticipated that possibility, and that was why he'd refused to sail. Maybe the palanquin allowed him to keep his charge boxed up and safe, or maybe being trapped aboard a ship would have left him fewer avenues of escape if fortune turned against him. Daigoro didn't need to understand his reasoning. It was enough to know that his last remaining *shinobi* was trustworthy, and that Shichio's knives might be in the very next room.

But if the other four ninja were Shichio's men, wouldn't they have struck by now? Daigoro almost voiced the question, but then thought better of it. He was not like Shichio. Deceit did not come naturally to him, and that left him defenseless. Better to trust no one than to risk another attack. "We must leave the rest of your clansmen behind," he said.

"At last your mind is clear."

Daigoro was hardly accustomed to being spoken to in this way, least of all by a hired hand, but in this case he was proud he'd finally gotten something right. "Like it or not, you're the one man I *have* to trust. And since neither of us is a traitor, we can travel by sea again. Unless . . . no. It's too late for that, isn't it?"

The *shinobi* made a grunting noise that Daigoro took for assent. It made sense. Ships were faster than horses. If Shichio's riders were already on Daigoro's heels, then his sea captains might well have reached Izu by now. Daigoro had no doubt that Shichio would send ships. He had the might of Toyotomi Hideyoshi behind him, and a fleet to rival the Mongol hordes of old. Daigoro could not set sail until this storm blew itself out, and by then, the swiftest sloop ever put to sea would not be fast enough for him.

"But where do we go now?" he said. "If the sea and the Tokaidō are barred to us, the only paths I can see are to travel overland or to sprout wings—and I'm not sure the former is any more realistic than the latter."

"You overlook the obvious."

"Do I?" Daigoro scrunched his eyebrows and thought about it. The back roads were laid not by the great houses but by farmers. They connected villages, not cities or ports. Some ran nowhere at all; they tapered out halfway up a mountain, for reasons only the local grandfathers could remember. Few were charted, all were winding, and none were well maintained. A night like tonight would wash many of them out of existence.

"I give up," he said. "What is so 'obvious' here? Where the Tokaidō has bridges, the lesser roads have fords. If this storm topples trees, they'll be cleared from the Tokaidō. Not so for the other roads. Shichio will hasten his wedding plans the moment he learns I am still alive. So tell me, how am I to outrace him by clambering over every obstacle between here and Izu? I don't even know where *here* is."

"Childish. You have a mind like thin ice. No flexibility."

"And afraid it might crack? Is that what you think? That I'm afraid?"

"Yes."

"Then teach me to think like water, damn you. Show me what leeway I have to adapt. My enemy commands the oceans, riding the back roads will take weeks I do not have, and the Tokaidō is watched."

"Not the Tokaidō. You."

Daigoro's shoulders slumped and his head sagged. "What difference could that possibly make?"

"Obvious. Send me in your stead."

"That's no solution. What I'm going to ask for is too outrageous for anyone but me to ask it."

"New disguises, then. Your limp, easy to hide. Your weapon, impossible. Do what must be done."

"Oh, no. If it weren't for this sword, I wouldn't be in this mess in the first place. I'm not getting rid of her now."

The *shinobi* snorted. "Then your mind is not clear after all. You are a child. As well ask for a square egg as to ask me to deliver you to your family's home. You wish to be there without going there. You refuse straight paths and then complain of curves and corners. You would go without being seen, without surrendering that which makes you seen. Pah!"

Daigoro made a sound somewhere between a laugh and a sob. Pain and weariness and despair bore down on him, so heavy that he wasn't sure he could stand. He was desperate, he'd run out of options, and now he'd managed to aggravate even his unflappable companion. He'd never seen *anyone* display as much anger as this nameless man now captured in a single scowl. And this was his last friend in the world.

He wanted nothing more than to go back to sleep. Even an hour would be enough. He was so tired he could hardly think. But Shichio's riders could arrive at any moment. For the hunted man, rest was an enemy, not an ally.

He forced himself to his feet. "You're right," he said, marshaling what little energy he had left. "I ask the impossible. But we have three advantages in our favor."

"Optimistic. Stupid."

Daigoro would not be deterred. "First, any good knife can make a round egg square. Second, my family's compound is not our destination."

"I am to deliver you to Izu. To prevent your enemy from wedding your mother."

"Yes, but doing that from my mother's house is impossible. The answer to that riddle lies in the house of Yasuda."

The furrows between the *shinobi*'s eyebrows grew deeper and darker. "This clan is unknown to me."

"To Shichio too. They're just up the road from my family's compound. Trust me; Shichio may have men on the road, but he won't be watching House Yasuda itself."

"You are certain?"

"Of course. Why waste the manpower? The Yasudas are no threat to him."

The *shinobi* breathed loudly through his nostrils. "You said three advantages. You named only two."

"Ah, yes," Daigoro said with a smile. "The third is that I have you with me. And there's no place the Wind cannot reach."

53

Daigoro stood proudly at the wheel, his ketch in plain view of the fleet blockading the Izu Peninsula. His starched *haori* snapped in the crosswind, whose gusts were so powerful that Daigoro had to brace his feet against them. Sometimes he had to clutch the spokes or else be lifted bodily overboard. The storm he'd weathered had finally broken, but by no means had it blown itself out. There were still clouds all the way to the horizon, and all of them were in a foul, blustering mood.

Another squall raked the ship, forcing him to hold tight to the wheel. His hands burned like hellfire. Fortunately his *shinobi* knew techniques for binding broken bones—techniques quite similar to Tomo's, in fact—and like Tomo he'd bound Daigoro's two broken fingers to a little curved splint. It allowed Daigoro to hold things like sword grips and the spokes of a ship's wheel, but Daigoro feared the bones would mend in a curve, so that he'd never be able to fully straighten his right hand again.

It was while his fingers were being bound that he got his first close look at the *shinobi*. The man's hair was shorter than a grain of rice, and he wore a thick beard of the same length. Judging by his pug nose and flat face, he'd never walked away from a fistfight in his life. His forearms were covered in coarse black hair, more than Daigoro had ever seen on a human being. There were even traces of it on the digits of his fingers and the tops of his toes. Daigoro had never heard of a man having hair on his chest, but he'd seen tufts of it peeking out from the *shinobi*'s jacket. Between the hair and that growling voice, Daigoro found himself thinking of his companion as more animal than man.

Daigoro had become something of an animal himself, sleeping under brambles and evading the eyes of men. He and his *shinobi* had used the storm's fury to mask their escape. It broke Daigoro's heart to abandon his favorite mare in the innkeeper's stable, and with her his saddle, the only one of its kind. Both deserved a better fate than to be forgotten in the hands of a stranger, to be sold off at a whim, but his emotional attachment was exactly why he needed to leave his horse and tack behind. Anyone pursuing him would think not that he'd ridden off in the night but that he'd simply vanished. They would try to figure out where his body was buried before they ever thought to track a highborn princeling through the muck.

By morning the storm had not slackened in the least. There was no sun, only a gradual lightening from black to gray. Rain became hail, pinging off Daigoro's breastplate. At last he could go no farther, and he and his *shinobi* found a stand of wind-battered pines that would ward off the hailstones, if not the wet and the cold. The princeling would have been miserable beyond description, but Daigoro the outlaw just looked for a rock flat enough to serve as a pillow.

Sora armor made a poor futon. He hadn't managed even an hour of sleep, and awoke with his hips and back feeling just like his broken fingers. He cursed sleep for a beguiling temptress, and cursed the gods of wind and thunder for their spite of mortal man. There was no telling when the rain would change to hail, driving every sane person into shelter while Daigoro and his *shinobi* soldiered on.

But no sooner did that thought strike him than he understood: the storm was the greatest gift the gods could bestow. Horses would not abide the hail. Daigoro's mare was lucky to be left behind in her stall. So long as the gods remained fickle—so long as their rain could turn to hail on a whim—Shichio's hired swords could never coax their mounts into the storm.

Daigoro's thinking had been wrong from the start. He'd confused his allies for enemies and his enemies for allies. Twice now, in the inn and under the pines, he'd wanted to sleep. The next time he would not forget: for the hunted man, sleep was a foe, not a friend. Even the hailstones, the worst of his tormentors, did him more good than harm. The real threat was a clear sky.

That was the realization that unlocked the Toyotomi blockade: the most dangerous enemy was the innocuous one, the one that seemed like a friend. As soon as that dawned on him, he'd arrived at a decision: it was high time he came to learn the arts of naval warfare. He decided he would become a pirate.

He and his *shinobi* had pressed on through a miserable day and a cold and miserable night. By the hour of the dog they'd put the worst of the storm behind them, and by midnight they'd reached their goal: a wharf, and in it a junk-rigged Toyotomi ketch rocking sleepily beside her quay. Dispatching the night watch had posed little difficulty; the *shinobi* was as silent as his own shadow, and Glorious Victory's long reach was more than a match for any seaman's dirk. Most of the crew were ashore, probably bedding whores and feeling thankful that they weren't the ones stationed out in the rain. Together Daigoro and his *shinobi* made short work of the watchmen left aboard. They slipped the little ship's hawsers unnoticed, and with a skeleton crew of two they rode the tide out to sea.

Daigoro was no great sailor, but he'd lived his entire life on the coast, with his family's harbor for a playground. He knew his way around a junk rig, and his *shinobi* was evidently an expert seaman. In fact, the man seemed to do everything with an expert hand. The Wind must have trained him since boyhood. He and Daigoro had that much in common: neither of them had ever been children. Daigoro spent his childhood learning swordsmanship, horsemanship, archery, calligraphy, poetry; the *shinobi* must have been raised on brewing poisons, moving silently, killing men with his bare hands. Daigoro wondered at what rigors the Wind must have put him through, and how many of its disciples survived the training.

At first light Daigoro had caught sight of other Toyotomi sails on the horizon, and feared the crew of the hijacked ketch might have sounded the alarm. Then he'd realized the truth: the ships already at sea weren't hunting him. They were just a part of Shichio's fleet. They couldn't have learned of Daigoro's piracy, because the ketch's crew had no one to sound the alarm to. They'd been alone in the harbor— hardly a typical deployment for naval vessels, so Daigoro could only surmise that Shichio must have stationed a ship in every last harbor along the coast. A lone ship was vulnerable, yes, but Shichio had a mind to place eyes and ears as widely as possible. No doubt he thought there was little risk of a crippled boy commandeering an entire warship on his own.

But Shichio had underestimated the prowess of the Wind, and neither had he accounted for Daigoro's own boldness. It was beyond bold to propose a two-man assault on a harbor; it was rash, even fool-hardy, but Daigoro vowed he would make Shichio realize the danger of driving an enemy to desperation.

Now, despite the pain in his fists, Daigoro wanted to howl at the sky. Shichio had made an animal of him, but not a mere cub. He was a prowler, a predator. As he approached the Toyotomi blockade, he felt the same hunter's glee a tiger might feel as it slipped through tall grasses toward its prey. Hidden by nothing substantial, invisible none-theless, the thrill of it made him feel he might actually grow claws.

Perhaps the other captains might have hailed him if he'd made straight for House Okuma's jetty, but Daigoro was too canny for that. He ran the blockade at its thinnest, giving the other crews no reason to point their spyglasses his way. Even if they had done so, he and his *shinobi* were both wearing Toyotomi colors, borrowed from dead men who no longer needed them. Shichio's fleet was spread too thin; at this distance even a hawk wouldn't notice the ketch had too few crewmen on deck.

Daigoro had run the gauntlet. He would reach Izu after all.

54

The Green Cliff loomed over the road, tall and broad and steadfast. It was not, strictly speaking, a castle, but rather a wall surrounding House Yasuda's largest compound. Not only was it the Yasudas' sturdiest stronghold; it was arguably the most obdurate structure in all of Izu. Blessed by the gods of good fortune or else by *kami* dwelling deep in the rocks, the Green Cliff shrugged off earthquakes as easily as arrows. The land was weak just north and just south of the Green Cliff, falling away from the road in deep ravines that swallowed bridges whenever the tremors grew violent. Each time the Yasuda carpenters shored up the trestles and rebuilt the spans, and each time the Green Cliff stood fast.

The typhoons that lashed Izu every autumn had no greater effect than the earthquakes. While other lords commissioned new roofs, new gates, even new walls, against House Yasuda the driving rains only brought more moisture for the verdant moss that gave the Green Cliff its name.

Behind the Green Cliff, inside the Yasuda compound, banners of muted green snapped on their poles, causing the white centipedes adorning them to wriggle and slither. The same wind bent low the flames of Toyotomi fires, making them gutter and crackle and return all the stronger. Twenty fires, maybe more. They should not have been there.

The little cookfires illuminated the skirts of long, multicolored tents with gently sloping roofs, pitched in two long columns like horses on a wagon team. Long banner poles flanked each tent, these ones bearing not the white centipede of House Yasuda but the black *kiri* flower of Toyotomi Hideyoshi. They should not have been there.

The thought paced back and forth in Daigoro's brain: they should not have been there. How had Shichio come to know of this place? Did his demon mask give him second sight? Or had he communed with actual demons, who spied on Daigoro from the pits of hell? Garrisons at the foot of Kattō-ji made sense, or at the Okuma compound, but there was no reason to place House Yasuda under guard. Daigoro had told only one person of his true destination in Izu: the *shinobi* right next to him, who had not left Daigoro's side since the night they'd disappeared into the storm.

And yet there they were: Shichio's sentries, dwarfed by the Green Cliff. Tiny points of firelight glinted on their spears. They should not have been there.

Daigoro was too tired to think of anything else. For such a long time he'd been pushing himself forward on willpower alone, always with the thought of House Yasuda as a safe haven. Seeing it besieged was enough to break his spirit. There was nowhere left for him to go.

His only refuge was the talus-strewn hilltop overlooking the Green Cliff. He could not even stand; he had to crawl from boulder to boulder, or else risk being seen. His *shinobi* moved like a spider, swift and effortless, but Daigoro's shoulders and thighs burned from exertion. He crawled on his elbows because neither of his battered hands could take the weight.

He assayed the Green Cliff once more, and the garrison encamped at its base. "They outnumber us twenty-five to one—and that counts only the enemy we can see. There's no getting in there."

"You lack imagination."

Not true, Daigoro wanted to say. He could imagine a hundred ways in which these men might kill him. The biggest part of him wanted to get it over with. Just walk up to the gate. The sheer audacity of it might take the enemy by surprise, at least for a moment. Long enough to cut a few of them down before he died.

There were fathers who raised their sons to think such recklessness was exactly what *bushidō* required of them. They said anything less was cowardice. But Okuma Tetsurō had raised his sons differently. He taught them to think strategically, to avoid combat whenever possible, so that when they drew blood the world would know it was necessary and right. Above all, he'd taught his sons to be of good use to their clan. Daigoro knew he could serve his clan best by gaining an audience with Lord Yasuda Jinbei. He just couldn't see how to make that happen.

"Maybe we can get Lord Yasuda to come outside," he whispered.

"You said he is ill," said his *shinobi*. "Bedridden."

And has been for most of this year, Daigoro thought. Truth to tell, he couldn't even be sure his old ally was still alive. No one would have sent word to him if Lord Yasuda had passed on. Daigoro had no standing now, no face, no family. He didn't even have a home where he could receive the news.

Daigoro set his jaw and steeled his mind. He was still samurai at heart, even if he'd given up any such claims in the eyes of the world. Speculating about worst-case scenarios was unbecoming of him. "To hell with it," he said. "I'm going in there."

"Better," said the *shinobi*. "At last you see clearly."

They retreated to the far slope of the hill, where they were impossible to see and less likely to be heard. Even so, they kept their voices low and their movements slow and seldom.

"When I first hired you," Daigoro said, "you didn't know I intended you to deliver me here, *neh*? You thought I was making for my family's compound?"

"Yes."

"And you thought to encounter soldiers there?"

"Many."

"What was your plan? How did you intend to get me inside?"

"Walk through the front door. Kill as many as necessary to do so."

"Oh. Right." I guess he doesn't share my father's beliefs about restraint, Daigoro thought. "And now?"

"Impossible now. Had six then. Now there is only me."

"But you had a second plan in place, *neh?*"

The *shinobi* nodded. "Sneak you in over the wall."

Daigoro could not keep the shock from his face. "That was your *second* plan? It's easier than the first."

"No. Killing men is easy. Easier still to make them desert their posts. Much more difficult to move among them unseen."

"But that's what you do. You're *shinobi.*"

"I am. Not you."

"And the message can only come from me." Daigoro frowned. "It will do no good for Lord Yasuda to hear it from anyone else. But why can't I just follow you over the wall?"

"Loud. Clumsy. Could have managed it before. Impossible now."

"Why?"

"Had many targets before. Now only two."

"No," Daigoro said. "There must be fifty targets down there—"

He cut himself short, because suddenly the *shinobi*'s meaning became clear. His concern wasn't with finding Toyotomis to kill; it was with Toyotomi arrows finding targets.

Daigoro didn't care for being thought of as a target. Still, he supposed the *shinobi* had a point. His initial complement of six could have created distractions in every direction. They were trained in such arts. Now there was only one to distract the enemy—enough for a lone sentry, but not nearly enough to draw every last arrow away from Daigoro.

"I don't suppose you have a second backup plan," Daigoro whispered.

"Ten plans. Twenty. No matter. What you lack is time."

It took Daigoro a moment to unravel what he meant by that—he was *so tired*—but at length he understood: Shichio was coming. Thus far he'd foreseen Daigoro's every move. He'd placed an assassin in Daigoro's bedchamber, he'd locked Izu under a blockade, and somehow he'd even stationed a garrison at the Green Cliff. The one gambit he hadn't expected—commandeering the ketch—was only possible because he *had* foreseen the need to put the entire coastline under watch. If the storm hadn't driven the ketch's crew to port, Daigoro might never have made it as far as he did. Shichio had known Daigoro was heading north almost as soon as Daigoro set out. That would only accelerate his plans to marry Daigoro's mother; in fact, he was probably already en route. If he came by road, Daigoro had a day or two at most. If he came as he did last time, by sea, he might arrive by morning.

Daigoro needed to deliver his message to Lord Yasuda, and he needed to do it *now*.

He looked at the *shinobi*, who still wore his pirated Toyotomi garb. The *kiri* crest drew his eye. "I know of one distraction compelling enough to draw off all those men," he said. "Me. I'm the only bait they're sure to go for."

The *shinobi* gave him a nod.

"Then what choice do I have?" Daigoro said. "It's time to give them what they want."

55

The Toyotomi lieutenant could hardly believe his eyes. There he was, the Bear Cub of Izu. He went disguised, wearing Toyotomi colors, but there was no mistaking that enormous sword of his. It flashed in the moonlight, and even from a hundred paces off the lieutenant could hardly believe the size of it.

The boy was in hot pursuit, chasing one of the lieutenant's own men. Both of them limped as much as ran. Rumor held that the Bear Cub had a lame leg; his quarry probably hobbled because the Bear Cub had wounded him. "Archers!" the lieutenant said. "Nock!"

Ten men leaped to their feet and put arrows to their bowstrings. "Mark," the lieutenant said. "Draw." His man was increasing his lead, but that made no matter; he should never have fled the enemy in the first place. If a stray arrow found him on its way to the Bear Cub, so be it. An ignominious death was exactly what he deserved.

Unless. Was there some conceivable reason to retreat? Or if not to retreat, to quickly return—and perhaps to report? That was it. General Shichio had authorized the lieutenant to handpick his detachment, and the lieutenant chose only good soldiers. Brave men, seasoned men, men patient enough to endure the boredom of garrison duty. Such men knew not to flee combat, especially not when the enemy was so a prized target. General Shichio had already promised a thousand *koku* to the one who claimed the Bear Cub's head. The lieutenant didn't approve of such incentives himself—it was merchant's thinking, offering a reward simply for fulfilling one's duty—and he'd chosen soldiers of similar mind. Not one of them would flee the Bear Cub unless he had something invaluable to report, something so important that the Bear Cub would risk exposure to cut him down.

The lieutenant ordered his men to relax their bowstrings. "You there," he barked, pointing at the four door guards, "go protect that scout. Drive off the Bear Cub if you must, kill him if you can—"

It was too late. The Cub's sword shone like a comet. It flashed in a wide glittering arc and the scout's legs died under him, limp as wet rags. He collapsed bloodlessly; with a sword large enough to chop a man in half, the Bear Cub cut just deep enough to nick the spinal cord.

"Go, go!" the lieutenant yelled. The door guards were already in motion, spears leveled. "Archers, loose! Loose at will!"

The Bear Cub stood his ground, waving his sword defiantly above his kill. Arrows sang as they took flight. The lieutenant redeployed eight spearmen to guard the Yasuda gate and rallied the rest of his unit into formation.

The first salvo from the archers fell short. They adjusted their aim and shot again, loosing haphazardly now, no longer in unison. Still the Bear Cub stood his ground, and with a deft swipe from that massive sword, he struck ten arrows right out of the air.

It was impossible. The boy must have been part cat; how else could he have seen an arrow in the dark? The thought of deflecting *ten* of them sent the lieutenant's head spinning. At last he understood why General Shichio deployed fifty men to dispatch a single teenage boy.

Still his men had not formed ranks. He knew they were well trained, knew it was only the heat of the moment that confounded his mind, but to him his unit seemed to be wading through water. "Pick up your feet, you damned sluggards! Move!"

At last the Bear Cub turned to run. The lieutenant could wait no longer. He led the first platoon himself, commanding the rest to follow as soon as they managed to form up. His archers fell in behind him, dropping their bows in favor of swords.

He was the first to reach the fallen scout, who still attempted to crawl, dragging his legs uselessly behind him. The man seemed so *small.* "Easy," the lieutenant said. "Easy, soldier." He crouched beside the scout and sent the rest of his platoon around the bend in the road. "Report. What are you doing out here alone?"

"Not alone," grunted the scout, his head hanging heavily between his shoulders. He clutched the lieutenant's sword belt as if trying to pull himself upright. "My patrol. All killed. Ran us down outside the Okuma compound. Killed us all."

A prayer for mercy escaped the lieutenant's lips unbidden. He did not want to believe in boys with magic swords and cat's eyes, but what else could explain what he'd seen tonight? There, twenty paces ahead, he spied another corpse along the roadway, lying facedown in the weeds and clad in Toyotomi colors. How many more littered this road? Could the Bear Cub have felled an entire patrol?

"You men, up here!" barked the lieutenant, his voice echoing off the Green Cliff. The remainder of his force came running, save the eight men reassigned to guard the door. "Our quarry is out there in these hills," he said when they reached him. "Watch yourselves; this one is as dangerous as they come. Half of you, over the hill. The rest, take the road."

The limp-legged scout still clung to the lieutenant's belt, trying to pull himself up though he lacked even the strength to raise his own head. He seemed to weigh nothing at all. The lieutenant hadn't even seen the scout's face yet, and he wasn't sure that he wanted to. He felt a pang of guilt for wanting to leave this man to die on his own, a warrior who had served his daimyo well. He felt even worse for not charging out to meet the enemy with the rest of his troops, who vanished over the hillcrest or around the bend in the road even as he watched them. He should have been at their head, facing the same danger, running the same risks as the two who now lay in the road, one dead and the other dying.

"Easy, son," the lieutenant said, not knowing what else to say.

"Much easier than I thought," the scout said, and he thrust a knife into the lieutenant's chin.

Daigoro did not let go of the knife because he wasn't sure the lieutenant was dead.

He'd expected to feel a great swell of shame and self-loathing after such skullduggery, but the sad and simple truth was that Daigoro was exhausted, and stabbing a defenseless man was much easier than facing him sword to sword. Later, he thought, he'd try to convince himself that deceit on the battlefield was no stain on one's honor, and that his ruse with this lieutenant was no different than his father's ruse with the "ghost army" that defeated Shichio and Hideyoshi. For now, it was enough that he was still alive, and that his enemy was either dead or dying, depending on how far the knife had gone up into his brain.

He gave a quick, low whistle. Twenty paces up the road, a dead body in Toyotomi colors got to its feet and picked its way out of the weeds. It was the *shinobi*, who moments before had made this lieutenant believe he was the infamous Bear Cub, then batted a volley of arrows aside, then transformed himself into a Toyotomi corpse, all without effort. He'd even draped his lifeless form over Glorious Victory Unsought, concealing it from all the troops that dashed past him in pursuit of a Bear Cub they would not find.

"I don't know how you managed that trick with the arrows," Daigoro told him, "but that was the most incredible thing I've ever seen."

The *shinobi* ignored the compliment. "Your sword. Too big for you."

Daigoro nodded and shrugged. "That sword is too big for anyone."

"Stronger than you look. Impressive."

For a fleeting moment, Daigoro's fear and fatigue lifted from him. An exchange of mutual respect, between himself and the deadliest man he'd ever encountered. Daigoro had to stop and think for a moment just to be sure it had happened. Then the moment passed, and Daigoro remembered the weight of what he needed to do.

He and the *shinobi* made a show of caring for the lieutenant, for the benefit of the Toyotomis still manning the gate. At this distance they would need eagle's eyes to notice their lieutenant was now the wounded one and their fallen scout had sprung miraculously to life. They would see only three men, one of them hanging between the other two like a field-dressed deer. With that disguise in place, Daigoro made the long walk to the Green Cliff.

At the gate all eyes were on the grisly form of the lieutenant. The cloying stench of his blood tainted the smoke and ash from the cook-fires. Together they stank of hell. Hinges wailed like tortured spirits as the Toyotomis put their shoulders into the gates. Then the lieutenant wailed too, giving Daigoro such a start that he nearly dropped the man. Somehow the lieutenant still clung to life, and also to his duty. He tried in vain to warn his garrison of the ruse, but with the knife pinning his jaws shut, he could only moan loud and long. It sounded like his ghost leaving his body, and between that, the wailing gates, and the smells of blood and fire, to Daigoro's weary mind the gate to House Yasuda had become the gates of hell.

He kept his head low and tried to take an accurate count of the enemy. Crunching on the gravel were eight pairs of booted feet. His own shadow stretched before him, bound to that of the lieutenant and the *shinobi*, as if the whole concatenous mass were the shadow of some hideous six-legged demon. Somehow the vision gave him strength: if this was hell, then at least *he* was the demon.

"Bar the gate," he said. "We can't let that Bear Cub get inside."

He waited until he heard the bar drop before he drew steel. He killed the first of the eight with his *wakizashi*, then drew Glorious Victory from the lieutenant's back. Together, Daigoro and the *shinobi* made short work of the rest.

56

Yasuda Jinbei had never been a large man, and illness had withered him even further. His cheeks were sharper than Daigoro remembered, as if the bones pushed through his skin with a mind of their own. His thin hands lay folded across his blanket, and there too the sallow skin sagged between the hollows of the bones. His white hair splayed limply across his pillow like a fan. The sight of it made Daigoro think of General Mio, and his mind reeled away from the memory of Mio's terrible wounds, fixating instead on the image of the giant man gleaming in his black armor, his hair as white as the snow atop Mount Fuji. By comparison, Lord Yasuda's hair seemed yellow, faded, brittle. His pale eyebrows were in the grips of a permanent, pain-ridden scowl.

"Lord Yasuda," Daigoro said, kneeling gingerly at the edge of the aging daimyo's bed. "Can you hear me?"

Yasuda opened his rheumy eyes. "Hehh," he said, forcing a chuckle that sounded more like a cough. "I must be doing worse than I thought. You look at me as if I'm already a corpse, Okuma-dono."

"It's just Daigoro now."

"So I've heard. A bold thing, that. Unorthodox too. Reminds me of your father."

"You honor me."

"Then it's time *you* honored *him*. He was bold, not reckless. And his every breath was in service to his clan and his code. Is this the best way to serve your family?"

Daigoro felt his face flush and changed the subject. "How are you feeling?"

"Better than I look, if that face you make is any indication. Just wait and see, Okuma-dono. I'll lick this yet."

Daigoro tried to smile. "I don't doubt it, Yasuda-sama."

"Oh yes, you do. And don't you sama me. As far as I'm concerned, you're still Lord Protector of Izu, the same as your father."

"That honor belongs to my son," said Daigoro.

"Assuming you have a son." He laughed and coughed. "Who's to say that lovely wife of yours doesn't bear a daughter? What will you do then, eh? Steal into her bedchamber every nine months? And who's to mind Izu when you're away? Those Soras and Inoues are back to squabbling like old hens. Don't look to me to shut them up. I'm too old for that nonsense, and even if I weren't, their houses outrank mine."

He was right. Worse yet, even on his deathbed he could summon more vigor than Daigoro could manage at the moment. An aging tiger was still a tiger. All Daigoro wanted was to lie down and sleep.

"I saw no other choice," he said at last. "Yasuda-sama, you must understand: if I hadn't relinquished my name, my whole family might already be dead."

"So what is it you prefer? To see your name dishonored? To see your mother saddled with more responsibility than she can bear?"

Daigoro smiled—a sad smile, but it was genuine, the first one in many days. "You never were one for small talk, were you, Yasuda-sama?"

"You stop it with that sama nonsense. She's not well, Okuma-dono. You know that better than anyone."

Daigoro nodded. "In fact, she's the reason I came here to speak with you."

"There's talk of some general from Kyoto wanting to marry her. Is that true?"

"That's what I've come to prevent."

"Then go back to your family. Reclaim your title."

"If I do that, the general doesn't need to marry her; he'll just kill her, and the rest of my house too. You don't know this man, Yasuda-sama. He isn't bound to the code as we are. He's mad."

Yasuda nodded weakly. "Then come at him from a position of strength. Your own position, the position of your birthright. Let a widow mourn the passing of her husband. Let a mother mourn the death of her eldest son. And if death comes, then such is a samurai's lot. Die in your rightful stead, Okuma-dono."

"No. I was no good at governance even while I had name and station. Let the other lords protector manage Izu's affairs while my mother grieves. Surely they owe my family that much."

Yasuda coughed, snorted, and spat a wad of mucus into a red-lacquered bowl held by a serving girl. "What they owe is one thing," he said. "How little they can get away with repaying is something else again. Someone has got to mind the difference between the two, and doing that will demand more vigilance than your mother can spare."

"Yes. I was rather hoping I might ask a Yasuda to hold things to-gether."

Lord Yasuda had another coughing fit. His face flushed, and the little veins visibly bulged in his temples. Whether it was from the coughing or emotional agitation, Daigoro couldn't say.

"I told you already," Yasuda said, "it's beyond my reach. Too old. Too many other things to worry about. This devil besetting my lungs isn't the least of my problems, but it isn't the greatest either."

"I did not presume to saddle *you* with this burden, Yasuda-sama. I had your youngest son in mind."

"Kenbei? He's responsible enough, I'll grant you, but none of the other lords will listen to him. Izu looks to House Yasuda for strength and defense, not for fair minds and level heads. And we don't look to the Inoues or Soras either, that's for damned certain. We look to House Okuma."

The devil, as Yasuda called it, possessed his lungs again, and he had to spit five times into the serving girl's bowl before he could rest his heavy head back on his pillow.

"Izu looks to House Okuma," Daigoro said, "and now House Okuma looks to the house of Yasuda Kenbei. I have surrendered my title as lord protector; I can only ask you as a friend. Will you help me? Will you speak to your son for me?"

"Nothing would please me more. If my Kenbei were to marry your mother, your enemy would have no recourse but to accept it. But Kenbei is already married, and his wife is at least as dangerous as this madman in Kyoto. They called your father the Red Bear of Izu, but let me tell you, they should have given that nickname to her instead. That woman is a bear if ever there was one."

Daigoro grinned. "Direct as ever, Yasuda-sama."

"Wait until you're my age and then see how much time you have for dithering." Lord Yasuda hacked and spat. "You're a clever boy, Okuma-dono. And this fever addles an old man's brain. You did not have Kenbei in mind, *neh*? You spoke of his house, not Kenbei himself."

"Yes, sir. Perhaps someone younger—and someone not married to a bear."

"Inventive thinking. Just like your father."

Daigoro felt his face flush. On any other day he would have enjoyed the compliment to his father. On any other day being likened to his father would have filled him with the warm glow of pride. On this night he could enjoy neither. He could only wonder if his father would have condoned his wife's marriage to another house, or whether he would approve of his son pawning her off as a political ploy.

Daigoro had neither the time nor the inclination to seriously pursue such questions. Shichio's soldiers were bound to return, and Daigoro had already tarried too long. "I don't wish to press you," he said, "but I'm afraid time is of the essence, Lord Yasuda."

"Then my answer to your request must be no," said Yasuda. "I would not see your mother wedded to any one of Kenbei's sons. The eldest got himself killed in a drunken brawl, and the younger ones are bound on the same path. Mountain monkeys, all of them. Would you set them loose in your mother's bedchamber?"

Daigoro tried to speak, but a spate of coughs and wheezes interrupted him, making him bide his tongue. This time the fit left Lord Yasuda struggling for breath, so his voice came out hoarse and ghostly, like wind rattling through a long, thin slit in a rice-paper window. "I am sorry, Okuma-dono, but House Yasuda has no men of marriageable age to offer you. Kenbei is too old for your mother, even if that she-bear of his were to keel over dead. I have groomed him to take my seat when I die—which will not be tonight, so you can remove that pitying look from your face."

Daigoro blushed, bowed, and regained his composure. "My apologies, Yasuda-sama."

Lord Yasuda ignored him. "And Kenbei's brothers are older still. They are not tigers anymore; they are trees, and their roots have burrowed deep. Their homes are far from here—and well they should be. 'The sword arm's strength comes from a strong stance.' Isn't that what your father taught you? My house defends Izu from a broad, strong stance, but that means we cannot bend even when we want to—not even to serve our most trusted friends."

He could not keep the shame from his face. It was enough to make Daigoro want to weep, seeing his family's strongest ally so vulnerable. Taking Yasuda's frail, cold hand in his own, he said, "I had not looked to your elder sons. They serve Izu best where they are. Please, indulge me in a flight of fancy, my lord. If your son Kenbei spoke with House Okuma's voice—*if*—then he could bring stability to the region, *neh*?"

The old man conceded the point with a nod. "Do you suggest he take on a concubine? He cannot—not a woman of your mother's stature."

"No."

"Then I've told you already: I would not have those wild stallions I call my grandsons see the Lady Okuma as a broodmare."

"No, Yasuda-sama, but suppose we take a longer view—"

A shout from outside made Daigoro break off in midthought. Daigoro turned to see one of Yasuda's sentries hit the floor on his back, his armor clacking like a metal hailstorm. Another samurai fell beside the first, struck by something invisible outside the doorway. Daigoro's first thoughts ran to musket fire, but there was no report. Next he thought of Toyotomi arrows, but neither of the fallen men was pierced. Daigoro had no opportunity to look out into the courtyard to see the attacker, for Yasuda spearmen instantly blockaded the doorway, their myriad spears stabbing out into the darkness.

"Daigoro-sama!" a lupine voice shouted outside. "Come out!"

Daigoro hurried through the door, pushing Yasuda spearmen aside with an armored forearm. The courtyard sprawled before him, its white gravel glowing as if the moon itself had rained down in a million tiny pieces. The *shinobi* crouched at the base of the stairs leading down from the veranda, his gaze flicking between the main gate and the green-clad samurai jabbing spears at him from the doorway to Lord Yasuda's chamber.

Daigoro glanced over his shoulder at the two men lying on their backs—door guards, no doubt. His *shinobi* must have kicked them, punched them, thrown them somehow, and that meant he'd only acted in self-defense. If he'd had a mind to kill them, Daigoro had no doubt both men would be dead.

And if he'd acted in self-defense, then they must have reacted poorly when the *shinobi* had tried to enter. That meant the *shinobi* must have come up too quickly for their liking, and Daigoro could think of only one thing that could make him hurry. The Toyotomis were coming back.

"How many?" Daigoro asked, drawing Glorious Victory Unsought.

"Twenty," said the *shinobi*. "More on the way."

Daigoro didn't know whether to be disappointed with Lord Yasuda's bodyguard or to be awed by how easily his *shinobi* companion had felled two of them despite being unarmed and unarmored. In any case, the lord of their house was in no condition to be giving orders. "You there," Daigoro shouted at one of the spearmen, "rouse every man House Yasuda can put in the Green Cliff's defense. The rest of you, hold this doorway. No one gets through. And put a line of armored bodies surrounding Lord Yasuda. There will be archers."

Armor clattered behind him; feet rustled against tatami mats; battle formations took shape. "And now," Daigoro muttered under his breath, "what in hell do *we* do?"

57

On the opposite side of the courtyard, the gate thundered like a *taiko* drum. It seemed the Toyotomis had found a battering ram.

"Lord Yasuda!" a voice bellowed from beyond the wall. "Send out the fugitive! Do not force us to put your house to the torch."

An empty threat, Daigoro thought. He'd seen no sign that the garrison was equipped with fire arrows, and there wasn't enough wood on the entire island to burn down the Green Cliff's outer wall. Nevertheless, Daigoro could not allow the ultimatum to go unanswered. The Yasudas were among his family's oldest allies. He would not risk turning the might of Hideyoshi against them. The Toyotomi captain had no need to level the Green Cliff *tonight*. He had only to dictate a letter declaring the Yasudas an enemy of the throne. Then he would have as many reinforcements and as much time as he liked to raze House Yasuda to the ground.

Again the gate strained against its hinges, struck by some heavy thing wielded by many men. Daigoro couldn't recall seeing an iron-shod battering ram among the garrison's equipment; then again, he'd had other things on his mind during his hasty pass through their encampment. In any case, straight, stalwart ironwoods stood in rank and file in the forest outside the Yasuda compound. A makeshift ram was easy to come by.

"Do you hear that?" shouted the Toyotomi captain. "Sooner or later, your gates will yield. If it is later, it will not go well for you. Deliver the traitor and we will leave you in peace."

The gate was huge—or so Daigoro had thought before his ride to Kyoto. Each of its two doors was broader than a wagon, all stout timbers and iron bands. Centipede motifs had been beaten into the metal, with a heavy ring dangling from the center of each door in the shape of a centipede devouring its own tail. The gate to the Okuma compound was a barn door by comparison.

But Kyoto had temples with doors this big. Daigoro's long journey had taught him what real fortifications looked like. The great gate at Hideyoshi's Jurakudai dwarfed that of the Green Cliff: twice as high, four times as broad, and so heavy that only a team of horses could draw it open. The battering ram that rattled the rings on House Yasuda's doors would not be enough to wake a sleeping guard at the Jurakudai.

Even so, the Toyotomi captain had spoken the truth: whether it took an hour or a month, there wasn't a gate in the world that would not yield. The soldiers outside had neither siege engines nor the training to use them, but they had manpower and time, and those were more than enough.

The gate boomed. Yasuda samurai shifted nervously; Daigoro could hear their gauntlets click against their spears. A warm and sluggish breeze carried the scent of horse feed. The moment he smelled it, Daigoro had an idea.

"I'm approaching the gate," he yelled, slowly descending the steps to the courtyard. In a low voice he explained his plan to the *shinobi*, who nodded once and loped off silently toward the stables. "Do you know who I am?"

"If you are anyone other than Daigoro the traitor, the Bear Cub of Izu, then I do not care who you are," the captain shouted. Again the ram thundered against steel and wood.

"I am the Bear Cub. Now stop that damned hammering. I told you already, I'm coming."

"Lord Okuma, no," said a voice behind him. He turned to see the captain of the Yasuda spearmen stepping forward from the formation. "You are an ally to this house. Please, stay here with us."

"I cannot."

"Then at least let us go out to fight at your side."

"I thank you, but no. I will not have Toyotomi blood on your blades. I've brought trouble enough to my own family; I won't bring it here too."

Daigoro took his time crossing the courtyard, certain that his crunching footfalls could be heard on the other side of the wall. Clicks and clacks came from the other side, hundreds of pieces of armor rubbing against each other like chattering bugs at dusk. Daigoro imagined men readying swords and spears. At least they'd set down the ram, but Daigoro wondered how many had picked up bows instead. A lone swordsman stood little chance against archers.

"I have no interest in fighting you," he shouted. "How am I to know you won't cut me down as soon as I open this gate?"

"You don't." There was a decidedly defiant edge to the captain's voice. "We will kill you if General Shichio wishes it. It is not for you to question his orders."

"And how can I know you won't assault the Yasudas once I give myself over? They have no part in this."

"You have my word as a samurai. Lord Yasuda and his kin will not come to harm. Give yourself over and they may go back to sleep."

Slow hoofbeats behind him told Daigoro that the *shinobi* had finished harnessing the horses. As soon as he saw the animals, Daigoro recalled his wedding present. These two could have been sisters to the horses he and Akiko had received along with Lord Yasuda's blessing. They were majestic animals. They didn't deserve to be harnessed so sloppily, but Daigoro was short on time.

He took the lines from one of the mares and tied her to the left-hand gate, hitching her to the big iron ring as if to a wagon. She was not stupid; she could sense the tension in the air and it had her spooked. Only the *shinobi*'s grip on her bridle kept her from bolting.

"I hear horses," the captain bellowed. "Do not attempt to mount a charge against us. You will only doom innocent animals along with yourself."

"How very noble of you," Daigoro said. He hitched the second mare to the right-hand gate while the *shinobi* held both animals steady. Then, slowly, silently, Daigoro put his shoulder to the heavy wooden beam that barred the gates.

"My patience wanes. Come out now and no Yasuda will be harmed."

"You gave me your word as a samurai," Daigoro shouted, setting his feet to take the weight of the bar. "How can I be certain that you are samurai at all, and not some shit-stained farmer's son like your master?"

"Enough! Break it down!"

Someone outside put a boot to the door, but it did not budge. Daigoro heard stones shifting underfoot, swords returning to their sheaths, men cursing and shuffling and taking up new positions.

Daigoro hefted the bar onto one shoulder. Its weight pressed back painfully against his hands. He retreated from the gates, and not a moment too soon. Outside, he heard big men grunting as they picked up their battering ram.

An instant before the ram's next strike, Daigoro loosed a deafening *kiai*, startling the mares that were already scared out of their wits. The *shinobi* released the lines. The horses bolted. Hideyoshi's gates might have required a team of horses to move them, but the Yasudas' were lighter; they all but burst from their hinges. Both gates flew open, leaving Daigoro in the middle of the gateway with a massive wooden beam in his arms.

He was not alone for long.

Six soldiers lunged for him with the ironwood trunk they'd been using as a makeshift ram. But their target was the gate, not him, and without the gate's mass to meet their charge, the weight of the ram pitched them forward. They collapsed in front of him in a tangle. They dropped the heavy ram, some tripping over it, others falling beneath. Daigoro heard leg bones breaking.

With almost ceremonious flair, Daigoro tossed the wooden bar onto the heap of men. It broke bones too. Then Glorious Victory was in his hands, and he rushed the first rank of Toyotomi invaders.

None of them were prepared for his onslaught. Many had returned to their tents, knowing hundreds of strokes would fall before the gate yielded to the ram. Glorious Victory claimed three lives with the first stroke.

For the first few seconds, Daigoro thought the battle was going well. He hacked off hands even as they were drawing swords. He let a mighty chop spin him all the way around, just in time to cut the knees out from under a samurai who had him outflanked.

Then the Toyotomis found their footing. In his opening gambit Daigoro had felled ten men, but thirty more now formed a wary circle around him. Most had swords drawn. Here and there an archer took aim.

Unwilling to be shot down where he stood, Daigoro rushed in like a madman. One, misjudging Daigoro's reach, lost an arm. Two arrows went wide, both hitting kinsmen. A third archer drew a bead on Daigoro's jugular. Then his bowstring snapped, cut from below by a *shinobi* who appeared out of nowhere. The whip-snapping string lacerated the archer's eyeball. Then the *shinobi* was gone.

Daigoro had no more luck tracking him than did the Toyotomis. He knew the *shinobi* was there only because now and then a man would have him dead to rights, and in the next instant that man would fall. Then the *shinobi* vanished again into the swirling melee.

Once, twice, a dozen times Daigoro tried to cut himself a channel to open ground. Each time the enemy denied him, closing back around him as inexorably as the sea.

Once, twice, a dozen times the Sora breastplate saved his life. Here it turned aside a *katana*. There it sparked as an arrowhead struck home. One of the Toyotomi commanders managed a clear shot with his matchlock. The ball knocked Daigoro two steps back but could not penetrate the Sora *yoroi*.

At last Toyotomi steel found flesh. Daigoro's right leg collapsed beneath him, blood spurting from his wasted thigh. Glorious Victory fell in a deadly arc, killing the one who'd struck him and two more as well. Daigoro fought from one knee, desperately parrying the attacks of six, seven, eight men at once.

Someone behind him let out an almighty scream. It was no shriek of pain; this was a war whoop. The ground shook. Either a horse was charging him or else a score of men. Daigoro slashed forward, driving a few assailants back, then turned to meet the new threat.

Katsushima rode through the heart of the Toyotomis, bellowing with a typhoon's fury. His sword flashed red and silver, claiming limbs every time it fell. His charging bay shattered swordsmen as easily as clay pots. When Katsushima saw Daigoro, he kicked his heels savagely and Daigoro had to throw himself flat or else be decapitated by a hoof.

The Toyotomis scattered in the wake of the leaping horse. Suddenly the field was clear enough that Daigoro could struggle back to his feet.

Katsushima killed two more before wheeling his mount around. "Come on!" he shouted. "This is no time for patience!"

Already the Toyotomis were regrouping—what few remained. Most were dead, dying, or crippled. Daigoro hobbled over a pair of broken men, settled his left foot in Katsushima's right stirrup, and stepped up to grab the saddlehorn with his left hand. "Good to see you again," Daigoro said.

"I'm glad to see there's something left of you to see," said Katsushima. "But talk later. We've work to do yet."

He nodded toward the gate, where the surviving Toyotomi swordsmen had formed a line to deny access to the keep. Heedless of the dead, deaf to the moans and cries of the wounded, they stared Daigoro down with grim determination.

Determined or not, footmen were no match for Glorious Victory Unsought. She was a cavalry sword, at her deadliest when she struck with the weight of a warhorse behind her. Katsushima charged the line. Daigoro, effectively a human outrigger, stretched Glorious Victory out long. Inazuma steel mowed down the right flank. Katsushima claimed one on the left. Their horse crushed two in the center.

Then the blood work was done. Daigoro would not honor the wounded with a clean death. Any man who bowed to a lickspittle like Shichio wasn't worthy of such a gift. Moreover, Daigoro didn't want killing them to burden his conscience. He hadn't asked for this fight. Had their positions been reversed, Daigoro would never have resorted to using Shichio's family allies as playing pieces in their private war. He chose to let his defeated foes explain why they still lived, and let Shichio bear the burden of sending them on to join their ancestors.

Daigoro limped across the courtyard, leaving a bloody footprint wherever his right foot touched the gravel. The Yasuda soldiers watched him in wonderment. Their spears still jutted out like quills from the doorway to their master's bedchamber, as if they hadn't yet realized the fighting was over. Daigoro looked down at his blood-spattered *hakama* and *haori*, then at their spotless moss green garb. He felt absurd: these ranks of older, wiser men gaped at him like he was a battle-hardened veteran—a veteran still months away from his seventeenth birthday.

He'd forgotten he was still wearing Toyotomi colors—what was left of them, anyway. He'd also forgotten that he was armored; only the sight of an arrow recalled it to mind. The arrow looked like it was sticking out of his gut, but in truth it had only caught in his *haori* after shattering against his Sora breastplate. He remembered first donning the armor on the banks of the Kamo not so long ago, remembered how heavy it had felt then, how awkward, how alien. Now he wore it like his own skin.

By the time he reached the stable to fetch tack and harness, the *shinobi* had reappeared beside him, noiselessly as always. Swords had sliced his clothing in a hundred places. He bled from his face, his forearms, his shoulders, his shins, but most of the blood on his tattered clothes was not his own. He gave Daigoro a silent, approving nod.

Halfway back to the horses still tied to the gates, Daigoro's throbbing hands prompted him to wonder why he hadn't walked the horse to the saddle instead of lugging the saddle to the horse. His mind was as exhausted as his body; his thoughts plodded along as if wading against an undertow.

"Who's your friend?" Katsushima asked when Daigoro reached his mare.

"He is of the Wind," Daigoro said, laughing weakly. "The Wind is without name."

Katsushima's eyes narrowed, and the smile of a proud father played at the corners of his mouth. "You found them."

"I did."

Katsushima looked at the *shinobi* with new eyes. "Whatever your name is, Wind-sama, I thank you for saving my good friend's life."

The ninja's only response was to grunt as he heaved his saddle up over his saddle blanket. If Daigoro hadn't known better, he'd have sworn his *shinobi* was actually fatigued.

"How did you find me?" Daigoro asked.

"I was on my way to your family's place when I heard the commotion," Katsushima said. I never expected to find *you* here. I thought I had a few days' lead on you on the Tokaidō."

"We came by ship."

"Did you?" Katsushima whistled. "You weathered an unholy bitch of a storm."

"A Toyotomi blockade too. Shichio's men are watching every last pebble of coastline."

"Then we're apt to find many more of them when we reach your mother's house."

Daigoro gave him a long, studious look. His friend looked back down at him, red spatter dotting his woolly sideburns. An hour's conversation passed between them in that single glance. Then Daigoro made a final adjustment to the girth, and with energy reserves he didn't even know he had, he stepped up into the saddle.

Katsushima had to dismount to lash Daigoro's right leg in place, and even then Daigoro felt on the verge of sliding off his horse. His own saddle, the precious one Old Yagyū had fashioned for him, was many *ri* behind him. Sitting in an ordinary saddle, the weight of Daigoro's left leg threatened to drag him down and his right leg wasn't strong enough to counteract it. He could only stay ahorse by balancing there, the muscles of his belly, chest, and back shifting constantly, as if he were an acrobat on the tip of a pole. It was exhausting even when his horse was standing still, and impossible at a full gallop.

It was necessary, then, that Katsushima lash down his right leg. Nevertheless, Daigoro could not help thinking that usually it was the injured and dying who were tied into the saddle. When at last they set out on the road, his coal black mare shied from the twitching of pained, bloodied men, nearly throwing him. Only by gripping the saddlehorn with both hands did he manage to stay mounted.

But soon the miasma of battle was behind them and Daigoro could settle into a rhythm. "If I didn't know better," Katsushima told him, "I'd swear you just stole a horse."

"Lord Yasuda knows I'm good for it," Daigoro said defensively, realizing only too late that his friend was kidding him. "I apologize, Goemon. I'm too tired to think. Why did you ever come back? Why do you want to have anything to do with me?"

"Don't you know?"

"I can't even imagine."

Katsushima's wry smirk faded away. "How did we meet?"

"You dueled my brother."

"And then?"

"You dueled me."

"Almost," said Katsushima. "We had tea first. Then dinner. Then we talked all night, at your insistence. 'I want to discuss swordsmanship with you, and *bushidō* as well.' That's what you said."

Daigoro nodded. Even through the haze of fatigue, he could recall Katsushima's response: *I expect we have much to learn from each other.*

"So let's discuss," Katsushima said. "*Bushidō* demands that you fight even against impossible odds, *neh*?"

Daigoro nodded.

"To describe your odds of besting Shichio as 'impossible' seems blithely optimistic to me. Would you agree?"

Daigoro nodded. It was easier than talking; the jostling of his saddle did most of the work.

"So why not give up *bushidō*? Following it is certain to kill you. You gave up your name. It only makes sense to free yourself of the rest."

Daigoro nodded again—due more to the rocking motion of his horse than to his own agreement. But Katsushima wasn't wrong either. Not entirely.

"A *rōnin* keeps his swords and throws the rest aside," Katsushima said. "Duty, family, lord, name, honor; they're shackles. All you have to do is give up the shackles and you'll be free."

"I can't."

"Why not? You've already given up the ones you value most."

"Yes," Daigoro said. "I've surrendered my family and with them my name. I have no other lord—save Izu herself, perhaps, but without my title I've abandoned her too. With every sacrifice I feel I've done what honor demands, but my only reward is to be hunted like a traitor and a criminal. There's no honor in that. I have no honor left."

"Then what else remains?"

"Duty."

"To whom?"

"To my father's memory. To what little sense of family I still have left. To *bushidō* itself."

"Your father's gone, Daigoro. When you gave up your name you gave up your family too. Why not shed the last of your shackles?"

It sounded so inviting. Done properly, it might even end the feud with Shichio. He could give up being samurai. Put down the burden of his father's sword. Make an obsequious and public apology. Cut off his topknot and go home unmolested. Comfort his mother. Share Akiko's bed. Be there for the birth of his child.

He could have had everything he wanted, and all he had to do was betray his code. "I can't," he said, near to tears. "I can't give up duty. I don't know how."

"That is why I follow you."

58

There was no shore party to greet him when Shichio made his landing at the Okuma jetty. In any other circumstances, failure to send an honor guard for the great Toyotomi no Hideyoshi might have got a daimyo and his family crucified. (Though not a convert to the southern barbarians' religion, Hashiba found their religion's obsession with crucifixion quite exotic. It had become his favorite method of execution.) But today the Okuma clan would receive a pardon, not because their honored guests had come unannounced—they should have seen Hashiba's flagship from ten *ri* away—but because it was Shichio's wedding day, and that had the regent feeling jovial.

The bile rose in Shichio's throat when he remembered his last visit to this wretched place. He'd left the Okuma compound in disgrace, no thanks to that giant pig Mio. Shichio would have thought the fat man's precious *bushidō* code would have forbidden throwing a fight to a cripple.

Shichio supposed he owed the fat man a debt of gratitude. If it weren't for his superhuman endurance—if he hadn't survived long enough to reveal Shichio's designs for marriage—the Bear Cub might never have approached the Wind, and then Shichio's informant could never have betrayed the boy. He knew now that his assassin had failed; the absence of a second communiqué proved the first message was false. But it was enough just to learn that the boy had made contact with the Wind. Shichio had stepped up his wedding plans, while the Bear Cub must surely have gone to ground. That typhoon had forced even Hashiba's flagship into port. No cripple could withstand it.

Shichio touched his hair, which was behaving peevishly in this all-pervading heat. He stepped out of the launch to walk side by side with Hashiba down the jetty toward the palanquin. Once inside, he carefully brushed all the sand from his fine silk stockings and smooth wooden sandals. There was little sand on the jetty to begin with, but Shichio would abide no imperfections on this perfect day.

As his palanquin rocked side to side with the footsteps of the bearers, Shichio looked out at the emerald tangle of kudzu strangling the black rocks. He wondered how long it would take him after the wedding to sell his new holdings and buy an estate in the Kansai. Only barbarians could make a permanent home in Izu. The humidity alone was reason enough to leave and never come back.

"What have you got in that scarf of yours?" Hashiba said, nodding at the little parcel Shichio unconsciously worked in his hands. It was wrapped in the finest Chinese silk, which did little to soften its horns, its teeth, its furrowed brow. Hashiba squinted at it, then laughed. "Well, I'm damned if I know what to get you for a wedding present. You name a gift that tops that mask and I'll buy it."

Shichio felt himself wince and quickly converted it into a coy smile. He couldn't let Hashiba see how he'd come to fear the mask, and yet he hadn't been able to leave the mask in their cabin, either. He wished he had. So long as they were behind closed doors, it was enough to let Hashiba ravage him. It wasn't hard to tempt him into being a little rough. The mask would not be sated, but it could be distracted.

Shichio had wrapped it up in the hope that he could satisfy his unconscious need to hold it while avoiding the touch of its iron skin. He envied the mask; even in this heat, it would never sweat. He wanted nothing more than to disrobe it, to press its cool cheek against his own, but that was out of the question. This was no time to compromise self-control. He had a madwoman to bring to heel.

Seeing Hashiba's expectant look, he said, "Gifts be damned. And let the wedding and the wife be damned too. Once I have her name, my mask and I come back home to serve their rightful lord."

"Already thinking like a trueborn samurai," Hashiba said with a wink. He smiled his impish, simian smile.

The palanquin's woven bamboo window screens were no proof against the sweat-stink of the bearers, who grunted in time with each other as they plodded up the cliffside trail. "These commoners smell like animals," Shichio said, grimacing. A tiny part of his mind insisted that the bearers' parents probably worked a farm no different from the one Shichio had grown up on, but he would not dwell on that. Soon enough he would have rank, name, station, and esteem. He would be above the commoners for ever after.

At last the countless switchbacks took him to the top of the cliff trail, and through the window screen he could see the high white wall of the Okuma compound on his right. Soon to be *my* compound, he thought—very soon, in fact. That fact hung over him like the rain clouds he'd endured the day before, and so it was especially irksome to hear a runner coming from somewhere ahead. The man stopped to kneel beside the palanquin, panting like a horse. Delay after delay; it was the only way the lower classes could exert power over their betters.

Shichio slammed the sliding door aside and looked down upon the messenger kneeling in the weeds. "What do you think you're doing, stopping your lord on the way to his wedding?"

The man bowed deeper. "General, your orders were to deliver any news of the Bear Cub, day or night."

The Bear Cub? How could any word of him have reached Izu already? Shichio's fleet had been the first to set sail after that storm, and it should have swept up all other ships in its net. No horseman could have outrun them.

He looked down at the mute messenger. "Well? Spit it out, boy."

"My lord, the Bear Cub stormed the Yasuda compound last night. We lost fifty men."

"*Fifty?*"

"He was said to have a rider with him. A *rōnin* of some years."

"No," said Shichio. His spies on the Tokaidō had reported that Daigoro and his haggard bodyguard had split ways at least a week past. His agent within the Wind said the boy had been alone when he hired his retinue to spirit him to Izu.

But this was not the first fantastic tale to have reached Shichio's ears. Just this very morning a skiff had come alongside Hashiba's flagship, delivering word that the Bear Cub had stolen a frigate after slaughtering the entire crew. It was preposterous, of course. Yes, the Okumas were a coastal power, but the boy was a cripple, not a seaman, and each of Shichio's vessels was teeming with armed men. The whelp would need an army of pirates at his command. The tale was so ludicrous that Shichio had ordered a broadside into the skiff that delivered the message. He would have sunk the bastards for their cheek had Hashiba not heard the sudden cannonade and ordered a cease-fire.

Out of sheer magnanimity Shichio chose not to kill this messenger either. "The Yasuda garrison is playing tricks on you," he told the kneeling man. "They take advantage of your gullibility."

"My lord, they were most explicit: a young boy with an *ōdachi* and a lame leg—"

"Quit while you still have a tongue in your mouth." Shichio had a sudden vision of blood oozing from the messenger's mouth, and he realized his fingers had worked their way under the folds of Chinese silk. He was touching the mask.

He withdrew his hand as if the mask had bitten it. Hashiba frowned at him but said nothing. Shichio banged on the roof and the stinking, sweating bearers resumed their march.

When he reached the gate, Shichio was pleased by what he saw. House Okuma commanded a grand vista. Kattō-ji, home to the abbot he was soon to kill, peered out from the pines on the next summit to the north. Below, on the saddle between the peaks, a double garrison was camped along the road flying Toyotomi colors. That road and the jetty were the only ways to reach the Okuma compound. Rumors be damned, Shichio thought. He would believe his eyes before he believed tales of captured frigates and samurai heroics, and his eyes saw no corpses lining the road, nor any pirate vessels anchored in the bay.

Just inside the gates, Okuma warriors formed columns of red and brown, their bear paw crests fluttering overhead on their banners. Opposite them stood a wall of soldiers in mossy green, with a fat white centipede winding its way up the length of each green banner. He remembered that crest from his intelligence reports: House Yasuda. He wondered how low a clan had to sink before it took a wriggling insect as its sigil.

In the center stood his bride, the Lady Yumiko, cradling an infant. Shichio remembered hearing the Bear Cub's wife was with child. That wedding must have been rushed along by spearheads if the cub's child was already born. Again exercising his generosity, Shichio decided he would let his new bride coddle her grandson for a few minutes before ordering the wedding to commence. He was happy to see the woman sober enough to stand. If even half of the rumors that reached him were true, she spent her days either sedated by poppy's tears or wailing and running about like a hungry ghost.

The primary reason Shichio had cajoled Hashiba into coming with him was not to have his friend, lord, and lover by his side on his wedding day, but to guarantee that the wedding would take place. The matron of House Okuma had yet to respond to a single one of Shichio's marriage proposals, and he needed a contingency plan if she chose to remain mute when her would-be husband arrived. That was where Hashiba came in: he could simply order her to marry Shichio. But seeing Lady Yumiko in her bridal dress, with her attendants and even the attendants of neighboring houses arrayed to honor the occasion, Shichio could see her will had finally caved.

"My lord regent," he heard a familiar voice say, "and General Shichio too, what a pleasant surprise! You honor House Okuma with your attendance."

Shichio stepped out of the palanquin and looked over the top of it. There stood the Bear Cub's tall, lean bodyguard, the one with the bushy sideburns and tousled paintbrush of a topknot—Katsuhara,

Shichio thought his name was, or Katsushira, something like that. He stood just inside the Okuma gate, looking tired and gray and not at all like a proper attendee at a wedding. Shichio expected no more of the man; he'd always struck Shichio as common.

"Why, we're just as surprised to see you, aren't we?" Shichio said. He set the mask in the palanquin; shabby though he was, the *rōnin* was dangerous, and Shichio needed to keep his wits. "Word reached me that you abandoned your little cub in his hour of need—and now here you are at his homestead. Fickle, aren't you? One who lacked manners might ask whether you had impure designs on the boy's mother."

"His designs on my mother are pure enough," said the voice Shichio hated most in the world.

The Bear Cub stepped out from the midst of the Okuma column, pallid as a corpse but somehow still standing. It was impossible. Every path to the compound was under watch. But there he was, with that long and lovely sword slung across his back. Its *tsuba* and pommel glittered in the morning sun.

The boy bowed deeply, and Shichio responded with the slightest dip of his chin. "I bow to your superior," the Bear Cub said, and Shichio turned back around to see Hashiba had hopped out of the palanquin.

"Ah!" said Hashiba, marching around so that he could see the gathering; he was too short to see over the palanquin. "An honor guard after all! I was beginning to think you'd lost your manners, Daigoro-san."

"The honor guard is my mother's," said that odious voice, "and she and I beg your pardon alike. We did not know you were coming, my lord regent."

"Forget it," Hashiba said, waving his hand as if shooing off a butterfly. He inhaled deeply, flaring the nostrils in his too-flat nose, and clapped his hands against his breastplate with a grandiose and flippant air. "Smell that breeze from the sea! So different from Kyoto."

Daigoro stepped forward to usher Hashiba inside the compound. Shichio noticed the boy's limp was much more pronounced than he'd seen before. "Why, young Daigoro," he said. "You seem to be limping more than usual, my lad. Is your infirmity growing worse?"

"I took a wound to the leg last night."

"Ah, yes. Getting out of bed, was it? What a trial it must be, being unable to do all the things the rest of us take for granted."

"It was a sword wound," said the whelp, grinding his teeth.

"Was it indeed? Can the rumors of your assault on the Yasuda compound be true? Do tell me who cut you; I shall have to decide whether to promote him or to chastise him for not cutting deeper."

"You needn't burden yourself with such difficult decisions. He's dead now."

"Is he?" Shichio found himself unable to keep the glee from his voice. It caused the boy such obvious pain simply to be standing on his own two feet. He so plainly wanted to rest that Shichio resolved to keep him standing and talking for as long as possible. Taunting him was just a garnish on a plate that was already beautifully overfull. "I shall add his murder to the list of charges against you."

"Why stop with one murder?" said the whelp. "Make it fifty."

"Fifty? That's the second time I've heard that number, *neh*? Yes, it is. You've become quite the little brigand, haven't you? Perhaps the lord regent and I should have you crucified now, and get to the wedding later."

Shichio saw Hashiba's eyes light up at the mention of crucifixion, but on the face of that despicable boy he saw an insufferable little smile—a tiny thing, so small it was barely there, yet it seemed to hold back a torrent of derisive laughter. Shichio had seen that smile many times as a child, stabbing at him like a dagger from the faces of countless village boys, and in fact he'd made a point of riding in the vanguard when, during the bitterest of the war years, he and Hashiba demolished the tiny hamlet where Shichio had grown up. Seeing that wicked, happy smile on the face of the Bear Cub was more than he could stomach.

"That's quite enough," he said, striding angrily across the road until he stood chest to chest with the boy. Daigoro stood just inside the threshold of the Okuma compound, Shichio just outside of it, each one matching the other's stare. "I'll string you up on the gates of your own house," he said, his voice so low that only the Bear Cub could hear him. "Your wife, your child, your servants, they'll walk past you for *days*. I'll nail your bones to the wood. I'll have you fed and watered, keep you alive for as long as I can. And then, right before you die, I'll kill your mother—my *wife*—right in front of you. I'll flay her with your own sword. Your wife too, and then your little boy. And then I'll drive that big sword of yours right through your—"

"My little boy?"

Shichio's heart pounded in his ears. A sweat broke out on his upper lip. "Yes, your boy, you little runt, that newborn son of yours. He's going to—"

"That's not my son."

"What?"

There was that smile again, that smallest, sharpest, wickedest of grins.

"That's not my son," Daigoro said again, desperately restraining a triumphant laugh. He'd never seen anyone look so baffled while trying to look malicious before. He wished he had a mirror, so Shichio could see what it looked like.

"My lords," he said, taking a step back into his family's courtyard—a step away from Shichio and toward Hideyoshi. "Your presence on this wedding day honors us all. Please accept my heartfelt thanks, and allow me to thank you on behalf of House Okuma as well."

"Thanks? Honor?" Shichio spat the words. "Of course I'm here. It's *my* wedding. You're the one who shouldn't be here."

"Oh, because of your garrison? You may want to have words with them. It seems they don't know about all the little lanes we've got crisscrossing the estate."

"What?"

"Of course," Daigoro said, enjoying himself every bit as much as

Shichio had been a few moments before. "Connecting the orchard, the bathhouse, that sort of thing. You'll understand when you have property of your own."

"This *is* my property—or it will be, as soon as you step aside and let me get on with my wedding."

"I'm afraid there's been some misunderstanding. Unless . . . did you bring a bride of your own? I'm afraid all the ladies present are already married."

"I'm here to marry your mother, you impudent little cur, and you know that damn well."

"But my mother's already got a husband," Daigoro said. "Allow me to present to you the newly married Lord and Lady Yasuda."

He stretched out his arm as grandly as Hideyoshi might have done it, and from the heart of the assembly his mother walked forward, positively glowing. Her steps were tiny—a bridal kimono did not allow the legs much movement—and so it took a delightfully long time for her to approach. Shichio fumed all the while. "This," Daigoro said, touching his mother's silken shoulder, "is Lady Yasuda Yumiko, and this"—he gingerly took the baby in his green swaddling clothes from his mother's arms—"is Lord Yasuda Gorobei, her new husband."

Shichio opened his mouth to speak; only a strangulated gurgle came out. Daigoro's mother blushed and looked with adoration and pride at her son, then at her rosy-cheeked husband in the crook of Daigoro's arm. Hideyoshi let out a howl, laughing so hard he had to cling to a bodyguard's shoulder to stay standing.

"We have *got* to come here more often," Hideyoshi said. "You bastards are a riot."

The little Lord Yasuda replied with a yawn, scrunched his eyes tight against the morning sun, and nestled himself deeper into Daigoro's kimono. He had no more hair than his great-grandfather, Yasuda Jinbei, whose compound Daigoro had just departed some scant hours before. Whatever Hideyoshi had to say next was choked off by another fit of cackling, which he tried to restrain out of respect for the baby's sleep. Shichio nearly choked too; apoplexy still had the better of him.

Daigoro decided to make the most of the opportunity. "Mother," he said softly, "how are you feeling?"

"Better, now that we have you home." She smiled at him, though he winced at the word *home*. Her face glowed with a radiance he hadn't seen in her in more than a year. She stroked baby Gorobei's fat cheek with the back of a finger. "What a beautiful little husband you found for me."

"I had hoped to speak of it with you first," Daigoro said. "It was not my intent to marry you off without your consent. This was the only way I could think of to—"

"It's fine, Daigoro. It was very clever of you, in fact—a much better solution than that horrid letter we got from you. I'm your mother and Akiko is your wife, regardless of what you write in any official decrees."

Daigoro felt his face flush. "I promise we'll have a talk about that—but later, if you don't mind. Do you know where Aki is?"

"I'm here," Akiko said, wending her way through the armored ranks of Okuma warriors. She wore ruby red silk, her face pale and inscrutable. It was the first time he'd laid eyes on his wife since departing for Kyoto, for though he'd reached the Okuma estate in the earliest hours of the morning, there had been distractions of every kind: introductions to be made, wounds to clean and bind, to say nothing of the hastiest wedding preparations in history. On top of all that, morning sickness had invaded Akiko's stomach like the Mongol hordes, waking her each day with a new incursion and showing no signs of decamping.

As such, Daigoro's first thought was to attribute her pallor to nausea. But then she narrowed her eyes at him, her shoulders stiffened, and Daigoro feared he'd angered her. But of course, his conscience said. Running off without so much as a farewell, disappearing for nearly a month—one-third of their entire marriage—sending a decree almost as soon as he was out the door, declaring that he'd disowned her; what was she supposed to do? Welcome him with open arms? Had she even read the accompanying letter, the one that explained his decision and explained how much it pained him? Or had she pitched it into the fire pit? Torn it up? Tossed the scraps into the wind?

All these thoughts passed through his mind in the space of a heartbeat. Daigoro braced himself, fearing the worst. She would hate him. She would slap him in front of the entire gathering—and he would deserve it. Aki took another silent step toward him, finally emerging from the forest of motionless soldiers. Despite his dread and self-loathing, Daigoro could not help finding her beautiful. The thought that he'd hurt her wounded him to the quick. He loved her and he'd abandoned her. Whatever retribution she visited upon him could not compete with how harshly he would punish himself.

She stepped closer. Her shoulders tensed. Her chin drew back ever so slightly, as if she were a cobra preparing to strike. Then she grabbed both of his wrists, stretched up on her tiptoes, and pecked a kiss on his cheek. "Get inside," she whispered, her lips tickling his ear, "as quick as you can. I want you to strip me naked."

She settled herself back on the ground, and though she tried to hide it behind a coy smile, Daigoro could see she was near to bursting. She'd missed him after all, *and* she was angry, and love overwhelmed the anger, and worry threatened to overwhelm the love. It was all she could do to give his wrists a little squeeze instead of wrapping her arms around him, clutching him close so he could not wander again.

Behind him Daigoro heard the faint click of a sword slipping a thumb's length out of its sheath.

"And who might this pretty girl be?" he heard Shichio say.

Stupid, stupid, stupid, Daigoro thought. He had a venomous snake in his courtyard and he'd brought his pregnant wife within striking range. He looked over his shoulder at Shichio, whose left hand gripped the mouth of his scabbard, the fingertips of his right hand stroking his *katana*'s cord-bound grip. The preening peacock's hair had become disheveled, as if his shock and disgrace had struck him like a physical blow. Daigoro only wished they'd struck hard enough to knock him dead.

"I might have guessed she's your wife," Shichio said with a smile, "but you don't have a wife, do you? Not anymore. Not since you signed that decree."

Daigoro did not take his eyes from Shichio's face, but in his peripheral vision he noticed his enemy's feet settling into the gravel, his thumb pushing that *katana* a little farther out of its scabbard.

Glorious Victory was sheathed across Daigoro's back. She was too long to draw at this range. Shichio knew it. And if any Okuma stepped forward to his defense, the whole clan would be guilty of high treason against the regent's adviser. Shichio knew that too.

"If she's not your wife, then what is she?" said Shichio. "Just some girl you spilled your seed into, I suppose. But what does that make you? Certainly not a husband. Closer to the truth to call you an oath-breaker and a liar."

It was more than any man should bear. Even as a *rōnin*, Daigoro was ten times the samurai Shichio would ever be. The man was a viper. Deceit came as easily to him as breathing. And even if he were not, for a commoner to accuse a samurai of being a liar was more than provocation; in truth it was immoral for Daigoro *not* to kill him.

Shichio knew that too.

"You wouldn't be trying to pick a fight, would you, Shichio-sama?" It was everything Daigoro could do to end that sentence with *-sama* and not *you son of a bitch.*

"I hardly need to. You're a fugitive, aren't you? Yes, you are. Come to think of it, the bare fact that you stand in this courtyard means the Okumas have harbored you. Ever so convenient, isn't it? I have no need to marry your mother; I can kill her right after I kill you."

"You might want to think twice about that," said Daigoro.

Toyotomi samurai formed a rank behind Shichio, summoned as if they could hear his thoughts. "Seize the fugitive," Shichio said, the very picture of nonchalance. "And his mother and girlfriend too while you're at it."

"Shichio!"

The shout came from Hideyoshi. "This is a *wedding*," the regent barked. "By the gods, you idiot, you don't threaten the bride."

"Toyotomi-dono," Shichio said, "she's colluding with a fugitive—"

"And you're violating every damned rule of civility ever written," Hideyoshi said. "Have you forgotten the laws of hospitality?"

"I'm sure he hasn't," said Daigoro, "as your own General Mio cited them when last we met. The guest who instigates a fight under the roof of his host is to be punished with death."

Shichio rammed his *katana* home with a loud *snap*. "Then face me in a duel," he said, his voice dripping with acid. He stabbed one finger toward the open gate. "Outside the compound. Outside the bounds of your precious hospitality."

Daigoro clenched his fists. Pain shot through them, broken bones in the right, deep cuts in the left. He hadn't slept in three days. His right leg had twenty-nine fresh stitches in it. And yet he wanted nothing more in the world than to eviscerate this prideful peacock of a man.

Daigoro took a breath, eyeing the distance to the gate. It was not so far, perhaps twenty or thirty hobbling steps. In his current state, just walking there would leave him dizzy. He would have the advantage of reach, but with hands so battered that he could not hold his sword after the first exchange. His opponent was well rested and well fed. Daigoro had just enough strength to stand. And then there was Glorious Victory herself. She knew about his burning desire to kill Shichio; she could feel it in her steel. How much more satisfying would it be to kill him in front of Akiko, his mother, and his former clan? Daigoro's mouth all but watered at the thought of such satisfaction. He would even seize glory and victory in front of the regent, who already held him in such high regard that he might well make Daigoro a general.

Indulging his need for vengeance was more than simple revenge. It would secure him victory and glory. And for that very reason his own sword would betray him.

Another breath, then another. He studied Shichio in every detail: the length of his sword, the hand he'd returned to its hilt, the tension in his forearm as if he were ready to strike.

Daigoro breathed again, trying to calm his racing heart. He knew he could not face Shichio with some other blade—or at least not face him and win. He was too accustomed to Glorious Victory's weight and reach. Nor could he ask Katsushima to fight as his champion. If anything, Katsushima was even more exhausted than Daigoro; he was thirty years' Daigoro's senior, and he'd been riding day and night for a week, all the way from Kyoto.

Yet Daigoro knew the simple truth: Shichio had insulted him more than honor could bear. Daigoro took a deep breath and released it slowly. It was his sixth breath since Shichio had laid down his challenge. Daigoro knew the old maxim well, for his father had quoted it many times: the good samurai makes every decision in the space of seven breaths.

A silence fell over the courtyard, so that Daigoro felt the whole gathering could hear his pounding heartbeat. He took in his seventh breath. "If the Lady Okuma will allow it," he said, "I will face my challenger here, on the spot where I bested General Mio."

Shichio's face blanched. In an instant Daigoro could tell he'd read the man correctly. He remembered his last conversation with General Mio—not the exchange of scribbles and questions while Mio was on his deathbed, but their conversation in the Jurakudai before Daigoro had gone on the run and Shichio had somehow tied Mio down and cut out his tongue. *No, our Shichio's no swordsman,* Mio had said. *He did all his generalship with an ink brush.*

Daigoro could only guess how many times Shichio had fantasized about killing the hated Bear Cub. No doubt he'd rehearsed it in his mind: the cuts, the parries, the vainglorious pronouncements of victory. But between his obsession over the Inazuma and his flights of fancy, he'd forgotten that in all his years of warfare he'd never done any fighting. He'd made the mistake so many opponents had made: he thought of Daigoro as a cripple, not a warrior.

And then Daigoro reminded him of Mio. Mio, who was Shichio's superior in in every aspect of swordsmanship. Mio, the giant that lame little Daigoro defeated in single combat.

Daigoro put his hand to Glorious Victory Unsought, knowing that if he drew her he could not support her weight for long. His hands hurt too much. He'd asked too much of them in the fighting the night before. His forearm twinged just from the effort of wrapping his fingers around his weapon's hilt.

"After you, General Shichio," he said, filling his voice with every drop of confidence he could muster, hoping it was enough to patch over the exhaustion that made his voice sound like a rasp. He motioned toward the other end of the courtyard, and the dispersing crowd opened a corridor to the very spot where Daigoro had propped his foot on the mountainous General Mio. "I'm tired of your nonsense; let's get this over with."

Shichio's eyes narrowed. He took a single step toward Daigoro, just enough to put him in striking range. His slender *katana* would be faster on the draw. A good samurai could cut Daigoro down before Glorious Victory even cleared her scabbard. A good samurai, or even just a fast peasant.

"You're bluffing," said Shichio.

"The fifty up the road thought so too," said Daigoro.

Shichio's eyes narrowed, scrutinizing him. No doubt they could read Daigoro's exhaustion for what it was. No doubt they would note how heavily he favored his left foot, and therefore how badly hurt his right leg really was. But they would see more, too. Shichio was a liar and a cheat. That was how he thought, and men like him thought all other men were just as devious. More than once Daigoro had assumed Shichio would act like a samurai, but only because Daigoro himself thought and lived and breathed the code. Now, for the first time, Daigoro found the advantage in thinking like an ignoble backstabbing cur. Shichio thought *everyone* was a backstabber.

A muscle fluttered in Shichio's cheek. He swallowed. A tiny tremor had settled into his right hand. Daigoro's first instinct was to remain stone still. But that was samurai thinking. Instead, Daigoro said, "Do you plan to keep us waiting all day? Come on, make up your mind."

He counted Shichio's breaths, which came fast and shallow now.

He wondered whether Shichio knew the old adage about the seven breaths.

"A duel to the death is too good for you," Shichio said, loudly enough that everyone assembled could hear. He took a haughty step back and rammed his *katana* back home in its scabbard. Brushing the hair from his sweating brow, he said, "When I kill you, I'll have you strung up like a common criminal."

Daigoro heard Aki sigh with relief, and his mother too, and more than a few of the guests as well. Shichio snorted at him. "Be gone from this house by sundown," the peacock said, proclaiming it as if it were an edict, "or I will have everyone here executed for treason." On his way to the gate he spared a sneer for Daigoro's mother, and for the infant Lord Yasuda in her arms. "My congratulations to the lucky couple. A lunatic and an infant! I'm sure you'll be very happy together."

Then he stormed away, and it was as if the sun had come out from behind heavy clouds. The mood was instantly lighter; a cool breeze returned where once the air was still.

A chuckling Hideyoshi waddled over to Daigoro, looking for all the world like a shaved chimp in armor. "Nice ploy," he said under his breath.

"Whatever do you mean, my lord regent?" Daigoro kept his voice low too.

"I reckon I'd have drawn on you."

Daigoro inclined his head. "Perhaps my lord has a keener eye than some of his generals."

"Perhaps!" Hideyoshi laughed, baring his sharp, mismatched teeth. "What would have happened if I'd drawn?"

"There are so many uncertainties in combat, my lord regent."

"Meaning you're wondering about the reach of my blade, *neh*? I'll tell you this, boy: you look worn down to me. You'd better have killed me on the first exchange. I don't foresee you holding your ground after that."

"A keen eye indeed, my lord regent."

Hideyoshi laughed again. "The balls on this kid! I swear, give me ten generals like you and I'd invade Korea right this minute. Damn, it's hot this morning. Come on, walk me through the formalities so we can get down to some drinking."

Daigoro bowed deeply. "Forgive me, my lord regent. Not a month since I became a *rōnin* and already I've got the manners of a barbarian."

He introduced his mother first, then Akiko, then the grandparents of the little groom, Yasuda Kenbei and his wife, Azami. Daigoro had known them for less than an hour, but his immediate impression was of unwavering seriousness. That was only natural, he supposed; they were wards of their grandson because little Gorobei's father was a disgrace to the family, killed in a drunken brawl before the baby was even born. Kenbei's hair was graying, though not nearly so white as his father's; it looked more like storm clouds than snow, and he had stormy, steely eyes to match. He had twenty years on Azami, yet she was twice as stern, a stout pillar of a woman with forearms as thick as any blacksmith's. She looked strong enough to punch holes in a wooden barrel.

Perhaps their severity had something to do with the fact that Daigoro had forced them to drag themselves out of bed and ride half the night to marry off their departed son's newborn. For all of that they looked remarkably genteel, both of them immaculate in twenty shades of green, and they did an admirable job of concealing their ire. When Daigoro saw how awed they were by his conversational tone with the most powerful warlord in Japan, he thought they might even forgive him someday for so thoroughly disturbing their morning.

Everyone in attendance walked through the requisite pleasantries— praise heaped upon House Yasuda's newest son for the strength of his grip, compliments on the surpassing beauty of the bride, kudos to both houses for choosing such an auspicious day under such auspicious signs and stars—and at last it came to the drinking Hideyoshi longed for so fervently. Daigoro, cheered at the prospect of relaxation for the first time in weeks, treated himself to three nicely chilled flasks within the first hour. He could not decide which pleased him more, the thought of Shichio sulking in some dark, stifled cabin of the regent's flagship or the promise of a few uninterrupted hours of sitting with no other obligations calling on his time. By the time he finished the third flask he decided it did not matter, and happily ordered a fourth.

Even so, he could not match pace with Hideyoshi, who despite his small stature could drink like a demon. Before the noon meal was halfway finished, the regent was singing boisterously. Daigoro was surprised at how gifted a singer he was, at least as far as drunken warlords went.

When Hideyoshi was drunk enough not to notice, Daigoro took his leave. He and Akiko never made it as far as their bedchamber, opting instead for the top of a sake cask in the cool shady recesses of a storehouse. When they'd reassembled themselves, they marched off quietly and with great decorum to the residence, where they flung each other's clothes off for a repeat performance.

Afterward, Daigoro could not bring himself to say what he must.

It did not matter; Akiko read his silence as if he'd shouted from a mountaintop. "I know your enemy will kill you if you stay here," she said. She nestled her naked back against his chest and hugged his arms around her belly. "And me too, and the little one that quickens inside me. But tell me you'll stay close."

"I wasn't sure you'd have me back. I thought you would be angry with me."

"I am. I was. The next time you plan on sacrificing our marriage, I'd prefer if you asked me about it first."

"Aki, I had no choice—"

"Yes, you did." She reached back and pressed a warm fingertip against his lips. She did not need to look back to do it; she knew his body as well as she knew her own. "You could have accepted defeat," she said. "You could have strayed from your path, from your father's path; you could have kept our family whole. And perhaps in time I might have learned to respect you again. Don't mistake me, Daigoro: I'm proud of what you did."

Daigoro blinked. He could hardly believe his ears. "You are?"

"Of course. My parents are samurai too; I know the path as well as you do."

Daigoro's skin prickled; an ice-cold wave rippled over him despite the midday summer air. He hugged Akiko tight, ignoring the pain in his hands, his arms, his legs, pressing his cheek against her ear. For the second time he found himself dumbstruck. He wished for a word that expressed thanks and love and longing, all in the overwhelming measures he felt in that moment.

And for the second time, Akiko heard his silence as if she could read his very thoughts. "Wherever the path leads you, stay close to me, *neh*? Never leave me again."

She pressed her back against him like a stretching cat, a kind of reverse hug, and Daigoro held her close. For the first time in what seemed like years, he felt truly at home.

BOOK TEN

HEISEI ERA, THE YEAR 22

(2010 CE)

59

"Mariko!"

Han had her in a half nelson before she knew it. She still had two fistfuls of long black beard. One of her officers came out of nowhere, holding Jōko Daishi by the armpits so that Mariko didn't have the whole of his body weight hanging from her two hands. Someone else assisted Han and locked down Mariko's right arm. Mariko was so angry she hardly felt them.

"Easy," Han said. "Let him go, Mariko. I did enough damage to this case already. We don't need you drawing police brutality charges to boot."

That snapped her out of her rage. She released her grip and stepped back, palms outspread in a peacemaking gesture, or at least an I-won't-press-the-fight gesture. The other two cops lowered Jōko Daishi back to a seated position against the wall. Han didn't loosen his grip. "I'm serious," he said, whispering in her ear. "That shit I pulled before, ignoring probable cause, it's going to make it hard enough to land a conviction. You just ripped this dude off a motorcycle, Mariko. If he's got short-term injuries, okay, he was assaulting you. But if jerking him around like that causes—"

"Long-term injuries. It'll sink our case. I know, Han. I'm cool."

Cautiously, he relaxed his hold. She could tell she'd taken him by surprise, pouncing on their suspect like that. In truth, she'd surprised herself. She hadn't realized the affection she felt for her city—a city that would never run short on garbage to heap on a female police detective. COs who treated her like a girl, subordinates who treated her like an equal, newspapers that hungered to make her an item, slavering for every exploit, spoiling any chance she'd ever have for doing undercover work, all to boost their sales for a couple of hours. How many times had she asked herself why she didn't go take a job in some Canadian police department, or an American one? Someplace where the pay was better, where the rent wasn't so high, where she might find a boyfriend who wasn't intimidated by her profession? And yet the mere mention of a bomb threat in her city was enough to bring her blood to a boil. Jōko Daishi had threatened her *home*. She hadn't felt at home in a long time, maybe not since she was a little girl. No wonder she'd reacted so violently; no wonder she'd surprised herself.

"Okay," Han said, and she could see his wariness recede. "Tell me what you got from him."

"A bunch of crazy cult bullshit."

"Come on, Mariko. Get your head in the game."

"Nothing, okay? He says his goal is to destroy order and harmony, whatever the hell that means. The guy's out of his mind, Han, and that means we're out of leads."

"That sounds like quitting," Han said, "and *you* don't quit." He took her by the elbow and turned her around, leading her on a slow march away from their suspect. He was right to do it; just having Jōko Daishi out of her field of vision was enough to slow her pulse a little. "Come on, now. Help me think."

Mariko frowned, ashamed of herself. Han was right: she needed to get her head together. But it was hard when her whole investigation had just been one frustration after another. First they had an upside-down drug buy. It got even loopier with the introduction of top-quality Daishi. Following up on that led to a pair of thefts that could have been drug related, except for the tiny little detail that the thief had no interest in selling the sword or the mask to buy drugs. Tie in a yakuza connection, a needless murder in the suburbs, and a domestic gas chamber and what did she have? Only the weirdest narcotics case she'd ever heard of—and that was before anyone mentioned the word *cult*.

In three days they'd uncovered more arcane secrets than Mariko would ever have thought possible, and every last one of them raised more questions than it answered. Mariko didn't want to give up. She wanted to push harder, but she didn't have anything solid to push against. Her whole case was made of smoke.

"What if we got everything wrong from the beginning?" she said. "What if the whole crazy cult thing is just a con?"

"Seriously? We're in midgame here, Mariko. You want to forfeit and go back to batting practice?"

"No, I'm just asking if he's playing the same game we are. What if we've got it all wrong? What if the Divine Wind is just a front operation for the Kamaguchi-gumi?"

Han gave her a quizzical frown. "Where is this coming from?"

"I don't know. Desperation. Just work with me. Who gained the most from that dumb-ass drug buy with the Kamaguchis?"

"The Kamaguchis."

"Exactly. They corner the market on the Daishi, and all they have to give up is a stupid mask."

Han shook his head. "How does that explain everything with the Bulldog? Every speed freak in town wants what he's selling; what's he got to be pissed about?"

"I told you, I don't know. I'm just spitballing—"

"And I'm all in favor, so long as it gets us closer to figuring out where those bombs are going to go off. So? Does it?"

Mariko didn't have to think about that for long. She didn't even have to answer; a resigned sigh was enough.

"Look, maybe you're right. Maybe he's been throwing us curveballs all along. But maybe you had it right from the start. You profiled him as a whack-job cult leader, *neh*? So let's stick with whack-job cult leader. What does that tell us?"

Mariko nodded. Han had a point. "If he's not playing us—*if*— then he really believes he's preaching the truth of the Divine Wind."

"And that is?"

She put her hands on her hips and looked at the ceiling. "Something about structure and order suffocating the mind. He wants chaos. He wants to shake people up."

"Finally something that actually makes sense."

"Huh?"

"The Daishi deal. If you look at it as a narc, the whole thing is a fiasco. World's dumbest dealer delivers top-quality product and forgets to call ahead to see if anyone wants to pay him for it."

Mariko nodded. "And walks right into a sting too."

"Exactly. But what if we look at it like a loony-tune cult leader?"

"Then kicking hornet's nests is some kind of spiritual exercise. Who cares about giving away a fortune in Daishi if you can flip the whole speed market on its head? It knocks the balance of power out of whack."

"That's it," Han said, giddy with the discovery. "It's got to be."

Mariko felt something relax in her mind, the way her body would relax if she peeled herself out of a skirt and slid into some old jeans. She and Han were back to their old repartee, the shooting back and forth, bouncing ideas off each other, the ideas getting clearer, not breaking apart.

"But then what?" she said. "Economic chaos? Collapse the black market and see how many legitimate businesses fall with it?"

"Why not? Let's face it, yakuzas run a lot more front companies in this city than we like to admit."

Mariko waved him off. "I don't buy it. Take one look at that guy and tell me if the words *mad bomber economist* spring to mind."

Both of them looked at their perp. They'd been pacing back and forth as they talked, working out nervous energy, but even from a distance Jōko Daishi's mask was creepy as hell—all the more so because the guy wearing it was sitting contentedly on the floor, a childlike grin playing at the corners of his mouth. Somehow Mariko thought he'd look more natural with a bloody ax in his hand.

As if he'd heard her thoughts, he looked at her. Locking eyes with him gave Mariko chills; her mind automatically conjured an image of him standing over her bed while she slept, watching her from behind that mask.

Han noticed it when she flinched. "Okay," he said, "we've got to change things up. All of this speculating isn't getting us any closer to finding those bombs."

Mariko noticed he'd changed too. His gait was different. He was bouncing on the balls of his feet. Jittery. She'd seen him like this in the SWAT van too, right before go time.

"Han, don't even think it."

"I don't want to, but we're desperate. Give me two minutes alone with him and I'm telling you, I can get him to tell us where the bombs are."

"Two minutes? Two minutes ago you were the one talking *me* down. What happened to not sinking our case?"

"What happened is this asshole is going to murder hundreds of innocent people. Sakakibara said it himself: who cares if we don't get a single conviction, so long as we save lives?"

"He wasn't talking about beating information out of a suspect, Han."

"Look, I'll be the one to take that hit, okay? My career is fucked anyway. We need to know where Akahata's going with those bombs."

"We're not crossing that line. Period."

Han's eyes were pleading and pained and frightened and angry, all at once. "Mariko, he took off a long time ago. On a fast fucking bike. What makes you think we're going to find him in time?"

"Because we've got his boss, and because I think our speculating actually did us some good. Jōko Daishi's a strategist, not a mental patient. It's like you said: from his perspective, everything he's doing makes sense. All that Wind imagery—scattering, randomizing, blowing what's orderly into disarray—*that's* the real mask. He's not following some divine hallucination. He's got a plan. He's got a timeline. He's got—holy shit."

"What?"

Mariko punched him in the arm. "The dope deals. Buying his

hexamine with speed instead of cash. He *was* conning us, right from the beginning."

"Slow down, Mariko. What are you seeing that I'm not?"

"As soon as we got onto the hexamine, what did we assume?"

"MDA. . . ." Mariko could almost see the shift in his thinking, a deft little slide away from desperation and back to their old give-and-take. "No way. You think he decided to cook his bombs with hexamine just to throw us off his scent? To make us think he was just another random speed freak?"

"It worked, didn't it?"

"Come on. You're saying he *knew* we'd get onto the hexamine before we got onto the cyanide?"

"Yeah."

"And he *knew* we'd leap to the conclusion that he was cooking MDA?"

"We didn't leap, Han; he pushed us. He's not just making bombs, is he? He's cooking boutique uppers with rare ingredients, and he knows exactly what any narc who runs across those ingredients is going to assume."

"And you and I never thought to question that assumption until we saw *that*." Han jabbed a finger at the cluttered folding tables lined along the right-hand wall—the explosives assembly line. He shook his head, flabbergasted. He couldn't even bring himself to look Mariko in the eye; he was too embarrassed by the idea that Jōko Daishi had so thoroughly duped them. "This dude is thinking *way* farther ahead than we are."

"Yeah."

"Like, months ahead. Maybe years ahead." He snorted a self-conscious laugh. "You don't suppose he writes it all down in a day planner, do you?"

"Years ahead. . . ." Mariko didn't even mean to say it aloud. She looked at the tables too, and at the hodgepodge collection scattered across them. Nails and screws: shrapnel. SIM cards, rubber-coated wire, outdated cell phones: remote detonators. Right beside them, gutted flashlights: handheld detonators. Any one of those items was totally innocuous. The only way to see them as dangerous was to take a much longer view.

And then she saw it. The Year of the Demon. Right above those tables. "Holy shit, Han, it's right in front of our faces. He's got a calendar!"

She turned and broke into a run. The cops watching over Jōko Daishi instantly formed a defensive barrier, just in case Mariko was ready for round two. But Mariko was headed for the explosives assembly line, and specifically for the astrological calendar hung above it.

Only one day was circled, smack in the middle. Mariko could make no sense of the rest of it—too many months, too many weird astrological squiggles—but she knew for a fact that Jōko Daishi had been hurrying things along lately. Preparing for the Year of the Demon. The appointed hour. It was a good bet that the circled day was today. Tomorrow if she was lucky, but there was no point in assuming her luck would suddenly improve.

No. She didn't need to be lucky. She'd already seen another calendar with today's date circled on it. That little wallet-sized copy of the Yomiuri Giants season schedule. She still had it in her pocket.

"Han!" She pulled the schedule out of its Ziploc bag, unfolded it too quickly, nearly tearing it. One game was circled. A home game. Today.

It had started three hours ago.

"His target is the game, the Tokyo Dome," Mariko said. "We have to go—"

"No," he said, and she followed his gaze to Jōko Daishi. The son of a bitch still looked as giddy as a little boy, but a boy who was anticipating something, not a boy who'd already won. "We haven't heard anything over the radio. If there was an attack, we'd have gotten the call—or at least heard about it, *neh?*"

He whipped his phone out of his pocket and pulled up the app that kept him up to date on box scores. "Come on, come on," he said. Mariko had far too much time to think about how long eight or nine seconds could be. "Okay, the game's not over yet. Bottom of the eighth, two outs, the Giants are up five to four."

"Han, I really don't give a shit about the scores—"

"I'm saying it's not a blowout. The stands are still full, Mariko. The stands are still full."

Of targets, Mariko thought. Han didn't need to say it. But as she saw it, his logic was flawed. "Akahata's late if he's trying to set off bombs in the stands. He should have done it midgame. It's like you said: if this had been a blowout—"

"The stands would be half-empty already. People trying to beat the rush to the trains."

"The trains!" Mariko's skin went cold. "Han, he's going to hit the subway."

"No. Oh no, no, no." Han began to quiver. "What if he . . . what if we can't . . . ?"

Paralysis through analysis, Mariko thought. There wasn't time to consider worst-case scenarios; she and Han needed to act. "Come on," she said. "The Giants are your favorite team. You've been to a million games. What's the train station down there?"

"Four stations. One is JR's, the other three go to the subway."

Mariko looked back at Jōko Daishi, who watched the two of them eagerly. "He wants to cause chaos, right? Remind people of old fears?"

"Then it's the subway," Han said. "Like the sarin gas attack when we were kids."

"Exactly."

"Then our best bets are Suidobashi Station or Korakuen Station. Kasuga's nearby, but it's the other two that are always jam-packed after a game. If he wants a body count, it's got to be Suidobashi or Korakuen." His face went white. "Mariko, they're going to be packed like sardines down there. It's going to be a massacre."

Mariko started running for the door, Han a pace or two behind her. She didn't have time to give orders to the rest of her detail; there was too much to explain, too many loose ends to be tied up on-site before she could even think about a mass redeployment to the subway stations. "You take Suidobashi," she told Han, "I'm taking Korakuen."

"Oh, hell," he said.

She heard him miss a step. Looking back, she saw him slowing, staring at the phone, halfway through the movement of trying to cram the phone back in his pocket. "Top of the ninth," he said. "Still five-four. We've got three outs before all hell breaks loose."

60

Mariko raced to Korakuen Station, lights running hot, siren as loud as it got and still not loud enough. Even before she became a cop, she remembered thinking people ought to go to prison for not pulling over to give emergency vehicles right of way. How these idiots failed to notice an ambulance or a fire engine riding their bumper had always been a mystery to her. Today she wished not pulling over was a capital offense. Death by strangulation, and Mariko wanted to do the strangling.

She clenched down on the steering wheel instead, thinking about all the mistakes she'd made in the last few minutes. She should have taken side streets, not the main thoroughfares. She should have ordered one of her officers on scene to call the Bureau of Transportation and order them to close Suidobashi and Korakuen stations so that she didn't have to call it in herself. She'd made the call to Dispatch easily enough, but she'd done it driving one-handed at maximum speed, and plenty of cops had put themselves in the hospital that way.

Most of all, she should have asked Jōko Daishi whether Akahata's target was a subway car or a subway platform. Maybe he wouldn't have answered. Maybe he would have been delighted to tell her. Now all Mariko could do was wonder which target was worse. Detonating a bomb inside a subway car would contain the blast, all but guaranteeing everyone aboard would die. Detonating it on the platform would let the bomb's fury disperse, trading guaranteed fatalities for a far greater number of injuries.

It was possible, of course, that Mariko and Han had it wrong altogether, that Akahata was bound for somewhere else, some other target they hadn't even imagined. But Mariko couldn't allow herself to think that way. She made the best guess she could on the evidence she had— and following that logic, she committed herself to another hypothesis: Akahata would hit a platform, not a subway car. For one thing, he'd prefer a fixed location, a place he could observe, timing the blast to maximize his body count. For another, there were dozens of train cars to choose from, and only two likely stations. Mariko *had* to believe he would target one of the stations; the other possibility left her feeling hopeless.

She heard Sakakibara's voice over the radio just as she was approaching her final turn. She ripped the steering wheel over, her tires shrieking in protest, and as soon as she could free a hand she snatched up the mic. "Sir?"

"We reached Transportation. They've got the stations closed. That game let out ten minutes ago, Frodo. You're going to have a crowd."

"I see them." Her tires screeched again as she stomped on the brakes.

"Backup's on the way, but you're the—"

Mariko didn't stop to hear the rest. "On the way" wasn't good enough news to wait for the details. She brought the car to a halt just a few meters from the mob that had gathered outside Korakuen Station.

Just as Sakakibara had said, someone in TMPD had reached the Bureau of Transportation and ordered them to close the station. They'd done it wisely too, posting an OUT OF SERVICE notice at the entryway. Mariko hoped that might turn some of the crowd away, because a good-sized blast down on the platform would send a shock wave up the stairs too. Anyone up top was standing in the muzzle of a flamethrower.

Fighting her way through the crowd, she wanted to shout at the top of her lungs, telling them there was a great big goddamn bomb right below their feet and they ought to get the hell out of her way. But panicked mobs were dangerous, and her next best plan—firing her SIG P230 in the air like a sheriff in a cowboy movie—would panic them too. So all she could do was lead with her elbows and knees and shout, "TMPD! Make way!"

She knew it was only seconds but it felt like it took forever to burrow a tunnel through the mass of fans. When she finally reached the turnstile, she planted a palm on it and got overeager on her jump, almost pulling a one-handed cartwheel as she cleared it. It cost her a stutter step when she hit the ground. She came close to rolling her ankle but didn't. Then her SIG was in her left hand and she was racing toward the stairs.

There were two flights, one for the eastbound tracks, one for the westbound. Which one would Akahata choose? The one with the greater promise for passengers, Mariko supposed. But she didn't know where the most Giants fans lived. She didn't know where people went after ball games. Han would have known. She wanted to call him but she didn't want to take the time. She wanted to pause for a few seconds, to mentally locate herself on the city map, to reason it out, but she didn't have time for that either. Paralysis through analysis. Over-thinking was the enemy. Sometimes you just had to act.

She took the closest flight of stairs and didn't even bother to look whether it led her to the eastbound or westbound trains. When she got to the bottom, she found the platform occupied. There were forty or fifty people down there—hardly crowded by Tokyo's standards, but Mariko was surprised to see anyone at all. Mentally she kicked herself for being so stupid: the station might have been closed at street level, but nothing could prevent people from disembarking trains they'd already boarded elsewhere.

It was the kind of platform with two sets of parallel tracks between it and the opposite platform. Every surface seemed to shimmer: the steel tops of the rails, buffed hundreds of times a day by the wheels of train cars; the pillars wearing their ceramic tiles like snakeskin; more ceramic tiles on the walls, still more lining the floor; the ceiling panels, flat and smooth as mirrors. Commuters ambled about in a kind of human Brownian motion, fiddling with book bags or sending texts.

Mariko spotted Akahata in their midst, loitering, dressed as a sanitation worker. He stood four or five paces away from a wheeled caddy that held a big blue trash can and a bunch of cleaning supplies. People were keeping their distance, predictably scared of the guy who looked like he'd just limped away from a knock-down, drag-out bar brawl. His face was still a ruin, a spatter pattern of purple and red. Mariko watched a girl, walking idly and texting, come close enough to catch him in her peripheral vision. The girl started, blanched, and backed away. Mariko wondered how many others had done the same.

Akahata looked at the girl, and looking past her, he saw Mariko.

His bloodshot eyes flicked to the trash can. It was big, heavy, but sitting on its stout plastic casters it would be easy for one guy to move. Perfect for housing a great big bomb.

Mariko put her front sight on him. Civilians crowded her backdrop; doubts about her aim infected her mind. A moment's hesitation was all Akahata needed. He grabbed a high school boy in uniform and held him like a human shield. One bruised forearm snaked around the kid's throat, tight as a python.

"Let him go!" Mariko shouted.

Akahata responded by chanting his mantra and taking one step toward the trash can on his caddy.

For a fleeting second Mariko wondered why she was still alive. Why hadn't Akahata unleashed his bomb? Then she understood: he didn't have a remote detonator. There was no need for one. He'd been waiting for masses of baseball fans to crowd the platform; the trigger was on the bomb itself, and he wouldn't trigger it until his victims had walled him in. As he took one more step toward the caddy, Mariko was surer than ever that his trash can was an enormous IED.

Mariko moved to flank him, trying to cut an angle around the kid so she'd have a clean shot at center body mass. But the kid was struggling, jerking Akahata this way and that. He wasn't strong enough to break Akahata's lunatic strength, but his tugging and twisting gave Mariko a constantly moving target.

She shifted targets, aiming at Akahata's head. Her backdrop still wasn't clear. Some of the commuters had the sense to flee, but too many panicked, frozen like so many deer caught in the glow of an oncoming light. Mariko kept moving to flank, yelling at Akahata to let the kid go, sidestepping until her backdrop was the empty black tunnel above the train tracks. It hardly mattered. A head shot behind a struggling human shield was damn near impossible even for an expert marksman. Cops went to sniper school to make shots like that—and they didn't do it southpaw either.

Akahata took another step toward the trash can. His eyes were wide and wild, his head lurching this way and that as his hostage tried in vain to break his grip. The kid seemed more scared of Mariko's pistol than of Akahata, flinching at the sight of it, squirming whenever it moved. Stupid, Mariko thought; if you'd just stay still for a second, this pistol will save your life.

"Last warning," she said, not at all sure she meant it, "let the kid go."

Akahata broke off from his mantra and said, "What difference does it make? He will die. We all die in the end. Don't you see that's what we're trying to teach you?"

Mariko had no time for the religious bullshit, but she saw a different truth in Akahata's words. If he reached that bomb, everyone on the platform would die. Just as well to start shooting, and if she killed the kid, so be it, so long as she brought down Akahata too.

Maybe Han would have pulled the trigger, but Mariko couldn't cross that line. If the kid was bound to die anyway, better for it to be at the hands of a mass murderer than a cop. Even so, she wished the kid was the type to freeze up and piss his pants. She had plenty of training hitting stationary targets. By now she could have slowed her breath, taken her bead, made that slow squeeze on the trigger.

And now she was overthinking it. She knew it. Paralysis through analysis. She tried to keep her front sight zeroed on Akahata's face, but the more she concentrated on keeping it steady, the more it wavered. Yamada-sensei would have told her to holster her pistol. She could almost hear him say it: the good swordsman would rather drop his blade than squeeze it tighter with the wrong grip. Drop it and pick it up again. That was the better course. But Mariko was too scared to drop her weapon.

Akahata switched the kid from his right arm to his left. Freeing his right hand to reach the detonator, Mariko thought. He was close to the bomb now. One more step and he'd have it.

Han would have shot him by now. To hell with the psychological games and moral dilemmas. That's what he would have said. And now Mariko was so entangled in her conscious thought that she'd spoiled any chance for her subconscious to do what needed to be done.

There was no way she could make the shot now, not against such a small target, a moving target, not with all the self-doubt. Yamada was right. There was no room for thinking, only for doing. And she couldn't—not while she was stuck so deep in her own head. Better to drop her sword and pick it up again. It was the only solution.

She had no choice. She lowered her weapon.

Akahata's eyes went wider still, glowing with triumph. He roared out his mantra and reached for the detonator.

Mariko's pistol snapped up and she put a bullet in the center of his forehead.

61

Mass panic erupted all around her. People were running for the stairs even as her gunshot's echo reverberated in the tunnels. Passengers on the opposite platform stood slack-jawed, frozen. Mariko watched as the high school boy fell, seemingly in slow motion, resisting the pull of Akahata's deadweight as best he could until finally he lost his balance. At first Mariko wondered whether she'd shot him, whether she'd somehow double-tapped Akahata without knowing it, whether her second shot had pulled left and hit the kid. She didn't remember firing two shots, but it was only when the kid rolled away from Akahata's body, shrieking and crying, that Mariko was certain she hadn't hit him.

She ignored the fleeing crowd for the moment, trusting that the transit authorities upstairs would know what to do with them. Her focus remained on Akahata, his weapon, and his erstwhile hostage. Akahata wasn't moving. The bullet hole was a neat, perfectly circular thing, just like in the movies.

That surprised her somehow. It was morbid of them, wasn't it, getting a detail like that just right? Of all the things a person could obsess over, some special effects artist had chosen to perfect the fatal gunshot wound to the head. Maybe there had been a pay raise in it for him, or a patent, or at least a pat on the back for a job well done. Maybe his mother boasted to her friends about how far he'd come.

The instant that struck her, Mariko wondered what her own

mother would say about what she'd done. A man was dead and it was Mariko's fault. Mariko had just killed a human being.

She knew she'd have to make a moral assessment of what she'd done, and she knew it had to come soon, but for now she had civilians to tend to. That high school boy was hunched on all fours, stupefied and shuddering. His face was red; his mouth hung open; tears flowed openly and a string of drool lolled from his lower lip. For all of that he seemed stable enough for the moment, not a threat to himself or others, so Mariko took a few cautious steps toward the massive IED.

She wasn't on the Bomb Squad and they hadn't taught her a thing about explosives in academy, but the big steel canister barely hidden inside Akahata's trash can didn't look like garbage. Neither did the gutted flashlight sitting on top. It was no more than a simple on/off switch now, with wires trailing from it into a little hole in the canister. To Mariko it looked a whole hell of a lot like a homemade detonator.

Part of her was thankful not to see a countdown timer. Another part of her said it was stupid to think Hollywood got that detail right too, and that prompted a sudden need to inspect the device all over, looking for a hidden timer clicking down toward zero. But that little voice was silenced by her common sense, which screamed at her not to get any closer to the really dangerous object that hadn't gone boom yet but very well could if she decided to poke at it. She decided to return her attention to the traumatized teenager who had been a hostage a few moments before.

"Hey, kid," Mariko said, holstering her weapon. She put herself directly in his line of sight, between the boy and Akahata's corpse. "Look at me, okay? You're going to be all right. Just look at me. Please?"

He was scarcely able to speak. His voice was harsh and squeaking, like a missed note on a violin, but at last he managed to say, "You shot at me."

"Not at you. Never at you."

"You could have shot me. You could have killed me." He still hadn't managed to meet Mariko's gaze; his eyes were locked on Aka-hata's ruined face.

And he wasn't wrong. Mariko heard herself say the words anyway: "I shot at your assailant. Not at you. At him. I promise you that. I never would have pulled the trigger if I thought I might hit you." She hoped the words were true.

"You shot at me," was all he could say.

"I want you to sit down, okay?" She did what she could to herd him away from the body, but though he consented to sit against one of the tile-faced pillars, she couldn't get him to pull his gaze away from Aka-hata's face, much less look her in the eye.

"I want you to know I'll be speaking to your commanding officer," said a voice from behind her.

It took her by surprise; she'd honestly forgotten anyone else existed apart from her, the kid, and Akahata. She turned to see a tall, blond *gaijin* with a little mustache and wispy beard. Only upon seeing him did it occur to her that he'd spoken in English. Now she heard the Japanese voices too: hurried whispers from the opposite platform, distant panicked chattering echoing all the way down from street level, just as her pistol's report must have echoed all the way up.

Mariko stood from her crouch beside the high school boy and as-sessed the *gaijin*. He seemed the graduate student type to her: he had a computer bag slung over his shoulder, and despite his Midwestern accent his shoes were European, vaguely hippieish. His face was grave, the sort of expression she'd seen before in people who had narrowly escaped what should have been a fatal car crash, or a house fire. She had a good guess of what he intended to tell her CO, and she wasn't in the mood at the moment. "There's no need to thank me, sir—"

She could tell she'd taken him aback, as happened all too often when she responded to *gaijin* in fluid, unaccented English. She as-sumed this was another case like that, but then she saw his expression shift from solemnity to outrage. "*Thank* you? Are you joking? You just shot an unarmed man!"

"Excuse me?"

"You just shot a civilian in cold blood. I'm going to stand right here until your commanding officer arrives, and I'm going to tell him exactly what I saw. You endangered that boy's life to shoot an unarmed janitor. In my country we call that reckless endangerment and excessive force."

We're not in your country, Mariko wanted to say. She could also have gone with *Are you fucking kidding me? I just saved your life.* She was still wired from her standoff with Akahata and now this skinny, self-righteous prick had her adrenaline spiking yet again. Politeness was beyond her, but she managed to resist face-planting him on the floor to slap handcuffs on him. She stood chest to chest with him and said, "Sir, I don't think you have the slightest goddamn clue what just went down here."

"I know *exactly* what 'went down' here, Officer. I study law at the University of—"

"Mariko!"

It was Han's voice, and hearing it made Mariko's mind do back flips. She was relieved and elated and discombobulated at once. How had he gotten here? Was all of this some sort of post-traumatic hallucination? But no, there he was, racing down the stairs. "You all right?" he said, his words tumbling out in one unbroken torrent. "Did you find him? Is he—?"

The *gaijin* law student was still talking, but Mariko ignored him. "I'm fine," she said, reverting to Japanese. "Akahata's down. We've got a kid who's pretty roughed up, but he'll pull through sooner or later. Akahata used him as a shield."

Han looked past her shoulder, and looking at no more than his face Mariko could tell the instant he saw Akahata's body. "You—?"

"Yeah."

His eyes flicked back to hers. "You okay?" He wasn't asking whether she was hurt.

Mariko hadn't had time to conduct her moral assessment yet. The high school boy wasn't far wrong: Mariko hadn't shot at him, but she'd sure as hell shot near him. And it seemed the kid and the prattling *gaijin* were thinking along the same lines: Mariko shouldn't have pulled the trigger.

The decision seemed right at the time. Or rather, trying to decide had fractured her composure, so she derailed the decision process and let her instincts do the driving. But her gut instinct seemed right at the time, and it seemed right with the benefit of hindsight too. So why were those two so pissed off?

At last the truth finally struck her: neither of them knew about the bomb.

They'd seen her shoot an assailant she could have talked down. She could have stalled, placated, waited for backup, pepper-sprayed. She could have done anything, but as they saw it, her response to an unarmed man with a hostage in a simple choke hold was to shoot to kill.

Mariko turned from Han to the *gaijin*, ready to explain the misunderstanding. Then she caught herself short. Should she tell him the truth? Let him know how close he'd come to dying? Show him Akahata's detonator? The guy was being a royal prick; did he even deserve an explanation?

More to the point, what were the ramifications of letting it slip that someone had managed to get thirty or forty kilos of high explosives into the Tokyo subway system? Mariko was perfectly happy for that decision to stay well above her pay grade.

"Mariko, who is this asshole?" Han pointed at the *gaijin*.

"He was just leaving," Mariko said. Switching back to English, she said, "Sir, I'll be more than happy to discuss the ins and outs of the Japanese legal system some other time, but for now I'm going to have to ask you to get the hell away from my crime scene."

"Do you think I'm going to stand for this?" the guy said. "I'm going to—"

"Fuck off," said Han.

The law student reacted as if Han had slapped him in the face. Perhaps he hadn't expected to hear a second Japanese cop speaking English. More likely, it was the first time he'd ever heard a Japanese person drop the F-bomb. Either way, it made him go stand somewhere else to wait for a lieutenant to complain to.

"Why, Detective Watanabe!" Mariko said, reverting to Japanese again. "I had no idea you spoke such fluent English."

"And I had no idea anyone in this department remembered it doesn't actually say 'Han' on my business card. No wonder you made sergeant. You've got a mind made for paperwork."

"Now that's low."

"So you're okay, then?"

Mariko felt her pulse quicken. Even while he was joking, his attention had never wavered from how she was coping with shooting Akahata. Now that things had calmed down a little, Mariko found herself feeling more conflicted than she'd realized at first. She knew she'd fired in self-defense, and in defense of the lives of everyone else on that platform. But there he was, staring blankly at the ceiling, a puppet snipped from its strings. And there was Mariko, with a second death on her hands. After Fuchida, that made two *this year*. More than the rest of Narcotics combined. And yet she didn't know what else she could have done. She'd given Akahata the option of submitting peacefully and he hadn't taken her up on the invitation. A bullet in the brainpan didn't seem out of line.

At least not to Mariko. A few dozen onlookers still lingered on the opposite platform, and by now one of them had probably recognized her. Her fame after the Fuchida affair might have been short-lived, but her missing finger was memorable and it only took one eyewitness to spot it. Reflexively she stuck her right hand in her pocket, knowing it was far too late to start any attempt at damage control. Even as she tabled her own moral assessment for later, even as she told her partner she was okay, she wondered what the consequences would be for killing a man that every last bystander would describe as being unarmed.

Whatever the consequences might be, there wasn't a thing she could do about them at this point. Even if there were, she could hear a platoon of cops coming down the stairs, and when they reached her they would need orders. She had a shell-shocked teenager to deal with, a body to zip up and roll away, a bomb to quarantine, a major subway station to restore to working order, and if she really got cracking she might get it done by midnight. "Seriously," she told Han, "I think I'm all right. Ask me again in a couple of days, maybe. For now, let's get this crime scene locked down."

62

"Tell me again why you don't want me to call the papers," Mariko's mother said.

She sat with her two daughters around her living room coffee table, all of them sitting on the floor and playing rummy. Mariko had been appraising both of them without saying a word. Her mom was wearing a polo shirt with a logo embroidered on it that Mariko didn't recognize, probably from the manufacturer of something related to her beloved sport of Ping-Pong. She seemed radiant, not careworn, as she'd so often been of late. Of course she'd panicked after she found out her eldest daughter had been in the same room as thirty-odd kilos of high explosives, but that was after the fact, after she knew Mariko was safely at home. More important, Mariko guessed, was that her second daughter was also safely at home.

Saori was looking good. She'd regained some of the weight she'd lost. Her hair didn't seem so brittle and her skin had regained its luster. The scabs she'd accumulated from when she was using, the bruises, the pallor, had vanished. Her teeth would never recover from the years of meth abuse, but otherwise she was back to being her contented, girlish self.

"Yeah," Saori said, "you're a hero, Miko. Didn't you save, like, fifty people?"

"Fifty-two," Mariko said. And killed one, she could have added. Akahata's death had a completely different character than Fuchida's.

With Fuchida it was a simple quid pro quo: he gutted her, Mariko stabbed him back. But Akahata hadn't actually done anything violent; he'd only threatened to. Mariko shot him preemptively. With a couple of days' hindsight she'd expected to feel some guilt over it, but still none had come. She didn't feel good about it, either. If anything, she was just apprehensive about what would come next.

A psychologist might have been able to explain the scientific reasons why she preferred to look ahead rather than back. Mariko knew she might seek out a psychologist someday. Every sensible cop in Narcotics had asked her how she was doing, and all the thoughtless ones had asked her what it felt like to shoot somebody. Sooner or later that would wear on her. And she hadn't been in the field since the incident. Sakakibara benched Han and ordered Mariko to take two days of vacation time, which meant Mariko hadn't so much as looked at her pistol since she'd checked out of post that night. Maybe she'd get the jitters when she came back to work, but for the moment she was thankful to be with her family, and that was all she needed.

Not for Saori, though. "*Fifty-two,*" she said, gripping Mariko's wrist insistently. "Shouldn't you get a headline for that? Shouldn't *I* get a headline for that? My big sister in the news again—and not for what they're saying now. Come on, Miko, you deserve better than this."

"I can't," Mariko said. "For one thing, the department's already given its statement. For another, you might have noticed they didn't mention the bomb in that statement. You have to understand how important it is to keep that secret. I told you two because I think you have a right to know, but if the bomb scare gets out, it gives Jōko Daishi exactly what he wants: mass panic."

It didn't feel good to say that out loud. It might be that fifty-two onlookers saw a cop shoot an unarmed janitor, but Mariko knew the truth. She knew how close they'd come. A dozen different theories were circulating on talk radio, doing the same kind of postgame could've-would've-should've analysis that followed every baseball game, and Mariko had the power to disperse all of their blissful ignorance with a simple phone call. So did her bosses. But TMPD couldn't exonerate her without explaining about the bomb, and that they could not do. The mere mention of it would cause a rash of panic, plus God knew what else on talk radio.

No, better for Tokyo's hero lady cop to take the momentary hit to her reputation. Everyone in Narcotics knew the score, the top brass did too, and if rumors of the truth managed to slip out here or there, at least there was no one to recognize them officially. Even Jōko Daishi couldn't do it. For one thing, he was more Tyler Durden than Osama bin Laden: not the type to claim credit for his political cause, most certainly not when his agent had failed. For another, inmates didn't have the right to call press conferences. So the department quashed his cause and considered Mariko collateral damage.

"You two have to understand," Mariko said. "Seriously, you can't talk about this. To *anyone*. Okay?"

"But what if—?" Saori began.

"If anyone asks you about it, tell them your sister thought the assailant was a direct threat to his hostage's life. You don't have to have a knife or a baseball bat to kill somebody. Crushing the guy's windpipe does the job just fine."

She flapped her cards on the table. "Oh," she added, "and I'm out."

Again Mariko found herself receiving a punishment she didn't deserve—a round of boos this time, though she supposed this was a whole lot better than the thrashing she was taking in the press. Those stories would lose their shine before the week was out, passing out of public memory just as quickly, though for the moment they really did sting. And unlike the press corps and the radio harpies, Mariko's mom followed up with another round of dessert.

"Okay, girls," she said after they finished their cherry cobbler, "one more game and then this old woman has to get to bed."

"Sorry, I can't," Mariko said. "I've got someone I still have to meet tonight."

"Oooh," Saori said. "A date! Is he hot?"

"No. Most definitely not."

"Who, then?" Saori said. At the same moment, their mom frowned and said, "It's someone from work, isn't it?"

"Sort of." The whole truth was complicated. She was looking forward to ending her professional relationship with this man, but she didn't particularly look forward to being in the same room with him.

She spent most of her train ride thinking about Han, about what to do with him, about where the moral lines lay. One way or another, her partner was going to stand before Internal Affairs. Her gut told her to stick up for him. Ten seconds of reflection on that told her she had a stronger obligation to stick up for the law. If a citizen broke the rules and got away with it, that was just a fact of life, but if a cop broke the rules and got away with it, that chipped away at the rules themselves. Law enforcement without accountability was a police state, not a police department.

What if Sakakibara decided to back Han's play? What if he found a way to wriggle around the fact that one of his officers ignored a suspect's civil liberties? Did it matter that the very next day the same suspect tried to murder Mariko and fifty-two other people? No. In civilian life it would matter, but legally, rights were rights.

The Americans had a good word for them: *inalienable.* A right that could be stripped depending on the situation wasn't a right at all. Sakakibara respected that. He was good police, and he was a real hard-ass when it came to playing it by the book. But he always said it was to protect his unit's conviction rate. What if, just this one time, he could boost Jōko Daishi's prison time by covering for a detective who strayed outside the lines and then came right back in? If he defended Han, Mariko would be left with the choice of crossing her CO *and* betraying her partner, or else looking the other way on a moral question that just wasn't up for negotiation.

With all of that on her mind, she walked up to the building she didn't want to walk up to and rang the doorbell she didn't want to ring.

When the steel doors slid open, Bullet was waiting for her inside, taking up half the elevator. Ever his chatty self, he said nothing on their ride up to Kamaguchi Hanzō's apartment.

"There she is," the Bulldog said with a sharp-toothed grin, "my hot little *gokudō* cop." He got up from his sofa, a huge Western-style block of black leather, tossed his TV remote aside and picked up a sweating bottle of beer. "Get your tight little ass in here and tell me what you got for me."

"Everything you want," Mariko said. She remained just outside the elevator, standing her ground just to show the Bulldog she wouldn't follow his orders. "We claimed your mask as evidence."

"So? Where is it?"

"A phone call away." She pulled a smartphone from her pocket and held it out as if to offer it to him. "If I deliver your mask, you'll call off the bounty on my head?"

"That's the deal, honey."

"And your dad? I'm square with him too?"

"He gave the contract to me. I'm the only guy you have to worry about."

"Then I've got you on record admitting to conspiracy to commit homicide." She came closer, showing him the phone's little screen.

Bullet took a menacing step forward. "Taking this phone from me won't do you any good," she told him, never taking her eyes off the Bulldog. "I'm not the one recording this. My department is. You getting all this, sir?"

"Loud and clear," Sakakibara said. He sounded gruff and authoritative even through the tiny speaker.

"Have a good night, sir." She dropped the phone back in her pocket. "So here's the deal: I'll give your mask back anyway, since it's yours, but you're going to call off the hit on me one way or the other. You do understand how this works, *neh*? We don't just come after you, we come after your dad. And yeah, I can't touch him, and yeah, there'll be blowback to cops in this city for a while to come, but at the end of the day cops and yakuzas are going to settle back into their old ways, and the only thing different is going to be you, implicating your old man on record. How well do you see that working out for you at the next family function?"

Kamaguchi rose from the couch, switching his grip on the beer bottle as if to use it as a weapon. He fixed her with a glare that said he might just chuck her phone off the balcony anyway, and her with it. Then his gaze flicked down to her left hand, which without her knowing it was resting on the heel of her SIG Sauer.

"You're not afraid to use that, are you?" he said. His tone was almost congratulatory.

"Nope."

"Heh. I heard about that. You and the guy in the subway. He's the one who stole my mask?"

"One of them, yeah."

"And the other one?" His grip on the bottle hadn't changed yet. There was still a tension in his knees and shoulders, harnessed there but ready to explode, like a dog pulling at an invisible chain.

"In custody. He'll see some serious time."

Kamaguchi snorted a laugh and set down the bottle. "Then we're square, sugar. Hell, I couldn't've killed you anyway. You're too much fun to fight. Come on, sit, have a beer."

Mariko shook her head and took as step back toward the elevator. "About your mask—"

"Don't worry about it. Get it to me when you get it to me. I know you're good for it." He snorted again and settled back into place on the huge black sofa.

"I am," Mariko said, "but that's not what I'm getting at. This guy, Jōko Daishi, he thinks the mask gives him divine power. He's a terrorist, plain and simple, and if he gets the mask back he's going to cause all kinds of harm."

"Blah, blah, blah." Kamaguchi flapped the back of his hand at her, as if shooing a fly away from his food. "It's my property, *neh*? I'll do what I want with it."

"That's just it," Mariko said. "He stole it from you once. He can do it again. I can't force you to melt it down, but I'm telling you, unless you want people on the street to think you can't protect your own property, you need to keep that thing under lock and key—"

"Already sold it." Kamaguchi flipped the channel.

"You what?"

"I already sold it to him. It's done."

"You sold it to *Jōko Daishi*?"

"Was that his name?" He settled on some sports channel covering a motorcycle race. "Yeah, I figured he wants it that bad, he'll pay a good price for it."

Mariko's balled her hands into fists. She heard her breath coming loud and angry and she had half a mind to reach for her pistol again. "Do you have the slightest idea what this man intends to do with that mask?"

"Honey," he said, twisting around to look at her, "I'm a gangster. This is what I do." Then the TV reclaimed his attention.

"Mass murder," Mariko said. "Mass destruction. Maybe killing your own people. Definitely hitting your own hometown. He thinks he needs the mask to make it happen. You want that?"

"Honey, I'm a *gangster*. I see a chance to make money, I take it. Shit happens to my people, I deal with it. Shit happens to other people, I let you deal with it."

Mariko couldn't believe her ears. All the work she'd put in, all the man-hours allocated by her department, all the fear, the tension, the worry, to say nothing of the quagmire Han had sunk himself into—all of it for nothing. For the second time in as many days, she'd surprised herself with her loyalty to a city that so often made her feel alien. Jōko Daishi wasn't just another criminal. His bombs weren't just a menace to the general public. He'd threatened *Tokyo*, damn it, Mariko's city, Kamaguchi's city, and Kamaguchi couldn't even be bothered to turn down the volume to hear her out.

All she could think of to say was "You selfish son of a bitch." There was nothing left to do but walk away.

63

Jōko Daishi's indictment was the following Friday. His legal name was Koji Makoto. Age fifty-one, though he looked a lot younger. A history of petty crimes in his youth, all linked to mental illness, resulting in some court-ordered psychiatric care but not a day of incarceration. No known residence, no known relatives. If he had a source of income, the National Tax Agency didn't know about it. As far as the bureaucracy was concerned, he'd stepped out of a psychiatric ward on the morning of his eighteenth birthday and simply ceased to exist.

The indictment was supposed to be at ten o'clock, on the first floor of a district courthouse around the corner from TMPD headquarters in the heart of Kasumigaseki, a neighborhood as schizophrenic as they come. The Metropolitan Police HQ was an enormous postmodern thing with a tower coming out the top that was striped like a candy cane. Across the street was the Ministry of Justice, Italianate, only three stories tall. Both of those fronted a moat of the Muromachi era, on the other side of which was the five-hundred-year-old sloping stone foundation of an Imperial Palace still decades shy of its one-hundredth birthday. Firebombing had eradicated the old palace, but the foundation had endured the bombers and worse—earthquakes, floods, erosion, an economy that valued downtown real estate over obsolete political heirlooms—emerging with a little more moss but otherwise hardly the worse for wear. Now that foundation was surrounded by brand-new skyscrapers, cell phone towers, hybrid electric vehicles, invisible waves of Wi-Fi. It stood stoically in their midst, unchanged.

Mariko wished she could say the same, caught in the midst of her swirling emotions. From the moment she woke up that morning, Mariko didn't know where she needed to be. Her friend and partner had a hearing before Internal Affairs. It was scheduled for ten o'clock, the same time Jōko Daishi's indictment was supposed to take place. Part of her wanted the decision to be as easy as supporting a friend, doing the right thing, letting the job come second. It was the same part of her that wished she thought of Jōko Daishi as Koji Makoto, not the religious title he'd given himself. It was the more charitable way to identify him—innocent until proven guilty and all that—but in her mind he remained the heartless cult leader, not the psychiatric case with a troubled childhood.

Her more cynical side doubted that Koji Makoto was even his real name at all. Most of her colleagues would have said she was grasping at straws, but they only thought in Japanese. Mariko read kanji characters as a native and as a *gaijin*, and the English-speaking part of her mind saw that, literally translated, Koji Makoto meant Short Path to the Truth. Too poetic to be coincidental, Mariko thought.

She wasn't all that fond of her propensity to find reasonable suspicion even in the most innocent of details, like names in the blanks of standard governmental paperwork. The sad truth was that her capacity to see the worst in people made her a better cop. Today it made her unsure about her partner. Despite that idealistic voice in her head, this had never been as simple as standing by a friend. He worked with her and he'd jeopardized their investigation. He reported to her and he'd undermined her authority. And now, at ten minutes to ten, she knew exactly where she needed to be but she didn't want to go.

It wasn't her lingering mistrust that told her to find another place to be at ten o'clock. If anything, her cynicism and pessimism would lead her straight to Han's hearing. But trumping those, overriding her feelings of betrayal, she was torn between wanting to be a source of support for her partner and dreading being there to see his verdict handed down.

She wanted to spare him that shame. The tension between those two desires had been building all morning, and now she had to walk it off, pacing up and down from the courthouse to the police headquarters. She'd seen Han pace like this, cigarette smoke trailing him. She'd never had much interest in smoking, but maybe today was the day to start.

Sakakibara caught up with her halfway down the block. "There you are," he said, walking fast on stilt-straight legs. Obviously *he* knew where he wanted to be. He hooked her by the crook of the elbow, spinning her on her heel and dragging her toward the courthouse. "Come on. Do you want to see this prick indicted or not?"

A simple indictment wasn't usually the sort of thing that drew a lieutenant's attention, or even a sergeant's for that matter, but Jōko Daishi had masterminded a plot to terrorize the city and run up a hell of a body count while he was at it—not fifty-two but hundreds. That train platform would have been packed if he'd had his way. If Mariko hadn't shot him. If Han hadn't put her where she needed to be. It had been a fifty-fifty shot as to which one of them would get to Akahata. Han had raced off the same as she did—had volunteered to be on a train platform with a madman and a bomb, the same as she did. It was blind luck that made her the hero instead of him. Again Mariko wondered what Han's fate should be.

"Sir, it's over."

"What?"

"Jōko Daishi's lawyer, Hamaya. He had the case pushed up an hour. Nine o'clock."

Sakakibara stopped cold. "And?"

"I saw it," Mariko said. It was sheer luck that she'd been there. She showed up early for Han because she couldn't sleep, and she happened to see Hamaya Jirō hurrying toward the courthouse. She nearly caught up with him, thought better of it, slipped in the courtroom behind him, and watched the whole proceedings.

Hamaya hadn't noticed her until afterward. "Sergeant Oshiro," he'd said. "A fine morning for a trial, wouldn't you say?"

He'd dropped the word *trial* on purpose. Jōko Daishi wasn't on trial yet. But Han was. "Do thank your partner for me when you see him," Hamaya had said. "If it weren't for him, I can only imagine how difficult it would be for me to mount my client's defense."

"That's because your client is guilty."

"Only of what you can prove in court, Sergeant. I'm afraid the district attorney will have a tough time of it, once it becomes clear how much evidence is inadmissible. If I'm not mistaken, your entire investigation would have fallen flat if your partner hadn't illegally tailed Akahata-san."

He had her on that one. The district attorney chose not to press charges on anything connected to the Kamakura house. The heroin, the cyanide, even Shino's murder. None of it would stick.

But Mariko wouldn't let him see the cracks in her resolve. "Too bad you won't be drawing a paycheck from him anymore. That breaks my heart."

"I'm sure. No doubt you're equally heartbroken that Akahata-san is not alive for cross-examination. If not for you and your partner, the case against Jōko Daishi would be ironclad."

Mariko felt herself fuming but refused to rise to Hamaya's bait. "You'll wriggle out of a charge here or there, but we've got your client dead to rights on the bomb-making factory. We got that from a search warrant on phone records, not from anything Han did. That means we've got your client on unlawful use of weapons, and believe me, the DA's office can turn that into five or six different counts by itself. Then there's conspiracy, furtherance, public endangerment—and after all that, your client gets to go to federal court, where we're going to smack him with every last terrorism charge we've got a law for. I hope your little cult believes in reincarnation, because Jōko Daishi's looking at back-to-back life sentences from here to eternity. Best of luck with that."

"The best of luck, indeed," Hamaya had said, giving her a little bow by way of a farewell. "I have no doubt of it."

That was nine thirty. Now, at nine fifty-one, Mariko's frustration hadn't cooled in the slightest. "He's going to walk on almost all of it,"

STEVE BEIN

she told Sakakibara. "How many charges should we have nailed him on just for the dope? Precursor chemicals, manufacturing, intent to distribute, you name it. Plus the two homicides, plus all the prohibited substances charges . . . I don't know *what* you charge someone with for having a gas chamber in his bedroom, but I sure as hell hope we've got a law against it."

"We probably do."

"And what does it matter?" Mariko clenched her fists, wishing she had a *bokken* in her hands and something to smash with it. "None of it's going to stick. I was thinking we had a lock on terrorism and conspiracy, but that cocky bastard Hamaya seems to think otherwise. He's a slippery little fucker. He's looking for ways out already."

"That's his job," said Sakakibara. "You know that."

"Yes, sir," she said, and she told him about what else was on her mind. Kamaguchi Hanzō. The mask. How Hamaya might already be on his way to file some paperwork Mariko had never heard of, something that would release the mask from police custody so he could hand-deliver it to Jōko Daishi.

It ended up becoming more of a tirade than an explanation, and at the end of it she felt deflated. She slumped against the side of the HQ building and threw up her hands. "What the hell have we accomplished, sir? Jōko Daishi will see some time—I hope. But after that, he's still got his mask and his cult, and we didn't even seize all of the explosives. He's got more people out there. We have no guesses about who they are. He'll have more targets. We have no idea where. And for all of this, I get my name dragged through the muck and maybe Han loses his badge. So what the hell was the point?"

Sakakibara grimaced at her, his thick Sonny Chiba eyebrows scrunching toward each other like hairy black caterpillars. "We're cops, Frodo. Not lawyers; not judges; cops. That makes us goalkeepers, and the simple truth is that sometimes the bad guys get one through."

He took her by the chin—an astonishingly gentle gesture coming from him, almost fatherly—and raised her eyes to meet his. "What did you think when you took this job? That we were going to stop every crime in the city? We stop the ones we can, but some of them are going to get by us. If you can't live with that, just hand me your badge right now. I'll fill out the paperwork for you."

"Sir, you know I can't—"

"Can't what? Take a cushy desk job for the same pay? Get off the streets, rest your feet for a minute? Sure you can. You don't need to be in the dirty little corners where the lines get blurry, where it's hard to tell right from wrong. Go take a job in a police box in the suburbs, where the worst problem you'll have for the rest of your career is not knowing the answer when someone stops in to ask for directions. How many COs have you served under who told you to do exactly that?"

Mariko couldn't help smiling a little. "Actually, sir, the last one told me he'd have me working the precinct coffeemaker."

Somehow he'd made the shift from concerned father to stern father and back to bitter, grumpy commanding officer. "Fine. Go take his advice. Or stop pitying yourself and recognize you did something magnificent. You saved fifty-two lives. You put a very bad man in the ground and you put another one in a cell. The day that's not good enough for you, just hand me your badge and I'll fill out the paperwork."

Mariko looked back down for a minute, then found his gaze again. "Thank you, sir."

"You know what happens now?"

"Sir?"

"The same thing that happens in any other sport with a goalkeeper. The other team gets the ball back and they try to score again. Now, are you ready to do your damn job?"

"Yes, sir."

"Good. Let's go to your partner's hearing."

Mariko glanced at Sakakibara's huge black diver's watch. "We're running late for that, sir. Do you think they'll let us in after—"

"They haven't started yet. I told them to hold off until I got there."

Mariko was glad he'd already started walking so he couldn't see her jaw drop. She knew her lieutenant had some swat, but she didn't know his arm reached *that* far. It made her wonder if IAD would allow him to get involved in their decision too, made her wonder whether Sakakibara would push to get Han off or see him hang.

True to his word, it was Sakakibara who unofficially began the hearing when he walked through the door. Mariko found it embarrassing, seeing Han being deposed, and she could only imagine what he was feeling. She thought of Saori, who, somewhere along the way of her Twelve Step program, had to make a list of everyone she'd every wronged while she was using, and then had to go out and apologize for each offense. It was no easy thing, admitting you were wrong. It took a kind of strength not a lot of people had. Saori didn't have it; she'd had to build it from scratch. It made Mariko proud to see Han push ahead, explaining everything he'd done and leaving nothing out. He held no one else to blame, nor did he shield anyone else from blame. If IAD found reason to investigate Mariko as well, it would start with Han telling them the truth as plainly as he could.

For an event that would see Han's whole career hang in the balance, the hearing was surprisingly brief. The review board adjourned after only an hour, sequestering themselves to make their judgment. Mariko found herself sagging back into her seat, and until then she hadn't even noticed she'd been sitting forward, hands gripping her knees, waiting for the board's ruling. Now she wanted to know how long review boards generally took to make their decisions—or, more precisely, how long she'd have to be waiting on the edge of her seat, tense as the skin of a drum.

And since she lacked anything even approximating the proper sense of decorum for a woman of her rank and station, she asked. The chair of the review board, a commander she hadn't met before, gave her the same kind of frown he'd have given a Tokyo Disney mascot walking into the room, a blend of puzzlement and offense. "Fifteen minutes," he said, making it clear that he was doing her a great honor even in recognizing her existence, and closed the door behind him.

Mariko found herself immediately at Han's side, which surprised her. The part of her that was still pissed off at him still had a loud voice, but it had lost its majority. "Fifteen minutes?" she said. "You'd think they'd take longer than that for something this important."

"Yeah," said Han. "You'd think your partner wouldn't say anything to ruffle their feathers before they made their ruling, too."

She blushed for a second, but he winked at her and even gave her a little grin. "You look awfully relaxed," she said.

"What's there to be nervous about? The worst part's over."

Mariko hadn't realized that was true, but now that she thought about it, it was almost self-evident. Working up the courage to make a full confession was agonizing work. After that, taking your licks was easy. Han had just looked his own guilt full in the face; he knew he deserved punishment and he'd already resigned himself to accept it, however harsh it might be.

A few minutes later the review board returned to render its verdict, and again, paradoxically, Mariko found herself more nervous about it than Han. The chairman sat down with what looked like a sheet of prepared notes that he didn't bother looking at, making Mariko so curious she wanted to jump out of her seat to see what it said.

His ruling was short and to the point: Han had violated Akahata's right to freedom from unlawful search and seizure; he had transgressed the boundaries of probable cause, though not the boundaries of reasonable suspicion; he had placed his CI, Shino, in a situation that might have become dangerous. All of that was clear. But there was no indubitable proof that he had directly endangered Shino's life. He would not be charged criminally, and that meant he'd get to keep his badge. But the board found him guilty of violating eight general orders regarding the proper handling of covert informants, and that meant his life in Narcotics was over. The review board busted him back down to general patrol, where every time he walked into a roomful of cops it would be like showing up to a black tie affair with a nice tuxedo and his pants around his ankles. Sooner or later things would get back to business as usual, but for years to come there would be stares and whispers everywhere he went.

As the members of the review board packed up their things, Sakakibara offered Han his stern congratulations; Mariko thought he seemed grimly pleased with the ruling. Afterward he offered to buy Mariko and Han a cup of coffee—or rather, he ordered them to sit down to coffee with him; lieutenants did not offer *invitations* to their subordinates. All the same, sitting down to coffee outside of their post felt like Mariko's father taking her out for ice cream after she'd run hard in a track meet and still finished second. That marked it as another fatherly gesture from Sakakibara, both the second Mariko had seen from him this morning and the second one she'd seen from him, period.

They sat down and Mariko and Han waited for Sakakibara to speak. Coffee shop or not, this wasn't exactly a social call. "Han, I don't want you coming in to clear out your desk until second shift. Wait until the unit's down to a skeleton crew. Save yourself that embarrassment, all right? Hell, save *me* the embarrassment."

Han swallowed. Mariko gave him an "it's okay" sort of nod, the kind no one really meant, the kind oncologists everywhere gave their patients when the news wasn't good but the prognosis wasn't terminal. "I worked general patrol for a long time, Han. It's a good job. An important job."

"And it's not Narcotics." He sighed and gave a defeated shrug. "At least one of us still has a spot in the lineup, *neh*? I'm really, *really* glad they didn't drag you down with me."

"I am too," said Sakakibara. "I'm shorthanded enough as it is. But you two need to learn a lesson from this whole fiasco. When you do the right thing and you break the rules, sometimes you need to ask yourself what that says about the rules."

"Sir?" said Han.

"Sometimes you admit you're in the wrong. Like your hearing today. You did your job. You did the right thing. But sometimes the rules aren't what they should be."

Han's eyes flicked between Sakakibara and Mariko, and Mariko felt her face go sour when she met his gaze. "What?" Han said. "Oh, hell. You went to Jōko Daishi's indictment, didn't you?"

YEAR OF THE DEMON

Mariko had a decent poker face, but not for Han. She tried to hold his stare but couldn't. "No," he said, and in that incredulous, angry tone it came out as a curse word. "He's going to walk?"

"On most of it," Mariko said. "They didn't even bother to charge him with Shino's murder."

"Because he murdered the only eyewitness who can put him on the scene."

"Yep."

Han was crestfallen. "So the same circumstantial shit that lets me keep my badge—"

"Gets Jōko Daishi off the hook, yeah," said Mariko. She broke down the rest of the details for him. "In the end, we're thinking—*hoping*—the terrorism charges will stick, but that'll be a federal thing, out of our reach."

Mariko hadn't thought it possible for Han to deflate any further. His color drained from him; he seemed to diminish in his chair.

Mariko knew the feeling.

Somehow, through heroic effort, Han mustered the energy to speak. "So what the hell did we accomplish?"

"A lot," Sakakibara said, "and don't you dare lose sight of it. You've both been at this far too long not to have figured this out by now: we don't have the luxury of total victories in this profession. You think we're in Narcotics so we can put a stop to illegal drugs? No. We stop one dealer. Then we go stop another one. If the first guy's out on the streets already, we go back and get him again. This is the game, boys and girls—the game *you* signed up to play. And you know what happens next?"

Han's gaze shifted from Sakakibara to Mariko and back, wavering, just as unstable as his own resolve. But Mariko felt steadier. She'd lost her composure when she couldn't pull the trigger on Jōko Daishi, felt it crumble, shot through with a million fractures. Even her victory over Akahata wasn't enough to restore it. But Sakakibara's words were like glue, seeping into the cracks, bleeding deeper into them, finding more, binding it all together, making her stronger.

"I do," she said. "I know what happens next. Their team gets the ball back. They try to get one by us again. And we block it, again and again." She looked at her partner. "Narcs, patrolmen, paper pushers, it doesn't matter. It's all the same job. We're goalkeepers, Han. This is what we do."

Han slumped. "And I was always a baseball guy. I guess I'm not cut out for soccer."

"Han," Mariko said, "you know that's not what I mean. I'm trying to say—"

"I get what you're saying. But the truth is, this goalie got benched, and now he's getting reassigned to direct traffic in the parking lot. It's fine. Seriously. It's no more than I deserve."

"Han—"

"No, Mariko. I'm out of the game for a little while. But I guess there are traffic violations in the parking lot too. I don't know how important they are, but someone's got to crack down on them."

"Take the rest of the morning off," Sakakibara said, as abrupt as ever. He stood up to leave. "Get your heads clear. Then put all this crap behind you. Get it out of your mind so you can do your damn jobs. Frodo, I'll see you at noon. Han, I guess I'll see you when I see you."

"Yes, sir," Han said. He stood up and gave the lieutenant a deep bow. "Thank you, sir. You taught me everything worth knowing about being a cop."

"Don't get weepy on me."

"Sorry." Han gathered himself and bowed again. "It's been an honor, Lieutenant."

Sakakibara gave him a curt nod and walked out.

Mariko finished her coffee and set it on the table with a loud *clack*. "Let's go to my place," she said. "I have something I want to show you."

Han prodded Glorious Victory's pommel with a single cautious finger. "Whoa. Are you sure you should keep this thing hanging over your bed?"

"What's the big deal? You've been here before. You saw my sword rack."

"Yeah, but not with the sword *in* it. I mean, look at the size of that thing."

Mariko rolled her eyes at him. "That's not really what I invited you over to see."

He craned his head under the rack like a plumber peeking under a kitchen sink. "You're sure these screws can take the weight?"

"What are you, a carpenter now? Just read this, okay?"

She handed him one of Yamada-sensei's notebooks, with her thumb marking a page referring to Jōko Daishi's iron mask. He reached for it blindly, his eyes still on Glorious Victory Unsought. "Aren't you afraid it . . . I mean, earthquakes and all . . . seriously, Mariko, hang it somewhere else."

"Where? Look around this great big penthouse of an apartment and show me another wall long enough to mount that sword."

Han didn't have to be a detective to see her point. "Well, I don't know . . . prop it up in a closet or something."

"Just look at the notes, will you?"

She explained who Yamada was—who he was to her, who he was to the study of history—and then explained about his notebooks. "See, none of this stuff ever makes it as far as the public eye," she said, "but I'm telling you, that mask is important."

"Even though I won't see a word about it in any history book?"

"Especially because you won't see it in any history book. I think Yamada-sensei's Wind and Jōko Daishi's Divine Wind are the same thing, and if I'm right, then they've been around for a long, long time. We haven't seen the last of them, and we haven't seen the last of that mask."

Han leafed through the notebook. "Are you for real? A five-hundred-year-old ninja clan in Tokyo?"

"Maybe, yeah."

Han's face lit up. "That is *so* cool."

"Men," she said, accidentally reverting to English. "It doesn't matter how old you get; you're all just eight-year-old boys."

"Huh?"

"Never mind." Exasperation clung to her like a wet cloth. At least he was studying the notebook a little more closely now. Not much progress, but it was progress. "Help me look through all these boxes," she said. There was no need to point at them; they were stacked four and five high along the back wall of her bedroom, taking up a lot of valuable floor space. "I need another pair of eyes on this stuff."

"Why?"

"Don't you get it? I should have seen the connection to Glorious Victory. I should have remembered it the second I saw the mask. If my memory was a little better, maybe they never would have stolen my sword in the first place."

Han looked up from the notebook. "You can't beat yourself up over this kind of thing. If your crackpot ninja theory is right, then there was nothing you could do to keep them from breaking in."

He stopped himself for a second—maybe to think of something more comforting to say. Mariko could have used it. But no. "I mean, can you imagine what kind of totally badass tools they must have invented over the last five hundred years? Relocking a door chain from the outside would be, like, the tenth coolest thing they could do."

Great. The eight-year-old boy was back.

"In case you haven't noticed, Han, I'm feeling pretty fallible right now. I can't afford to overlook details like this anymore. We've got a cult running around our city with high explosives. If these notes can help us find them, then I need someone else reading them, someone to help me connect the dots—"

"And now that I'm not working as a detective, my workweek is about to get a whole lot shorter, *neh*?"

Mariko sighed with relief. She felt the tension seep out of her shoulders. They were thinking along the same lines again, and that was a blessed thing. "I figured maybe a couple of nights a week?"

Han flipped through Yamada's notes again. "I don't know," he said. "Looks like pretty dry reading."

"Maybe over a few beers?"

"Getting better."

"I'll give you the play-by-play of my goaltending duties."

"Ow! Just kick me in the nuts and get it over with." Han made a show of wincing. "First I get taken out of the game, and now you're going to rub it in?"

Mariko laughed. "Come on. You have to admit you're interested, *neh*?"

"Oh yeah."

"Me too."

GLOSSARY

A-side: for SWAT operators, the front side of a building

ama: traditional Japanese free divers, best known for diving for pearls

ambo: ambulance

Aum Shinrikyō: Supreme Truth Cult, responsible for the sarin gas attack on the Tokyo subway system in 1995

B-side: for SWAT operators, the side of a building to their left as they approach the A-side

bizen: an unglazed style of Japanese pottery

bokken: solid wooden training sword, usually of oak

bushidō: the way of the warrior

C-side: for SWAT operators, the side of a building to their right as they approach the A-side

CI: Covert Informant

D-side: for SWAT operators, the backside of a building (or, for irregularly shaped buildings, the side opposite the A-side)

daishō: katana and wakizashi together, the twin swords of the samurai; literally, "long-short"

dono: an honorific expressing great humility on the part of the speaker, more respectful than -san or even -sama

foxfire: magical lights said to be carried by foxes or fox-spirits

Fudō: a Buddhist deity, typically depicted as an angry, red-skinned demon with sharp horns and fangs, often wielding a sword and a lariat

gaijin: foreigner (literally "outsider")

geisha: a skilled artist paid to wait on, entertain, and in some cases provide sexual services for clientele

gokudō: extreme, hard-core

gumi: clan (as in Kamaguchi-gumi)

haidate: broad armored plates to protect the thighs, usually of lamellar

hakama: wide, pleated pants bound tightly around the waist and hanging to the ankle

haori: a Japanese tabard (i.e., short, sleeveless jacket) characterized by wide, almost winglike shoulders, often worn over armor

hazmat: Hazardous Materials Team; alternatively, hazardous materials and items

Ikkō Ikki: a peasant uprising, largely disorganized and only nominally Buddhist, whose political and economic influence endured for over a hundred years until the Three Unifiers quelled it in the late sixteenth century

kaigane: a sharp, stiff tool with a blade like a spatula used by ama to pry shellfish from rocks and coral

kaishaku: a samurai's second, charged with virtually beheading him if he should cry out while committing seppuku

Kansai: the geographic region around Kyoto, Nara, and Osaka, and the locus of political power for nearly all of Japanese history

kappa: a water-dwelling mythological being, humanoid with reptilian features, with a topless head and a water-filled bowl in place of a brain

katana: a curved long sword worn with the cutting edge facing upward

kenjutsu: the lethal art of the sword (as opposed to kendō, the sporting art of the sword)

kiai: a loud shout practiced as a part of martial arts training, usually uttered upon delivering a strike

kiri: a paulownia blossom, the emblem of Toyotomi Hideyoshi

koku: the amount of rice required to feed one person for one year; also, a unit for measuring the size of a fiefdom or estate, corresponding to the amount of rice its land can produce

MDA: methylenedioxyamphetamine, a hallucinogenic amphetamine

Mount Hiei: a mountain overlooking the city of Kyoto, home to hundreds of monasteries and the traditional locus of political power for Buddhism in Japan

ōdachi: a curved greatsword

ōyoroi: "great armor"; a full suit of yoroi armoring the wearer from head to toe; literally "great armor"

Raijin: demonic god of lightning, thunder, and storms

ri: a unit of measurement equal to about two and a half miles

rikishi: sumo wrestler

rōnin: a masterless samurai (literally "wave-person")

Ryūjin: dragon-god of the sea

sama: an honorific expressing humility on the part of the speaker, more respectful than -san but not as humbling as -dono

sarin: a potent neurotoxin

seiza: a kneeling position on the floor; as a verb, "to sit seiza" means "to meditate" (literally "proper sitting")

sensei: teacher, professor, or doctor, depending on the context (literally "born-before")

seppuku: ritual suicide by disembowelment, also known as hara-kiri

shakuhachi: traditional Japanese flute

shamisen: traditional Japanese lute

shinobi: ninja

shoji: sliding divider with rice-paper windows, usable as both door and wall

sode: broad, panel-like shoulder armor, usually of lamellar

SOP: Standard Operating Procedure

southern barbarian: white person (considered "southern" because European sailors were only allowed to dock in Nagasaki, which lies far to the south)

sugegasa: broad-brimmed, umbrella-like hat

Sword Hunt: an edict restricting the ownership of weapons to the samurai caste; there were two such edicts, each one carrying additional provisions on arms control and other political decrees

tachi: a curved long sword worn with the blade facing downward

taiko: an enormous drum; alternatively, the art of drumming with taiko

temari: embroidered silk thread balls; alternatively, the craft of making temari

tengu: a goblin with birdlike features

Tokaidō: the "East Sea Road" connecting modern-day Tokyo to modern-day Kyoto

tsuba: a hand protector, usually round or square, where the hilt of a sword meets its blade; the Japanese analogue to a cross guard

wakizashi: a curved short sword, typically paired with a katana, worn with the blade facing upward

washi: traditional Japanese handmade paper

yakuza: member of an organized crime syndicate; "good-for-nothing"

yoroi: armor

yukata: a light robe

yuki-onna: a predatory winter-spirit that hunts on snowy nights, taking the form of a pale (usually naked) and very beautiful woman

AUTHOR'S NOTE

This book required a lot more research than the last one, for many reasons. For one thing, it's longer. For another, Mariko isn't working on her own; as soon as I reassigned her to Narcotics, I signed myself up for more cop research. And of course there's the obvious: I'm not a historian by training, and between Daigoro and Kaida, more than half of this book is historical fiction. Compounding that, Daigoro spends his time interacting with Toyotomi Hideyoshi, one of the most influential figures in Japanese history. When you put people like that in your story, you've got a certain obligation to get them right.

The first thing to know about Hideyoshi is that Hideyoshi isn't his real name. He doesn't have *a* real name; he changed it many times over, as did many of the great figures of his day. This habit of theirs is enough to drive historians to apoplexy, and so even the most esteemed scholars of Japanese history resort to using just one name, usually the name the figure is best known by.

But a Hideyoshi by any other name would still be a badass. He had so much working against him—he was born of peasant stock, he was so ugly that his nicknames were "the Bald Rat" and "the Monkey King," and he showed no promise whatsoever as a fighter—yet he made himself the most powerful man in the empire. Through sheer force of personality, he earned his seat as one of the Three Unifiers, the three warlords who created the nation we now know as Japan.

The other two Unifiers are Oda Nobunaga, who raised Hideyoshi from lowly manservant to one of his top generals, and Tokugawa Ieyasu, who was first a rival, then an ally, then a usurper. All three were brilliant strategists, each in his own way. Nobunaga is best known for his ruthlessness, Hideyoshi for his honeyed tongue, and Ieyasu for his patience. In brief, their stories run as follows: Nobunaga, who was so merciless that he could scarcely retain even the loyalty of his own family, saw great promise in Hideyoshi and elevated him to the rank of general. With him and a coterie of other now-legendary commanders, Nobunaga conquered a third of Japan.

When Nobunaga was assassinated by one of his inner circle, Hideyoshi swept in to kill the traitor. He then pressured the emperor into making him samurai and appointing him as imperial regent and chief minister. Hideyoshi was no swordsman, but he was a cunning strategist and a negotiator nonpareil, and he crushed every warlord he could not recruit as an ally. Enter Ieyasu, whose preferred method was to sit back and allow Nobunaga and Hideyoshi to do all the heavy lifting. Then he ousted Hideyoshi's heirs, appointed himself shogun, and established the greatest dynasty in Japanese history. Hence the mnemonic, recited in one variant or another in classrooms throughout Japan: Nobunaga mixed the dough, Hideyoshi baked the cake, and Ieyasu got to eat it.

Because Daigoro and Shichio are my two lenses for viewing Hideyoshi, I have chosen to characterize him rather differently than you might see him elsewhere. In Kurosawa's *Kagemusha*, for example, Hideyoshi is portrayed as a deadly serious samurai warrior. This is by no means unfair, for Hideyoshi desperately wanted to be thought of as noble and refined. He was fascinated by the tea ceremony, he performed kabuki, and fancied himself an accomplished singer. His palace, the Jurakudai, was real, and if there can be such a thing as an excess of elegance, this was it. But if Hideyoshi was pretending at nobility, he certainly was not pretending at being charismatic. By all accounts he was positively magnetic, but because Shichio is effete and Daigoro is highborn, they see my Hideyoshi's charms as being quite coarse.

Shichio himself is purely fictional, but homosexual relationships were common among men of Hideyoshi's station and era. These ritualized relationships, known as *shudō*, usually coupled adults with young boys; grown men were not supposed to be penetrated (hence the tension in Shichio's relationship with Hideyoshi). Mio Yasumasa is also fictional, but Hideyoshi certainly had high-ranking samurai advisers like Mio. I'm sorry to say that Mio's death is based in truth; the method is called *lingchi*, and it is the origin of the proverbial "death of a thousand cuts." We don't know for a fact that Hideyoshi employed it, but we do know that he developed a penchant for cruel and elaborate executions.

On that note, I should mention that including Mio's torture was a considered choice. My agent and my editor found the scene quite disturbing—so much so that my agent was only willing to read it once, and my editor suggested that perhaps I ought to take it out. Obviously I didn't.

I chose to keep the scene because of what the story arc demands, not because I think torture is cool. Quite the opposite: I joined the Campaign to Ban Torture years ago, and I remain a member of the Center for the Victims of Torture today. Milan Kundera suggested that the true measure of our morality lies in how we treat those who are at our mercy, and I happen to think he's right. Regardless of whether or not you agree with me, I hope you will grant that I have not glorified torture here.

Shifting from philosophy back to history, all of the military conquests I attribute to Hideyoshi in this book are true to life. Oda Nobunaga's Sword Hunt was real, as was Hideyoshi's, though on that count I must confess that I got extremely lucky. I don't recall why I picked 1587 as the setting for Daigoro's story in *Daughter of the Sword*, but it certainly wasn't because I anticipated writing a second book, or that I planned to make the Sword Hunt a plot element in Daigoro's continuing story. This was just one of those cases where you do your research and it gives you better ideas than you could have come up with on your own.

The Wind is a fictional clan, but ninja clans did exist, and they were more active in the Kansai than in any other region. Despite what you may have seen in pop culture, samurai were not "the good guys" and ninja were not "the bad guys." *Shinobi* (or *shinobi no mono*, the period terms for what we now call ninja) were the original secret agents, routinely hired by the great houses as spies, forward observers, assassins, saboteurs, and the like. Their clans trained them in a wide range of skills, by no means limited to martial arts; they also learned a wide range of professional skills, the better to blend in and take on any disguise as necessary.

Incidentally, such disguises did not involve the trademark black bodysuit and face mask that we all know and love today. These would have been about as subtle as James Bond wearing a ghillie suit. The black garb that has become their emblem actually dates back to the theater; stagehands would wear all black, the better to go unnoticed as they moved certain props. (Stagehands do this in modern theater even today.) Somewhere along the line, a clever playwright needed to figure out how a ninja could sneak up on his protagonist, catching even the audience unawares. The answer was—like the ninja themselves—hiding in plain sight: just make one of the stagehands the assassin. The audience was delighted and a new tradition was born.

Featuring as prominently as the *shinobi* in this book is the *rōnin*, or masterless samurai. According to *bushidō* ideals, the samurai was to commit suicide at the loss of his master. Needless to say, not everyone lived up to the ideal. Many samurai became itinerant swords for hire, wandering the countryside as freely as waves on the sea—hence the name *rōnin*, or "wave-person." (Katsushima Goemon is one such case.) Other samurai chose to abandon their caste, shave their top-knots, and join a monastery. (The abbot of Kattō-ji is one such case.) Then there were those who gave the *rōnin* their bad name: they became highwaymen and bandits, either falling in with criminal elements or forming gangs of their own.

The third profession to feature prominently in this book is the *ama*, usually translated as "pearl diver." Literally, *ama* just means "sea-woman" (and with a swapped character, "sea-man"). The *ama* occupies a strange cultural space in that it is, to the best of my knowledge, the only profession in Japan that is defined by strenuous physical labor and is yet a profession that belongs to women, not men. The reasons for this are not entirely clear, though the U.S. Navy did yeoman's work in trying to discover the answer. This was one of the gems you are only likely to find while writing a book and wanting to get the details right: a 380-page study on breath-hold diving, with detailed descriptions (and even diagrams!) of *ama* diving techniques, published in 1965 by none other than the Office of Naval Research. The SEALs were brand-spanking-new then, and it seems the navy was interested in training them to dive deeper and longer—an interest it has since suspended, officially designating breath-hold diving as "an extremely dangerous practice." To my mind this tidbit only makes Kaida cooler. If at age thirteen she can outswim a SEAL, then the Wind will make a fine *shinobi* of her.

This book closes with recent history—namely, with the Divine Wind. My cult is fictional, but the inspiration for it is based in fact. In 1995 the Aum Shinrikyō cult carried out sarin gas attacks on the Tokyo subway system, killing thirteen and injuring over a thousand. I think it is fair to say that the sarin gas attack was to Tokyo what 9/11 was to New York City. By this I don't mean to liken thirteen deaths to the 2,606 in the World Trade Center; rather, I mean to say that while terrorist attacks are hideous no matter where they occur, for such an attack to happen in one's hometown is terrifying in a way nothing else can be.

This, of course, takes us to Mariko, who demands a totally different brand of research. I should mention at the outset that I interviewed (and in some cases trained with) law enforcement personnel in three different states, from I forget how many different organizations, which means any commanding officers who happen to be reading this should not assume that *their* officers were the ones who showed me such a good time. I find the cop research to be much more difficult than historical research, but for all of that, it's also a hell of a lot of fun.

I've had the chance to do ride-alongs, search houses, shoot machine guns, run combat courses, and work hand-to-hand control tactics. I will neither confirm nor deny that I violated ATF regulations when someone let me chuck a flash-bang grenade. I can answer that one definitively after the statute of limitations runs out.

Copspeak is every bit as much a foreign language as Japanese. In both cases the translator's job is to walk that fine line between authenticity and readability, and in this book that meant taking certain liberties. For instance, I'm well aware that the Tokyo Metropolitan Police Department has Special Assault Teams, not SWAT teams. Since most of my readers know what SWAT means when they see it, and have no idea what SAT means when they see it, I've chosen to translate SAT as SWAT. I've also chosen to omit almost all of the abbreviations and number codes that are the epitome of copspeak—avoiding, for example, the kind of sentence I once heard a cop tell his dispatcher: "I'll be seventy-six one J-5 to dicks." (In English, that's "I'm en route with a woman I'm taking to see the detectives.")

If oddities of translation and historical context are of interest to you, I'll recommend that you visit my Web site. I've got an appearances page there, with links to interviews and guest blog posts on topics like this. I post updates on my writing there too, and free sample chapters, and links to some of the Web sites I use in researching my work. You can find all of that stuff at www.philosofiction.com.

—Steve Bein
Geneseo, New York
March 2013

ACKNOWLEDGMENTS

First and foremost, I have to thank my brother Dave. He comes first this time around because I was a jerk and forgot about him last time. He was the one who first suggested that *Daughter of the Sword* should have a glossary, which was a really good idea. So cheers to Dave, and jeers to me for forgetting to credit him last time.

Thanks also to everyone who helped in researching this book. Alex Embry is my point man on cop questions, and I worked him a whole lot harder on this book than on *Daughter*. I'm very fortunate to know Diana Rowland, who in addition to being a former cop is also kicking ass on the writing scene; someone who knows the details *and* the craft is an invaluable asset. D. P. Lyle is invaluable for similar reasons, and is most generous with his medical and forensic expertise. My thanks go out to all the other cops I interviewed and worked with but who asked not to be named. Props again to the Codex hivemind, and to Luc Reid, aka He Who Shall Not Be Named, aka The Man.

Special gratitude is due to Cameron McClure, my agent extraordinaire, and Anne Sowards, my wonderful new editor. (Kat, I still miss you!) Structurally, *Demon* was much harder to put together than *Daughter*, and Cameron and Anne were pivotally important in that effort. To Cameron especially, thanks so much for bearing with me through all the outlines and story lines and worry lines.

Of course my deepest and most heartfelt gratitude goes to all of my readers. Special thanks to Jess Sund and Kati Strande for being early readers and for their general effervescence; to Dave and Kris for being early readers too, though neither of them is known to effervesce; to our mom, my proofreader, and dad, for his enduring belief in my future as a writer; to Chris McGrath for two kick-ass covers in a row; to Stephen Baxter, Jay Lake, Diana Rowland, and Kylie Chan for their kind and very humbling blurbs; to Kirsten Lincoln and her hubby, Naoto, for help with lesser-known Japanese idioms; to my publicist Lindsay Boggs, and to the host sites she hooked me up with for my blog tours; and to anyone else I may be omitting due to general absent-mindedness.

Begrudging thanks to Michele for getting me a Facebook presence, and sincerest thanks for everything else. Our dog Kane also deserves an honorable mention. He and his brother Buster were both present in the earliest draft of the manuscript, but Kane's scene got cut. Sorry, buddy.

ABOUT THE AUTHOR

Steve Bein teaches Asian philosophy and Asian history at the State University of New York at Geneseo. He has a PhD in philosophy, and his graduate work took him to Nanzan University and Ōbirin University in Japan, where he translated a seminal work in the study of Zen Buddhism. He holds a third-degree black belt and a first-degree black belt in two American forms of combative martial arts, and has trained in about two dozen other martial arts over the past twenty years. His short fiction has appeared in *Asimov's Science Fiction, Interzone, Writers of the Future*, and in exclusive e-Special format from Penguin. He has been anthologized alongside authors such as Isaac Asimov, Ray Bradbury, William Gibson, George R. R. Martin, and Ursula K. LeGuin. Please visit Steve on the Web at www.philosofiction.com and like him at facebook/philosofiction.